Keep it Dark

Will Jonson

To Ben, Philippa and Flora.

It is better to speak
remembering
we were never meant to survive.

'A Litany for Survival' - Audre Lorde

From the place where we are right, flowers will never grow in the spring.

Yehuda Amichei

CONTENTS

Chapter One: Tommy I

I'll never forget the day I saw my Uncle Jack cry. I'd never seen a man cry before because in those days, you never did. Just didn't happen. Unless they were all drunk and laughing. Or drunk and reminiscing and maudlin. But everything was different back then. Men were different, I suppose. Or something was. Anyway. Maybe it was just that Uncle Jack was different. I dunno.

It must have been when I was seven or eight. I remember my mum had sent me round to Uncle Jack's butcher's shop for some bacon and black pudding. It wasn't just because Jack was family – everyone round our way said it was the best butcher's shop on the Old Kent Road. It's not there now. I walked past where it used to be a few months ago. It's a discount booze and fags place now.

I know it was in spring for sure, because London's plane trees had started to get that light green sheen of freshness that seemed, if you were eight, to be some sort of natural beacon of hope after a grey, wet, grinding winter. And I also had to get some hot cross buns from the baker's. So it must have been around Easter. Now you can get hot cross buns in the supermarkets whenever you like - at any time of the year. Now. Things were different then. And stuff doesn't stay the same forever. I thought it would. I was so convinced that some things would never change. But I was wrong. Lots of shit changes. Even shit changes if you leave it long enough. Shit comes in different colours to start with, but then it changes. Very much like life, I've found.

Anyway, the sun was shining fit to burst and I was eight and on the top table in my class at school and Spurs were doing well that season in the League and *Passport to Pimlico* was on TV that afternoon and everything was all right in my little world. Uncle Jack was a tall, strong man with broad shoulders and black hair and smiling, kindly eyes, and he was always cheery and smiley with family and with customers, so an errand to his butcher's shop was the opportunity for some badinage – though I did not know that word yet.

Being family, I went round the back of the shop to surprise him – I always did, maya dorogaya.

But then I saw Uncle Jack cry.

And I don't just mean cry: he was heaving great broken sobs of sadness that seemed to start from way down below his waist as he hacked with his huge cleaver at the great red and white marbled haunch of something – beef or lamb or pork, I suppose.

I shivered and started to creep back out of the shop. Gob-smacked – though we didn't say that then.

Uncle Jack happened to look up and our eyes met. In his I saw an unfathomable, unreachable sorrow that froze my soul to its core.

But Uncle Jack suddenly broke into a grin and said, wiping the wetness from his face with his heavy forearms, "S'all right, Tommy. Nuffin to worry about. Best go round the front, kid."

And he added, as an afterthought it seemed, "Tommy – what you just seen – keep it dark, eh, sunny Jim? Keep it dark."

So I quickly went round to the front of the shop and pushed the glass door open. The little bell tinkled and Uncle Jack appeared, right as rain, bright as tuppence. With every appearance of a man who had never cried in his life.

"Wotchya, Uncle Jack," I faltered.

"All right, Tommy. How's it going? What does your mum want today?"

And it was many, many years before I found out the reason why, on that bright, spring, full-of-promise morning that made you want to stand open-mouthed like a daffodil in the sun and dance for the sheer joy of being alive on this wonderful, amazing planet, Uncle Jack was crying.

I've got a lot to thank him for – Uncle Jack. He taught me how to cry. He taught me how to live. And, in a way, a roundabout, circuitous, perigrinaciousy kind of a way, he is why I am here now, sitting in a café, sipping a coffee, waiting for the woman whose laugh and voice and smile and eyes have taught me how to hope and to live again.

But Uncle Jack. Well, I'll never forget that day. Nor the day I found out why he'd been crying. Sort of. Nor today for that matter. Days? Where do we live but days?

We were a big and close-knit family. My mum and dad were the youngest of families of five and four respectively and I was surrounded by a noisy network of older cousins, jolly uncles, and aunts, who were housewives or maybe had a little job two afternoons a week – pin money, a little bit of extra readies, moulah, brass, mawanga, shekels, spondulicks, wonga, dosh, doshoola, greens. See – I always liked words. And where do stories come from if not from words?

And Sundays were the gatherings of the tribes. At the grandparents'. Alternate weekends. One weekend with my mother's loud and sentimental bunch; the next with my father's more reticent, more sober clan.

And Uncle Jack always seemed a bit detached, a little out of place, as if he were dreaming of a life elsewhere, a world elsewhere perhaps, beyond his butcher's shop on the Old Kent Road.

And the tribe, as I recall it, was very pleased with itself. They had cars – rust-ridden old Ford Populars, but cars! They started to have TVs – all of them in time for 1966. They had foreign holidays that their parents had never even dreamed of. In places their parents hadn't heard of or scarcely imagined. They had freezers and central heating and children and all the bragging rights that gave you.

And Uncle Jack had those things too. Except for the holidays. I can't remember him going away at all. He never left the flat above the shop. Except to go shopping. Or for one of the gatherings of the tribe. Or to go and watch Spurs. And my grandparents, his great uncle and aunt, were only a couple of bus trips away or a brisk, quick walk if you were feeling energetic. And he didn't have a car. Or children come to think of it. No telly.

Uncle Jack always walked carrying some huge hunk of meat in a box that fed us all. And he always refused a lift home. "Gotta walk all that food off," he'd cheerfully banter, when my father offered him a lift. "Walk'll do me good."

And he'd stride off quickly, as though running from some bad dream.

Now – I knew all this. No – I didn't know it. I had seen it - but with a child's eyes - without understanding it. I had heard it – but with a child's ears. With innocence, an unquestioning faith that that was the way things were. We took so much on faith back then. Or maybe it was me. And, you know, it was only when I was old enough to have my own children and my own freezer that I started to put all this together. Like some giant, complicated jigsaw with a big expanse of blue at the top and a swathe of green stuff at the bottom. Really hard to do. Gives you headaches and bad dreams. Like the best things in life actually. But worth the effort. Though I did not realize that until these last few months. And it was only when I found Uncle Jack's missing piece that it all made sense. And then it didn't make sense at all. Life can be like that, I've found.

So at the time I did not ask Uncle Jack why he was crying that morning when I was eight. It would not have been the thing to do. I was eight. I was English. Eight-year-old English boys did not ask their elders and betters why they shook with tears so much that streams of their sadness dropped from their faces as they hacked huge haunches of meat apart. He wouldn't have told me anyway. It took him years to tell me. And the funny thing is – in the end, I didn't even have to ask. I sort of worked it out. Almost. But I still needed help.

I knew my times-tables. I always got ten out of ten in the weekly general knowledge quizzes at school. I had a stamp collection that was clearly and unequivocally the third best in my year at school. I could name all the countries of the Commonwealth. And all the kings and queens of England. In the right order too. I was on the top table at school and I knew big words. And I could spell some of them. Everything was all right with my little, innocent world.

So I didn't ask Uncle Jack why he was crying. Then. I didn't ask him then. But I know now. And, you know something, I still don't understand, maya edinstvenniya.

I don't understand how he didn't break down with those big wrenching sobs and gasps and sighs every minute of every hour of every day he walked this earth. As he served his customers. As he walked the streets of South London. As he ate with us all at those Sunday gatherings. On the terraces at Spurs. Every fucking waking moment.

So what were they like the gatherings of the tribe? To tell the truth, I can remember only general impressions. Loud noisy laughter. Everyone chipping in. Helping to prepare the food. Clear away the dishes. A few drinks for the adults. A glass of beer or shandy for my older teenaged cousins. A sip of sherry for me at Christmas. (Wine hadn't quite reached our part of south London – that was to come. And when it did arrive it was, for a few years, confined to Liebfraumilch, when what we really craved were several cases of Zeitgeist.)

But I remember the talk. And the laughter.

A piano. All of us gathered round the old Joanna. Songs. Carols at Christmas. Sentimental songs of love everlasting and hearts broken by that bastard Life. Bawdy music hall songs full of innuendo that made the adults all laugh like drains. And made the children laugh too – though I didn't understand and spent endless introspective hours wondering which of my many cousins I could interrogate about why everyone was laughing, without being laughed at and dismissed for being five. Or nine. Or whatever.

But lots of patriotic songs too. Songs they had sung during the war. My parents and their sisters and brothers all knew the words. And, whatever the season, towards evening, when the beer flowed and the scotch came out, the tribe would become sentimental. It was usually the war. Nights spent down tube stations during the Blitz. The blackout. The rations. The sound of the Luftwaffe bombers. Noisy angry wasps. Deep thundering boomings. Random events. The family at number 28 all killed when their garden bomb shelter took a direct hit. The Doodlebugs and the V2s later – their keening whine bringing a chill of spine-breaking fear into all who heard them and Auntie Rita had seen grown men wet themselves in the street. The Blitz spirit – 'London can take it, but Hitler can't take London!' My gran, my father's mother, hearing that her eldest son (my Uncle Charlie) had been left wounded in a Belgian hedgerow, hearing it from Billy Higgins who lived in the next street (not from the Ministry of War – their telegram – Missing in Action – came later) and who had been in Charlie's platoon. They had left him with some water, two packets of fags and a white hankie, and had put a tourniquet on Uncle Charlie's leg before leaving him to the mercy of the Wehrmacht's medical staff. They wouldn't hear from Charlie for six years.

"He was all right, Maggie. Just a bullet in the thigh. We had to leave him. He'll be all right, love."

He'll be all right. He was all right. But Uncle Jack wasn't.

Uncle Bill and my father who together had fought through the desolate desert sands, those deserts of vast eternity, and walked all the way up the hill and all the way back down again and then walked again all the way through Italy. Monte Cassino. A vision of Hell, my father told me later, just before he died. A vision of Hell come down to grab you and force you to look straight into its eyes, smell its dirty, reeking breath, hear its hoarse, wheezing cackle and taste its shit.

And Uncle Sam who'd been in the sweaty rank dank of the Malayan jungle and come back with a touch of malaria and a visceral hatred of anything Japanese. He died before we knew about sushi. And the decline of the British car industry. Lucky in some ways.

And my Auntie Rita's husband, Arthur, who had ended up in the same prison camp as Uncle Charlie. And Stan, my oldest cousin, who had landed in Normandy and, from the way he told it, had fought all the way to Berlin on his own. And Auntie Doris's husband who had been a paratrooper and had been at Arnhem and who was scared of heights and flying.

"Well, just got to conquer your fear, ain't ya? Stands to bleeding reason. World'd be a sorry place if we all only did what we liked, eh?"

Words, words, words. When you're eight you believe it all. Stories.

But no-one mentioned Uncle Joe who (I later learnt) had spent five years in a British military prison for selling weapons and supplies to the Mafia in Sicily. I met Uncle Joe just the once. He turned up unannounced at our house sending my mum into what she described as a 'tizz'. He drove a gold Jaguar convertible with leather seats, a polished elm dashboard, wore a silk suit, smelt of brandy, gave my mother a bottle of champagne and left with the young, attractive and heavily made-up young lady whom he'd turned up with. And who my mum, later, in the righteous indignation of the righteously flummoxed, described as a 'tart'. A word I hadn't come across before – except in the context of jam or rhyming slang. I liked the glimpse of Uncle Joe that I saw. Though I understood I wasn't supposed to. I wasn't stupid. Though I now know the tribe was a little stupid. Stupid enough to keep the truth about Uncle Jack as dark as the grave. And Uncle Joe. But they didn't know about Uncle Jack. Not really.

Uncle Joe pressed a ten shilling note into my hand as he left, and his girlfriend winked at me and laughed so you could see her teeth and her breasts wobbled a bit and her heels click-clacked on the pavement and she set off a tiny seismic reaction in my pre-adolescent loins. I can still feel it. Just about.

Perhaps Uncle Joe was the life that Uncle Jack thought of when he seemed so detached. That's what crossed my mind back then. But it turned out it wasn't. No way. And it was all so self-congratulatory. Bragging rights. Tales of derring-do and heroics.

And Uncle Jack took no part. He'd been in the Merchant Navy, never fired a gun in anger, had it easy – so the family myth ran. Had a cushy war. An easy billet. That's what they said. Though not, in truth, as easy as my Auntie Doreen's husband who had been in the Bahamas guarding the bleeding Duke of Windsor. Never even saw a German. Unless you count the Duke of Windsor – which I do, of course.

Words, words, words. When you're eight you believe what you're told. Stories.

"So Jack," one of the others would goad, "while I was facing crack Panzer divisions, you were sailing the seven seas, a girl in every port, living the life of old Reilly."

And Uncle Jack never responded. Never. Not a dickie bird. Only the once.

I remember it well. It must have been Christmas 1964 or '65. Why then? Search me. He must have been drinking that night. Normally he never touched a drop. But that night he was totally pineappled. Abso-fucking-lutely pineappled. Although I had not discovered then the joy of infixing.

All I remember is his standing up, swaying a little and saying in a quiet voice,

"You lot. You don't know nuffin. No fucking idea the lot of you. Fucking morons!"

And then he left.

And he left a silence so shocked with his outburst that it wasn't broken until Auntie Rita struck up the opening chords of 'The White Cliffs of Dover' and we all sang lustily.

After that Uncle Jack did not come to the gatherings until next Easter, preferring to stay alone every Sunday in his flat.

Another piece of the jigsaw. But at the time it was just something that happened. Something I observed. And it became, inexorably, a family story.

We didn't do feelings back then. The English. Or at least we didn't do public feelings. That was somehow un-British. As bad as giggling in church. Or swearing in front of children. Peeing in the font. Talking at Sunday lunch. So my parents never commented on Jack's outburst. Never remarked on it to me, though I did overhear my mother in our kitchen say to my father that Uncle Jack was a funny bugger, wasn't he, and do you remember that look on his face when we told him we were going on holiday to Spain?

Life just went on in our complacent little world.

As I got older and started meandering through my teens, I started, by a sort of accident, to spend more time with Uncle Jack. He lived close to us; I was the eldest, the geeky, bookish one and the noise from my younger brothers and sisters led me to seek sanctuary in his flat where I could work on homework undisturbed. And, I suppose, we had a lot in common. A bit of a loner. Iconoclastic. A word I would learn about and love in the sixth form. But that word and solving the mystery of Uncle Jack were many years in the future on the evenings and weekends when I lugged my bursting school satchel round to his place and set to work.

Uncle Jack's flat was spartan, bare, but immaculately neat. He had books which I leafed through on Saturday mornings when he was busy, but no ornaments. Only three pictures. Black and white – from when the world was simpler. They were no-one I recognized. One showed a sailor on the deck of a ship covered in ice and snow, looking off into the distance – a blank of sea and cloud. His grin the only sign of life all around; chunks of ice floated in the water around the ship. The second showed a young woman with shortish dark hair and big, soul-filled eyes. She wore a smile that breathed life and warmth into you if you gazed long enough into her eyes. She stood, frozen in a time I didn't recognize. She wore a rough uniform of some sort, but with no badges or insignia. A military-looking leather battle top, the buttons undone at the top, so you could see her skin and the initial swelling of her breasts. Behind her a few straggly trees. A forest. Looked foreign. Well – it didn't look like South London, put it that way. The third showed the dark-haired girl alongside her blonde doppelganger. They were grinning broadly for the camera and cradled in their arms, lovingly, like two fatal babies of death, long rifles which looked like they were designed for hunting. Which in a way, I now know, they were.

And as I gazed into that woman's eyes – woman's? She looked like a girl. Not much older than me – I did not know that it would be her eyes and their solemn, laughing gaze that would lead to me being here today – sipping coffee in a café in a city on the River Volga.

Stories. You believe it all when you're eleven. All the myths, the lies, the stuff they tell you about the stuff they want to keep dark. Words, words, words, maya edinstvenniya.

So how did Uncle Jack spend his free time? Not sure, to tell the truth. Cross my heart and hope to die. Truth. Just words.

He read a lot – I know that. And he was also the reason I had the third best stamp collection in my year at primary school. He'd give them to me in a brown paper envelope – not steamed off or anything but torn off their original envelopes. And they were from all over the place. Spain. Germany. France. Australia.

"Still got mates in the merchant, ain't I, kid?"

Words, stories – you believe anything when you're ten. Or eight. I still have a tendency to believe now, at fifty-four. Hope. Faith. Love. The eternal quest.

Turned out, in the end, that Uncle Jack knew everything. I knew nothing – despite all those years of coming top of the class in the weekly general knowledge tests. And, although I'm enjoying this coffee and can spell iconoclastic, I still know nothing.

Mind you, I knew more than some. I remember a school trip up West to the Commonwealth Institute and standing with John Baxter, my best mate, looking at a huge wall map of the world. And John wouldn't have it that Britain was Britain. On the map.

"Gerroff. We're an important country – not that poky little island."

Oh, John – nothing stays the same, my friend. Nothing. There's nothing you can count on. Except that it'll be gone. Oh, John. Where did you get to, mate? I lost you along with my stamp collection somewhere down the road. But John'll be back soon, sunshine. Soon.

And the only obvious thing Uncle Jack spent his money on was football. And books. From the age of eight every other Saturday he took me up the Lane. He used to open at six on Saturday mornings and shut up shop at twelve and then it was the number 49 to London Bridge and change to a number 55 which said Leyton on its board but we got off at Seven Sisters and it was then a tramp up the Tottenham High Road. One of the poorest places in England. Even poorer than the Old Kent Road. Poorer than the North - no matter what they tell you. The streets awash with navy blue and white on match days.

Those days at White Hart Lane. Formative. Words. Where I learnt to swear. Learnt the big words somewhere else.

I worked hard at school. Because it was expected. But there were only three things that really held my interest. Books and sport and stamps. Until I was twelve and then it was books and sport and women. The stamps got lost along the way. And none of these was rationed for years after the war. Unlike just about everything else. Except women. They were to remain a mysterious unexplored dark heart of Africa and where-on-earth-really-is-the-Hindu-sodding-Kush for a while. And they still are. Even today. Especially today. And still rationed it seems.

Books and sport have held their sway. And books about sport – don't get me started.

Stamps – my introduction to the world. Must have been six. Big kid comes up to me in the playground and says to me:

"I hear you collect stamps."

I nodded.

"Can I add to your collection?"

"Yes, please."

And with that he stomped with all his power on my foot. I didn't cry. Not like Uncle Jack anyway. Seems like I've been crying ever since though. Inside. Well, inside mainly. But not today. Not today. Please don't let me cry today. Not even if I'm happy.

Books were easy. A cinch. Piece of cake. Piece of piss. Books I could do. Comics had started it, I spose. 'The Victor' mainly – where I read strips that appeared to show me how my male family members had won the war. You believe anything when you're twelve. I'd consumed all the things you were expected to read. Swallows and Amazons. Sherlock Holmes. Biggles. *Wind in the Willows*. The Famous Sodding Five. Words, words, stories – two a penny.

You know, *The Wind in the Willows* is another reason I'm here now, I spose. Though it's mainly down to Jack. I hated that book. Still do. What was I when I first read it? Eight? Nine? Whatever. I liked Ratty and Moley and Badger. What I loved about it was that when the weasels and the stoats took over Toad Hall it was just the best thing I'd ever read. The weasels and stoats were so cool. Beyond cool. Coolatastic. The very zenith of coolocity. The peak of coolocitude. Sick, as Talha Ahmed would say. I spent several days walking down the Old Kent Road doing what I thought was my best weasel impersonation. I imagined a whole gang of us weasels going up the

Lane and watching the Gooners getting stuffed. Taking over Highbury – now the Emirates, of course. See – everything changes.

But you know how it ends. The weasels and stoats get chucked out and Toad gets his ancestral home back. And that really upset me. And by my early teens it got up my nose. Then it got my goat. Then it hacked me off and pissed me off and fucked me off, until finally, as I got to know more words, it offended my aesthetic sensibilities. Still does. Toad-tosser. Toad cunt. You don't see that species on wildlife documentaries.

Words, words, words. Stories. At least *The Wind in the Willows* taught me not to believe all stories. And, while it still annoys me, I now know that it's all an allegory and the weasels are the working class and their defeat is inevitable because Kenneth Graeme was a closet fascist whose fictive narratives were designed to reinforce the values of the bourgeoisie. Or the élite. Take your pick, sunshine. Take your bleeding pick. So while most things change – Highbury becoming the Emirates – *The Wind in the Willows* has the enduring ability to annoy me. And the posh-boy spawn of the toad-tosser keep getting elected.

And the one thing Uncle Jack had was books. Thousands of them. Like in the film *Zulu* where someone runs up to Michael Caine and says:

"Zulus, sir."

"How many?"

"Thousands of 'em."

Stories. Words. You can't do without them. But, actually, if you want to get technical, and I almost always do want to get technical, maya dorogaya – then nowhere in the film does that exchange occur. It's just words, mate.

And, paradoxically, you probably can do without books. Stories are different. We all need stories. Stories are where we live. Stories to tell. Stories to live in.

Except Uncle Jack really did have lots of books. Which was another reason to hang round his flat of a weekend.

Anyway, what I can't pin down exactly was where Sherlock Holmes became Hamlet, and Dr Watson Winston Smith, but it happened somewhere back down the road. Where Biggles was exchanged for Phillip Pirrip. And Ginger for Ivan Denisovich. And Ratty and Moley for Humbert Humbert.

I do know Uncle Jack had a big butcher's hand in it somehow. I remember because for my thirteenth birthday he gave me a copy of *Animal Farm*. It's in my suitcase back at the hotel.

"You want to read about animals? That's the real deal, my son. Better than that Toad any day of the week."

And that was just the start. Read all of Orwell. Everything. And I found a copy of *Homage to Catalonia* on Uncle Jack's shelf. Read it in a day. Read Solzhenitsyn and then – irony of ironies – borrowed *Lolita* from the local library at Greenwich cos the librarian, knowing my interest in Solzhenitsyn, said would I like to read another Russian émigré? Beautiful, bleeding beautiful.

You like Guinness and Riverdance – you'll love Finnegan's Wake! Go on – have a read! You'll love it! Seen the film?

Mind you, I wouldn't put it past those wankers at Disney to try.

Words. They can really get to you. Really really really. Got *Dr Zhivago* in my pocket now. On my Kindle. We never saw those coming, did we? Kindles? When I was a little kid we were all going to be living in lunar colonies, being moon farmers and using the special powers of moon rock to grow the food that feeds the world that reads the papers that tell us shit like that, mate. And all the rest of the smoke and mirrors they use to keep the truth dark and to tell us a different story.

Like John Baxter and the Lane, we'll be seeing more of books a little further down the road.

Sport was less easy. Easy to play. Less easy to understand. I remember my mum waking me in the night in 1963 to whisper to me that she'd just heard on the radio that Spurs had won the Cup Winners' Cup. Athletico Madrid. 5 – 1. Easy. And I remember almost <u>not</u> watching the World Cup Final in '66 because Alf Ramsey hadn't picked Jimmy

Greaves and we were a Spurs house before we were anything else and Greaves was our God and my dad almost willing West Germany to do us over good and proper. Plus we didn't like the way England played – too reminiscent of Arsenal. And my mum going shopping in Lewisham High Street that afternoon and not knowing the result until she got in and her not wanting to be in because my dad used to shout and swear at the telly – honest to God, I bet they heard him in Wembley – and she bought me a book – one of the Jennings series and that set me off on another false trail. I was still in the Biggles and Swallows and Amazon period and just looking for some words to hang my dreams on. Christ! Biggles! Swallows and Amazons! Jennings! Toad! Wankers. Word wankers. Word-wanking mind-weasels.

Stories, stories – just words. Until you realize you're living a story. And you're telling stories. But with no control of the plot. The destination. The final score. The denouement. Our finale. What larks!

And, what's worse, you have to use words. To tell stories, I mean. The irony.

Everyone knows about '66. Looking back, isn't it obvious? Of course, the third goal never crossed the line – I didn't believe it then and I don't believe it now. But if you're England playing West Germany in the World Cup Final a mere twenty–one years after the end of the Second World War, what country would you want to provide the referee and linesmen other than the Soviet Union? And the ref and the linesman were in their forties.

Remember the political commissars who, if captured, were routinely doused in petrol for the fun of seeing them burned alive? Remember Stalingrad, moy droog? Remember the siege of Leningrad, maya kamrad? Remember the Red Army soldiers who were used before the Jews to check that the gas chambers at Auschwitz worked, moy tovarishch? Twenty-seven million Soviet citizens dead.

Of course, the ball was clearly over the line. You could tell it was going to be clearly and inevitably over the line on the morning of January 27th, 1945 – twenty-one years before Geoff Hurst kicked the bleeding thing.

Words, words, words. Stories.

Words – you have to be careful with them. And women. I've learnt that much. And Uncle Jack had learnt it too. Words and other people can make or break you, maya padrooga.

There's so much you don't understand about the world when you are little. Why did the opposition fans hiss at the Spurs fans in lulls and quiet stretches in our own singing? I now know why they hiss a deafening stream of toxic gas, and I'm reminded of the bloke who thought it so funny to add to my stamp collection.

I said twelve with women, but I probably lied. I do that a lot. As you will see. I know Debbie Chapman told me at playtime at primary school how to make a baby. Sounded very queer and would have put me right off except Janet Taylor, one of the twins, told me that Debbie was wrong. Which was a relief. Of sorts. The Taylor twins were exceptionally beautiful, real tasty treats, walking ice-cream with strawberry sauce running down the sides - and even at the age of eight we would drop our pens 'by accident' in order to scrabble around on the floor for the chance to sneek-sneak a quick treat-peek up their skirts, our eyes travelling up their perfect pre-pubescent thighs to see that triangle of navy blue regulation school knickers. They were lovely. The Taylor twins, not the knickers. Janet and Karen Taylor – tripping and tootling and titillating off the tip of my tongue perfectly in their tempting, trochaic synchronicity. Often wonder where they got to. The Taylor twins, not the knickers. Hope they are happy. And loved. I hope they have a good story to tell.

And Yvonne Atkins. I will never forget her. I suppose you could call her my first love. We had spent the whole of the last year at primary school catching each other in games of kiss-chase in the playground and I walked her home and struggled to carry her satchel. She had dark brown hair and huge eyes a boy could be lost in and a wide, expressive mouth, and I could make her laugh. I used words to make her laugh. And crazy dancing.

"Look, Yvonne, look! Only I can walk backwards and talk and dance at the same time while clinging to the earth with my special powers, despite my anti-gravity trousers."

Yvonne would laugh, although I don't think she believed me entirely. I was always fluent in high-sounding gibberish.

And then – our last term before big school - must have been July – it was steaming hot, humid, clammy – that clothes-stick-to-your-flesh heat that you get in London and you know the day will end in some spectacular thunderstorm with huge gobs of rain, when Gloria Smith came up to me just after the start of lunch in the playground and said,

"Come with me. Yvonne's got something she wants to show you."

So I went. Indoors. Up the stairs. Pushed into the girls' bogs. And there she lay – Yvonne – stark naked. And I stared at something I hadn't seen on that world map, transfixed by the dark triangle where her thighs met, where the whiteness of her legs became a fuzzy black. An unknown peninsula. Unexplored promontories. My pre-pubescent Hindu Kush. I didn't know a thing. I didn't even know the right word.

"Touch me if you like, Tommy – it might be fun."

And walking home that night to her house we kissed. It was like an angel had put her hands on me and let me taste heaven – but this angel had no wings and wore no knickers. Oh, so young. Me, I mean. Not Yvonne.

That was Thursday. On Friday Yvonne went home from school in the morning. She had a very bad headache. By Sunday morning she was dead. Brain haemorrhage. I didn't know until Monday morning. School assembly. All of us in tears. Gloria howling some primitive animal noise. I stood speechless. No words.

Don't kiss too many angels, Tommy. They die.

Chapter Two: Jack I

All night they had to endure the moans, the cries, the agonized screams of the men captured in that afternoon's raid. Individual voices and shouts for pity or mercy blended into one primeval howl of anguished pain, and Jack, on sentry duty after midnight, could not block out the sounds and yet at the same time could not stop trying to distinguish one heart-rending screech of sheer fear from another guttural squeal of protest. Was that Bob the Scouser, who had made them laugh last night with his jokes about his work in the docks? Or was it Jamie from Glasgow who had written a letter every night to his girl back home? Or could that bowel-emptying howling be the miner from Nottinghamshire who kept himself to himself and spent all his free time carving chess figures from bits of wood he had carried with him into the trenches from the woods behind the lines?

The attackers had carried off the unit's two dogs as well – Lupito and Bandito – and the cold night air was pierced by the savage and manic sounds of animals dying slowly. Jack tried not to think about what was happening to the dogs. In any case, they would find out soon enough: there was to be a counter-attack tomorrow – that is, if they could hold this trench in the meantime.

Jack sucked slowly on his cigarette and sipped the black strong tea that came from somewhere strange and tasted like no tea he knew in England. He hadn't taken to the local coffee, but this tea was like nectar and in other respects, he smiled to himself, he'd become a soldier quite quickly, learning to rest whenever he could, relax whenever he could, look busy if an officer was around, eat when there was food, drink when there was drink. The dogs had been useful in the trench too: he felt that tonight he had to be more alert than usual having relied at night on the dogs' senses of smell and their hearing for warning of any intruders. Mind you, with the inhuman sounds coming from the enemy trenches, an attacker could easily approach the trenches without being heard.

He lit another cigarette and saw his fingers still shaking. His first taste of war and he was still shaking. The attack had been over by midday, over twelve hours ago, but still his body and mind had not recovered, replaying every slow, quick second in minute detail. The attack had actually lasted only two hours, but now, in the slow replaying of events in Jack's mind, it seemed as if it had taken days, from the initial bombardment from the bombers – Stukas, Robbie had called them - screaming through the air directly at them, during the bombardment by mortars, then the enemy infantry assault and finally the hand-to-hand scrabbling for life or death here in the trenches.

It was easier when he could stand on the parapet and fire his gun at a target; he felt he'd achieved something. The new Russian rifles that had arrived a week ago looked crude but were good to shoot and the bayonet slid on easily and quickly when the time came: Jack hadn't waited for any order – it was obvious when to do it. Terrified and doubly terrified that he would lose control of his bowels during the plane attack and the mortar bombardment, once the enemy advanced he'd been too busy staying alive to worry about fear, too busy staying alive to worry about killing. Now he shivered and his hands shook, but he knew he would do it again – it had to be done; someone had to do it; and he and Robbie were here now. If not them, then who?

He heard someone stumbling along the trench towards him and, as he lowered his rifle, said, "Stop!"

"Sallright, me old mate. It's me – Robbie."

He felt Robbie sit down beside him.

"Got a fag going spare?"

"Course, Robbie. There you go. I thought you didn't smoke. You started?"

"Certainly have, sunshine. It's the latest Party directive – the more you smoke the less you shit yourself when the fascists attack. Didn't you know? That was always your problem, Jack – you are an idealist; your heart's in the right place, but you got no time for the details of Party doctrine – which is why I'm unit commissar and you, sunshine, are a mere plodding, droopy-arsed foot soldier of the proletariat."

"Sod off. I'm a Defender of the Proletariat. Staunch Father to the Homeless and Valiant Guard of the Motherless Orphans of the Bleeding Working Class. If you don't mind."

Robbie chuckled. He made a good Commissar, Jack thought. Serious and committed but not *too* serious, unlike the German Communist who had given them lectures during their hellish time outside Madrid before this posting above the Ebro.

"Sorry, Jack. I mean, sorry Staunch Defender of Whatever the Hell you just said."

Their shoulders bumped together as they laughed.

"Jack. I was frightened today. Absolutely bloody frightened."

"Me too. More frightened than someone called Algernon "The Frightened One" Frightened from the small hamlet of Frightened near the town of Petrified in Shitscaredshire in the United Cowardly Kingdom. But I tell you, Robbie, those sounds we can hear make me even more frightened of myself and what I'll do to those bastards when we attack."

Robbie was silent for a few seconds. Jack was aware that he was silently crying. He felt a slight movement of Robbie's shoulder and a short intake of breath.

"Jack, I was more frightened of showing fear than of the enemy, but I found myself praying to a God I don't believe exists that I wouldn't get hit and that if I did that I wouldn't show pain or cry. Also I was frightened that, when it came to it, I'd be frightened of killing, but, you know, after the first I enjoyed it. And then I got frightened by that. How did you feel?"

"Same as you really. It's all a con, isn't it – some of it? All of us more scared of showing fear and worrying about killing. But I tell you, Robbie - the bloke I stuck with my bayonet – it was him or me. I want to live." Jack paused. "And I also thought - sod it! You ain't here on holiday, Jack Wilkinson, you come here to kill fascists and – crickey – there right in front of me was a fascist. So I killed him.....Robbie, I didn't like it either, but I ain't going home. We got a job to do. We are here – who else is there?"

"I know. We could be good at this. Listen, I'm going round all the blokes what's awake and telling them. Tomorrow we're getting more ammo, some machine guns and they're sending up two snipers. Russian apparently."

"Russians? Snipers?"

"Like us - in that they've volunteered. Top blokes an' all. Good shooters, so I've been told."

"Crikey! I still can't believe this. Just think, Robbie, six months ago we were in South London living our little lives and if you'd've told me that I would soon be in Spain fighting alongside people from all over the world - I'd never've believed you. And for something we believe in – not for the bosses, not for our country, but for our principles. I've never been so happy, despite being so frightened today."

"Me too. I think this is what I wanted to do all my life, but I didn't know I wanted to do it till now. Think of all of them back home now. Our mates'll be wandering out of the pub right now, scoffing chips, thinking about getting up for work tomorrow morning and how much they hate it."

"Yeah, and we have tomorrow's counter-attack to look forward to. I'd kill for some chips and a few pints of grog just now."

"Yeah, but at least I feel alive. I feel important for the first time in my life. I feel that what I'm doing is important. I know this sounds daft, Jack, but I hope I live to tell the story of this war. And I hope you live, so that you can tell our story so people know what this feeling of solidarity is like despite all the fear."

"Robbie, I even like being in the Army. Well, this army. I know there are the boring bits – doing drill, counting the minutes down when you're on sentry duty and waiting to be relieved, but I like the order, the structure, the comradeship. When we're finished battling it out here it might be a good idea to join the Army again – we're bound to be taking on Hitler at some stage."

"Mmmmm, I wouldn't be too sure about that. A lot of our politicians seem to admire his policies too much. I wouldn't trust many of them, but you're right. I think it might come to a fight sooner or later. Look, Jack - got work to do. How much longer are you on?"

"Another hour and I can get some kip, if I've calmed down enough and if those sounds from the other trenches stop."

"All right. See you in the morning, sunshine."

"Yeah, see you, Robbie."

And Jack was left alone to count the minutes down until he was relieved. There was no respite, however, from the raw cries and primal howls that drifted across from the enemy trenches. Jack was thrilled with horror and revulsion at whatever it was, whatever appalling torture was being practised a mere four hundred yards from where he was sitting.

In the morning when Jack awoke from his disturbed, fitful, nightmare-filled sleep, he noticed immediately the continued agonized sounds from the enemy lines, but also the complete absence of birdsong and put it down to the terrible sounds which dominated the cool, gloomy and chilly early-morning air.

With the full light of morning came the usual bustle and slow coming-back-to-life-again rituals of fighting men anywhere in any country in any century. Breakfast was scavenged and devoured with the desperation of men who had not slept well or comfortably. The equipment was checked. Cigarettes were smoked. Idle banter filled the gaps, while some men shaved, others cleaned their rifles, and still others wrote – letters and journals, diaries and notes, wills, poems.

At some point before mid-morning – Jack seemed to lose precise track of time when he was not on sentry duty – the promised Russian snipers arrived and reported to the brigade commander.

Jack was amazed to discover that they were women: one blonde, the other with jet black hair, but apart from that, almost indistinguishable at first glance. They had small packs on their backs and carried long rifles with telescopic sights – not slung from their shoulders, but carried in front of them, cradled almost as if they were children who needed the protection and nurture of their mothers. Jack was amazed partly because he had been expecting male snipers, but also because he came from an England in which it was inconceivable that women should be given any combat role. Robbie, as ever the loyal party apologist, was less shocked – or, if he was shocked, he pretended not to show it.

"Stands to reason that, Jack. I've heard that factories inside the Soviet Union organise crèches for working mothers."

"What are crèches?"

"Like nursery schools where children stay while the mothers work. It's different from back home."

"A lot of things are different from back home, but can they fight?"

Robbie laughed.

"Hark at the great warrior! Jack, twenty four hours ago, you didn't know you could fight. Let's give them a go and see how they do - then we can judge them. Apparently they passed through their sniper school with flying colours, but today will be their first real action."

"I fancy being a sniper. How do you get to be one in the British Army?"

"Forget it, sunshine. You have to be an officer and to be an officer…."

"Yeah, you have to go to public school. Ridiculous! They'll be missing out on some good snipers then – more fools them."

"Jack – thank your lucky stars you're not in the British Army, my son. You'd be on a permanent charge for being such a subversive little twat!"

"Oh, Robbie – that's the nicest thing anyone has ever said to me."

There was a meeting to discuss the tactics for the counter-attack. Token sentries were left in the front line, while the others retreated to a small hollow about one hundred yards back where the battalion commander could address them.

"Come on, everyone. It gives me special pleasure this morning to introduce you to two comrades from the Soviet Union. Halya Reznik…."

At this the one with short black hair stood up and acknowledged very slightly the smiles and nods of encouragement and approbation, and the muted applause.

"And her comrade sister-in-arms – Katya Tyutikova. Like you, Halya and Katya have volunteered to be here. I'm sure their fighting abilities will add to our combat effectiveness and, in a way, it is thanks to them that we can even contemplate a counter-attack like this at this time of day.

"The plan is very simple. The men left in the trenches now will remain there during the attack to provide covering fire. At the same time Halya and Katya will position themselves about twenty-five yards on either side of me and the command post. Their job is to provide covering fire, but obviously theirs will be more accurate and once we have reached the enemy frontline and all hell breaks loose, Katya and Halya will advance rapidly behind us, slightly back from the action, but selecting their targets carefully to cause maximum damage to the enemy. Halya, Katya will explain what you must do."

They both nodded and grinned and Halya said, with a grin and a blaze of passionate fury in her eyes, "Fascisiti officieri!" and drew her right thumb (with her palm outstretched and at right angles) slowly from left to right across her throat.

There was general laughter. They all understood that.

"Comrade commander, how will we advance?" someone enquired.

"Forwards, I thought. It's usually best."

There was a general chuckle.

"No, comrade – I meant to ask what the plan was."

"I am pleased you asked me that. We won't be doing our usual mad dash across no man's land. We will be creeping, silently and stealthily under the covering fire and then – no yelling and screaming, comrades – we will really go into the enemy trench at precisely one o'clock – just when they're looking forward to lunch and a little siesta."

"Comrade commander, this is new. Will they be expecting us?"

"I bloody well hope not or we are, as we say in the military, completely fucked. It's all about surprise. We can't get artillery cover or any air support, but we have got our two new Russian secret weapons. I don't know what you know or what you think you know about sniping, but the Soviet Army uses snipers differently from other armies. For a start every infantry company has two specialist snipers. They don't take static, defensive positions, but are more mobile and used offensively to more effect. Katya, is that right?"

"Da. Of course, we can defend when the situation calls for it and then we would have special hiding places, but here we are attacking and we will be very mobile, using our telescopes to pick out the officers and target them – or just causing general mayhem amongst the defenders."

She gave a slight smile which the commander returned, nodding and smiling encouragingly at Halya and Katya. They each gave a slight smile back. War is a serious business after all.

"One last thing, comrades. From what we have heard during the night our lads have been tortured and –"

"And the dogs."

"And the dogs. I want there to be no reprisals, no retribution. We are a fighting battalion, who go to liberate not to conquer. The enemy are fighters like us. We will show them respect. There are some of them who are alive at this very moment who will not be alive when the sun sets. Those who do not wish to go on that journey to darkness, we will not send. As for those who resist us – well, let us rock and shock and terrorise and annihilate their world. We will give them death, if that is what they choose. But if you are ferocious and valiant in battle, remember to be magnanimous and compassionate in victory. If there are casualties of war, remember that when those men woke up and got dressed this morning and had breakfast, just as you have done, that they had no intention to die today. Give them due dignity in death. Bury them as you would your own and mark their graves.

"It is my main intention to take the enemy trench, but also to bring every single one of you out alive. However, there may be some among us who will not see the light of the moon tonight. We will bury you with great honour and enormous respect, but there will be no time for futile sorrow. We are here to do a job and we must steel ourselves and our spirits to accept whatever the day brings. The enemy should be left in not the slightest doubt that we are his nemesis and we will bring about his rightful destruction. As they die, they will understand the truth that their attitudes and beliefs have brought them to this place. Just as our ideals and beliefs have brought us here. In that sense we must show them our nobility, our dignity, our integrity. War is a terrible, awful, monstrous thing, so it behoves us to act as humanely as possible when the fighting is over. And do not forget the justice of our cause. Whenever death may surprise us, let us welcome it, if our battle cry has been heard by one receptive listener and other hands reach out to take up our arms.

"It is a big thing to take another human life – one that should be not done lightly. I believe that if you take any other life without just cause, then you live forever with the stain of blood upon you. If some of the enemy choose not to fight, then remember that they have the right to go home one day to their families and to live happily in peace. We must remember the values to which we are dedicated, despite our hunger for revenge. So no matter what we find – and I imagine it will be quite grisly - just get on with your job: take the trench, take prisoners, stay strong, stay brave and stay alive – if you can.

"Now on our mammoth crawl – across no man's land – no talking, no standing, no smoking – they might see or smell the smoke - and, if you need a piss, you'll have to piss in your trousers where you lie. And if you reach the line early, wait until one o'clock. Our chief weapon – apart from ourselves and Halya and Katya - is surprise."

"Comrade commander, do you still get scared before an assault?"

"Me? Of course not! I was at the Somme and the Third Battle of Ypres, so no – I don't get scared – although in the Great War I did notice that every time I went into action, just in the last second before the whistles were blown and all hell broke loose, I had a marked tendency to urinate copiously and completely without any conscious volition. But I wasn't scared."

There was laughter amongst the men. Katya whispered a translation to Halya.

"Listen – we are all scared, but it is the truly brave man – or woman," he glanced at Halya and Katya, "who knows fear but shows none."

The men laughed and broke up to chat and smoke and enjoy a few moments of calm before the attack, fiddling with their equipment, performing their good luck rituals as any soldier at any time over the centuries has done.

Robbie approached the two Russians.

"Commissar," he pointed to his own red tabs and then to Halya's. "We are awfully pleased to have you."

"Ochen priyatno."

"Nice rifle." Robbie stroked the muzzle of Halya's rifle. He was mesmerized by the unblinking smile that leapt from her eyes, the wayward shock of her short black hair and the cadences of her voice, the ineffable grace with which she moved – despite the unflattering army fatigues. Even the way she tilted her head back to stare at him straight in the eyes, mesmerized him. Robbie felt a blaze of hard, savage tenderness in her eyes and a bright flare of deep, shining longing in his whole body.

"Da, ochen harrasho. Mosin Nagant."

"She says: yes it is very good. Mosin Nagant is the name of the rifle."

This was Katya.

"Very good," Halya mimicked.

"Halya has no English," Katya explained.

"And I have no Russian. Well, please tell her, comrade sister," Robbie said, "that we are pleased and proud to be fighting alongside soldiers of the Red Army. My name is Robbie."

He was speaking slowly now and pointed to himself.

"Robbie," repeated Halya slowly, trying out the unfamiliar sound in her lips and in her mouth. Her lips moved to accommodate the strange new sound.

"I will," Katya assured him.

"And good luck in the attack."

"There is no such thing as luck. We make our own luck, Comrade Robbie. Sorry, Comrade Commissar." Katya smiled.

Robbie grinned. "'Robbie' is just fine. This is my mate Jack."

He looked around, but Jack was several yards away cleaning his rifle.

****

The crawl across no man's land was exhausting both physically and mentally. They proceeded at snail's pace, aware that the slightest sound would alert the enemy to their stealthy approach and the impending attack. Jack felt a rising sense of fear mingled with excitement and alarm, and had to consciously stop himself from standing up and running straight back to their own lines. Their watches had been carefully synchronized and at the appointed hour Jack looked sombrely into Robbie's eyes for a split second, before they rose and made a frenzied mad, crazed dash over the last few feet and, yelling and screaming, jumped into the enemy trench.

Run run run run stab stab stab stab kill kill kill but fight crouch stab stab fire fire fire stab stab thrust stab sounds explosion stab stab kill fights stab kill shoot shoot where should shoot reload reload the high dive dive right in Robbie stamp stamp butt stab stab fire fire reload duck duck little duck butt punch kick run grenade thrown blood blood God God stab kill kill kill kill kill duck dive reload kick kick lunge stab in the stomach into the chest all kick crouch punch but fire with fire fire kill kill kill blood blood blood die die diediediedie killkillkillkill

When the enemy trench had been taken, it was clear to them all why the sounds in the night had been so terrifying.

Beyond the front trench, beyond the supporting trench in a level, lower-lying piece of ground, they found two of their captured comrades and Bandito and Lupito, the platoon's dogs. All four – both the men and both the dogs – had been buried up to their necks in the ground. Above them, each one of them was surrounded by a makeshift cage, firmly pegged into the ground, from which no escape was possible. Still in each cage were three evil-looking feral cats which had done unspeakable things to the men and the dogs who had been powerless to defend themselves in any way.

What remained above the ground in each cage was an unrecognisable stump of life or half-life – battered and pulpy, beaten and mutilated, shredded flesh and hanging eyeballs and globs of brain, a bloody, eviscerated mass of suffering.

The third man was in a bigger cage: he had been spread-eagled, his feet and hands tied to thick stakes driven into the ground: his stomach had been sliced open and his genitalia hacked off. His tongue had been ripped out. The cats were still using their claws to feed on unrecognizable bits of his flesh.

One of the dogs was still alive – weakly whimpering. Jack realized it was Lupito and in a flash of memory recalled how the little terrier would beg on its hind legs for food. Halya calmly walked up to the cage, took out her revolver and ended its misery. Katya calmly shot the cats.

One of the fascist soldiers was lying a few yards away, wounded in the stomach and watching the platoon's horrified reaction to the torture they had found. Jack threw himself on the defender and began to strangle him. Robbie strode over and pulled him off.

"No retribution. We are better than they are and that is our victory."

But elsewhere a member of the platoon was jubilantly urinating into the mouth of a dying man, while another was hacking off another's penis to compound his agony and complete his humiliation. The commander shot once into the air.

"Kill those who are too injured to save with one bullet. The others – treat them as you would want to be treated yourselves. Jack Wilkinson – back to our lines sharpish and bring some medics with you."

****

A few days later. Behind the lines. The unit relaxes. Weapons are cleaned. Scratches and bruises tended to. Long letters home are written. Uniforms are repaired. Weapons are cleaned and checked. Sleep. Sunshine. Quiet. The buds on the acacias start to show.

Robbie and Halya are walking by a small brook that chuckles, giggles and chortles past on its way to a small mill surrounded by olive trees. They are learning each other. They are learning how to be with each other. As they walk their shoulders and upper arms brush together impelled by the swaying rhythm of their walk. Halya laces her arm into Robbie's slightly bent right arm and together they walk a little further, trying out this new position to see how it feels.

Then Robbie stops. He turns to face Halya. He looks directly into her black, soul-sparking, love-wide eyes. They have a common language but it is one that is so ancient it has never been written down and cannot be transcribed. They laugh. And as they laugh their hands and arms excitedly reach out to touch and enclose the other.

"You are beautiful," Robbie says.

"Ochen krasiviye," replies Halya.

Robbie points to his eyes. "Eyes."

"Glaze." Halya points to hers.

"Nose," and Robbie reaches out his right forefinger to touch Halya's nose.

"Nos." Halya repeats the gesture, her finger on Robbie's nose.

They laugh.

"Tongue." Robbie sticks his tongue out.

"Yazick." It is Halya's turn.

Robbie reaches his hand towards Halya's face and softly, gently, tenderly, strokes with his fingertips the skin on her cheek.

"Your skin is so soft," Robbie sighs.

"Kozjha." Halya says and reaches out to stroke Robbie's cheek. The touch of an angel.

Robbie's secretly intense forefinger traces delicate circles of soft swirling touch on Halya's cheek. Halya's eyes light up with fire and suddenly she half-bites Robbie's finger, laughing cheekily and with her eyes fixed on his, mischievous, laughing.

Robbie takes from his shirt pocket a chunk of bread, breaks a small piece off and offers it up to Halya's mouth. Her lips part slowly and, with a tiny smile, she allows Robbie to feed her the bread, letting her tongue linger fleetingly on Robbie's finger as it withdraws and allowing her teeth to scrape softly on his skin.

They laugh. Their eyes cannot leave each other. Immutable, fixed, ineluctable – for the eternity of the moment.

"I want you," murmurs Robbie.

"Ya hochu tebya," Halya murmurs.

"More?" Robbie offers another morsel.

"Da! Da!"

Halya opens her mouth in anticipation.

Unable to wrench his eyes away from the playful, dancing fire in her eyes Robbie, with gentleness and sweet care, puts the piece of bread between the white pearl-snowdrops of her teeth and, sensing the warm wetness of her tongue, delicately places the bread on it.

Halya chews, smiling.

As they were both later to admit to each other, for a few moments of caught-in-amber time, the world and all its tortured tears and screaming suffering and slouching, snarling, arrogant slaughter, simply stopped.

And they heard eternity in the beating of their hearts and the near-silent yet ceaseless susurration of the rhythms of their breathing.

Halya opens her mouth for more.

Chapter Three: Tommy II

Iconoclastic, not plastic, but fantastic,

It's so fucking drastic

Across the nation in your imagination.

Mental stagnation, spiritual incarceration

Is all you get in the great British nation!

Yeah, I should say so. I should coco, moloko. I remember during the build-up to the World Cup in '66 being asked in the corridor at my primary school who I thought would win. Well, no actually it wasn't quite like that. There were six of us - confronted by the top class primary school teacher, Mrs Douglas. The six of us stood in a line. You will understand this more when you hear about what she was like. She interrogated us one by one, using our surnames. The other five all said England when asked who would win the World Cup and then she got to me.

"What about you, Wilkinson? You're rather quiet. Who do you think will win?" She half-barked, half-insinuated, half-demanded. It certainly wasn't a real question. I got the impression she wasn't really interested in my answer.

"Portugal, Mrs Douglas," which I have to say was probably not a very politic or sensitive thing to say in May 1966 and in truth I only said it because I'd read in my dad's newspaper that Portugal were the dark horses and might do well plus I'd seen clips of Eusebio on the television, the new television, and his grace and spirit and imagination on the field had caught my eye. Mind you, I've never been one for being politic – I speak my mind, when I can find it.

Mrs Douglas was unperplexed. Perhaps one could have detected a look of mild surprise in her face, but no doubt she was used to the strange ways of pre-pubescent boys.

"And why do you say that?"

"Well," this was when I faltered and hesitated. "Well, I think they have a good chance. And Eusebio is a very talented player."

"Mm, good! Independence of mind!" she barked.

I have to explain that to get praise from Mrs Douglas was like winning the British Empire Medal and the Victoria Cross with Triple Bar. She was 'Old School' in 1966. What did that mean? It's hard to explain to the younger generation, maya dorogaya.

'Old School', if you were Mrs Douglas in 1966, meant that you smoked in lessons, only occasionally but quite openly; that you used corporal punishment regularly without regret, without hesitation over the slightest infringement or questioning of your will; and that you were treated with a veneration and awe and respect that held pupils and parents in a mesmerized trance of star-struck reverence. She seemed to love using the ruler on our outstretched palms. But what she really loved was concentrated, intense, precise intelligence. Curiosity. And the ruler and her magnetic, charismatic personality were the weapons, her weapons of choice.

And what did we get the ruler for? Well, certainly for talking when she was talking, doing any of the mischievous mayhem that young monkeys at English primary schools might get up to - flicking ink, throwing a rubber at Debbie Chapman, gazing too long at the Taylor twins. But she had a rigorous dedication to accuracy. Remember this was South London. We also got the ruler for saying "ain't", "nuffink" and saying "bottle of water" with glottal stops.

Her eyes would widen slowly; her hair would seem to stand on end. She 'gathered', I think, is the word we would use now. She certainly took a deep intake of breath before she bellowed.

"Bow'er o' Waw'er! Bottle of water! The letter 't' is there for a reason, you horrible little boy. My goodness, where were you brought up? Brung up more than likely! Come to the front," and coming to the front inevitably meant the ruler. Too many omitted full stops - the ruler; don't get the apostrophe - the ruler; smudgy work - the ruler.

It was a different world. We had ink monitors and those scratchy pens, bits of wood with a piece of fashioned metal on the end. No cartridges.

And a pet monitor, a plant monitor and a window monitor, a board monitor and I think there was even an unofficial ashtray monitor, who emptied her over-flowing ashtray before it threatened to engulf her desk. In appearance she reminded my primary school self of Churchill, and I suppose in a small way she embodied a certain Churchillian steadfastness. And she had the resolute jaw-line and the unwavering gaze. She ran all the sports teams and, yes, from the age of seven we played competitive sports against other schools. I wish I could remember her team talks before we played rival primary schools at football. All I can remember is the lavish praise she heaped upon me when I came third in the one hundred and ten yards under 11 All London Schools Hurdling Final. And on another occasion when I had scored the only goal in our 5 – 1 defeat against our closest, nearest, deadliest rivals. (The local Catholic primary school – where did all that sectarianism disappear to?) Perhaps it was because she knew what had happened to me when I was five that she seemed to like my determination, my willingness to keep going, to never give up, to never say die.

Yes, I know! Don't tell me 'to never give up' is, of course, a split infinitive - but listen to the rhythm. It's got to be like that. It's got to be iambic. It's got to be 'to never give up' or all the more important rules of the English language are blown out of the water. Just like *Star Trek*. To boldly go - and I've been boldly going whenever I got the chance, I can tell you, maya padrooga. Even today, mate, especially today.

So she was like Churchill. She frightened everyone. Her husband, whom I met once, seemed to be frightened by her too. She was a personage of enormous mystery and yet curiously we knew things about her life, her private life. Once she'd got a class where she wanted them (by perhaps early October of the school year) she would open up and reveal a more vulnerable, sensitive side. We knew, for example, that every Saturday she went to watch rugby, travelling either to Twickenham or to Richmond. We knew that her first husband had died at El Alamein and that her second had been his best friend who had only met her because he brought her husband's personal effects back to her in 1946.

And the funny thing with Mrs Douglas was that, if you used the apostrophe correctly, if you omitted no full stops, if you didn't flick ink at Paul Sturrock, if you didn't spend too long looking at the Taylor twins, if you didn't say "nuffink" and "ain't" and if you avoided the glottal stop – well, then you could say almost anything to her. I owe her a lot. She praised me when I thought I was worthless. She made me speak. She gave me confidence. And in a strange way she made me say that Portugal might win the World Cup.

Some would say she was a bully, but that wasn't true. She abhorred bullies. I'll tell you this story. I can't remember the origins, but there was one unpleasant, muggy afternoon. We were maybe nine or ten, I'm not sure. Nine or ten, practising to be men, the girls thinking they might like to be women but not sure of their role, not sure of where it was going, what to do. The school bully, Steven Foster was, I recall, out to 'get me'. You know, I can't remember why. Perhaps I'd offended him with my quick and agile tongue. Perhaps he didn't like skinny, clever, short-arses like me. Perhaps I'd been snarking about him. Steven fought people once a week, chosen (on Monday), it seemed to me, at random, and always on a Friday (the fight). It was his 'thing' we would say now, his 'bag'. What was worse was that his intention to 'get' someone would be announced sometime early on Monday morning and so his victim had all week to think of what might happen on the Friday, at lunchtime, when the 'getting' would commence.

Steven at nine was huge, a man-mountain of wobbly flesh and almost muscle, an Everest of threat to someone like me. I can still see his red hair and freckles, the way his face reddened with anger and exertion as he crushed his victim in his bear-like grasp.

I'd always avoided him and for the life of me I can't remember what I'd done to offend him on that particular week. Why I was his chosen one. But it turned out differently from the way anyone might have expected, despite my being half his size.

Krav Maga - I didn't know about it then. I didn't know about a lot of things. But now I like Krav Maga. I like the fact it's so different from karate and judo and Tae Kwon Do. And all those posturing, preening, let's-get-to-your-centre, elegant, elaborate, aesthetically-pleasing modes of self-defence or martial arts, as they prefer to call them. I like the fact that you don't have to wear fancy dress and look like a twat while practising Krav Maga. I liked the very first lesson of Krav Maga – from which I learnt to carry an almost-empty glass bottle of beer late at night through hostile, dark city streets. So practical. And inexpensive. I especially like the two tenets of Krav Maga.

1.   Get home safe.

2.   Avoid conflict.

Any self-defence system that has those two tenets as its central pillars is my kind of self-defence system. So I didn't know about Krav Maga consciously, but instinctively I did, and it was Krav Maga that did for Steven, the school bully.

Krav Maga is also not yet a recognized Olympic sport – which is good. Seems like everything else is these days. If you are going to allow Beach Volleyball, then Masturbation can't be far behind, but I'm not sure how it would be scored: obviously not speed or quantity of ejaculate, I would suggest; perhaps you'd need judges like Gymnastics and Diving. Or why not introduce an English Pentathlon: drinking 16 pints of lager; picking a fight with some strangers; intimidating women; casual acts of xenophobia; and finally downing a very hot curry while belittling the waiter – that would increase our medal haul at a stroke. We'd always get Gold. You gotta play to your strengths.

In Krav Maga they say that when faced with a difficult situation you have three alternatives. Flight, fight or freeze.

I was later to apply Krav Maga to my relationships with women, which you will hear about later, and it's not a strategy that really works in personal relationships. But it's a good way of thinking about the school bullies in large South London primary schools.

I'd seen Steven's victims freeze. They would end up tearful, snotty, bludgeoned and puffy, bloodied at the nose and the mouth, pummelled and humiliated in front of the whole school who would stand around in a huge circle, goading and chanting and bleating for blood. I'd also seen them flee, but that's not a good long-term strategy in any school or organization, if you want to be able to walk the corridors with your head held high.

And I'd also seen them fight. Try to fight as Steven did - with punches, with grappling, with in-your-face wrestling. They too ended up tearful and bloodied and pummelled and humiliated. Steven would always be confronted with Mrs Douglas and retribution; the official retribution of the school was inflicted on Steven, but he reigned supreme in the playground. He did not stop his bullying.

Fight. Flight. Or freeze.

That week I'd spent a lot of time fleeing. On our school field, before you got to the football pitches and the running track, we still had, would you believe, the air raid shelters from the war. And though we were not allowed to go in them at all, we did, of course, and they were quite effective hiding places. Very few people liked them because they stank of urine, were littered with indescribable rubbish, and there were rumours that the ghosts of dead pilots and bombed-out families haunted their eerie, cobwebbed blackness, but Friday lunchtime came, as it has a tendency to do every week. And I, slowly and with the deepest reluctance, left the shelters to face my fate.

I then slurked around in the bushes at the top of the playground. It must have been Yvonne who found me and told me that Steven was still looking for me. There were only maybe ten or maybe fifteen minutes of lunchtime left. Yes, lunchtime. Mrs Douglas had taught us to call it lunchtime and not dinner time, you uneducated rapscallion.

By now the whole school was in a circle around the playground. I wish I had winked at Yvonne and said, well, I wish I'd said, "Babe, I've gotta go," but I know I didn't. I only say that in the unmade Hollywood blockbuster, my biopic. I'm more likely to be in the Mister Men cartoon series – Mister Inadequate. Mister Egregious, as things have turned out, in fact. A fucking disaster of a human being. Mister Tosser. But I didn't know that then. I probably said nothing. Back then I was the archetypal weak, silent type.

All I can remember is being half-pushed out from the circle of screaming children to confront the man-mountain. His rage had intensified because my fleeing had been so successful all week that he had barely seen me. I remember standing there freezing momentarily and it flashed across my mind that he was like the boy who had added so generously to my stamp collection just a few years before. And I couldn't help wondering: why me? What can I have possibly done to justify your wrath? Why me? I've hardly ever spoken to you. I was also very conscious that my two younger sisters, Julie and Caroline, were watching and at the time, I have it on their own authority (although against all the evidence), they thought I was a god (erroneously as it was to turn out). Couldn't let them down. Plus whatever happened would all be recounted to my mum and dad that night.

I knew that I couldn't fight fair with Steven. I knew what happened to those who did. I knew I couldn't flee anymore, so flight was out and there was the shame to deal with. And, as I was freezing, something shifted in my brain and I moved – small, lithe, agile - towards Mr Everest. I'm not proud of what happened next. Even writing this makes me cry.

Like England's best fly half ever, my right leg swung up and caught him straight in the genitalia. His hands flew down, his face went crimson and he bent over double. With my hands on his head, I kneed him hard in the face. His face rose slightly, so that it was now at the level of my face and, hard and fast, I head-butted him across the bridge of the nose and then I ran, ran, ran.

I ran, not because of fear of Steven - I think his nose was broken. I ran through fear of Mrs Douglas. I sought sanctuary in the air raid shelters, maya edinstvenniya.

I froze; I fought; I flew. I had not avoided conflict. But would I get home safe?

After a few, fear-filled minutes, I heard the bell that signalled the end of lunch, a hand bell, carried around the playground by that week's bell monitor. Further flight was out of the question. I must leave the black, eerie safety of the air raid shelter and face the official retribution of the school.

But nothing happened.

Mrs Douglas at registration that afternoon simply paused after my name and said, "Wilkinson, stand up."

I did.

"Wilkinson, there is a lot more to you than meets the eye. In future try and play fair. But never, never, never give in to bullies. Bullies are not renowned for their inherent fairness."

"Yes, Mrs Douglas. Thank you, Mrs Douglas."

"Good, Wilkinson. With you I sense a condign propinquity of like minds. Yvonne – bring the dictionary, please!"

And that was it. Steven did not 'get' anyone again. I hope he treats his wife and children well. I hope they have a good story to tell.

Chapter Four: Halya I

When the task of burning all the bodies that they had retrieved from the pits to the west of Kiev was finished, they were marched to the west for three days. Old Tuvya, whose task it had been to keep count, since his crippled legs prevented him from any other work, told the SS Officer, "92, 770."

The S.S. officer nodded, withdrew his pistol and shot Tuvya between the eyes.

"92, 771," he said with a broad grin to the sergeant clerk who duly noted it down in the thick black ledger in which the unit kept its meticulous details.

"Fucking Jews. All this fucking paperwork."

And with that Tuvya's body was doused in petrol and set alight as all the others had been.

And so the march began.

The late May sunshine had roused the earth alive again, and Halya could almost ignore her missing eye and the intense pain in her right leg, and think herself either back in Spain or on an outing to the countryside around Ulyanovsk with her parents and Nikita, her son. The thought of Nikita far to the East in the safety of her parents' house consoled her and kept her going.

And there was something else. Indefinable. Ineffable. Hard to understand or even begin to express. From time to time on the three late afternoons of the march, they were convinced that at their backs from the sanctuary of the East could be heard the distant rumble of artillery. Sometimes it was not even a rumble. Just a minute tremor that seemed to be rippling towards them and the life-filled landscape which craved the return of summer. A tremor that carried death for their enemies, but life and hope for them. An angry shout of resistance that reached them as a mere whisper of promise, a soft zephyr of hope.

But then maybe it was just a thunderstorm.

"Our boys are giving it all back to you, you bastard fascists," grinned Isaac at one of the guards.

Like Halya he had been captured at Stalingrad. But he died that day at the roadside, the guard shooting him twice for his jibe – once in the groin and once in the back of the knees. He was just left to die as the marchers continued their trek to the west. But Isaac was grinning broadly through his pain – they weren't just thunderstorms.

Towards the end of the second afternoon, during a roadside break so that the Germans could make coffee and smoke, Halya surveyed the landscape and inhaled the sweet summer air deeply, so that it seemed to fill up every sad, grieving cell of her being.

What a wonderful world this could be! she thought to herself. My victory is to keep on living. Our victory is to keep on living. The birds were singing more cheerful notes, fresh leaves and blossoms were budding all around, and Halya's spirits were momentarily elevated. The past seemed a distant galaxy, the present was an abhorrent cancer, but the future must be gilded by bright rays of hope and anticipations of joy.

During their work at the pits, a rumour had spread about a huge German army encircled and then captured at Stalingrad, but Halya had no way of knowing if it were true. But if not already, then soon. Soon. Soon. Halya kept her faith and she felt the warm sun on her face.

She shut her left eye and cried only for Robbie and Katya and the other millions whose names she did not know. Was Robbie alive? Was Katya alive? Where were they? Could they feel this same benevolent sunlight on their faces? Was Robbie wounded or lying maimed and dead at the bottom of the Arctic Ocean? Or was he alive and laughing with Jack while thinking of her?

And Katya, sweet Katya? Had she been captured as Halya had been? Tortured as Halya had been? Was her decaying corpse slowly rotting beneath the rubble of Stalingrad? Or was she part of the distant thunderstorm that they sensed approaching them?

The sunlight and the time of year – even the time of day - reminded her of the afternoon on the hills overlooking the Ebro when she had first felt Robbie's delicate fingertips touch her face. Her hand reached up to her right eye and she tentatively touched the throbbing crusted hollow where her right eye had been. She had torn some material from her uniform and fastened it across the eye and around her head to fashion a crude eye-patch which quickly became stained with the blood and pus that oozed from the violated socket.

When the SS had discovered she was right-handed, they had gouged out her eye, softening-up the jelly with cocktail sticks and cigarettes before finishing the work with a bayonet. The SS had said it was their special operation for captured Red Army snipers who were Jewish and commissars to boot. But Halya's victory had been to show no suffering, to remain silent and to resist wordlessly through the freedom of her mind and spirit.

If Katya had been taken, Halya thought, or even killed, Halya hoped that her suffering had been less. If Robbie had died, or was dying even at this moment, she hoped it had been quick and that he had died with her name on his lips. Despite the intense throbbing of her eye, and the stabbing pain from her right leg (an SS Doctor had cut her ligaments, "To stop you running so fast, Comrade Commissar!"), she smiled at her own selfishness.

And smiled again to remember the Party's catechism that personal desires must be subjugated to the revolutionary needs of the proletariat and laughed again having decided that her and Robbie's love was wholly compatible with revolutionary zeal and a commitment to the revolution. What larks! She thought, as Robbie, she knew, would have said.

In Spain she and Robbie had felt like gods, but now they were apart and she was a lame Cyclops, an expert sniper with no rifle, who couldn't run and could make no decisions about when she walked or where she walked or why she walked. By now the terrible ironies were making her almost giggle in their absurdity and then, just as the guards called on the group to resume the march, she knelt down at the roadside and picked very carefully, very gently and very deliberately four forget-me-nots; one for Robbie, one for Jack, one for Katya, one for Nikita.

When they finally arrived at the railhead - there was no station: it was just a clearing in the woods with half a dozen wooden huts scattered either side of the tracks - they found a frightened mass of humanity. A mass of humanity that had been ravaged and harassed; ripped and wrenched and torn from their homes and their daily lives; reviled and beaten and forced to live in ghettos: a mass of humanity frightened, vulnerable, human; a mass of humanity staring almost in unison at the black and dark green uniforms which held their survival in their hands and in their guns.

To Halya's single eye, they seemed to consist mainly of small family groups overdressed for this late May heat wave, weighed down by bursting suitcases, all showing a willingness and determined, steadfast resignation to endure whatever might happen to them. Who else? they seemed to be saying: we are here. Halya's heart and all her sympathies expanded to try to encompass them all, and she attempted to comprehend unsuccessfully the sufferings of these thousands of people gathered at the railway station – themselves merely a small drop of the human river of the marginalized who were on marches and soon to be on trains to an unknown, unknowable and deeply frightening future.

And yet their humanity remained. She saw one small child imploring his mother for sweets which might duly appear from underneath the many layers of clothing that all the adults wore; here in their small groups, children played catch or hide and seek; girls were playing hopscotch. Halya saw small children being entertained with games of I Spy and enough of a sense of humour remained to her to imagine how they might go if one were determined to see the blackly humorous side to all this.

"I spy with my little eye something beginning with S."

"The SS."

"I spy with my little eye something beginning with E."

"Einsatzgruppen."

We are here, thought Halya. And I am here. And I can still laugh.

Looking at these thousands of people, Halya reflected on how only twelve months before these were happy families – who laughed together, prayed together, who played parlour games together and ate ice cream together. The men, she knew, had been plumbers, bakers, lecturers in literature, dentists, postmen, businessmen, factory workers, but now all those useful rhythms established with the human ingenuity of usefulness, of social organization and in the need for a humanized sense of order – the simple beauty of the quotidian - had been obliterated and the rhythms of its life, the very human yet deeply aesthetic yet ordinary order of its life, and the very light of its life seemed to have been extinguished all across Europe. Shattered. Obliterated. Annihilated. Drenched in a raging flood of hatred and blood.

The tattered rags of Halya's uniform were barely recognizable, but nonetheless she was approached by several people, noting the remnants of her red collar tabs, and all wanting answers and directions and orders. What could she tell them, knowing nothing herself? Halya felt tired, tired as death, tortured and far away and isolated from her dearest man and from her son. Some strong spirit within her roused itself to reassure these people who needed her more.

"Tovarishch, Commissar. What is going to happen to us? Where are they taking us? Did the Germans take Stalingrad? Or was their army surrounded and forced to surrender? Is that thunder in the East?"

Halya told them all she knew or had heard.

"What shall we do?"

"I too have heard that rumour about the fascist defeat at Stalingrad," interjected an elderly man.

"But we have no way of knowing if it is true," said someone else.

"And that the Red Army is advancing on all fronts."

"And that America is in the war."

"Yes," grinned Halya, "and that specially-trained British paratroopers, each unit with its own commissar, and its own designated Rabbi will be parachuting in in an hour's time, to prevent this train from leaving to take us to the French holiday camps on the Riviera that the magnificent SS in their wisdom and charity have reserved for all captured Soviet citizens, military and civilian, Jews and non-Jews."

Halya concluded this speech by clicking her heels and with a brisk military salute. "That is the official party line. Tovarishch Stalin told me in a dream last night so it must be true."

Everybody laughed.

"But Comrade Commissar –."

Halya grimaced. "Please, I am not your Commissar. I am just Halya."

The woman smiled.

"But Comrade Commissar Halya, what shall we do?"

"Live. Laugh. Live and laugh and let our lives and laughter be our victory."

"But Halya –"

"Look around you. This earth is renewing itself no matter what these bastard fascists want, and our revenge and our victory will come."

The small group of people who had gathered around Halya set their teeth with determination and defiance, their faces masked by stony stoicism.

"We could sing *The Internationale*," suggested one woman, slightly younger than Halya herself.

"We'll save that for later, if things get worse," replied Halya. "I suggest we simply burst out in loud raucous laughter, just to show them we are still alive." She paused. "And when the British paratroopers arrive, I insist, as your Commissar, that their commander be brought to me immediately, so that we can co-ordinate our anti-fascist operations."

And at that they all burst out laughing and with broad grins returned Halya's ironic salute.

"My dear comrades, beloved fellow citizens, I would wink at you, but the SS seem to have forbidden Bolshevik winking."

And that set the crowd laughing even more.

Things did get worse.

After a night of broken, ragged sleep in the clearing, brightly lit by floodlights, and patrolled by guards with vicious, snarling dogs, at eight o'clock the following morning the train arrived.

"Oy, looks like we're travelling fifth class," a middle-aged man near Halya commented.

Halya nodded. She had counted the trucks as the train pulled in. There were one hundred and fifty. Cattle trucks. A frenzied two hours of frenetic activity followed as the prisoners were ordered, squeezed, crammed into the cattle trucks. The harsh, sharp orders came for them to get in the trucks. Anyone who complained or showed even the slightest reluctance was simply shot on the spot.

And things got worse.

One woman in her thirties, her strident voice rising above the general hubbub, demanded to speak to the guards' commanding officer. Her twin daughters had a debilitating brain condition and needed to lie down on long journeys.

And so the daughters were shot. And the woman was stripped. And then she was tied to the sloping boot of an SS car. Even then she loudly complained that the ropes on her wrists and ankles were too tight.

And so the SS Sergeant took his bayonet and made two deep slashes on the outside of her thighs. And then he cut a deeper slash across her abdomen and two deep slashes at the base of both breasts. And then they set the dogs on her.

Halya saw all this and inside she wept.

The day was blisteringly, soul-sappingly hot. None of them had eaten or drunk since the previous evening.

But the one young man who begged for water for his pregnant wife had had to watch while the SS bayoneted her in the stomach. And laughed. And threw her to the floor – without emotion - for the dogs to eat their fill of her unborn foetuses.

Halya asked around and managed to scrounge a scrap of paper and a pencil from a family recently ejected from the ghetto at Kiev. She felt she had to write something to Nikita and hope beyond hope that it would somehow reach him one day. She scribbled furiously for ten minutes and slipped the note to the engine driver – a Russian – who said he would do his best to pass it on by hand if he could, to send to Nikita on its way back East. With one eye missing, she had lost perspective and the writing was slow and at times almost indecipherable, but Halya persisted. She would do it. She had to hope that much later, despite the screaming bedlam of war, it might be delivered to her parents far back in the East. She had to write quickly: having made all these people wait for so long with no food and no water, the fascists now seemed anxious to fill the train as quickly as possible.

And things got worse. It stated clearly on the outside of the cattle trucks that each truck was intended to carry sixty cows. Halya calculated that there must be nearly two hundred people crammed into her cattle truck.

Crammed in a cattle truck with hundreds of others with only standing room and the heat and the lack of water and food, Halya became aware of the sheer human-ness of those around her. She imagined many hours would pass before they reached their destination: people would need the lavatory but would have to do it where they stood; some would die from dehydration or simple exhaustion; some would die through lack of hope; some would become too tired of being here. But we *are* here, thought Halya to herself. If not us, then who?

Halya knew that to love another human being is to love the way they smell. To refuse to love her fellow travellers would be to deny the overwhelming love she felt for them, despite the contaminating disgust the fascists were trying to enforce. Shit and piss prove that we are real and that we are here, Halya reflected and smiled at this new thought: I shit, therefore I am.

She spoke loudly and clearly:

"Comrades, we must learn to get along in these conditions. We must communicate with each other. We must support each other. Let us sing. I'll sing the first line and you will repeat it, please, if you have the strength and the energy."

Halya sang:

Never say this is the final road for you!

They heard the door to the cattle truck slam shut and the bolt pushed firmly home.

Halya sang.

Though leaden skies may cover over days of blue!

The train's whistle hooted.

Halya sang.

As the hour that we longed for is so near,

Shouts in German punctuated the train's hooting.

Halya sang.

Our song beats out the message: We are here!

A woman towards the front of the carriage broke out in uncontrollable sobbing.

From lands so green with palms to lands all white with snow,

They felt the enormous wheels of the train slowly, slowly, slowly, lente, lente, currite noctis equii, begin to turn and there was just the vaguest suggestion of forward momentum.

We shall be coming with our anguish and our woe,

The sound of involuntary retching came from further forward in the truck.

And where a drop of our blood falls on the earth

Through the slats in the truck Halya could see - sunlight, dappled beautiful green, and, if she tilted her head back towards the roof of the truck, the sun.

Halya sang.

It is there our courage and our spirit have rebirth!

"Now we'll do it all together," asserted Halya.

Never say this is the final road for you.

The fields were spinning by in a weird, insane kaleidoscope of blurred colour and motion.

We are here, thought Halya. I am here. Our anguish and our woe are weeping to be heard. Will it get any worse?

Chapter Five: Jack II

That grey morning they had marched from barracks all over the city, Robbie and Jack, and Halya and Katya from the Caserna Lenin to the Plaza Catalunya. The atmosphere was an odd combination of pride and regret. Happiness and sadness wreathed the faces of men and women from every continent on the earth who could be seen bursting into tears and huge star-bursts of laughter from one minute to the next. Resolution and despair were sweetly and bitterly mixed with the feeling that something was over, that something had died. Some wept openly; others marched with their shoulders squarely back, proud and defiant.

All around Jack could see a mass of flags and banners: a few hand-painted with Spanish or Catalan slogans on them, the flags and banners of the brigades themselves, here and there the flag of the Soviet Union with its characteristic hammer and sickle, but overwhelmingly the tricolour of the Spanish Republic with its bright red, yellow and almost purple blue. Jack wondered how long that flag would continue to fly over Barcelona, and also, when it had been torn down, how long it would be before it flew freely again in the gentle zephyrs that slooped in from the Mediterranean or with the gusty breezes that slipped down from the Pyrenees or the screeching gales that slapper-thwacked the city in the grey days of winter. Would it ever fly freely here again?

Katya could sense Jack's unease and gently touched his arm, whispering to him, "My friend, moy droog, what troubles you?"

"This!" Jack's curt reply was to keep the tears at bay, not from impoliteness. With his left hand he gestured broadly around the plaza.

"I understand, Jack." Katya took Jack's right hand from his trouser pocket and gripped it in hers. "One day, Jack, all will be well."

"I hope you are right, Katya. Hope you are right. Can't come too soon." He paused and looked around the plaza. "That day – can't come too soon."

As the crowd waited for the promised address from the balcony at the northern end of the square, a deep, rhythmic chanting had begun somewhere and now rolled over all the assembled soldiers like an unstoppable wave of futile defiance:

El pueblo unido jamás será vencido!

El pueblo unido jamás será vencido!

El pueblo unido jamás será vencido!

Even Jack, normally so reticent, took up the chant with a desperate, defeated gusto, but sadness wreathed his face in gloom. As if summoned by the crowd itself a small figure emerged on the balcony. It was clear the speech was about to begin. The crowd settled down to listen.

"It is very difficult to say a few words in farewell to the heroes of the International Brigades, because of what they are and what they represent. A feeling of sorrow, an infinite grief catches our throat - sorrow for those who are going away, for the soldiers of the highest ideal of human redemption, exiles from their countries, persecuted by the tyrants of all peoples - grief for those who will stay here forever mingled with the Spanish soil, in the very depth of our heart, hallowed by our feeling of eternal gratitude."

Robbie whispered something in Halya's ear and poked her affectionately in the ribs and she laughed. They were inseparable – relishing these last few hours together. Jack and Katya stood a few feet away, their hands chastely interlocked, exchanging occasional whispered remarks.

"From all peoples, from all races, you came to us like brothers, like sons of immortal Spain; and in the hardest days of the war, when the capital of the Spanish Republic was threatened, it was you, gallant comrades of the International Brigades, who helped save the city with your fighting enthusiasm, your heroism and your spirit of sacrifice. And Jarama and Guadalajara, Brunete and Belchite, Levante and the Ebro, in immortal verses sing of the courage, the sacrifice, the daring, the discipline of the men of the International Brigades."

Robbie and Halya's interlocked fingers squeezed hard together. Jack said to Katya, "She might have mentioned the women too!"

"They never do," Katya muttered under her breath. "It's as if we do not exist, but we are here. I'm a better shot than you are, Jack Wilkinson."

"Never said you weren't, Katya." He nudged her playfully in the ribs.

"For the first time in the history of the peoples' struggles, there was the spectacle, breath-taking in its grandeur, of the formation of International Brigades to help save a threatened country's freedom and independence - the freedom and independence of our Spanish land."

Halya began to cry at the thought of the long separation she and Robbie were about to endure. Jack squeezed Katya's hand – a futile attempt at osmosis to pass to her the strength and courage and stamina she would probably need in the future. Katya squeezed back harder – she sensed everything and more that Jack might have to undergo – and Katya was stronger, strong enough for both of them.

From the barrios around the Plaza Catalunya could be heard the distant but incessant sound of clapping that had accompanied their progress along the Ramblas and which still rippled through the air in audible tribute to these freedom fighters.

"Communists, Socialists, Anarchists, Republicans - men of different colours, differing ideology, antagonistic religions - yet all profoundly loving liberty and justice, they came and offered themselves to us unconditionally. They gave us everything - their youth or their maturity; their science or their experience; their blood and their lives; their hopes and aspirations - and they asked us for nothing. But yes, it must be said, they did crave something - they aspired to the honour of dying for us."

"But I am pleased to be alive!" Robbie said to Halya, more loudly than he intended, and Jack and Katya grinned broadly at his remark in mute but laughing acquiescence. Halya gripped Robbie's shoulders, turned him round to face her directly and kissed him long and hard. It was the kiss of lovers about to be parted for an unknown, unknowable and hazardous future.

"Banners of Spain! Salute these many heroes! Be lowered to honour so many martyrs!"

"Jack," Katya said, "look after Robbie – I worry that his idealism will get him killed." Jack squeezed her hand by way of reply. Robbie and Halya were hugging each other and whispering to each other incessantly.

"Mothers! Women! When the years pass by and the wounds of war are staunched; when the memory of the sad and bloody days dissipates in a present of liberty, of peace and of wellbeing; when the rancour has died out and pride in a free country is felt equally by all Spaniards, speak to your children. Tell them of these men and women of the International Brigades."

"We will always tell everyone!" Katya asserted, although Jack put his fingers to his lips to indicate silence.

"Tell the whole bleeding world!" Robbie, ever more demonstrative than Jack, shouted at the top of his voice. "Tell everyone! Tell the unborn children!"

At this, tears sprang suddenly into Halya's eyes. But Robbie did not notice.

"Recount for them how, coming over seas and mountains, crossing frontiers bristling with bayonets, sought by raving dogs thirsting to tear their flesh, these men reached our country as crusaders for freedom, to fight and die for Spain's liberty and independence threatened by German and Italian fascism. They gave up everything - their loves, their countries, home and fortune, fathers, mothers, wives, brothers, sisters and children - and they came and said to us: ``We are here. Your cause, Spain's cause, is ours. It is the cause of all advanced and progressive mankind."

Yes, Halya thought, we are here. We are many. We are strong. But tomorrow we will be apart. And we won't be here. Is my life beginning to unravel?

"Today many are departing. Thousands remain, shrouded in Spanish earth, profoundly remembered by all Spaniards. Comrades of the International Brigades: Political reasons, reasons of state, the welfare of that very cause for which you offered your blood with boundless generosity, are sending you back, some to your own countries and others to forced exile. You can go proudly. You are history. You are legend. You are the heroic example of democracy's solidarity and universality in the face of the vile and accommodating spirit of those who interpret democratic principles with their eyes on hoards of wealth or corporate shares which they want to safeguard from all risk."

"You are my example of solidarity and universality, maya dorogaya Halya," Robbie whispered in her ear and easily slipped his arm around her waspy waist. Halya smiled back, but her eyes were troubled by a shadow of the thought of being apart from Robbie.

"Solidarity! Solidarity! Solidarity forever!!" A swelling chant was rolling round the square. "Solidarity!"

"We shall not forget you; and, when the olive tree of peace is in flower, entwined with the victory laurels of the Republic of Spain - return! Return to our side for here you will find a homeland - those who have no country or friends, who must live deprived of friendship - all, all will have the affection and gratitude of the Spanish people who today and tomorrow will shout with enthusiasm."

"I will return after the war, I promise you." That was Robbie.

Katya nodded approvingly.

"Long live the heroes of the International Brigades!"

There was a deep roar of approval as the speech came to an end. And a slowness to depart, a desire to prolong the moment, not kiss the joy and see it fly away. Robbie and Halya were in tears. Jack and Katya held hands and seemed closer than they had ever been.

Halya said, "I want to stay here with you. Ya hochu ostat′sya s toboi. Я хочу остаться с тобой."

"Perhaps I could come back with you," Robbie said.

"Robbie – you are a romantic fool. Come, we must go: your train and our ship are waiting," interjected Katya.

"Katya's right. We have another fight on soon. Halya, Katya," Jack smiled with regret but determination, "God speed. See you in Berlin! If you're there first, don't eat all the cakes and remember – I'll have a black tea with lots of sugar."

He embraced them both and hugged them tightly.

"You must stay. We will win eventually. Ty dolzhen ostat′sya. V kontse kontsov my pobedim. Ты должен остаться. В конце концов мы победим," Halya pleaded.

By now Halya was weeping openly. Katya was tugging forcefully at Halya's sleeve. "Come! The boat will not wait for us. It is the last one out of Barcelona. None of us can stay!" she took Halya by the shoulders and shook her. "Look at me! Success is not final; failure is not final: it is the courage to continue that counts. You must believe this."

"Oh, Katya! I don't think I can. You don't understand."

Jack was steering Robbie to the north of the square towards the avenue that ran to the railway station.

"Come on, kiddo. We've got a train to catch. Katya will look after Halya. She'll be fine. Just you wait and see." He was dragging Robbie at this point, hauling him in the general direction of the railway station. Robbie was not resisting, but his eyes were fixed on Halya's, receding further into the distance behind him.

Halya forced herself out of Katya's embrace and shouted at Robbie:

"Robbie! Robbie! I'm pregnant! Ya beremenna. Я беременна."

Robbie sprinted back to Halya's waiting arms and hugged her as if he would never let go. He was about to speak, but Halya put her hand over his mouth:

"No words! Words would break my heart! Be strong! Ne nado slov! Slova razob'yut moe serdtse! Bud' sil'nym! Не надо слов! Слова разобьют моё сердце! Будь сильным! "

"I will be strong… for you!" Robbie shouted.

Katya was grim-faced and determined: "You can't be too strong!"

Chapter Six: Tommy III

Heteroglossia - don't you just love it? It sounds like it should be something else, something contagious, something you suffer from.

After a successful career in the West End he retired to the South of France, although his later years were dogged by frequent attacks of heteroglossia.

Or sexual preference.

I used to be heterosexual, but now I'm heteroglossic.

Or maybe a Greek Island.

I spent a month with Samantha on Heteroglossia. It's so quaint. We were doing a Tai Chi/Zen/Buddhism course to find our real selves.

Find your real selves? Get an A – Z, girl, and you'll know where you come from. And where you're going too. That's my advice to you. Where you come from! FFS!

For four days as a thirteen year old in my eyes and certainly in my parents', I was an outlaw. It was very exciting.

It started in the most mundane way imaginable and began at the top of my road. John had called at my house as usual. We cycled to school every day. At the top of my road we stopped. We had a Geography test that morning.

John said, "Done much revision for that test?"

"No, not really," I lied.

"Well, let's not go. Who says we have to?"

"All right then."

And so we didn't go to school that day. It was the one and only time that I played truant and I can't say I'm proud of it, but this is what happened.

We weren't experienced outlaws, John and me. Our bright blue grammar school blazers made us very conspicuous on a school day when we should have been in school. And even removing our caps and ties and trying to make ourselves look slightly more dishevelled didn't really work, so we cycled and cycled and cycled out to Dartford Heath. We also had no money which became a problem when we got hungry, but the Heath first of all - the Heath!

Heaths have a curious place in the English imagination. They were places of mayhem and chaos where highwayman would ask people to stand and deliver. Uncultivated, messy, untended, recreational now - I suppose everyone has a car these days. Well, everyone except the demonized, unemployed underclass. It was deserted the day John and I were there. We tramped through the fallen leaves of autumn, found huts with discarded beer bottles, no cans. This was before cans and, strangely, in every hut there were messy, random caches of single sheets torn from pornographic magazines - which to our thirteen year old eyes were quite astonishing in their graphic overtness. Were women really like that? Did they really do those things? So gloriously pneumatic. So strangely gymnastic. So physical. So happy, it seemed. So ecstatic. So this was why people got married. It started to make sense. Better than Geography, maya padrooga. Any day of the week.

What had we stumbled on, a secret den of hidden iniquity? Or just some tramp's hideout? Or was it the place where our slightly older teenage fellow students would come to feel free from the restraints of life in South London? I may have known all the countries in the Commonwealth (South Africa had just been expelled – good thing too!), but our school and our parents, who ironically were so keen to impart their wisdom on some subjects and to pass judgment on our personal comportment – *Sit up straight! Don't read while you're eating! Don't drop your aitches! Keep your tie straight! Wilkinson, go to extra cover!* – were more taciturn on matters sexual.

I don't know. I do know it was very boring. We had no money, but we hit on a scheme. It was a rather cunning scheme.

We went back off the Heath to civilization, found a big pub and realized that we could take from their rubbish bins round the back as many deposit bottles as we could which we then would take to the local grocers' to claim the deposit back. Quite what the grocer thought occurs to me now, but didn't occur at the time: two fresh-faced (neither of us were shaving), two fresh-faced, blue-blazered grammar school boys on what - seven, eight visits with hordes of bottles, slowly accumulating a cash loot prize. With this money we bought fish and chips and then so well behaved were we, so in tune with the school ethos, we ended the day at the Borough library which was next door to the school.

Perhaps we were playing with fire. Perhaps we wanted to get caught. Perhaps we just wanted to gauge the reaction of our peers who we knew would pass the library as they left school at four o'clock. I can't remember, but that's what happened. We ended up - these truanting, work-avoiding, test-dodging, outlaw-reprobates, but essentially good pupils - reading books in the public library.

That's how my outlaw weekend began. It got much more exciting. Well, at least for a thirteen-year-old me, it got much more exciting. I didn't want to go home that night because I was convinced the school might have telephoned my parents to enquire about my health so I went to Uncle Jack's. I said nothing about the truanting then. That was to come later in the weekend. Had a wash: truanting had made me feel dirty and had literally made me dirty. And got stuck into what? *1984*, I think. Quite a good choice really, given the day's events so far. In my mind, I was Winston Smith, pursued all day by Big Brother but with no Julia to make it better. Was Uncle Jack Goldstein?

I'd still not forgotten the mystery of Uncle Jack crying. And by chance that night I put more of the jigsaw together.

Jack kept the shop open later on a Friday, but when he'd shut up and come upstairs at about half six, he started to cook something. I can't remember what. There was a knock on the door.

"See who it is, Tommy, and send them packing, son."

I went down to answer and send them packing but when I opened the door the man who stood there, tanned, swarthy, dressed in foreign clothes and wearing a flat black cap, was not for sending packing. I could tell that from his body language and something inside me told me that Jack would welcome this intrusion from, well, from wherever this bloke came from, so I beckoned him in and he followed me up the narrow stairs to Jack's flat, and Uncle Jack beamed for England and welcomed him with open arms.

"Xavi, Xavi, ben venuto, mi amico. Com ès axió?"

Xavi answered, "Bona nit, Jack. Long time, mi amico."

"Ah, Xavi, what on earth are you doing here?"

More words and in a language I didn't recognize. I was doing French and Spanish and Italian and Latin at school and it wasn't one of those, but it wasn't a million miles away either. Jack packed me off to the New Cross Tavern to get some beer from the Off Sales. You could do that then, if they knew you and they knew me and they knew Uncle Jack. Now you have to show ID if you look under twenty five. Everything changes.

But who was Shavvy, as I thought of him then? What was that mysterious language that he spoke? I hurried back along the Old Kent Road, beer bottles clanking and clinking, desperate to see Jack and his interesting mate. I didn't learn very much so I'll just tell what happened that night.

The stranger was shorter than average, very short black hair, dressed a little out of place. You could tell he wasn't from round our way. A blue denim shirt, a shapeless dark blue jacket, a red neckerchief, a bit of stubble, eyes that looked as tired as an angel's, sick of - you've guessed it - sin.

Jack introduced us. "Aquest ès Tommy. My nephew."

"Tommy," Xavi smiled and held out his hand. "Com ès axió?"

"Tell him 'Axió bon', Tommy," prompted Uncle Jack. "Oh, and Tommy, aquest ès Xavi. This is Shavvy."

I did as I was told. I always did what Uncle Jack told me to. It started with a sneeze and a word for good. I wasn't stupid: I was doing French and Spanish and Italian and Latin at school and I could recognize the word for 'good'.

Jack and Xavi drank beer. They even let me have a glass, and talked and talked. It seemed as though they talked all night, but they didn't because Jack and Xavi had plans. They were going on an excursion and I was invited. Uncle Jack explained.

He said, "Don't worry Tommy. I've phoned your Mum and Dad. It will be fine. You nip back home, get a change of clothes for tomorrow, something simple, jeans, a shirt, maybe a pullover and a coat. We are going on a long trip. Oh, and ask your mother if she'll tend the shop tomorrow."

This was important. Uncle Jack never let people tend the shop on Saturdays. Other days yes, but on a Saturday - never. And Spurs were at home that weekend. Xavi must be someone important, but I never really found out who he was. Then. Merchant seaman, I thought that evening. As the weekend went on, however, I managed to put two and two together and made five – as we used to say.

I was woken at six the next morning by Uncle Jack with a cup of tea. A quick bacon sandwich and we were on our way, all three of us, Uncle Jack, Xavi and me. I had no idea where we were going. We had a brisk walk to London Bridge, took the tube to Kings Cross. Uncle Jack went to the ticket booth and then in next to no time it seemed we were sitting on a train. I hadn't the guts to ask where we were going, but I trusted Uncle Jack completely.

He said to me, "Tommy, you're a clever boy and you go to a good school, but this weekend, this weekend, my son, is going to add to your education."

It was then that I told him about the truancy and he laughed.

"Good for you. Everyone has got to do it once in a while. I'm pleased you were bored though. You'll never do it again will you?"

"No," I admitted sombrely.

"Take that frown off your face. Look happy. Today might change your life. Don't worry about school. I'll write them a note. In any case you're not going to be in school until Tuesday, cos we're not getting back from Glasgow until Monday night. Today you will witness something astonishing."

Glasgow, I thought, why were we going to Glasgow? I had no idea. Luckily I'd brought a bag full of books and that's remained with me on any long trip to this day, and, yeah - I do a lot of long trips. You never know where my kind of work will send you next. I get paranoid, really, really paranoid, really upset, tearful almost, if I run out of things to read. My trips abroad are planned with the books in mind, then I book the tickets, then I worry about the insurance and then I get a visa if I need one. It's the books that come first. Thank goodness for Kindles. Before Kindles, I had a suitcase for my clothes and a suitcase for the books. I've even searched foreign airports for English language novels because I'd run out. The number of things I've read on obscure Greek Islands, even Heteroglossia, simply because I've run out of things to read!

I have always loved travelling by train, especially as the night turns to dawn and then full day. What I like and am in awe of is all the lights in all the houses coming on and in each house a family or a group of people, all individuals, all doing the same things: teeth, shave, wash, tea, coffee, toast. And here all of us in this country and in each home, behind each lighted window, a human being with their own thoughts and worries and dreams and completely unknowable to the rest of us. How to reach out to all these people? How to connect?

On our trip to Glasgow it was Orwell's *1984*. I remember because somewhere like Grantham when there was a lull in Jack and Xavi's conversation, Xavi looked, nodded appreciatively at my book.

"Orwell?" he said.

"Yes, it's George Orwell - it's really good. Have you read it?"

"Sí, in Catalan."

Catalan! So that was the language he spoke. Uncle Jack roused himself a little and realized seemingly for the first time that I was there.

"Tommy, I owe you an explanation. I've not seen Xavi for years. We first met way back in the thirties in Spain. We've got a lot to talk about and he's brought you… well, brought me, brought you some presents. Where we go you're gonna need one of these."

In his hand he held out two lapel badges: one was circular and grey and said on it 'Voluntarios Internationales de la Libertad 1936 – 1939'. There was a five pointed star towards the bottom, but above it all was an angry, clenched, left fist.

"Or this one - it's a bit more colourful."

The other one was rectangular, bright red with hammer and sickle in one corner and then in gold lettering Caserna Lenin and then some initials which at the time I didn't understand but which now make complete sense to me - POUM. What on earth did they stand for? Some memory of Orwell's *Homage to Catalonia* skittered across my brain. I was tempted to ask to wear both, but I thought that would be excessive, and I am English and well brought up and have a low sense of self-esteem. I picked the red one and pinned it clumsily on my windcheater. Which is what we called anoraks back then, and years before people were afforded that unkind epithet. I like the word windcheater: I am Thomas of England, Cheater of Winds and Defier of Gravity, Lord of the Words and Ruler of Splorge. I just made the last word up.

"Good," said Jack. "I think now you're ready. Where we're going these badges will show people that we're on their side."

Not the Merchant Navy then. The Spanish Civil War. Wow! My Uncle Jack had fought in the Spanish Civil War. I knew enough from Orwell to guess that, in a way, that was just the start: my Uncle Jack must have volunteered for the Spanish Civil War! Crickey! To my mind, that was something to be proud of and it troubled me vaguely that the family hadn't made more of that. Or that Uncle Jack himself had not bothered to mention it when he was being criticized for having had a cushy war. That was clearly bollocks: he'd done his bit before 1939. What had happened in Spain that had upset him so?

Jack and Xavi talked almost non-stop from King's Cross to Glasgow Central Park mainly in Catalan and partly in English. Jack seemed reborn, full price, brand new and free. He even started telling jokes.

"One night I was walking home across Southwark Bridge when I saw this young man standing on the parapet of the bridge about to jump in the Thames. I can't stand to see people in distress and I feel a deep sense of duty to my fellow citizens so I thought – I'll try to save his life. So I start talking to him to try to get him off the bridge and stop a pointless suicide:

"What's the matter, mate? What's so bad that you feel you have to end it all?"

"He says to me: 'Well, my girlfriend's left me and she was everything to me, but what makes it worse is living under a Tory government. I can't stand it. I can't take any more. There will never be any meaningful change in this country.'

"So I said to the young fellow, 'Look I feel impotent politically but I ain't about to throw myself off a bridge. We gotta fight the system. Don't waste your life – join the struggle. Are you in the Labour Party?'

"He says, 'No chance - they are too moderate for my liking.'

"I says, 'I agree with you there. They will never really change anything fundamental. The problem is that their manifesto promises are always watered down by the realities of government. Are you a member of a different party?'

"Young fella says, 'Yes, I'm a Communist.'

"I goes, 'Well, my son, it really is your lucky night because I'm a Communist too. I can help you, comrade. We have everything to live for. Are you a member of the British Communist Party or are you a member of the Communist Party of Great Britain?'

"Young man says, 'British Communist Party.'

'So am I! You are lucky we met, I'm telling you, mate. Are you British Communist Party (Marxist Leninist) or British Communist Party (Trotskyite)?'

"He says, 'British Communist Party (Marxist Leninist).'

"I goes, 'Amazing! Me too! Tell me - are you British Communist Party (Marxist Leninist) Maoist Tendency or British Communist Party (Marxist Leninist) Stalinist Tendency?'

'I'm British Communist Party (Marxist Leninist) Stalinist Tendency.'

We are soul brothers. Now we've met you might as well get down off that bridge. We have a revolution to prepare for. Just one thing: are you British Communist Party (Marxist Leninist) Stalinist Tendency pre-1956 or British Communist Party (Marxist Leninist) Stalinist Tendency post-1956?'

'I'm British Communist Party (Marxist Leninist) Stalinist Tendency pre-1956.'

'Then DIE, you counter revolutionary waster!'

'And I pushed him off. Bastard!'"

Xavi laughed and laughed, but his tears changed to ones of real sadness and, shaking his head, he murmured, "So sad. It was like that in the war – always divided."

"When," added Jack, "we most needed to be united."

There was silence for a few miles. I could see the glinting of the hint of tears in Jack's eyes and I looked out of the window to see the flat bit on the east – Lincolnshire, where, as I would later discover, sea and sky and sausages meet.

Hesitantly I said, "I've got a joke, but it's not very good."

"Won't know until we hear it, Tommy, will we?" said Uncle Jack.

This was my first foray into the adult world with anything designed to gain a specific result.

"O.K. It goes like this:

There are two men travelling on the slow train from Moscow to Samara and they get chatting. Eventually one turns to the other and says, "So what do you do?"

'The other one says, "I'm a history teacher. What about you?"

'I'm in the K.G.B. I'm part of the division that hunts out those who are dissatisfied with our great Communist society."

*"So the history teacher says, "Oh!" And then he has a little think and he says, "Hang on! You said you hunt out those who are dissatisfied – are you telling me there are some who are **satisfied**?!"*

"Of course," the K.G.B. man replies, "but they are dealt with by a different unit."

"A different unit?" asks the history teacher, still amazed.

"Yes, it deals solely with Embezzlement and the Misappropriation of State Property.""

"Nice one, Tommy!" Uncle Jack, chuckling softly.

Xavi smiled, "Yes – accept no authority except yourself."

Accept no authority except yourself. Easy to say, but when you're thirteen, what you crave is an authority – not necessarily the one you're given or is foisted on you, but some sort of guide, a bit of direction. But I liked Xavi's idealism: I simply didn't yet know who I was, so baulked at the idea of myself as an authority on anything really. Still do. Especially myself. And on that day in particular I was prepared to submit to the authority of the train driver, the ineluctable destiny of the railway tracks. Seemed like a plan.

Then it was Xavi's turn to tell a joke. He told it in Catalan and Jack translated:

The United Nations decide to hold a competition open to all the nations for the best book on elephants.

The French submit a lavishly produced book entitled 'Love and Sex in the World of Elephants.'

Great Britain produces an erudite treatise: 'The Importance of Elephants in World Trade.'

The Germans produce a twenty-four volume encyclopaedia with the title: 'Elephantology: an Introduction.'

The USA submitted a million hand-outs: 'Lottery: $10 only. Win your own elephant.'

The USSR sent three volumes with the following titles:

'Volume One – The Role of Elephants in the Glorious October Revolution.'

'Volume Two – The Happiness of Elephants under the Glorious Communist System.'

'Volume Three – Stalin: Friend and Staunch Defender of All Elephants.'

What larks!

When the conversation lagged, Uncle Jack would include me in the conversation. We spent so much time together that our conversations were ritualized learning sessions and I also got the impression that he was showing off his favourite nephew to Xavi a little. Can't remember exactly what it was that day, but it was probably our recurring debate about the best general in the whole of world history. Ever.

"Alexander the Great," he'd say, just to provoke.

"No chance, Uncle Jack! As far as we can tell, his weaponry was far in advance of his opponents'. A well-trained Jack Russell terrier with good communication skills could have achieved as much with the same army. Over-rated. What about Robert E. Lee?"

"Ignoring the morality of his cause?"

"Course, Uncle Jack – what's the morality of the cause got to do with being a good general. Rommel was good."

"All right. Lee – yes, brilliant use of limited resources, I'll give you that."

"His use of his troops' mobility in 1863 prevented a full-scale assault on Richmond."

"Yeah, but look at his opponent. McClennan was a timid general whose intelligence was poor."

"Whose intelligence agents were manipulated by Lee's brilliant tactics and his use of limited resources. Come on, Uncle Jack!"

Uncle Jack turned and smiled at Xavi who nodded his approval.

"All right, Tommy, but what if Lee had been facing Zhukov?"

"That's irrelevant – you can't cross historical periods. Otherwise you can argue that if Wellington had faced Zhukov, we'd have lost Waterloo."

"But we didn't." Uncle Jack grinned.

"Now you're just winding me up, Uncle Jack. In any case, who would have guessed that Lee would then have the nerve to invade the North? Gotchya!"

"But, Tommy, Antietam virtually destroyed his army: it made the outcome of the war inevitable."

"The outcome was always inevitable, given the North's industrial and financial advantages, not to mention their superior manpower."

Uncle Jack laughed out loud: "Tommy Wilkinson, you are a precocious little twat sometimes."

You've probably guessed already where we went, where we were headed: the Clyde Shipbuilders' yard. I'd seen it on television, but Uncle Jack thought I should see it for real, in person. We eventually got there late on that Saturday afternoon; outside the gates there was quite a festive atmosphere.

All the yards were controlled by the shop stewards. No one could leave or enter without their permission and when we arrived their wives, girlfriends, family members formed a big throng outside the gates, having brought food, presents, all sorts of things for the men inside the yards. The old bill were out in force too as well as journalists and TV cameras. The gates to the yard itself were massive as you'd expect, but virtually hidden in flags and banners, mainly red... with a bit of black thrown in for contrast.

Uncle Jack astonished me. He spoke to the shop stewards and then beckoned Xavi and me towards him.

"Come on! They've let us in. I've got something to give these boys."

You have to understand - back then I wasn't the talkative, flamboyant person I am today. I was in private, with Uncle Jack or my brothers and sisters, but in public I shut up, I watched, I listened, I watched my p's and q's. I watched carefully, fascinated that the Uncle Jack whom I thought I knew so well was becoming someone else in this new strange world.

We wandered through the yard. I wandered and wondered through it too. We were being taken, it turned out, to the headquarters from which the yard was being run. One or two people clocked my lapel badge and the one that Jack was wearing and Xavi had one too, and nodded approvingly and finally up some outside steps and into a spartan office, foggy with cigarette smoke.

"Jack! Jackie boy!"

"Fucking hell! Eric! Eric, good to see you. It's been a long time."

"It certainly has. Too long, my friend. When was the last time I saw you, Jack?"

"Must have been in the Plaza Catalunya the day we left – except you were staying."

"Och, aye – we stayed in Barcelona for when the Nationalists arrived."

"Bad?"

"Unbelievably fucking bad, Jack. Then we took to the hills and mountains. I didnae make it back to Glasgow until 1946." Eric paused, on the verge of saying more it seemed, but he just shook his head and smiled, then grinned broadly. "Is this your boy?"

Jack laughed. "No, no, it's my nephew. Do you remember Xavi, or have you heard of Xavi?"

"I've heard of Xavi. Who's not heard of Xavi?"

I wanted to interrupt and say, "I haven't. I haven't a clue about what is going on or who Xavi is." But I didn't, of course.

Jack said, "I've just come to give you this," and with that he took an envelope from his rear trouser pocket which quite obviously contained money. I've no idea how much, but Jack thought it important to deliver it in person. At this point too Xavi pressed a thick envelope into Eric's hand and said something.

Jack translated.

"This is a donation, Xavi says, from the shipbuilders of Barcelona. They had to have a secret collection. Xavi has come all this way to deliver it in person."

I can't remember seeing Jack so happy, so animated, as he was that day in the Clyde shipyards. People seemed to know him or know of him or had heard of him and treated him with respect that had nothing to do with being the best butcher in the Old Kent Road. He shook people's hands, stopped to give words of encouragement to young men, who had never heard of him I'm sure, and he and Xavi, with me dragging along behind, were treated to a tour of those mighty shipyards.

Looking back all I can remember are the posters everywhere forbidding alcohol. And the red flags and banners proclaiming the work-in. Everywhere red. Blood red.

The people's flag is deepest red:

It hovers o'er our martyred dead.

Eric saw me gazing at one of the anti-drinking posters and explained. "It's the lads, Tommy, you can't keep them off the booze, but if they stay in all night boozing, the press will have a field day so for the duration, no alcohol. It's revolutionary discipline. You see, Tommy, the press in this country are so biased towards the establishment. They're all secret fascists."

"Leave it out, Eric!" Uncle Jack had joined us. "He's a clever lad – he'll work it out for himself."

What a day! Good place to live. But not somewhere you can live forever. We stayed that night in the shipyards, singing songs, sharing food with the ship workers. And there was some booze around. Uncle Jack gave me a quart bottle of brown ale and told me to drink it nice and slow. I scrounged a lantern and found a little place late at night to escape the group singing: it was deep in the bottom of a huge ship that was half-built on one of the slipways. You know me – I still had thirty pages of *1984* to get through and I wanted to try the brown ale in peace.

In the darkness my lips found the top of the bottle and I raised it expectantly to my lips.

"Don't drink it too fast, wee man, or you'll make yourself sick."

A voice. A girl's voice. Here in the ship.

"I'm sorry – what did you say?" I faltered.

"You heard what I said, wee man."

"You're right. I was just surprised. I thought I was on my own."

"Gie us a taste of your drink, wee man. I'm Siobhan. What's your name?"

A pale face framed by bright red hair materialized from the semi-darkness. I felt my new friend smile as she plonked herself down against the curved iron of the ship's hull.

"I'm Tommy. Nice to meet you, Siobhan."

A hand touched my lower arm and I guided the bottle of brown ale into it. I heard Siobhan gulp some beer down.

"Dinae worry, wee Tommy. I can get some more when this runs out. My da has a stash and he's well away, singing wi his mates."

I was frozen into silence. What should I say?

"I'm fifteen, but my da treats me like I'm ten." Siobhan sighed.

"I'm fourteen," I lied.

"Really? You looked about twelve when I saw you with that big fella wandering around the yard. Is he your da?"

"No. He's my Uncle Jack. He fought in Spain you know – for the International Brigades."

"Well, he would nae be here if he'd fought for Franco, now, would he, wee Tommy?"

"True – but he really did it. He's a real hero."

"Aye, wee Tommy, but can he do this?"

I felt soft fingers stroke my face from my forehead down to my neck, and then one thin, inquisitive finger traced the outline of my lips faintly.

Suddenly I jerked the lantern up so that I could see Siobhan's face: big, blue, astonished eyes, a shock of red hair, freckles, and a wide amused smile.

"Have you seen a naked woman, wee Tommy?"

"Well, actually – yes, I have."

"Not including your mother, any sisters or any photos in those pervy magazines?" Siobhan said in a big rush like a five-year-old.

"Yes, I have. I really have." Poor Yvonne.

"So, wee Tommy, do you know what to do with one?"

I think the brown ale made me honest. I laughed.

"Siobhan – I haven't the foggiest."

"Well, neither have I." There was a long pause. I could see Siobhan's eyes twinkling in the light from the lantern. Twinkling with mischief. "I'm clever and you must be clever cos it's Saturday night and before I got here you were reading a book: round here that proves you're clever."

"So?"

"So I think we should work it out, Tommy. Put our heads together –so to speak."

"It's not our heads that worry me, Siobhan…." I tailed off.

A soft, gentle hand reached down and entangled itself with mine.

"It'll be all right. It might be fun."

Cider with Rosie. Brown Ale with Siobhan. The softness of angels. Ah!

We stayed all day Sunday too. Someone gave me a book, Trotsky's *On Permanent Revolution*, and told me I had to read it before we caught the train back to London on Monday morning, so I did. I always did what I was told. Siobhan found me again and I did what she told me to do as well: we stole a kiss when Uncle Jack and her da weren't looking. I wonder where she is now? I hope she has a good story to tell. I owe her a lot. Caught the early morning train back to King's Cross. Got back home around mid-afternoon, full of my new experiences.

Uncle Jack wrote a letter to the school. I have no idea what he wrote, but I certainly didn't get into any trouble – apart from a few sarky remarks from the Geography teacher about mine and John's convenient absence from the test – which we had to do one lunchtime anyway. Uncle Jack fell out with my parents who thought he was becoming a dangerous influence, but the bonds between Uncle Jack and me had grown stronger. But we were still slightly reticent about the past: I didn't ask him all the questions about Spain that were fizzling and sizzling around in my head until much later. I was too busy growing up, and any questions seemed to make Jack ill at ease, so I avoided the subject.

I couldn't quite understand why something that should have been a source of pride to him was kept so dark. And for the life of me – apart from Franco's victory and the defeat of the Republican government – I couldn't quite see quite what had happened in Spain that could explain that scene at the back of the butcher's shop. That terrible sobbing. I still had a lot to learn.

Remember that lapel badge – I'm wearing it today.

Chapter Seven: Jack III

It was September – our first run on what were to become notorious: the Arctic Convoys. We were moored off the Langanes Peninsula near Hvalfjördöur in Iceland and had just been cleaning the ack-ack guns when Robbie shouted out, "Jack, come look. Here's the convoy!" I joined him on the port bow, but by the time I got there he looked disappointed because this wasn't the convoy. It couldn't have been really: it was coming from the east. I can understand his mistake though.

From the distance it was such a huge formation of ships that to our very inexperienced eyes it could hardly have been anything else. It was the escort and it gave me and Robbie a feeling of great relief for it seemed to us as if the whole of the British Navy had gathered there. We were still new to the sea and we weren't sure we'd got all the silhouettes right. But I recognized two battleships, at least a dozen cruisers, forty or fifty destroyers and lots of smaller craft: freighters converted into auxiliary aircraft carriers, recognizable by their ungainly, oddly-tilted launching decks. I counted more than sixty ships; it seemed a huge fleet for just one convoy. Ours was PQ1 – only the second – and the Navy and the enemy, it seemed to me, were still learning how to fight in this new type of warfare.

Robbie and I had only been in the Merchant Navy for six months and the novelty of life on board ship had not worn off. We had had some very basic training in Portsmouth and then joined what was to be our first ship. We were ordinary seamen, but our military experience meant that our main duties in battle were to man the ack-ack guns that each merchant ship carried as a matter of course. We'd left a London kept dark and ravaged by the Blitz. Train to Liverpool. Embarkation and then a meandering but frantic scuttle through the Scottish Islands and then a mad dash to Iceland. We were learning quickly, and our ship seemed a haven of safety after the relentless bombing in Portsmouth and London and even Liverpool. The Britain we had left smouldered and smoked by day and by night it glowed and blazed.

A little while later the convoy itself rose out of the western horizon. I'd tried to visualise forty-nine ships sailing in formation and had found it difficult. Now I realized that I'd never included the escort in that image. The armada bearing down on us consisted of an enormous cruiser with an aeroplane on its deck, two destroyers, a dozen coastguard cutters, smaller craft - all American apparently. They didn't seem as impressive a force as the British escort, but then the run between Halifax and Iceland was a relatively safe one. Apparently the Germans had concentrated their U-boat packs on the Murmansk route and their planes based in Norway could not reach west of Iceland. The ships of the convoy itself hadn't taken up their new formation of two lines abreast. They came towards us in the pattern of counters on a draughts board – all spread out and easy to attack if the enemy had been about.

As they drew closer, it occurred to me how huge some of the ships were. I'd never seen such enormous ships. It was an immensely impressive sight that struck me mostly by its size, the sheer material wealth represented by those forty-nine ocean-defying giants and, from me and Robbie's perspective, they were carrying the things our allies needed the most: food, munitions and the weapons to fight fascism.

The Non-Aggression Pact that Stalin signed with Hitler had made me feel very uncomfortable, but Robbie was a hard-line, true believer and, in any case, he always said to me privately that he reckoned Stalin was just playing for time, trying to put off the inevitable. As it turned out, Robbie was right, and the fascists had invaded the Soviet Union. Robbie was doubly biased anyway: he missed Halya and the child he had never seen, and, despite his natural easy cheerfulness, he could get terribly morose – just because he and Halya were apart.

Which is funny in a way, because Robbie had had quite a reputation round our way as a ladies' man. Course, he was handsome and charismatic, and could be really charming when he turned it on: 'jazzing up the glatz', he called it. Me – I could barely speak to women cos I got so shy, so embarrassed. Way back, after Spain, I'd asked him one night in Portsmouth after we'd been doing our training:

"Robbie, how come all these women fall at your feet? What's your secret?"

Robbie smiled. "It ain't no secret, Jack, my lad – it's my natural sex appeal, my good looks, my magic words, and," he pointed a finger at me insistently, "a certain biological urge: they just wanna have my babies. And there's only one way to do that, I reckon. Tried and tested. Old as the hills."

"Ha- bloody-ha!" I had paused. "But seriously, what do you say to them? What poetic charms do you use just to speak to a girl? I never know what to say."

"It's not magic, Jack – honest! If I see a bird I fancy I just go up to her and say, 'Oi, do you wanna fuck?'"

"Christ, Robbie! You don't! Tell me you don't!"

"It's true – it's easy."

"I bet you get your face slapped a lot."

"Yeah, sure, that does happen – you're right. Sometimes they look all shocked and whack me round the face." He paused. "But every so often I find one that does want to get fucked. And I always like to please."

"You are fucking incorrigible."

"Jack – I swear you're a walking, talking fucking dictionary. Incorrigibubble, my arse!"

"Robbie, I read the dictionary every day, cos this world is full of clever bastards who know big words and my dad says my life might depend on knowing what the clever bastards are telling me and trying to get me to believe with their lies. Words give you power, Robbie – even more than those fucking torpedoes."

"So, Jack – what went wrong with you and Katya? Your big words didn't help you there, sunshine."

"Nothing went wrong," I said defensively. "She just wasn't my type."

"You should have the women swarming all over you – big, strong bloke like you."

For a few seconds I stared into Robbie's dark laughing eyes, so bright and full of life, and for a frozen sliver of time, I almost said something, but I knew that there were no words for what I had to say and that our friendship might survive, but everything between us would change a little, so I deliberately changed the conversation.

"What I don't understand, Mr Charmer Thompson, is what changed when you met Halya. I ain't seen you look at another woman since you met her. What's going on? Deptford Lad in Soviet Love Plot?"

"Deptford Lad in Love. Full fucking stop!" Robbie returned. "Jack, you've never been in love, so you ain't gonna understand what I say, but Halya…," he looked out into the sea, down into the waves closest to our ship, then up at the far horizon. His eyes were starting to fill with tears.

"I've never met anyone like Halya. As soon as I met her, I knew: I knew I'd found the only woman I could ever love - ever."

"But what's special about her? Just anuvva bit of skirt to you, I'd've thought, judging on your record."

"No, you couldn't be more wrong, Jackie, my boy. Halya and I have a deepness that I didn't know could exist. I don't want another woman after her. She's for life – and my son, Nikita."

"Well, that's wonderful, Robbie."

"So if I look a little blue or down from time to time – don't worry: I'm just thinking about Halya and Nikita. Hey, Jack! I got this wizard fucking idea: you know a couple of the ships – those huge fuckers with the cranes – are going to stay in Murmansk so they unload the cargoes of the convoys that follow us? Well, I can put in a transfer to one of those ships, so I can be in Russia where Halya is and, who knows, maybe I can get to see her somehow."

I roared with laughter. "Robbie, you might get the transfer, but you are a bleeding idiot to think you'll be able to find Halya on your days off: the country is at war. She could be anywhere."

"Well, she'll be fighting in the front line, and -."

"A front line that is thousands of miles long. You are a daft ap'orth, Robbie. Transfer if you like, but you won't find Halya."

Robbie looked disconsolate.

"I'm sorry, Robbie, but you gotta face facts: you have no idea where she is in the biggest country in the world which happens to be fighting an extremely nasty and vicious war against an evil and violent ideology. What if she's in Leningrad? It's besieged – they won't let you in."

"Oh, Jack! You're right, of course. I was just dreaming. I'm desperate to see her is all."

"Come on, Robbie, let's get back to our proper job."

We watched the convoy again. There were tankers carrying aircraft to protect them but filled with fuel, the fuel loaded so deeply that from a distance their fore and aft castles (from which the planes would be catapulted) looked like two small craft; there were huge freighters chock full with war equipment - planes with folded wings like giant butterflies lined up on their decks. There were ships of almost every nationality that had by now joined the British: Panamanians, Norwegians, Greeks, Canadians, Free French, Americans, Danes, the Dutch. Their crews lined the rail and, as they passed us, everybody waved, but there was no cheering. It was a strangely serious and solemn occasion. We did not wave at each other like crews on buses passing in the solitude of the ocean, but like knights preparing for battle or gladiators about to enter the killing arena.

The convoy slowed down, as a flag signal fluttered on a huge British freighter, obviously the flag ship. When the signal was taken down, there began a general re-shuffling of the convoy. It brought my heart to my mouth when all those vessels slowly, deliberately, very carefully fell into their new positions, two lines abreast but without stopping going forward. It was done without any accidents, but there were some narrow escapes as twenty thousand ton tankers got too close to the mammoth freighters carrying the aeroplanes and tanks to the Soviet Union.

When all the merchant ships were in the right position, the actual escort began to distribute itself around the convoy and it turned out to be much smaller than I'd thought: six destroyers, ten rather weird-looking smaller craft and two ships like us - merchant ships converted, but fitted out with ack-ack guns and Katyusha rockets. The rest of the comforting and impressive fleet of war ships took off at high speed in various directions. The American ships that had escorted the convoy so far turned around completely and headed westwards. The British ships now vanishing on the horizon were split into two forces, one presumably going back to Britain and the other, our shadow covering force, given licence to roam in circles at a greater distance from the convoy itself. At last, just as the sun was beginning to sink below the western horizon, a signal went up on the flag ship.

"Convoy: proceed at full speed ahead! Keep your distance and stay in formation. God speed!" and off we went, steadily increasing speed until we were running at fifteen knots.

Robbie and I were just pleased to be back in action, fighting fascists, and, as the convoy cumbersomely made its way through that radiant, evening sunshine across the tranquil, deep blue sea, a sense of security that I'd never felt before took hold of me again. It seemed impossible for raiding U-boat packs to get past those two massive concentrations of war ships ahead of us and the triple ring of defence of the endlessly circling destroyers scanning the darkness below the surface with their asdics ready to pounce on any U-boats that came within range with depth charges, gun fire or torpedoes.

As for the planes, there were the improvised ships of the shadowing force studded with catapult planes. There were these ungainly anti-aircraft vessels which sported gaunt, unfinished-looking scaffolding. This included conventional ack-ack guns which Robbie and I mounted, but also the Katyusha rockets which were a Russian invention capable of firing whole clusters of rockets which would decimate any formation of approaching planes.

I wanted to see them in action. Who would dare to challenge the tremendous destructive power of all these forces protecting the convoy? That first evening it seemed unimaginable that anyone would. I almost came to believe that we might sail all the way to Murmansk unchallenged. But events were to prove me wrong.

The night passed quietly, but an hour after dawn the Germans struck. The U-boats' captains were very cunning and skilled, although it hurts me to admit it, because they managed to evade three lines of defence, the last one our own escort which was circling around our ship with a dozen asdics pinging away. Apparently, although I didn't know this at the time, the asdics were adversely affected by the temperature and the strong, deep sea currents.

Out of the blue on a calm morning, with heart-stopping suddenness, two ships in the convoy exploded almost simultaneously: the first one quite close to us and to starboard and then the American freighter immediately in front of us. If you weren't watching closely (and Robbie and I were new to this, remember), you'd miss the white shimmering trail of the torpedo gliding straight towards its target. Our lifeboats were lowered in record time and there was a mad rush to save as many sailors as we could.

But Robbie and I were busy on the ack-ack guns. Messerschmitts and Fokker Wolfs were attacking us from above, swooping down and pouring an endless stream of automatic fire right at our gun positions and smaller bombs designed to damage the ship and help in the process of destruction. Stukas joined the assault, their sickening scream adding to the sense that this was hell, and death was coming. I was half aware that by then we were sailing through wreckage and through human bodies, some of whom were lucky enough to be hauled up black from the oil, black from burns, into the lifeboats. I saw sailors dragging black slippery bodies over the rail. They were a grizzly sight - scarcely human because of the oil that covered their faces. Many were badly wounded and their screams as they were dragged over the rail were harrowing and haunt my dreams still. And my days. All I could concentrate on though at the time were the planes trying to kill us and destroy our ship. Every now and then I heard further explosions as either plane bombs or torpedoes hit other parts of the convoy.

Meanwhile our destroyers were still circling, desperately, frantically dropping depth charges, trying to locate the murderers beneath the waves. The whole scene was one of complete mayhem, chaos and confusion, and then suddenly around midday it all stopped.

The attack had been going since dawn. I looked around me. I looked over at Robbie. He was grinning broadly, his face blackened by the cordite from the guns and the grease which had to be applied continually to the swivels so that the ack-ack batteries would turn efficiently. I laughed back: I like a man who grins when he fights.

"Time for a cigarette, Jackie boy," Robbie joked.

"Time for a nice cuppa tea, sunshine!"

It was a blue, brilliantly clear, cloudless day now, the sun was blinding, and the sea now was unruffled, untroubled and smooth – nature returning to itself. But it had turned noticeably colder. I watched with fascination the shadow of our ship glide over the water, so clearly outlined that Robbie and I were silhouetted on the cold water. The wind was cold – a biting, bitter cold that seemed to numb my cheeks and amaze my eye-balls. It was, in a small way, just a foretaste of the conditions we were to face in the depths of winter on this same route. This was just the back-end of September: I could not imagine what these seas would be like in January when my breath would come in a stream of steam which instantly turned into frost on my balaclava and my scarf. All the adrenaline in my body had made me strangely excited. Fighting, war is horrible, but if you survive, and we had survived, you feel a strange elation when it stops.

But it wasn't over. There was a sudden eruption of another explosion from the forward hatch of a tanker on our starboard side. A devilish obscenity in that beautiful, sunny, bright morning which reminded you so much of life while, under the water, death lurked for us all. The tanker exploded with clouds of steam and a burst of flame. As I watched, the satanic pre-meditated evil of it all seemed to me more overtly revealed than ever before. In Spain during our posting to Madrid we had seen first-hand what fascists with bombers could do to cow and intimidate and murder a densely-populated area of a city. But it wasn't until I was on the Arctic convoys that I started to understand what they meant when they talked about the Nazi War Machine.

Then another ship suddenly exploded in a boom of noise and crumps and fire on the port side - a freighter: she must have been carrying munitions as she blew up with such force and a havoc of violence that you felt the air buffeted and slapped, as well as the noise – and it started: I could see the bodies and wreckage still high in the air after the ship had already disappeared under the waves in clouds of seething steam and black eruptions of oil, detritus and further intermittent explosions.

As I stood there watching the whole scene with disgust and revulsion, yet unable to tear myself away, I was overcome by an intense, violent hatred, a mad desire to rush to the port gun and start firing blindly into the water, into the air at these hidden fascists, these surreptitious, malevolent killers, sinking our ships and slaughtering our men in an orgy of destructive and strangely calculated lunacy. Before, even in Spain, I'd never felt such fierce hatred and mindless violence surge up inside me. But now I stood there, shaking with a wrath that seemed impotent, fragile, individual, in the mad hope that one day I would get a chance to throw myself, bare-handed, on a fascist bastard, any German, strangle him, break his neck, gouge his eyes out, grind my boot into his teeth, piss in his eyes and shit in his mouth for all the terrible things he had done to 'our' ships. And that is why I hate war, though I'm proud of my part in that one and in Spain. War forces us to forget our better angels and become darker, more savage, more malign. But, as the man said, "If you're going through hell, keep going." Robbie and me were there: who else but us?

It took an act of will to stop thinking like this, and Robbie's punch on my arm saying, "Come on, kid, let's clean the guns. Then we can go and get a nice cuppa tea."

Chapter Eight: Tommy IV

A deep red stain darkened the road.

Nine eleven. September 11th. I can't forget it, but the images that crowd my mind are probably slightly different from yours. My image is of a wide, tree-tunnelled suburban street, the horse chestnuts still with their leaves – some a fading, dying green, some with a faint tinge of yellow, others more orangey, the conkers ready to drop. Sunshine, sunsheen and a green canopy like a green wash on a theatre stage, bathing everything and then - in the centre of the road - a big red stain. And police cars and that milk float and there are other images too: black and white, a foreign country, a man, my age now, in a suit and a tie, with a machine gun, staring into the air above him as jets fly over the presidential palace. So all in all a bad day, though when I saw the stain of blood I had not seen the grey flickering, faltering, forget-me-not images that would appear on that evening's news.

It was on my way to school. A big leafy road, not very typical for our area. It was near the golf club and, to be honest, I knew no one who went to the golf club. I could tell something was up that morning because the traffic was lighter. I was in good spirits: I'd just started the sixth form. Life was good. We were preparing for a school election and I was the Independent Socialist. There was a Tory candidate and a Liberal candidate, but ten different candidates of the left: Labour, Independent Labour, Socialist, Independent Socialist, Communist (Marxist Leninist), Communist (Trotskyite), Communist (Stalinist), Maoist. And a Green whose policies were indistinguishable from the others of the Left. Oh, and a Feminist/Marxist.

The Liberals won that school election. But the Left together garnered the most votes. Oh, and there was no far right candidate, in case you were wondering. The times were different. We thought the times were changing, but they weren't: they were soon to revert.

My bike flowed almost effortlessly on this bright promise-filled autumn morning and then I stared at this irregular jigsaw of police cars, the milk float, the stain of blood on the road. A young copper told me to turn back, find another way. And I knew something was terribly wrong.

When I got to school the rumours had already started. How does that work? How do people know? I can understand now with the internet and text messaging and instant updates on your mobile phone which can fix your car and make you coffee and cut your toe nails and your nasal hair and do your shopping if it's a voice recognition phone. But back then how did word spread so quickly?

Because it was our town, our area, and because the blood in the road had been shed by one of our own.

Now we talk about neets. People who are not in employment, education or training. We didn't talk about neets back then. Lee Jackson was just a bad lad, according to my parents and the neighbours. We'd somehow lost contact. No, that's not true. We'd not lost contact. We had suspended communication. When you're eleven you want to be like everyone else, but then you get to fifteen and you want to be different from everyone else. Lee was different. But at primary school we were friends or friendly rivals. We were similar: we both had crew cuts; we were both short for our age; we were both good at running and football – we were even twin wingers - him on the left, me on the right – for the school football team. Lee lived near me too, so we occasionally had tea at each other's houses. Not afternoon tea – but the main evening meal, before we learnt to call it dinner. He lived in that long straight road that adjoined the Post Office Sorting Office. His house was memorable, because it was one of those tiny, single-storey prefabricated houses that the government had thrown down everywhere after the war just to solve the housing shortage. I thought they were snug and cosy, but I also knew that some people despised them and those who lived in them. Not me.

At primary school if you're good at something – in this case running – then you tend to do every event, because they and you haven't really worked out what you excel at. So I knew that when we ran the 100 yards, or the 200 or the 400 – or their hurdling equivalents – I would usually come first and Lee second. And when we ran the half-mile or the mile the positions would generally be reversed. It was just the way things were. Like me, Lee used get bright red and drip with sweat after the first two yards of any race, so we were alike in many ways. I have two very sharp visual memories of Lee: the day we won the Inter-House Football competition at school in our last year, our red shirts crimson with sweat and a shared embrace; and three years later at Crystal Palace – some All London Schools' Athletics Competition. I grinned and nodded at Lee; he ignored me completely. I had passed the eleven plus; Lee had failed and that changed everything – although it shouldn't've.

Lee left school at fifteen - you could still do that then - so I don't know what had happened in the fifteen months from his leaving school to that blood stain, but I know that it filled me with sadness. There were other rumours round our way: a young girl was pregnant and the father was Lee; he had started experimenting with drugs; he'd been stopped in a stolen car near the Blackwall Tunnel; he kept bad and dangerous company. Words. Words. Words. I had no idea how much was true.

But I felt an instinctive sadness for the whole situation. Sadness for the milkman who left a wife and three children (oh, yes, and sadness for whatever had made Lee stab him, so much, so wildly that he died in the cramped front cabin of the float and his blood flowed out onto the tarmac of the road - the rumour mill got that detail right), sadness for the fact that Lee so desperately needed that money, so much so that he would kill to get it.

Killing is wrong, but it doesn't mean that you can't stand in the killer's shoes and feel sorry for the fact of what he did. And though I would never know in detail what was going to happen in the rest of Lee's life, that morning at school, as his name was mentioned and gossiped about and speculated about and bandied back and forth by people who had never spoken to him, I cried inside for the rest of his life. You don't need a weatherman to know which way the wind blows, and you don't always need to throw the I-Ching to predict the future. Perhaps he turned it round, perhaps he has a good story to tell, but I doubt it and I cried for the other people. No, not for them, but because of them. The milkman was dead. Lee's life in all probability was about to take a course from which he might never recover and which would stain the rest of his days.

But all people were interested in were their own idle, stupid, narrow-minded opinions.

Always was a wrong 'un. You could see it coming when he was in the first year. Mind you, not surprising when you look at his mum and dad – and them divorced too. I always said he'd turn out bad. His eyes were too close together.

I'm sorry: "His eyes were too close together." "Always knew he had it in him." "Have you seen where he lives?" I'm sorry – is this supposed to be in-depth analysis of another human being? Where is your fucking compassion?

Of that other death thousands of miles away in Santiago I saw a few seconds on the television news - it's famous footage. They say he committed suicide with forty-three bullets in him.

Thanks, CIA. ¡Muchas gracias, yanquis!

So there were three people at least whose lives were ruined on that other, largely-forgotten September 11th: the milkman's, Salvadore Allende's and Lee's – oh! and the milkman's family and Lee's mum and dad and that's before you get on to the tens of thousands of desaparecidos who got lost in Chile in the decades to come. A fucking bad day on the planet. But aren't most of them?

As someone very famous and much cleverer than me once said, "Let us get out of our grooves and study the rest of the globe." It all depends on your perspective. Robin Hood - Anglo Saxon freedom fighter. To the Normans - a terrorist, quite clearly. Hereward the Wake - Anglo Saxon freedom fighter. To the Normans, another terrorist.

Look at them now! They've been appropriated, haven't they? You can go to the Robin Hood Study Centre in the middle of Sherwood Forest and buy a Robin Hood hoodie and a t-shirt and a rubber and a sharpener and place mats and commemorative plates and Maid Marian fudge in fifty different flavours and Friar Tuck Chicken Tikka Masala sauce and a Will Scarlet kazoo and wooden swords and shields, but his spirit lives on somewhere on the streets of any city where the rich ignore the poor, where a woman pleads for mercy, where the unemployed beg for money and scrabble through the rubbish for a crust to eat.

Mind you, the unemployed beggars, '50p for a cup of tea, guv?' which *seems* such a bargain in the West End. But I've often paid and you know they've <u>never</u> <u>ever</u> brought me the tea. I'm a generous man, but if I pay for a cup of tea, I expect to get it.

Lee was caught, of course, but it took them three and a half months and ironically they found him living rough in the woods where John and I had truanted, just – what? - four brief years before. Unkempt, unshaven, uncelebrated - a modern day Robin Hood perhaps. Lee would have laughed at the thought of me truanting. LOL.

Everything changes. But outlaws still get caught.

Unless you're a Zapatista. ¡Ya basta!

Chapter Nine: Katya I

As soon as we were west of Samara we were greeted by fascist planes which made several attempts to bomb and strafe the train. We had to jump out of the carriages and start digging. One night a plane came at us from behind. Halya and I were in the last carriage. The blast and the impact of the explosion tore off the roof of our carriage. But in the neighbouring carriages three men were killed and another three were wounded. The train stopped somewhere in the steppe. We buried our dead comrades. The inside of the graves were lined with planks that we took from the bunks in the carriages – it was all we had. The train stopped about fifty kilometres away from Stalingrad. We were ordered out of the carriages and marched the rest of the way. We could only move after dark. It was tough, hard going. It was not simply that we were exhausted and we were dying of thirst: the route was well-known to the fascists and it was under attack at all hours. The tramping and marching of so many soldiers' feet brought up clouds of thick dust into the air. I found it difficult to breathe.

"Look, Katya, look!" Halya touched my arm and pointed to the west: there was a faint reddish glowing on the horizon.

On the horizon ahead of us there was a continuous glow. It was Stalingrad burning. By day it smouldered and smoked, and by night it glowed and blazed. As we slowly got closer to Stalingrad, along the edges of the road from villages even twenty kilometres away and right up to the Volga, everywhere was covered with banners and posters calling for Stalingrad to be defended. They were hanging from posts and trees and shacks, telegraph poles and fences, abandoned trucks and bombed-out tanks.

Before we crossed we were given our orders: we were to dislodge the enemy from the Red October housing estate. The command was given to prepare and about an hour and a quarter later we were already heading towards the crossing. The infantry were marching and vehicles were dragging the guns and carrying the munitions. The horses harnessed to the carts were snorting from the unbearable dust; the night was ravaged by the sound of explosions and the deathly rattle of machine gun fire from the west bank. The road was covered in potholes; in places floor boards been laid on the surface of the road and they had been strewn with bundles of brushwood.

"This looks like a fight to the death," Halya said to me as we marched along the dusty road. "I have a feeling this is going to be worse than anything we saw in Spain, Katya."

"I think you're right. I was committed in Spain, but this is our country. I will die many times if I have to in order to keep it free of fascism." I looked at Halya. I had not seen her cry since the day we left Barcelona. "Halya, what's the matter? You're crying."

"Oh, I'm just having a moment of weakness. I'll be fine as soon as we're in action – doing something."

"Are you thinking about Nikita?"

"No, not really. I know he's safe with my parents." She paused. "Katya, you're the only person I can say this to." She blinked back a stray tear. "I miss Robbie. I miss him so much. I never thought I would meet a man who consumed me so much. Why can't life be simple? Why can't we be together?"

"You know why, Halya. You know why – it is our governments' fault – ours and Robbie's. And now this war."

"Perhaps one day we'll be able to do without governments; then men and women can love who they like and do what they like."

"Halya, there'll be time enough for that when the city is saved. Come on, we've got to cross the river first."

"Katya, you're right. If I ever mention Robbie again – you have my permission to shoot me on the spot."

We arrived at the crossing: smashed boats were lying on the banks; we were sitting in ditches and trenches waiting our turn to cross over to the right bank of the Volga to Stalingrad. The city was burning and was lit by one continuous glow. The whole ground seem to be burning; there was nothing to breathe, it seemed, but the order was given to cross.

The night was very cloudy and dark: the moon and stars could not be seen - only the bright lines of tracer bullets racing into the sky looking like a weird fan made up entirely of demented, multi-coloured, manic fireflies. Searchlights swept the sky looking for fascist planes. It took us five hours to cross; we saw eight planes caught in the searchlights' beams and shot down. We had not yet seen any fascists.

Stalingrad was completely ablaze with flames – an inferno, turning the right bank now yellow, then orange, then red; light and dark chased one another around in a weird, whirling dance of death. Then suddenly, as we got to the top of a slope, it became as bright as day. Dozens of parachute flares were shining in the night sky illuminating the whole of Stalingrad and the crossing. As we crossed the Volga that night we could see the water lit up by the blaze of explosions and fires from the west bank and the faint glimmer of our lights on the eastern side. I had a terrible apprehension that the water was filled with human blood. But I dismissed that from my mind, although my mother, who was working as a nurse in a field dressing station on the eastern side, told me many years later that I had been correct and that the water had run black with oil and red with human blood. The blood of our soldiers. The blood of our militia. The blood of our workers. The fascist planes dropped burning fuel. All the air around you felt as if it was enveloped in fire. The ground was on fire. The corpses were on fire. The shattered remains of houses were on fire. We tried to find a way through it, but we had to make a detour. We ran through trenches hunched up to avoid the flames. Part of the problem was that on the top of the bank where the Staff Officers were quartered there were many oil tanks which exploded as a result of enemy shellfire, starting huge, new fires. These fires were the greatest danger to all of us as the burning oil was spilling downhill, setting alight everything in its path including the officers' dugouts. The burning oil flowed out onto the Volga where it spread over almost the entire surface of the river just as it had done on land, burning boats, barges - everything that was in the water. The Volga glowed like a huge flow of molten lava whose flames had been blown to the bank by the wind, even setting fire to the dressing stations and the jetties on the eastern bank. We also started, about half-way across the Volga, to smell the city: we'd smelt war before – the sweet but nauseating stench of death mixed with cordite and the metallic bitter tang of burned metal, but at Stalingrad that smell was intensified and over-powering - death, excrement, cordite, burned flesh, burned buildings – all mixed up together in one hellish miasma that assaulted your senses. I was not aware of it at the time, but I would encounter that smell again – in Berlin.

The river was alive with vessels of all types – rowing boats, summer pleasure steamers, fishing smacks, military boats of the Soviet Navy – because the situation in the city was so desperate and we needed to get as many soldiers into the city as quickly as possible. But it was very organized too: an NKVD officer ushered us to a waiting motor boat. What we found on that hazardous crossing was dangerous chaos: the fascists were bombarding the river and the light from the city allowed their pilots to see our boats. So many comrades did not reach the western bank, but perished in the water. We were lucky.

Just before we reached the west bank, Halya gathered our sniper unit together in a circle – all ten of us. We huddled around her and put our hands on hers as she shouted above the angry boomings of battle:

"Comrade sisters, we are in for a hard fight and some of us will not survive. But let us say these words together as a reminder of why we are here and to serve as an inspiration in the coming hours and days and weeks of battle."

And there, as the motor boat swayed in the river, as the spray from falling bombs spattered us with water, as our faces were lit up and then darkened as the flares and the fires and explosions intermittently flashed around us, we repeated Halya's words:

"For the burned cities and villages; for the deaths of our children and our mothers; for the torture and humiliation of our people – I swear revenge upon the enemy. I swear that I would rather die in battle with the enemy than surrender myself, my people and my country to the fascist invaders. Blood for blood! Death for death!"

As soon as the boat reached the shallows, we were over the side, led by Halya and we ran through the water and pressed on: we knew the fight for the city was desperate. Immediately we took a defensive position in a large two-storey building in the basement of which we found the families of workers in the Red October Factory. The children were crying, asking their parents for something to eat, but they had no food to give them. They had chanced upon two freight cars full of wheat for the factories, but the railway trucks caught fire from the bombing. They gathered up the burned grain and made uncooked flatbread, but the bread had an unpleasant taste of ashes and oil. One of the women treated us to some of this bread. You may find this hard to believe, but every man and woman in our platoon gave the children our emergency rations.

Halya and I took up our usual positions about forty metres from one another - Halya to the left of the centre and our commander, and me to the right. This was our standard defensive position. We were close enough to communicate and, if things got worse, we would move to the centre in an attempt to consolidate the command post and preserve communications. That was the plan. But we had learnt in Spain that the realities of battle make such plans almost irrelevant - when under fire, intense fire, and in the chaos of war even the best soldiers fight hard to keep their discipline. Usually we drifted further apart and with the explosions, the bullets, the screams of the wounded, the howls of the dying, the screech of enemy fighter planes, the desperate struggle to kill, kill, kill, and, of course, to ensure that we lived – well, then the frenzied, whirling chaos infects even such dedicated soldiers as Halya and myself. And remember that is before the terror, the hatred, the panic of hand-to-hand fighting, when the bayonets are fixed and you get so close to the enemy you can count the bristles on his cheeks, glimpse the dead blackness in his pupils and smell his courage, his fear and his sweating's stench.

Our unit was moved up to an attack line north of the factory canteen; when I left Halya, the boiler house was on fire. When the riflemen went into attack, we covered them from our sniping positions, but whenever we changed our positions, the machine gunners changed theirs too. The Maxim apparently is a heavy machine gun, but they didn't feel its weight: it was manoeuvred with such power and speed.

By the end of the day our tunics were soaked in sweat and clinging to our backs; the grit was crunching in our teeth; our mouths were completely dry. We had to sling our guns over our shoulders when we moved and that made it difficult for us to run. Bullets were whistling past and mortars were exploding, but we hardly saw the Germans at all. They had taken cover behind piles of rubble and wrecked buildings. I came across a trench in which a machine gun had been mounted and started feeding a cartridge belt into the bandolier. It seemed to take forever, but in fact it couldn't have been more than a minute. Halya helped. I squeezed the trigger. The machine gun was working fine.

Everywhere we could see our soldiers frantically digging in; every minute, every second, counted. The deeper you dig the better you'd be able to repulse enemy attacks and hold on to your position. It's probably been the same for foot soldiers, for infantry, for thousands of years. Dig, dig, dig – put your faith in Mother Earth. At that moment a cloud of dust soon appeared from the west. Fascist tanks were coming and, behind the tanks, masses of infantry. Several of the tanks turned and started heading straight towards us. It's difficult to describe your feelings at a moment like that. There's a continuous growling, rumbling and roaring in the air. The ground seems to be alive and groaning; the air is shrieked with blast. The tanks were firing as they went; from every gun they had shells, and in addition mines and mortars were exploding all around us, throwing up huge quantities of earth and brick and rubble and parts od dead bodies. All around there was hissing, roaring and wailing. It seemed as though thousands of splinters and shrapnel and bullets were flying through the air.

Halya and I were running dangerously short of ammunition so, wanting to save our sniper rounds for better targets, we grabbed whatever we could find - grenades, ordinary infantry rifles. There was only one thing to do - shoot at the fascists with everything we had and hurl grenades at them. The battle lasted for another two hours: two tanks were burning in front of us, but the rest of them were continuing to fire on our trenches. Behind us there was an anti-tank gun. It managed to disable one tank before being smashed. The second gun was firing at point blank range. It was mounted in a window on the ground floor of the brick building. Things had reached the stage where we were using anti-tank grenades, though we didn't have many of them. Someone not far from us disabled a tank with a grenade. The tank turned around on one caterpillar track, revolved its turret and started firing at our right flank. Anti-tank riflemen from the 118th Independent Machine Gun Battalion came to our aid and we held our positions.

There were a lot of dead and wounded people. We stayed there until nightfall. During the night we took the opportunity to move the dead and get the wounded back to field dressing stations and consolidate our position. That meant digging deeper and moving the machine guns and also for Halya and me trying to decide on our best position for the morning. We'd decided that it was best if we moved out beyond the front line trench, so we could snipe from what was effectively no-man's land, but we needed to rest first.

It was a dark night and I was only able to keep watch over the forward position by lying down and looking at the horizon against the background of the sky. You couldn't make out any moon. It was hard to stay awake. The sleepless nights were really taking their toll; my eyelids were getting heavier and heavier with every minute. I couldn't keep my eyes open any longer, so I had to report this to the commander of our platoon. He gave me permission to keep crawling around rather than stay lying on the same spot. Halya and I made sure we didn't fall asleep by whispering loudly to each other from time to time. In the basement, the narrow corridor led up to the window. They had mounted a machine gun quite high up and, since we didn't have a ladder, I had to use some beer and vodka crates that were in the basement to climb up to it. There was a little cupboard on the back wall which everyone was using as a place to sleep. It was too short and you had to bend your legs, but you could sleep in it and with luck you might get twenty minutes of oblivion.

The next morning the Germans opened up with heavy artillery fire again. It felt as if they wanted to obliterate the factory canteen from the face of the earth. In the basement, in the darkness, we could only sit tight and wait behind the thick walls. It looked at times as if the ceiling was about to come crashing down. The air in the dark, murky basement was filled with dust from all the collapsed plaster. When bombardment stopped, of course, the Germans attacked. We flew to the windows or to the trenches. This time the Germans' main effort was directed at the right hand of the factory canteen; ten or so fascist tanks were moving along the hollow towards School Number 35. We could all hear the thundering roar of their engines, even though they were stationary. But we had to ward off sub-machine gunners that were coming towards us shrieking loudly as they came. We could hear the yells of the officers and the shouting of the men. They were just coming and coming. Halya and I concentrated on shooting the officers: that was the best way to make the attack break down and eventually our fire forced them all to the ground and they stayed there.

I remember hearing that our machine gunners had used up nearly all their cartridge belts, but the battle seemed to be over for now and we had managed to hold on to our position. Halya and I had been firing so much and for so long that it was impossible to touch the barrels of our sniper rifles. The palm of my right hand was hurting and my right finger had a blister. My shoulder was in constant pain, battered by the rifle butt from all the shooting. I was probably in need of a good sleep. Towards mid-day on October 14th the Germans took the boiler house: only one soldier managed to get out of it alive. There were lots of wounded men in the basement with us, but there was no way to get them across the Volga. The battalion commander sent a messenger to the regimental command post to report this and he must also have asked for reinforcements since about two hours later dozens of sub-machine gunners arrived. The sub-machine gunners brought us cartridges, grenades and bottles of inflammable fluid. We immediately set about re-taking the boiler house. Halya and I were deployed on the flanks, our mission as usual - to kill fascist officers. All the others shouted one long "Hurrah!" and rushed the ruins. After a brief engagement the Germans retreated. All around lay the bodies of dead Germans and some of our lads too. Two disabled tanks were still smoking; they had probably been hit by our anti-tank riflemen. I heard the rumble of tank engines coming from behind the ruins of the boiler house.

On the right flank the fascists had taken our trenches: the battle was still raging but not as intensely as it had that morning. I saw five or so of our men surrendering. I saw them running towards the Germans with their hands in the air. I fired at them several times from my rifle, but I didn't hit any of them. That's not like me. I was normally very accurate. There's nothing more painful than when your own comrades betray you to save their own skins. The loss of the boiler house meant our left flank was exposed to the enemy. The battalion commander telephoned the regiment's command post to report the situation, but almost at exactly the same time the communications broke off. The battalion commander sent a messenger, but he was killed. There was no way of getting through, so those of us who were still alive were stuck in the basement of the factory canteen. Only then did we realize how difficult it would be to escape from the basement by day, so we decided to wait until nightfall. We gathered up the last cartridges and grenades. We didn't have any food or water left and the pit of water was full of debris from the ceiling which had finally fallen in. We tried to dig it out, but the water was now an undrinkable gruel of soil and dirt and lime.

Halya looked exhausted.

"Are you all right?" I asked her, knowing that she would give an optimistic response.

"I'll keep going. What choice have we got?" She grinned. "I don't care if I fall as long as someone else picks up my gun and keeps shooting!"

We both laughed out loud: what else could we do? We were there; there was no one else and we had a job to do. So we did it.

Halya even said, "This is no time for ease and comfort; it's a time to dare and endure." She seemed possessed with an indomitable spirit.

That night we managed to make our way to the factory's power station where we found three tanks full of water. This was a tremendous stroke of luck. We made use of this water and also supplied the neighbouring units that were fighting in this sector. Later a huge water tank was discovered in the ground close to the factory's offices which probably served as the factory's reserve supply. I set up a twenty four hour guard around it, so as to prevent any possibility of its being spoiled or contaminated since the basement of the factory's offices housed the dressing station where the wounded were sent. This reserve water proved invaluable as it supplied all the units in that combat zone including the 308th Siberian Division.

There were still workers from the factory around and they found us fifty sacks of flour, thirty-eight kilos of butter and several boxes of expensive cigarettes, in the ruins of the stores. When the supply situation became dire I gave the 308th Siberian Division over thirty-five sacks of flour and half the butter.

This is how we were kept supplied with munitions: we'd pick up any rifle rounds, sub-machine gun rounds, mortar shells that we found and store them in the boiler room. When provisions were low, the soldiers would make butter and flour pancakes in the cellars.

In the middle of October the German attacks on the factory area were relentless, fierce and unceasing; we stopped being human and became just savage fighters intent on killing, killing, killing and keeping in our hands any pointless scrap of territory, while they were desperately trying to drive a wedge into our right flank. A lieutenant ran up to me and asked me to give him as many cartridges as I could spare as the Germans were starting to encircle them from the flank. I recalled Zhukov's dictum that even if you perish in the attempt, you should come to the aid of your comrade-in-arms. I handed over seven boxes of cartridges and poured some more into some kit bags. Day and night embrasures were made in every building; connecting trenches and concrete underground passages were dug between all the sectors and the dug-outs including the trenches and machine gun foxholes and so forth. I shall never forget the second company's battle by the maritime workshop. It was the 16th or 17th October, I think.

The Germans launched several co-ordinated attacks into the factory and managed to break through to the main gates with tanks, disabling our two anti-tank guns outside the power station. It was desperate stuff. The second company fought for over four hours – hand-to-hand where necessary. I saw our men using bricks, lumps of concrete, jagged scraps and shards of shrapnel to bludgeon enemy skulls to a mass of bloody pulp; bayonets to strike the enemies' eyes or genitals. Contact with the Siberians to our right was lost. The Germans were breaching the line of defence in the area of the boiler room and the main gates. There was a high risk of our being surrounded by the Germans as they had more men, more weapons, more munitions than us. The company therefore fell back to the next line of resistance, repulsing the enemy as it went with sub-machine gun fire and grenades.

Halya joked across at me: "I get this sneaking feeling that they don't like us, you know? They're making such determined efforts to kill us. What do you think, Katya?"

"I think you're right but it's good in a way. When you have enemies like this, you know you've stood up for something you believe in – otherwise people like this would not be your enemy!"

She laughed out loud. But that was a respite: we had work to do.

Halya and I kept up a continuous sniper fire in a defensive formation, close together, so that we were almost within reach, moving sideways, moving whenever we'd fired off one shot to avoid detection. On the evening of the 18th October the factory's defensive line had gone as far back as the southern edge of the factory. On this line there was continuous fire for several days. By the last days of October the Germans were attacking the Red October Factory at several points. The wail of sirens and dive bombers, the blasts of bombs and grenades and the crackle of machine guns never let up. The area was veiled in smoke and dust which covered the buildings.

The next four weeks were a struggle to survive on three fronts at least: the hardest winter for ten years set in early and the city was enveloped in snow; getting enough food and drink was always a struggle – on the river crossings the priority was usually given to fresh soldiers and to ammunition; and, of course, we were fighting a grappling, desperate fight for every square centimetre of our city against an army that had conquered most of Europe and swept all before them.

War can bring out the worst and the best in human nature: in a sense I had already seen that in Spain, but the four weeks immediately before Halya's capture led me to admire anew her stamina, her determination and her skill as a soldier. She knew no fear and seemed to know no tiredness; she was always happy and optimistic; when I was most in despair, she always lifted my spirits and made me laugh. She told jokes which were quite critical of the Soviet system, but she also managed to convey a complete and utter devotion to that system and that ideology, and a belief that it was the only way to achieve some sort of betterment for the whole human race. And she did all this while fighting every day and night to keep Stalingrad undefeated, to stop the Fascists crossing the Volga, to stop the brutal, inhuman carnage that this malevolent human maelstrom of hate and viciousness had unleashed on everything we loved and the values we held so dear. And remember that she did all this while separated from her son and from her lover. She never did mention Robbie again all the time we were together, but I am sure she thought of him. And who can blame her? She had boundless energy and courage and could single-handedly, with one anecdote, lift the spirits of an entire infantry company.

Once she found a red rose – perhaps a remnant of someone's balcony garden – and put it behind her ear, with a defiant and yet coquettish glint in her eyes. So that the fascist sniper spotters, if they saw her, she said, would know that their men had been shot by the Red Rose Sniper. She kept it there for several days; it simply became whiter and whiter with the dust.

I remember one morning was particularly dangerous. We were in a house just to the north of the city centre. We had endured a constant bombardment all night and had sustained many casualties. Halya kept seeing the sunny-funny side of things.

She told us:

"You know, comrades, this last night as I slept in my fox-hole, there was a knock on the sheet of corrugated iron that I'd used as a roof. It was the NKVD.

"The officer barked, 'Does the sniper Reznik live here?'

'No,' I said.

'Who are you?'

'Halya Reznik!'

'And aren't you a sniper?'

'Yes, I am.'

'Then why did you say you didn't live here?'

I said, 'Seriously – you call this living!'

Or she'd come up with little sayings that made us all chuckle and remember that there was a life outside this hellish war.

"Remember," Halya used to say, "it takes forty-two muscles to frown, and fifty-five to shout, 'Go home, you fascist bastards', but it only takes one finger to pull the trigger of a decent sniper rifle."

"And, oh," she'd say, smiling at me, "a sniper partner who covers your back and in whose hands you know your own life is completely safe."

But there were other times when more quietly she spoke to me about Nikita and how pleased she was that he was safe, far back in the east.

For those four weeks we never stopped fighting. We had hardly any food to eat; getting even water to drink was an achievement; tea was an unaccustomed luxury. We lost the ability to sleep and to relax because we were in action every day. The German attacks were continuous, and, with the snow and the plummeting temperatures, a new desperation and savagery entered their conduct. Neither side had been taking prisoners for some time now: the fighting was so intense that there were hardly any opportunities to take prisoners, but if they did occur they were ignored. Sudden summary executions were taking place all over the city – on both sides. At least the cold stopped the decay of the dead bodies that by then littered the city streets or protruded from piles of rubble, so we did not have to cope with the sick, sweet, rank scent of rotting flesh for a few weeks.

Where do we live but days? I will never forget the day Halya was captured. I blame myself in my darker moments, but it was probably her own bravery or her foolhardiness – she was so unconcerned for her personal safety, so committed to our cause, that sometimes she took too many risks. In fact, it was probably no more than the messy mists of muddle that war consists of. I will remember that day for the rest of my life. She was the only real friend I have ever had, and every day I wonder about how exactly she died. And I pray to a God I don't believe in that her death was quick and easy.

Every day I weep for Halya. And I weep because I do not know how she died. In a sense that is a consolation, but as a consequence of this she continues to die in a thousand different, equally barbaric ways every night in my bad dreams. Buried and rotting beneath the rubble of our murdered city? A bullet in the back of the head, the head that had fallen asleep on my shoulder in the middle of the night as we lay trying to get a little sleep during the nights in Stalingrad? Doused in petrol as so many of our captured commissars were? Gassed in a death camp, naked and frightened?

Every day I weep for Halya.

Chapter Ten: Tommy V

Abroad! What an adventure! I don't know what it is, but there's something about being abroad that is wonderful and liberating and magical. If I say I don't like holidays in England, that sounds very snooty and snobbish, but it's not meant to be. It's just that abroad is so different that it's like being in another country. Honest!

Is it some faint race memory that inspires the English to explore while at the same time trying to escape this sad little, wet little, narrow-minded country? Or is it simply an escape from the mundane nature of quotidian life, a chance to get out of our grooves and see how the rest of the world lives? Whence our need to emulate our Anglo-Saxon forebears and the later ones – Drake, Raleigh, Frobisher, Clive, Cook, Livingstone? Perhaps it's just the chance to drink cheap alcohol, smoke cheap fags and feel a little semi-detached from everything going on around us, while doing all this in a climate which is far better than our own. Maybe it is just the weather.

Shangri-La, Atlantis, Nova Zembla, Xanadu, Calais – why do they hold such a magnetic grip on the English imagination?

I had been on package holidays with my parents to Spain and on day trips to France with my school, and I loved what I saw: the sheer difference in everything – the little things, the street signs, the way people walked, the domestic architecture, the gestures, the facial expressions, and, of course, the language. The problem is, as a visitor, you still don't see the real country: I suppose you have to live there to do that and so we become itinerants, precarious, vicarious consumers of the cultures which seem on the surface so much more attractive, organic and sensible than our own. Or maybe it is the cheap fags.

I was in my second year at university when Uncle Jack asked me if I would accompany him on a trip to Spain. He would pay; I would drive. I acquiesced, desperate to immerse myself in French culture, to try out my French language skills and, without getting too pretentious, smoke myself silly on cheaper cigarettes. And to see the newly democratic Spain.

And so it was that in late June we found ourselves racing down the Autoroute from Paris to Lyon. Jack's intention was to see a little, fleeting bit of France before we arrived at our final destination – Barcelona. The trip down to France was to be punctuated with occasional stops at cheap hotels. Jack had not retired yet, but now employed an assistant who ran the butcher's shop in his absence. I loved every minute, every second of that trip and even now, in retrospect, I still love it. But then I like being abroad. I like being in motion, not stuck in one place. I feel foreign all the time in England anyway, but at least abroad that feeling is substantiated by logic and common-sense. Will I always be a stateless person, I have often wondered to myself, a sans-papières forever?

Yes, like being in a foreign country – but everything really <u>was</u> so different. The smells in the cafes were different; the houses, although recognisably houses, were different; the people sauntered, seemed to do no discernible work and used their hands and faces to communicate in different ways from ourselves. And the booze was so cheap!

Some people say that the rivalry between the British and the French is because in one sense we are so alike: the British are arrogant and expect everyone to speak English; the French are arrogant and expect everyone to speak French.

Hélas! Speak French! Speak French? Not too much of a minefield really. Although over the years I have sometimes been frustrated at the inability of French people to understand my French. Those situations where you amble into a boulangerie and say,

"Bonjour. Je voudrais un baguette et six pains au chocolat, mademoiselle, s'il vous plait."

And the shop assistant looks at you with a glare, a stare, a mixture of incredulity and horror and, for a split second, you worry that you have invited her to have penetrative anal sex there right there in the middle of the shop in front of all the customers. Où est la beurre?

But those incidents are few and far between and, as I've said, being abroad can be liberating. And me being me, I am almost tempted to pooch into the boulangerie and say,

"Bonjour, mademoiselle, je voudrais te donner toute ma jouissance sur tes seins – maintenant! Ici! Et vite!!!"

- since the reaction might well be the same, but I might end up with a baguette and six chocolate breads. You never know, maya dorogaya, you never know.

But on reflection that might have gone down better back in England: I would just have been dismissed as a crazy Frenchman.

And French women are already a good enough reason in themselves to visit France and all of them so unashamedly high-maintenance. I like high-maintenance women; I like low-maintenance women – with both types you know exactly where you stand. But there are women who should carry health warnings for the safety of the male sex and these women are high-maintenance women who believe (against all reason or logic or common sense) that they are, in fact, low-maintenance. Their adherence to this belief as an article of faith has been the cause of many unsuccessful and unsatisfactory liaisons.

But women were not part of the subject matter in the almost unceasing conversation that preoccupied Uncle Jack and me as we smoked southwards on the autoroutes, apparently towards the sun and certainly towards higher temperatures. We had a lot to talk about. He showed an intense curiosity about my university course and, because he had read so much himself, it felt like talking to an equal.

He too had lots to tell me. I'm not quite sure when this had happened but it had been, looking back, certainly before our trip to Glasgow. Uncle Jack, it seems, had felt strangely liberated in the late 1960s and, although still tied to the butcher's shop, had begun a more active life in his older age and was always off to political meetings, writing letters to local councillors, to his MP, writing to the Prime Minister, to the Ruler of the Universe, to the Grand Wizard of the Cosmos, writing to the newspapers, attending fringe meetings of obscure political groups or minor demonstrations to draw attention to some injustice or inequality somewhere in the world. His eyes would light up with a feverish animation and a childlike enthusiasm as he recounted his exploits to me.

"A demonstration a week and every day a letter, Tommy. I tell you, my son – it's keeping me young."

Letters for Amnesty; letters to the Shah; letters to King Faud; letters to Beelzebub; letters to Yahweh; letters to every repressive government all over the world. In Trafalgar Square getting people passing South Africa House to sign anti-apartheid petitions.

"Is it for the stamps, Uncle Jack?"

"Sod off, Tommy."

After years of repression it seemed Jack had started to find himself, as we might say now. We may even have said that then. I prefer to think that he was starting to have the confidence to do openly what he had always believed in, and certainly the 1960s must have helped in contributing to his newfound confidence. Mind you, the '60s makes me laugh. Hippies? LSD? Free love? Not down our road. Nor any road I knew.

I had worked out by now, of course, that Jack had fought in the Spanish Civil War on the Republican side and that he did so from a sense of political conviction, the desire to fight fascism – Xavi's visit and our own trip to Clydeside had confirmed that. But I was still uncertain why he had been crying that day in the shop. And it bugged me.

And I wasn't stupid. I knew Barcelona had been the capital of the Spanish Republic during Franco's insurrection. So I could see why we were undertaking this trip at this time. Also I was older and so perhaps he felt more able to tell me things. But there was still so much I didn't know.

When I don't understand something, now that I'm an adult, I ask openly and frankly: I admit my ignorance. My younger self was still in awe of Uncle Jack and so my questions about his part in the Spanish Civil War were tentative and deliberately delayed until we were south of Lyon. Add to that the macho English reticence that speaks not of that which it hasn't a bleeding clue – and you have a recipe for total ignorance. I needn't have worried – Jack's new confidence unleashed a flood of reminiscences that kept us going to the outskirts of Perpignan.

"What can I tell you Tommy? Robbie and me organized an Aid for Spain Committee in Deptford and that meant we held meetings every week in the top room of the Nag's Head. Robbie and me - we went round the houses knocking on doors and asking people for money, or tins of food, anything they could spare. Sometimes we got food, sometimes we got money: we even got a blanket or two. We had street collections in which we'd go round with a tin. We went to the Docks - stood at the gates when the men left work. We went to the market - you know, the one up at Greenwich - a lot of the stallholders were very sympathetic. I honestly think the Aid for Spain movement is probably the most popular and one which aroused more feeling than perhaps any other single issue in this country before or since, but people forget and where can you read it? As for going, well, I first felt that I should go without any sense of romanticism. I just felt that I wasn't able to sit back and content myself with collecting tins of food and money and speaking at meetings. It wasn't enough. Something important was happening and I wanted to be part of it. Plus I was seventeen and I'd never been abroad. I was excited. It made me feel important.

"The situation in Spain too had become very serious very quickly. In 1936 it was touch and go whether Madrid would be captured by the fascists. If they captured Madrid it would have had an enormous effect on the whole war. Despite the fact that the Government had gone down to Valencia, I just felt that I wasn't doing enough and the situation in Spain was reaching a dreadful state and Robbie and me we just wanted to be in on whatever could be done to fight fascism. I didn't think of myself as a hero. And I don't even now, you know, Tommy. I've always been timid, and I've never gone out of my way to pick fights. On the other hand, it's a big thing for anyone to knowingly put himself in a position where his life is in danger or where God knows what injury or mutilation is possible. Until you are in that situation you can't imagine it, no matter what they say.

"Anyway, Robbie and me, we both tried to go in January 1937, but the only way we could hope to get to Spain was through the British Communist Party. No one, but abso-fucking-lutely no one, Tommy, had a passport in those days. No one round our way. Certainly no one I knew. The British Communist Party weren't very impressed with our offer.

"In the first place we proved we were complete wazzocks. Robbie phoned them at King Street and said, "Can you help me and my mate? We want to go to Spain.""

"They said, "For Christ's sake, get off the bloody phone. You think such things are talked about over the phone?""

"He put the receiver down: seemed like our plans to save the world from fascism were scuppered. I suppose they had a point. As it happened at that stage they were only taking men with military experience. Which ruled us out, but by April 1937 things had got so desperate in Spain that they would take just about anyone, provided they were alive, vaguely left-wing and unmarried - they didn't want too many dependants. I had no commitments; Robbie had no commitments. So we just jacked in our jobs at the factory in Brockley, told the boss what we thought of him and fucked off. So they accepted us. We were told to keep quiet and not to tell anyone at all. All we had to do was to get British passports and book a ferry to France and a train to Paris, as if we were going on holiday. Because in a way we were deceiving the British Government. The Government had signed a non-intervention pact and so by going to fight in Spain we were breaking that pact and so we had to, you know, keep it dark.

"You know, Tommy, in a way I was terrified, but also it was so exciting. I had never been out of London, except to go to Brighton once on a Bank Holiday, so to go to France and Spain - just the thought of it was astonishing."

"And so the young bloke on the ship is Robbie?"

"Who else? But that photo was taken a couple of years later. Anyway, Robbie and I went to Victoria Station, but we had to pretend we didn't know each other, so we travelled in different carriages. We caught the Dover train and then the midnight boat for Calais, still pretending not to know each other. We changed trains a few times. It was pretty obvious the French police were looking out for people like us. We got to Paris. Robbie and me could speak only English, but as we came out of the station the taxi driver said, "English? English?" He packed us both in a taxi. He didn't ask us where we wanted to go. He seemed to know and drove us straight to a recruiting office. The Paris office was illegal - the French were constantly moving it around. It was the recruiting office for the all the international brigades. Later on it was so well organized, people even got a medical check there, but there were none when Robbie and I passed through. There were so many people: there were hundreds and hundreds. They came from everywhere in the world and, just as the taxi driver had known where we wanted to go, so did other people. There we were - two foreigners with spare vests and spare socks, but no other luggage and no money, but they knew where we were going. In fact, a sweet old lady on the train to Perpignan, who was knitting, looked at us both and said, "You Spain?"

"So even she knew where we were going. I suppose it was obvious. There are a lot of horrible stories about crossing the border - about the French shooting people like us. It didn't happen to Robbie and me. The French were shutting their eyes at that particular moment. They packed us all in a darkened bus and we went up to the French border. The French border guards said something to the driver, waved us on and – hey! - we were in Spain. We arrived at the old fortress in Figueras on May 1st 1937. We bedded down, and slept for the first time in three days. We only stayed two nights. The place was packed with hundreds of people, more arriving every day, so they gave us each a rifle and put us on a train for Barcelona. We demonstrated through the streets of Barcelona. We got a huge meal and then marched to the Lenin Barracks, the Caserna Lenin, where we started our training. After Barcelona we got on a train to Albacete where our real training began. Most of our instruction was given in Russian. The interpreter was American of Ukrainian descent. He was formal, but very friendly, very accessible. We got on with him very well. He said you should always take action. He said it was like sitting in a room with an attractive woman, would you just sit there and do nothing - no. I laughed at that in private, of course. The training consisted of a lot of marching to harden your feet - that was essential. We learnt the Spanish formation of marching in threes. We fired fifteen rounds from our rifle. We pulled pins out of hand grenades; we learned to give them a good throw. We learned to get out of the way. We learned Spanish instructions for the battlefield, how to oil and clean and put our rifles back together again blindfolded, and I tell you Tommy, after three weeks of that, we were ready to go.

"Oh, Tommy. You can't imagine it. I'd never been abroad before and it wasn't just the fact that the women looked different and the men looked different and the houses were different, all the road signs were different. When we first got to Barcelona, everything was different."

"In what sense, Uncle Jack?"

"The anarchists were still in complete control of Catalonia. The revolution was still in full, glorious swing. Can you believe that? It was the first time I'd ever been in a city where the workers and ordinary people were in complete control. Every building, every public building of any size, even the little post offices, had been seized by the workers and were draped with red flags or the red and black flag of the anarchists. Every wall was scrawled with the hammer and sickle and the initials of the revolutionary parties. Almost every church or chapel or shrine had been destroyed and its images thrown away. Churches all over the city were being systematically dismantled by groups of workers' militia. It was heaven, Tommy. You would have loved it. Every shop, every café, every factory we passed had a sign up saying that it had been collectivized. Even the shoe-shines had been collectivized and their little boxes were painted red and black. Everyone, waiters, shop assistants looked you in the face and treated you as an equal. All the old fashioned forms of speech had simply ceased to exist in everyday speech. Terms of address such as 'Señor' or 'Don' or even 'Usted' were no longer heard. Everyone called everyone else 'Comrade' or 'Tovarishch'. 'Salud' instead of 'Buenos días.'

"The anarchist government – yes, I know, that sounds like a contradiction in terms - but the anarchist government had passed a new law that abolished tipping. There were no private motor cars. They had all been commandeered by the party. All the trams, all the taxis and all the trolley buses and the trains had been painted red and black. The revolutionary posters were everywhere flaming down from walls in clean reds and blacks. On the Ramblas, which is like the main drag in the centre of Barcelona, there were public loudspeakers and all day and all night revolutionary songs, mainly in Spanish, but some in Catalan and some in Russian, were played at very high volume. But I've always prided myself on noticing the trivial little things and it seemed to me that it was an entire city where the upper classes had practically ceased to exist or at least were in hiding or in disguise. There were a small number of women and some foreign journalists who seemed what you might call well-dressed, but everybody else wore blue overalls or uniforms of the militia or a rough white shirt and a jacket. You know, Tommy, I found this all strangely moving. Clothes are so superficial. People just dress to impress - a sort of 'power dressing'. I've seen you do that a few times, sunshine. You always look a complete plonker."

"Cheers, Uncle Jack."

It was getting palpably hotter the further south we drove. Once we had passed Paris the characteristic chattering cacophony of the cicadas could be heard through the open windows – a sure sign that we were leaving northern Europe behind. As we crossed the River Loire we finally lost Radio Four.

"So you found revolutionary Barcelona exciting?"

"Yes, not half! And different and inspiring. There were no beggars, no buskers, and no little kids begging for money. When we left later in '38 everything had changed. Things were returning to what other people would call normal. I thought it was a fucking tragedy. Smart restaurants and hotels were full of rich people scoffing expensive nosh. But for the working classes food prices had jumped horrendously with no rise in wages. Apart from the astronomic price of every commodity there were shortages of this and that, something basic - sometimes bread, sometimes oil. And those shortages, you know, all over the world, Tommy, they always hit the poor rather than the rich. You didn't see the anarchist colours any more, just the hammer and sickle and the Russian flag. The restaurants, cafés and hotels, mind you, seemed to have no trouble at all in getting whatever they wanted, but in the working areas I saw queues for milk, bread, flour, sugar - queues hundreds of yards long.

"In late '38 there were lots of beggars, lots of them obviously injured, militia men, many with limbs amputated and, outside the delicatessens at the top of the Ramblas, hordes of emaciated children were always lingering and waiting to swarm round anyone who emerged and they would beg and plead for scraps of food. The language had changed too. Strangers never addressed you as 'tu' or 'camerada' or 'tovarishch' by then. It was always 'Señor' and 'Usted'. The waiters, the shop assistants, the barmen were back in their smart clothes, cringing, bowing, scraping to customers. I went in to a - well, what you would have called a hosiery shop - in the Ramblas to buy some socks. The shopman bowed and rubbed his hands. He fawned all over us like we were special, and the law forbidding tipping had been revoked. The workers' patrols that had replaced the police force had been ordered to dissolve by the central committee of the Catalan Communist Party and the pre-war policemen were back on the streets."

"So why did it change Jack, what went wrong?"

"Well, I hate to say this, Tommy, but it was the Soviets, the Communist Party - they had to be top dogs. They said you can't have a revolution until the war is won, but I couldn't see why you couldn't have both. Having a revolution made people more keen to fight but, no, if you're being totally honest, it was the Communist Party."

"But you are wearing that badge - POUM. Jack, I know what it stands for: Partido de Obreros Marxistos Unificados: the anarchist organization. You were never in the Communist Party, were you?"

"Well spotted, sunshine. No, I was never one for joining. I'd seen how good it was under the anarchists, but there was Robbie. Robbie was a commissar. He had to follow the party line, and he was my best mate. What could I do? I couldn't shoot my best mate, could I? Added to which Robbie had taken quite a shine to a Russian woman we met there. A sniper called Halya. Her sniping partner, Katya, was a good friend of mine. Tommy, I was torn: naturally for me friendships are more important than party dogma. You gotta follow your heart, kid. And I never have done – that's my problem. All my life that's been my problem"

"You met Russians in Spain? Really?"

"Yeah, there were lots of advisors there, but Halya and Katya weren't advisors – they went to fight and had volunteered just like us. They were regulars in the Red Army and volunteered out of a sense of duty. They were about our age too, so it was sorta natural that we should get together. They were specialist snipers too and someone higher up had decided they should be attached to our battalion. They were bloody good soldiers."

"And that picture in your flat of the two women is Halya and Katya?"

"Yes. Halya didn't survive the Second World War. I don't know about Katya – I've not heard from her in years, but you can't just send a letter to the Soviet Union, can you? I know – I've tried: they don't get through."

The mystery of Uncle Jack's sobbing at the back of his butcher's shop. The broken dreams of a romantic leftist whose cause had been lost in Spain, and I now realized - the life-long separation from the woman he loved. Things were starting to make some sense. I could have cried.

I changed the cassette. The tapes we'd brought represented an interesting if eclectic collection. Mine were all the latest punk – I'd recorded my copy of *Never Mind the Bollocks* onto a tape especially for the journey. Uncle Jack had brought a lot of very early Delta blues stuff – Leadbelly, Robert Johnson, Blind Willie Johnson: the authentic voice of suffering transformed into art. And several Woody Guthrie tapes.

"What I don't understand, Jack, is why you haven't been back before? You saw France, you saw Spain, but to my knowledge in my lifetime you never left South London."

"Well, you don't know the half of it, Tommy, my son. I've done enough travelling for a lifetime. After the war, not the Spanish Civil War, the Second World War, I didn't want to go anywhere really. Every time I went abroad someone died, usually someone close to me, so I stayed at home. I couldn't come back to Spain while Franco was in power. It doesn't look very good does it - former International Brigade soldier at the passport and customs checks. I don't think they would have let me in."

"But what about Katya? Couldn't you have kept in touch with her if you'd really tried?"

"No, Katya... Katya wasn't the type, if you know what I mean, and neither was I really. Plus the Cold War and all that phoney American rhetoric changed everything. The Soviet Union was our ally for a few brief years and then it all went fucking pear-shaped. There's even a Woody Guthrie song which was a hit in 1943. It's called 'Miss Pavlichenko' and it celebrates a famous Russian sniper. Lyudmila Pavlichenko even toured the USA – fêted wherever she went. I've got the song on one of these tapes. You know, people forget, because they are taught to. Suddenly the Cold War had begun and everything Russian was suspect. But you know your mother spent her afternoons at school knitting balaclavas and socks to be sent to the Soviet Union."

"Which goes a long way to explaining eastern European fashion disasters. It still seems a shame, Jack, that you lost touch forever with all these people. And what about Robbie?"

"I can't talk about that now, Tommy. Robbie died in the Second World War on the Arctic Convoys. Let's just enjoy the view."

It was a good point: the view of the Rhône valley as we headed south was superb. Neat vineyards dominated the gently sloping sides of the valley – as they had probably done for centuries.

"When it was all over we headed for France and went across the border. They interred us briefly. Robbie and I got out because we were British. All the Spanish lads and the women who came across with us were put straight in concentration camps. Well, good as concentration camps. Hemmed in with posts and barbed wire, the defenders of democracy. That's how the French treated them. Mind you, it was worse for the soldiers in the Republican Army who didn't manage to cross the border: half a million were shot by Franco after the war.

"And the remnants were kept by the French in those bloody camps until the Germans invaded and were only released by the French when Germany declared war. These Spanish Republicans were drafted en masse into the French Army. And then, Tommy, when the French surrendered, the Spanish blokes kept their weapons and went on to form the backbone of the French resistance. There's not a lot of people know that."

"Uncle Jack, there's not a lot of people care, I'm afraid."

"And Tommy, did you know, I read somewhere that if you were Jewish in the Second World War, whether you survived or not depended on which country you lived in?"

"I didn't know that, Jack."

"Yeah, if you lived in the Baltic States and were Jewish you had the highest chance of being exterminated. Guess where was second?"

"Go on then! Tell me!"

"France. Ironic isn't it? Jews were hidden in Berlin and they were safer than in the Baltic States and France."

"All that reading, Jack, has done you a power of good."

"And it's done you good too, sunshine."

"Well, sometimes I doubt that, what good does it do, what fucking good does it do? W. H. Auden said, 'No poem saved a single Jew from the gas chambers.'"

"Bloody hell, Tommy, haven't I taught you anything but to be rigorous? Everyone quotes that. Everyone knows that quotation: "No poem saved a single Jew from the gas chambers." It's typical: be selective; never tell the whole truth. What they never ever do is they don't quote the sentences he wrote after that."

"You mean there's more to it?"

"Too right! What he said was: "No poem saved a single Jew from the gas chambers. It doesn't matter. Write the poems anyway!" See – puts it all in a completely different light, don't it? So, Tommy, you ain't wasting your life, not like I've wasted my life."

"Jack, you are the best butcher in the Old Kent Road. How is that a wasted life?"

"Tommy, it's a wasted life. This world is so wonderful, so beautiful, so precious, so rare, and I've sold meat and hacked up the corpses of animals. I've achieved nothing, and all the people I cared about have died or were out of reach, unattainable. What a life! Don't they say that we make a living by what we are given, but we make a life by what we give? I don't feel I've given enough. Yet."

"How did you end up with the butcher's shop anyway? I've never really understood that. No one ever mentioned it."

"No one ever mentioned it because everybody knew. You musta had your head buried in a book for the whole of your childhood. I inherited the shop from my mum's parents – your Gran's parents. She'd been an only child and your granddad had a steady job, so they wanted to make sure I had a chance in life – as opposed to working in that poxy factory in Brockley. They both were killed when their bomb shelter took a direct hit. I felt I didn't have a choice. I felt somehow I was destined to hack at corpses. It reminded me of the war. And don't ask me why. Not today."

Uncle Jack grinned blackly and ironically. I glanced at him as quickly as I could whilst driving very fast on a French motorway. His eyes were glittering with tears – like transparent pearls of intense rancorous regret. I decided to change the subject.

"Geez! Jack, you must have been really committed to go and fight in Spain."

"Too right, Tommy, I'm committed now, but look how we live: give people a television and a car, foreign holidays and they forget how oppressed they are. Give them a choice of colours for their car and they think they've got choice. Give them the choice of television stations and they think they've got choice. Anyway they've got no fucking choice. They're still ruled by the people who've been ruling us for centuries, still being sent off to fight in their lousy wars. We call it democracy, but it's not. What did the man say, "In a democracy the oppressed are allowed once every few years to decide which particular representatives of the oppressing class are to represent them and repress them in parliament?" We haven't got a real choice about who to vote for, just different versions of the status quo. So, yeah, you can grow your hair long now and you can watch films from all over the world, and you can listen to the latest pap off the radio and you can watch three different television stations and you can support Spurs or Millwall, or West Ham, so yeah, you've got a choice. But you got no choice, no real choice. You, Tommy, you've got a choice. You are a lucky bleeder."

"But why did no one in the family ever mention Spain and your part in it? As I remember it, they were always taking the piss outta you for having an easy war, but you volunteered to fight for your beliefs. I don't get it."

"Dunno really. I think they didn't understand why I went and when people don't understand something, they often ignore it or try to pretend that it didn't happen. I suspect they were slightly embarrassed. Remember too that our departure for Spain had been very hush-hush. And to be fair they were very quickly at war themselves: the whole country was mobilized and focused on the fight with Hitler. So it was easy to forget or dismiss my little jaunt in Spain. Plus I don't brag much; I like to keep some things dark. Plus I was taught to be cautious."

Uncle Jack chuckled softly. "And, if I'm perfectly honest, Tommy, I think some of them thought I was the black sheep of the family – doing what I did. Mind you, your Uncle Joe turned out to be the real black sheep of the family. At least, you knew about me and grew up near me. Poor old Joe was simply ostracized completely after he was released from the military slammer. Don't think he gave a toss though."

Jack gazed to his left: there were glittering glimpses of the sea in view. "The only people who made a big thing of it were your dad's grandparents. Hence the butcher's shop maybe. They were really proud of me. But, of course, you never met them and I'm betting you don't know their story."

"Only what my dad told me: I know they were from Scotland – which is why he gets sentimental about tartan and shortbread and bagpipe music and Glenmorangie."

"As always, there's a bit more to it than that. Why did they move to London?"

"To find work – that's what I was told."

"Well, Tommy, that's true — but only partly true. Your great-grandfather left Glasgow to find work in London, because he was black-listed. He was black-listed because he was an agitator, a union man. And guess where he had worked in Glasgow?"

"In the Clyde ship-yards, I'm guessing — because you took me there that time. Jeez, it's all starting to make sense — of a sort."

"Tommy, it gets better. What was your dad's grandmother's maiden name?"

"Is this a quiz? I have no idea."

"Her name was Rachel Lehmann. Not especially Scottish, is it?"

I said nothing. I had hoped to find out more about Jack, but this trip was one of self-discovery for me too. I was adding two and two and kept getting five.

"Your father's great-grandparents had arrived in Scotland from eastern Europe in the second half of the nineteenth century. They were fleeing the pogroms."

"Uncle Jack, so now you're telling me I'm a part-Russian, part-Scottish, Jewish boy from Deptford? What else don't I know?"

"Lots of stuff I expect. But, you're not Jewish: the Lehmanns were secular and, besides, your ancestry is from the male line cos of your dad. Mind you, I think you'd've been Jewish enough for the SS."

"Even so, that's a helluva story. Can I play some music real loud, please? I gotta take this in."

I've always been proud of my background: I think we all should be, and, while I can spell xenophobia, I've never understood it. But what kept nagging at my mind was why all this had been revealed only now: why had it been kept dark? I said as much:

"Why didn't I know this stuff? Why did mum and dad not mention it before?" I asked Uncle Jack.

Without waiting for Uncle Jack's answer, I scrabbled around for the Sex Pistols' tape, and we passed Perpignan to the strains of "God Save the Queen" and "Anarchy in the UK."

"Search me, Tommy. I don't know. Maybe it's because we're English. We don't talk a lot about feelings, do we?"

"But these aren't feelings, Uncle Jack. These are just facts about my family history."

"Your family history's not important. Where you're from means absolutely nothing, Tommy. It's where you're going that's important, sunshine."

"Yeah, I agree with that – where you're going – and I don't give a monkey's about where anyone's from, but, still, I don't understand why it was all kept quiet."

"Look, Tommy, I don't know, do I? I can't speak for your mum and dad, but I do know that after the war, life changed for ordinary people, and things got better, and I think they wanted to forget the past and move on. Can't blame them for that, can you?"

"I see that, Uncle Jack, but those family gatherings – all they did was talk about the past and the war. They wanted to remember that."

"Only cos it made them feel good about themselves. And they were right to be proud – before Hitler attacked the Soviet Union we stood alone. Mind you, some of your uncles' stories about the war…."

"Should be taken with a pinch of salt?" I hazarded.

"No! A whole fucking warehouse filled with Saxa! But, Tommy, everyone needs a good story to tell."

"Yeah, I suppose you're right, Uncle Jack. But what about your story? Did you see any fighting in Spain?"

"Are you pulling my chain, Tommy? Of course - they sent us to a village called Majacar. It was a dreadful little place. The poverty was breath-taking. I come from Deptford, but I'd seen nothing like this. There were no pavements, just a dirt track down the middle of the street. There was one water supply: a stone column with a lead pipe. It might have been there for centuries. The people in the village were very good to us, but they had nothing to give us - nothing to sell us even: no corn, no wine, no oil. There was no tension with them. I am proud to say it was wonderful all the time. One thing I have to admit we did far too much drinking. We didn't have our own canteen: we shared the village canteen, the bar. We used to stagger back to our billets in the dark, singing *The Internationale*. We must have been a nuisance to the villagers who were trying to get children to sleep, but they never, never once complained. I have been told that to this day people still proudly boast that the British stayed with them during the Civil War.

"It wasn't long before Robbie got appointed the Political Commissar for our company. By this time the Republic had realized that to have a successful army they had to have a chain of command. We had heard that some of the anarchist companies had no officers, which sounds good - but resulted in chaos during battles. The duty of the Political Commissars was to look after our welfare, our political instruction, to see that everybody wrote home and everyone was satisfied with the way things were going. A couple of people wanted to go home, so Robbie arranged that they should go home. It was the Political Commissar's job to organise meetings, to get people to ask questions, to get up to speak, to state opinions. Anyway at the end of June we were taken on a train to Madrid. We were about to take part in the Battle of Bruñete.

"At first things went well and we pushed the fascists back. That winter, Tommy, I'll never forget it. Read the history books - it's all there for those who want to know. After Bruñete, after the defeat, we moved south to defend the Ebro. Again it's in all the books - the books people don't read any more. It was at the Ebro that we first met Katya and Halya. To meet real Russians was astonishing for me: they were living in the system I believed in and a few months before we met them I'd been working in a dead-end job with nothing to look forward to at all.

"Honestly, Tommy, fighting in Spain changed my life. It's one of the proudest moments of my life. Fighting fascism in Spain."

"You deserve to be proud, but you lost. It may say 'No pasarán' – 'They shall not pass!' on your badge, but they got past and you ran."

"We never ran. We failed because the democracies let us down. We fought for our ideals and it was a good fight - a fight worth fighting, but we never had enough equipment. Everywhere we went we weren't fighting the Spanish; we were fighting Italians, Germans, Moors. A lot of the Russian stuff had to come by sea, via the Mediterranean, but the Mediterranean was controlled by Italian submarines which sank a lot of the ships. People forget, but I've never forgotten my time in Spain. And you know as far as I'm concerned it was never a defeat, just a strategic withdrawal. Don't fucking laugh at me, kid. Anyway - to cut a long story short - when Robbie and I went to join up in the British Army, Robbie was refused because he'd served as an officer in a foreign army. Truth was, they was a bit suspicious of committed lefties like us. So together we joined the Merchant Navy, but that's another story. It was the only way we could get in the frontline really, but that story is for another trip, sunshine."

"Which explains why Robbie is on a ship in that photo in your flat surrounded by huge lumps of ice…?"

"Give the monkey a peanut!" Uncle Jack laughed. "Tommy Wilkinson, you're a clever boy and you know a lotta big words and you're gonna end up with lots of letters after your name, but you ain't half slow sometimes."

I took my eyes off the road to grin at Uncle Jack. "So now you'll be telling me that all those stamps were not, as you maintained, from friends in the Merchant, but from International Brigaders scattered across the globe."

"You know, Tommy, sometimes a really clever monkey deserves a crate of bananas."

"Great! I like bananas!"

"Sadly in the capitalist world you don't always get what you deserve, but I'll buy you a beer – lots of beers – in Barcelona."

Chapter Eleven: Katya II

Of course, for me everything changed after Halya was captured - which happened just two days before the encirclement was completed. From an individual point of view, I regarded it as my personal duty to kill as many fascists as possible in revenge for whatever awful things I imagined they must be doing to Halya. We had all heard the sort of torture meted out to captured Commissars, and Halya, as a sniper and as a Jewish sniper and as a Jewish sniper who was the company commissar as well – I just forced myself not to think of it. I could only concentrate on revenge – and not solely for Halya, but for all our murdered soldiers and civilians.

In a military sense, the Germans were now completely on the defensive and it was easier to organise our attacks. I was in charge of a sniper group consisting of seven snipers. We began our work in the area surrounding the Red October housing estate. The Germans were about twenty five or thirty metres away at that time and were laying down a persistent, never-ending barrage of extremely accurate fire: they knew their situation was desperate and, although there were rumours that a German force would break our lines and relieve them, I never believed it: once the encirclement was complete, I sensed it was just a matter of time. There were also crazy rumours that Paulus, the German commander, would try to rally his forces and break out, but on the ground they seemed demoralized, beaten, fighting to live – no longer to conquer and subdue. The barrage wouldn't let us lift our heads. At night we crept closer to the enemy and found spots for ourselves in attics, near the windows in foxholes, trying to find as many different angles and places from which to fire at them. We called this tactic 'hugging the enemy' – it was designed to nullify the effects of their artillery: we were so close that if they tried to hit us they would most likely hit their own lines as well. From there we started to take out the German snipers. We'd usually put out a decoy target, a shop dummy topped with a discarded Soviet helmet, and, when the Germans shot at it, we'd use the direction of the bullet hole to pin point the shooter's hiding place.

In our first five days we killed four lone snipers and three machine gun teams. We were always in threes except for me. I was the leader of the group. The girls worked in teams of three: one to spot, one to shoot; one to guard the rear and organize a safe exit.

Sometimes we had to seek out the enemy by more complicated means. One time we put a sniper in the centre of town, knowing that his shots would attract the attention of the enemy to a dressed dummy which we placed very close to our girl's foxhole. To the sides were two observers, also snipers, whose job was to spot the German when he shot. Once we knew where the German sniper was located, we closed in on him secretly and took him out: we didn't try to shoot him, but got into the building and used our bayonets.

Over the course of six weeks before the New Year we killed eighteen German snipers, thirteen machine gunners, six machine gun teams and seven anti-tank teams. I used to give each sniper in my group a kill sector of her own, an area of anything from fifty to six hundred metres. Each one of us had two or three reserve firing positions, so that if we thought we'd been spotted at one location, we could move unnoticed to another. As a rule, you would always be spotted by the time you killed five or six fascists from the same position. The Germans would then usually try to flush you out with mortar or artillery fire, so it was important to keep on the move. It was tense, draining work, but there was, I'll admit, a lot of excitement too.

In the second half of January 1943 the whole nature of the fighting changed. I remember the morning of February 2nd, the day of the surrender, with absolute, complete clarity. The frost had been very heavy. It was thirty-five or forty degrees below zero. The remains of our battalion gathered together to be formed into two units, one of which was put under my temporary command. There were very few officers left. The commander of our platoon had already been wounded.

The lieutenant in charge of our company ordered us to blockade a building about one hundred and fifty metres from our position and to clear it of fascists. The building was in ruins, and the windows were empty like gouged-out eye sockets. We advanced .We went in single file, one behind the other. We began to notice packages on the snow - supplies dropped on the German positions during the night. We picked one up - it was a frozen loaf of bread. We could see the heads of some Germans bobbing in and out of view at the dead windows. They did not bother to shoot. We were walking upright in broad daylight, so I suppose we were not expecting them to shoot. They knew or sensed that something was ending.

The situation was hopeless, after all. We approached a little opening on the front of the building where once there must have been a front door. The shadow of the soldier passed across it. I shouted in German, "You may as well surrender. We will treat you well."

After a few shouts there appeared the dirty, stubbly face of a crawling soldier. We then called to him to come out to us. After a little hesitation he stood up. I told the lads not to point their guns at him. I held out the bit of bread that we'd picked up. He grew bolder; he came nearer, grabbed the bread and straight away began to gnaw at it. Then a second soldier came.

We asked them, "Are there many of you down there?"

"Lots and lots," came the answer - which surprised us. We gave them all the bread that we had picked up and told them to go back down into the basement and come out with all the others. Then we waited. After five minutes the same man came back with three or four others.

We said, "Is this all of you?"

They replied that there were others, but they were afraid to come out. Especially the officers. So we sent this party back too and said that everybody had to come out.

A long time passed. We were bored and took a cigarette break. We prepared for the worst. We could hear dull shots coming from the basement. Something bad was going on down there. Then we heard noises getting nearer and nearer, talking. First out was our new acquaintance and many more behind him. We saw they were carrying a wounded officer. He was tied up and lying on a stretcher.

We asked, "Why has he been tied up?"

It turned out that he'd woken up to see the soldiers preparing to surrender and had drawn his pistol to threaten them. Someone had shot him in the leg and then they all tied him up. They all had their hands up and were unarmed.

"Where are your weapons?"

"Down there," they said.

We told them all to go back, apart from the officers, and to come back with their weapons. They very quickly did as they were told and piled up their guns in the place we told them to. We were astonished at how many people came out of that basement. A whole battalion at least.

Around that time our own officers turned up and began to organise the process of officially taking them prisoner.

Our commander came over to us and said, "Well done, comrades. Just one more job for you today. Go and clean up that building across the square and then you can relax."

It was about two in the afternoon by now. It was extremely cold - so bitterly cold that my rifle would barely fire because the grease had frozen. I had to swap it for a different one. We went forward to carry out the order. We went about it the same way as usual, single file, one behind the other, me in front.

Suddenly, and it was the most terrifying moment of my war, I realized I was in a minefield. Here and there we could see countless tiny wooden crosses poking above the ground. This meant they were anti-infantry mines. If you touched a wire and set one off, it jumped in the air and exploded. We called them frogs. They could take out everything in a four or five metre radius. We stopped in our tracks and discussed what would be for the best - to go on or to turn back.

The lads all said, "We've seen this before. Let's go on. Going back is just as dangerous."

No Germans were shooting at us and there were none to be seen. I began to move forward slowly and carefully. The lads followed in my steps. I should add that the square was full of ruts and holes. There were abandoned rifles lying around on the ground, helmets, ours and German ones, all kinds of kit, bits of brick, pieces of broken equipment, excrement. It was hard to make progress and hard to make out the tell-tale signs of the mines.

I had not gone six or seven steps when I stumbled and fell forwards. Before I could straighten up, I heard the deafening sound of a mine exploding behind me. In that instant there was a hard blow in my right shoulder and something wet on my back. I knew it was blood, but strangely I felt no pain. I glanced behind me in time to see the lads falling down: some of them front ways, others on to their backs. It was sickening. The mine must have gone off at their feet. I managed to see not only my lads as they went down, but also the sharp and jagged objects on the ground around me. I managed not so much to fall as to slowly lower myself on to the snow.

I remember nothing more. I lost consciousness. When I woke up it was night, and I woke with the sensation that someone was pulling me about, rifling through my documents, taking away my things.

Then I heard a voice, "Hey! This one's alive. She's moving."

A second person came close. I was slowly coming round and with a huge effort I opened my eyes. I could see the clear night sky and the twinkling stars. I felt a dreadful pain in my neck and my right shoulder. The medic leaning over me in the darkness was trying to find out whereabouts I was wounded.

He was saying, "Where is she hurt? Her arms and legs are in one piece - her head too. I see no blood."

Seeing that I had opened my eyes he asked me, "Where were you hit?"

I tried to answer, but I could not open my mouth. I was completely numb. He could feel my trying to speak and waited.

"Where are you hit?"

At long last I forced out some kind of sound. The medics were prodding me all over, my face, my nose, the top of my head. I managed to pronounce the word "neck." One of them shoved his hand down my collar and brought it back out covered in blood.

"There it is."

The medic got a pair of scissors and cut all the way up the sleeve of my quilted jacket. He got as far as the place where I was wounded. Then he got a field dressing on the wound and bandaged it. After that he bound up the sleeve of my jacket with some wire and put me on a sled. I asked him to help my unit.

"They are just here," I said.

But one of the medics showed me a wedge of Red Army pay books and said, "There is no one here who needs my help. You are the only one we found alive."

As for me I was dragged across the bumping, shell-pocked square. It was sheer torture. Although the field hospital where they were taking me was not far away, they had to take me over all kinds of obstacles and rough ground to get there. At one point they tugged at the rope as we went over a shell hole and the sledge shot out from underneath me. I ended up in a hole full of snow. They swore out loud, hauled me out and told me to hold on tight to the edge of the sled. Then the same thing happened again. My hands were freezing. I couldn't hold on to anything. Finally, they dragged me to a large canvas tent and put me down on some straw at the entrance to the operating room.

Inside the tent there was a surgeon and his team of helpers. I waited there until deep into the night and all the time there were operations going on. A helper would come out from time to time and pick out the less badly wounded person who would then become the next to go in. As the rest of us waited for our turn, we could hear the screams and groans of the wounded being operated on without any anaesthetic. It made me shudder.

I was one of the last. They led me in and made me sit down against the wall on the floor. One of the helpers held me very tightly. The doctor opened up the entry wound with a kind of pair of scissors, rooted around inside me and found a tiny piece of shrapnel which he pulled out and showed to me.

"That's what got you," he said and tossed it into a big bowl.

After a long sleep they let me go and I was able to walk through the city standing upright for the first time in months.

Every street, every house, every room in every house of Stalingrad had been a battle-ground. We had begun by defending every street. And then we had defended every house and then we had fought for a wall of each house. Stalingrad was a mincing machine, a charnel house of war.

As I walked over the freezing, tortured earth, I felt I was treading on human flesh and bones. And sometimes I was. I walked up the ravine which had come to be known as the Gully of Death. There had been houses on both sides of the ravine - now there was hardly anything left. In the main building of the Red October tractor plant trenches ran through the factory yards and through the workshops themselves: at the bottom of the every trench there still lay frozen Germans and frozen Russians – now covered in a thin layer of fresh snow - and frozen fragments of human shapes. There were tin helmets - German and Russian - lying among the brick debris and the helmets were half-filled with snow. There was barbed wire here, half-uncovered mines, shell cases, rubble, fragments of walls, human limbs, human hands, and tortuous tangles of rusty steel girders.

How anyone could have survived here is hard to imagine, but we had done. We did it. We were there and we won. Hardly a house was standing in the six miles between the Square of the Heroes of the Revolution in the city centre and the Red October works in the north. Around the central square tall buildings showed their bones to the air - the skeletons of buildings that housed the skeletons of men. The trees, the lovely squares, the roofs which the birds left last August were no longer there. Millions of shell-pocked bricks, monstrous mountains of twisted metal were all that remained of the famous tractor works, the factories of Red October and the Red Barricade. Deep thousand-pound bomb craters filled with ice pitted the trackless streets. And here and there a frozen corpse stared up pale through the ice.

And all over the city hung the sick smell of rubble and blood and death and decay.

Chapter Twelve: Tommy VI

The day he died was miserable. It wasn't raining and it wasn't that cold, but it was still miserable: it was one of those horrible spring days that you often get in London when the clouds are low and it's muggy. One of those April days where you put on more layers than you need and end up sweating; too few layers and you die of pneumonia or leprosy or something.

I didn't even know him. It was just a name that was in the newspapers the following day, so I'm not sure exactly where he died, but I know he definitely died that day. Somewhere near where we were. And the report at the time said it was, of course and inevitably, an accident and then what? Thirty-two years? Thirty-two years later the police admit they killed him! They killed him. Kept that pretty dark, didn't they? The blows to the head were not from the three foot high front garden wall he was said to have hit. The blows were from police truncheons. Thirty-two years and we call ourselves a democracy - we have an open society. WTF. Although then it must have been the World Trade Federation.

What was I doing there? What was Jack doing there? Uncle Jack, though pushing sixty at the time, had wanted to come as soon as he knew that me and Sue were going. He said he hoped it would remind him of the Cable Street riots. He was always up for a fight, Uncle Jack, when there were fascists marching, but why was I there? Not a very romantic day for Sue. Although in those days she seemed to care.

Hey, come with me to a street demonstration. We will fight some fascists. It will be fun. I'll let you wear my lapel badge.

Always the smooth talker.

But why was I there? And where, where on earth do we come from? I don't mean the gooseberry bush and the stork and that bizarre inaccurate, rather disgusting exchange of bodily fluids that Debbie Chapman had envisaged for me what, some forty five years ago, as I write this. I mean how do we become who we are. I know. I finally worked it out - how I became who I am.

Rather dead than red? No chance, mate, I'd rather be red than any other colour. It's my favourite colour. I want to live in Krav Maga House on Krasnaya Street in Jerusalem in England's green and pleasant land. With my burning golden bow to hand. And many arrows of desire. Yes, sirreee. So I've always been searching for another country where the Jerusalem project stands a greater chance of complete fruition.

I could blame *Trumpton*. I was exposed to *Trumpton* at a formative age, ready for convincing stories, and I spent too much of my life believing that I was living in *Trumpton*, my one desire to be the greengrocer singing to his customers:

Come buy my vegetables, fruit ripe and beautiful.

Fine fresh and fancy, come buy them from me.

Come buy, come buy, come buy them from me.

Cabbages, carrots and tender spring greens,

Broccoli, brussel-tops, fresh runner beans,

Peaches and plums, pears by the pound,

Parsnips and beetroot, straight from the ground.

Apples and oranges, strawberries too.

Mushrooms gathered in this morning's dew.

Radishes, lettuces, onions, shallots,

Tomatoes, potatoes and lots and lots - of spinach.

Come buy my vegetables, fruit ripe and beautiful.

Fine, fresh and fancy, come buy them from me.

Come buy, come buy, come buy them from me.

That was clearly my vocation: to be a greengrocer in *Trumpton*, selling vegetables on behalf of the local collective farm and attending occasional meetings of the South East London Revolutionary Front. Sadly, *Trumpton* doesn't exist and Thatcher changed the political landscape. AND I don't know a mange-tout from an artichoke, a pomegranate from a medlar fruit, a persimmon peach from a permanganate pear. And, as we are all children of our upbringing and all my daughters asseverate that my laugh has a Sid Jamesian quality, one can't help seeing the invitation to "buy my vegetables" as an innuendo worthy of the worst *Carry On* film. Or the best. Fine, fresh and fancy – in your imagination, mate. *Carry On Commissar. Carry On Up Your Volga.* Who's a Volga boy, then? Matron!

Tommy, bootee bandh! Shookria!

OK. Sorry, Talha.

And what I had really wanted to be from a very early age was a postman. Not a footballer. Not a pop star. Certainly not an astronaut. A postman. Such an important part of the community – delivering joy (birthday cards, Christmas cards, billets doux, job offers, Valentine's Day cards, invitations to all sorts of things, presents) and tragedy (missing in action, redundancy notices, Dear John letters, notifications of death) in equal measure. The guardian of the community's emotional life.

Or a meteorologist – except I stopped doing Physics at thirteen which ruled me out. Quite fancied being a lighthouse-keeper at one stage of my teens – all that solitary phallic grandeur, the isolation perhaps ingrained in me from my childhood experiences in hospital – with GPS I'd be redundant now – which I still am, but with a sense of resentment. Oooops! No – I have one of those too: a sense of resentment, that is. Very well-developed, thank you. Perfectly balanced – a chip on each shoulder. And I know now that in reality I am still living in a neo-liberal Trumpton, prey to globalization, living a tragic *Carry On* film – *Carry On Capitalism* and I'm the artist from Episode Five of *Trumpton* who sings:

I wander through the countryside

With easel, brushes, paints and stool

And settle in a leafy glade

By willow tree and shady pool.

I draw a picture first of all

With simple lines of green or blue

And then I fill the drawing in

With painted shapes of every hue.

And when at last my picture's done

I pack it carefully away

And wander on across the fields

To return another day.

Actually I blame my grandparents, my grandfathers and Uncle Jack's continued influence, especially the more I found out about his past.

My grandfathers were real Union men, both shop-stewards, one in the Dockers' Union, the other in the Transport and General Workers' Union. They used to refer to our little bit of south London as the Socialist Republic of South London.

Huh! In their dreams. But what good dreams to have! How inspiring! How idealistic! I think they are grave-turning now and they would have been grave-turning in 1979. I'll give you an example.

When I told my maternal grandfather which university my school had suggested I apply to he said, "Tommy, Tommy, that's wonderful. You know the economics faculty there is the most left wing this side of Leningrad?"

I hadn't the heart to remind him that I wasn't reading Economics. And the saddest thing - and I want to get this down so everyone knows - the saddest thing is the year I started at University he gave me £100. Now it's not a lot now, is it? And it wasn't really a big sum then, but he died in the autumn of my second year. And in his will he left only £120. What a man! Left school at ten and had to work. An autodidact. Never crossed a picket line.

So it was from my grandparents that I got this desire to live on Krasnaya Street, Jerusalem in Krav Maga House. I could write it in the front of all my books:

Tommy Wilkinson

Krav Maga House

Krasnaya Street

Jerusalem

England,

FU2 8ME.

Writing your name in books – always a good habit – proves its worth when the divorce kicks off.

But it's got my name in it!

Things were different then. You remember the school election – well, that's how things were.

So it was natural that I should find myself in Southall on that grey April day when the National Front decided to march through the Asian community. My grandfathers and my father and my Uncle Bill had fought alongside Sikh and Hindu units in the 8th Army. They wouldn't hear a word said against them. Against anyone except the Tories. And the Liberals funnily enough. They had a sort of visceral hatred for the Liberals and they never told me why. With the Tories it was easy – they were class enemies: they even wore a uniform of sorts. But the Liberals were chameleons, the serpent in the left's Garden of Eden. That's another thing I've been thinking about my whole life. What happened to the Liberal vote after the First World War? Why didn't it stand up? I know now. I think we all do. You force-feed Suffragettes in prison and you send the working class to fight in the First World War, to the slaughter house of industrialized, capitalized carnage and people soon forget you introduced National Insurance. And as for Uncle Jack, he felt compelled to take to the streets whenever fascists marched. He'd been involved two years earlier, in August '77, when the National Front had marched from New Cross to the centre of Lewisham and retained strong and bitter memories of the futile attempts to prevent the march:

"All the interested anti-fascist groups met in the Dog and Flagon in Deptford about a week before the march, but they couldn't agree on tactics. My lot were there along with a variety of the different communist parties, and the independent socialist parties, but there were also community groups – one representing Lewisham itself – the local Labour and Liberal councils, church leaders, community leaders - the whole shebang; and another church-led organization – with the same types of people in it, but purporting to represent the whole of London. Then, at the start of the meeting, a member of the Central Committee of the Socialist Worker's Party turns up and agrees to co-operate with everything the meeting decides provided that the SWP stewards are allowed to control the event. Well, that got up everyone's noses because, for starters, the SWP are fucking nutters, and, secondly, numerically they were the smallest group there and that even includes my lot.

"I was just pissed off: it seemed simple enough to me – all we had to do was get all the people connected with those organizations to sit down peacefully in the New Cross Road and – hey presto! – no fucking march! But they didn't listen to me, so the march went ahead and reached Lewisham High Street, and the four different groups – the SWP, the Lewisham group, the All London group, and the rag-tag rump of assorted lefties – we all did different things."

Uncle Jack sighed. Then he smiled; he grinned broadly.

"Still it went well at the end. The filth completely lost control of Lewisham High Street and we broke the police lines at the back of the march, so we bloodied a few noses and burnt their flags. Tommy, you were there weren't you?"

"Yes, I was Uncle Jack, and I remember getting in amongst them at the end." I smiled. "Don't tell my dad, Uncle Jack, but I borrowed his short detective's truncheon and kept it hidden down my trousers until I needed it."

"Good choice of weapon, sunshine! In that mayhem you might get mistaken for a rozzer in plain clothes."

"Don't ever tell my dad – he'll go fucking mental."

"Do I look like a snitch?"

"What I still don't understand, Uncle Jack, is who your lot are?"

"You will one day, Tommy. You will."

More mystery.

"Looking back," I mused, "I think I was safe: there were more of us than there were of them."

"Yes – we are many; they are few! That's why the past is so important, Tommy. The further backward you look, the farther forward you can see. That's why you have to fight fascists on the streets, our streets, so the fuckers never get elected."

Anyway fast forward nearly two years later to the day he died: grey, muggy, angry voices, banners, everywhere, the National Front militaristic, surrounded by coppers for protection, Union Jacks with 'NF' painted on in white; us lot, shabby, hippy, a diverse bunch, divided, the left always has been, but in a kind of good way. Some blokes in balaclavas, so you could only see their eyes – scary. And lots of local Asians who'd brought food – samosas, stuffed naan bread, chapattis, onion bhajis. It was great – the first time I'd been fed while fighting fascism.

And always tricky, according to Jack, trying to assess the shorthaired men in black leather - were they on our side or were they from the Branch, spotting faces? We didn't think then there might be police informers amongst us. We didn't care too much about the bobbies on horseback taking photos of us. I was twenty-two and I didn't care. I cared about doing what I thought and Uncle Jack assured me was the right thing.

My parents were different about politics. Funny - I had this insatiable curiosity as I was growing up and would always badger them: which way did you vote, which way did you vote? And they always said that was a secret between them and the ballot box. And as a father I can see now that that was a very worthy attempt not to influence me. And now that I know the way they did vote, I can see why they didn't tell me. Just so embarrassing.

Well, I've not been like that with my kids. A propagandist for the left. I figure you got to balance out all the lies in the media, all the half-truths and the official police reports that say he died because he collided with a three foot garden wall. Just keep it dark, toe the official line; tell the masses what it's best for them to hear; don't worry about the truth. Keep it dark.

We had a fine, if somewhat frightening, time. Jack's eyes glistened with tears, nostalgia probably. Ever since employing a manager at the shop, he had become more buoyant, more relaxed. He posed for the umpteenth time for a Polaroid on the Tube: Jack standing next to that injunction "Keep left." It had become a ritual of any day out with him in London. He seemed to be remembering his younger, more radical self and if he was happy I'm sure it wasn't because the National Front were marching through West London but because he knew who he was and he could see the direct line between the Cable Street riots and that day when that student died.

We got there early on the District Line. Long walk. Had sausage and chips from a fish and chip shop. I think I had a gherkin as well - that's a regional thing, isn't it, gherkins? I remember being in the north a few years later and making everyone fall about with laughter when I asked if they had got any wallies because in London a wally was a gherkin. But in the north - well it was the northern word that came to dominate the language and now I know, though I didn't then, why they were convulsed with laughter when I asked him if they sold wallies. All I wanted was a gherkin. You see, northern chip shops and boulangèries. There's a pattern here: I'm an idiot, sunshine – it's a wonder I can even feed myself.

Words. Words. Words. Still causing problems. Is it true that kangaroo means 'I don't know' in the Aboriginal language spoken by the first

Aborigine who was asked by an early English colonist: "What is that?" when he saw a kangaroo for the first time. I hope it is true. If that is true, then I hope too that when the first European asked, "What do you call that river?" and pointed at the river, he was told – "Mississippi" – which might mean, "Fuck off and go home, white man." I hope so.

Can't remember much about the day really: lots of red banners on our side, Union representation, but most of us a straggly, united, cheerful and angry scraggle of long-haired lefties, though I never had long hair, even then. Plus the friendly locals who actually outnumbered us. The National Front marched like a military column, surrounded by a three-thick protective cordon of policemen.

Sue, I think, felt diffident, but then I could never really tell how she was feeling; Jack felt angry and joyful; I was thinking about my work as always - you just can't get away from it. A bit of chanting, a few bricks lobbed towards the National Front, which ended up hitting policemen. And then the truncheons and the horses.

We kept one position: the National Front were marching past. Less than half of us were white, because of the heavy presence of the local Asian community. The National Front, unsurprisingly, exclusively white, of course. The black people I knew at that time in my life were so used to getting into trouble with the police that I think they had decided it would be pointless turning up. They would be arrested, just on sight. We were there because we felt that we <u>had</u> to do something, though I don't think any of us had reckoned on dying from blows to the head.

I'm not sure how many mounted officers were there, but it seems to me that at a certain moment, the police tactics changed: they stopped merely protecting the National Front, and started actively trying to disperse those of us protesting against the Front-cunts. Horses are quite intimidating when they are coming towards you down the street, as I was to discover time and again over the years. I wouldn't have wanted to be an infantryman up to about 1900. All that horseflesh bearing down on you – sabres, lances, bits of wood with sharp stuff on the ends - though I'm exaggerating: that day it was just police truncheons. Still I saw several completely defenceless Asian mothers with their children running as fast as they could down side streets pursued by mounted rozzers, their long truncheons flailing indiscriminately.

So how do they do it? Keep it dark, I mean? What about the people near him? The ones who saw the police assault him: where did they go? where did they live after 1979? The ones who knew the truth, the truth that wasn't revealed for thirty-two years? Where did they go? How did they live? Or were they just angry, like Jack, their whole lives?

So where we come from is important. That day we'd only come from Hammersmith because we were living, Sue and me, in a flat in West London, but I never got used to it. West London is so flat, you see, and though there are poor parts there are some very rich parts too. So our road, the road we lived in, was poor and multi-cultural and fun, but you walk 400 yards and you're in Kensington. I miss South London; I miss its hills; I miss the sense of unity that I perceived and that probably never existed. Yeah, my grandfathers, the Socialist Republic of South London.

Huh. When we were at school it was a donnée, a given truth, a tenet of life that you had three choices.

Number 1 - You got out and moved to the suburbs.

Number 2 - You became a criminal.

Number 3 - You joined the Police.

I got out. But I wanna go back. I've been stealing words all my life, you see. Word crimes. Dad crimes. It's where I belong.

When it was all over, the last insult thrown, the last brick hurled, the last banner rolled up, we went to a curry house. Sue looked beautiful that night. We talked about the coming election. We knew the outcome. The Tories didn't stand a chance, not with the way things were. Lower than vermin. Lower than fucking vermin. We had no doubts.

Chapter Thirteen: Nikita

When the order finally came to move out of Wenceslas Square, Nikita breathed a sigh of relief. It must be over, or close to being over, he thought to himself, but leaving Wenceslas Square was not as easy as his superiors must have assumed it would be. Each tank had half a dozen infantry who rode on the tank and were an integral part of the team. He spoke to Sergeant Ivanov and explained the situation. He gave Ivanov thirty minutes to get his men together. A couple were within sight, drinking coffee outside a Czech café. A third was, it was believed, in a local apartment. He'd become very friendly with a young Czech girl, but now it was time to part. The fourth and fifth – well, they could be anywhere. Well, anywhere in Prague.

Nikita prided himself on being a good soldier, a good, loyal tank commander, but there had been something in the atmosphere of this city, particularly in the last week of a long and sometimes intimidating month when his military discipline had become a little lax. Despite his loyalty, his pride in being a tank commander in the Red Army, despite his almost unquestioning obedience, he had had some strange nagging qualms about the last month or so, but he consoled himself with the thought of his family. He simply wanted to get back home as quickly as possible to his wife and three children in the barracks just south of Warsaw where they had been living for the last eighteen months.

He thought of his three children - Ilya, Yuri, and Olga - and he felt how blessed he was to have three such wonderful children. When he got home to the barracks he knew that they would want to hear everything about his trip and he would entertain them with bizarre stories of the wizards and witches he had met on his travels. And his recurring, never-ending story of Misha who was always on an errand to the shops for his mother with huge lists of bizarre things to buy: six pelicans, five camels, four monkeys, three talking parrots, two tanks and a glass of kvass.

Of Czechoslovakia, of Prague, of his doubts, he would breathe not a word.

And yet he liked what he had seen of Czechoslovakia, this strange country where every village was called Dubcek. Where the graffiti everywhere read 'Rusové jděte domů' or 'Russki ot doma." Where the young people wore their hair long (as in the West, he imagined). Where groups of students and workers had not thrown stones or petrol bombs at him and his infantry team, but had come up, made them tea or brought them coffee and talked to them.

'Russki ot doma'? Nikita sighed. 'Russians to the house'? Was the standard of Russian teaching so bad in Prague that they could not get it right? Could they not write their slogans in grammatically correct Russian? The pedant in Nikita, whose wife taught Russian Language and Literature, half-thought jokingly to himself that this mangling of Russian might well be enough justification to let the tanks roll. Get it right!

'Russki idi damoi!'

Nikita wanted to get damoi as soon as possible. He was pleased: he had avoided conflict, against the odds and against all expectation, and he was heading for home in safety.

The young people had asked him, "Why are you doing this, comrade?" They had tried to reassure him: "We are good communists. You do not need to attack us with tanks. We are peaceful."

Nikita's stony reticence, as a Russian, as a man, as a tank commander in the Red Army, had no weapon against the flowers that the students had put down the barrel of the tank's gun. No weapons for the disarming way that middle-aged women, young women, old babushka, familiarly touched him on his lower arm while pressing tea, hot sweet tea into his hands. And every morning the pastries - he'd probably gained a few kilos during his time in Prague.

But he had other more basic needs. He needed a good bath and he needed his family. He tried to work it out in his head. It had taken him nineteen hours to get from the barracks to Prague. So it would take them at least that to get back. So this time tomorrow, Nikita thought, I might be back with my family. It might even be quicker. They had been hampered as soon as they crossed the Czechoslovak border through the lack of maps and every village being signposted Dubcek. When they got into Prague all the road signs, and all the street signs had been removed, so it was like trying to find your way in a strange, beguiling maze. The Czechs didn't use Cyrillic either so he felt doubly alienated, triply alienated, far from his family, far from Russia, far from the people who loved him, in this bewildering city with no map and where people misdirected you and hated your presence, while at the same time giving you flowers and pastries and hot sweet tea.

The square had been a good place to get a sense of what was going on every day. For a month the students had gathered, had fraternized with the Russian troops, had had large raucous but peaceful meetings around the statue of the king in whose shadow young demagogues took it in turns to make speeches, read poems, and young men and young women with long hair and guitars, had serenaded the crowd. Nikita felt a sense of brotherhood, and all the young Czechs he had spoken to had asserted that they were good communists. Many of them were party members.

He wasn't quite sure why he was there. It had all been kept rather dark. After the first day it had been impossible to move the tank anywhere. If he had made any attempt to move the tank, the young people, gathered in their thousands around the statue of King Wenceslas, simply went and sat in the road and no orders came to move them, to shoot them, to roll the tanks over them, or to do anything, and Nikita began to dread any order like that. He was confused and wanted badly to get home. To hold and hug and cuddle his wife and to laugh and play with his children. To tell them stories of the wizards he had met. And of Misha.

At last the errant infantry men were rounded up - the last one stumbling, sprinting, and doing his flies up with a sheepish grin. He had certainly fraternized well with the Czechs. Nikita's tank was the lead tank and he was the commander of the whole tank group. Looking behind and checking on the radio, he waited another five minutes to ensure that every one was ready and that was it. He gave the order to go and slowly in the dark September after-midnight-dark, the Russian tanks rolled noisily, clumsily out of Prague, the city that they had liberated less than twenty-five years before and the city that was now so strange to them and yet friendly.

No one was around. The streets were deserted. Evidence of the uprising was visible: some buildings were pock-marked with bullets.

Scorched pavements and trees bore evidence, as they got further away from the square, of petrol bombs, scuffles, wanton destruction. There was more litter than when they'd rolled in, but it seemed safe and Nikita settled down, vigilant, but, at times like this, when travelling, he always thought of his mother.

And in his head he composed a letter that his mother would never read, that he would never write and that would never be delivered. It was his custom to do so. He had had a happy childhood brought up by his mother's parents. He was proud of his mother's achievements in the war. She had posthumously been awarded a medal for courage and a medal for the defence of Stalingrad and then a third, the Order of the Red Banner which was rarely awarded – and must have been awarded posthumously. But Nikita had no memories of his mother, just a single letter written in the summer of 1943 and delivered, eventually, by hand, by January 1944, according to his grandparents, and, every now and then, maybe once a month, even now at the age of twenty-nine, he still composed his reply in his head.

Dearest Mother,

I wish that I had met you, I wish that you had survived the Great Patriotic War and that you could have come and joined us at Ulyanovsk and seen me as a successful schoolboy. But I won't harp on what I missed because I know you did your duty and I know that you were brave. My aunt, Katya, although not my real aunt, has told me what a good sniper you were, what a charismatic woman, what a disciplined party member you were and the fact that you fought and died against the evil of fascism has always inspired me. I think you would be proud of me now. Of course, I'm not a sniper and so you may be disappointed, but I am a tank commander.

Dearest Mother, because I do not know where or how you died after being captured, my imagination has seen for you a thousand different deaths – all of them different, distressing and infinite in their power to make me cry. Were you shot for some act of disobedience? Did you die from an injection of phenol in the chest? Did you fling yourself at the electric fence of the death camp you were sent to? Or were you slaughtered like all the others in the gas chamber? I can never rest, for I can never know and so, each night, my dearest mother, you die a different brutal and agonizing death.

Oh mother, I wish I'd known my father too. You don't know, but I have made enquiries and my father is buried here in Russia. In Murmansk. It's hard to get the details: things are still kept dark from ordinary people, but he must have been a British sailor when he died or somehow attached to the British Navy who were bringing us supplies to Murmansk. One day, mother, when I can, when I have some leave, I will visit his grave. It will be a pilgrimage to the grave of the father I never knew and I will go in late spring or early summer and put forget-me-nots on his grave. I have three children now: Ilya, Yuri and Olga. You would be so proud of them. Part of me wants them all to follow me and you into the Army, but as a father I simply want them to be happy, to be good communists, and to go as far as their talents will take them, to live a long and loving life, to have a good story to tell.

Oh dearest mother, I am writing you this letter from Prague. I don't understand history. Katya was here to liberate Prague. And now twenty-three years later we are back to suppress it, to stop it liberating itself and I do not understand. The people here are good communists, but with laughter, with song, with flowers, as it should be. We are leaving the city, but the last month has been rife with rumours. What would the West do? The thought of the irony of a British and American intervention, and the irony of a British jet bearing down on my tank column, me with a British father that no one knows about, has made me chuckle a little to myself.

Mother, there are so many things to say to you. I've -

But at that point he broke off in the wide boulevard leading north out of Prague. Nikita's driver, more attentive than he, had slowly rumbled the tank to a halt. In the street lights Nikita could make out a frail, fragile figure, staring at the tank. A six year old boy, seven, eight, a small boy with a broken satchel clutched under his arm, blonde hair, wide cheek bones, huge eyes. He stood implacable in front of the tank. One small boy against a Red Army tank column. One small boy with a brown leather satchel. With his socks down around his ankles. And a slightly nervous half-smile on his face.

"What does he want?" Sergeant Ivanov whined.

"Go and see," said Nikita.

The boy was lost. Nikita looked and was reminded of Ilya and Yuri back home.

"I'll take him."

He hoisted himself out of his turret. The infantryman took his greatcoat to put it round the young boy's shoulders, but it was replaced almost immediately by Nikita's own, shorter, fleeced tank commander's jerkin.

The young boy's wide-eyed innocence turned, it seemed, to curious fascination as he touched with awe the parts of the tank. He was perched on the front with the infantrymen. Through a mixture of Czech and Russian and sign language they seemed to work out where this boy lived and after another two or three kilometres the driver, tapped on the shoulder by Sergeant Ivanov, again brought the tank to a halt.

After further consultation with the boy, they left the boulevard and the rest of the tank column to penetrate the dark labyrinth of apartment blocks that lay some fifty metres back through the trees, through the grass, past the cafés. By now Jan was balanced in the tank's turret, supported by Nikita's arms. Down an alleyway rumbled the tank, through to domestic yards, squares, until finally, in the darkness, the boy's squeezing of Nikita's hand indicated that they had reached their destination.

The boy was flown down through Russian arms to the pavement still clutching his satchel. And Nikita offered him his hand. The boy took it and smiled.

"Now, young man, what's your name?"

"Jan, sir."

"Right, Jan, I will take you safely to where you live. Show me the way."

"It's that apartment block in the middle."

"Which staircase?"

"This one over here. Twenty-one."

"Come on then. I'll take you right to the door. Your mum and dad must be terrified with you being out so late. Didn't you think of that?"

"I got lost," said the boy. "I had been truanting from school and I've been hiding. Oh, mum and dad are going to be so cross with me."

Nikita did his best to reassure Jan. "You'll be all right. They'll be angry, but they'll also be so relieved to know you are safe and well: these are dangerous times we're in, Jan."

They climbed three floors of the staircase until Jan said, "Thank you."

Nikita knew a Russian uniform was probably not the best thing to greet Jan's parents with, so he retreated three or four steps down the staircase as Jan knocked boldly on the door. He waited, saw a glimmer of light and heard, presumably Jan's mother say, "Ah, Jan, thank goodness," and Nikita, satisfied and content that at least young boy was reunited with his family on that dark night, left without another word. He reached the ground floor when he was assaulted from behind.

It was very quick.

There were two. One pinioned his arms from behind, the other grabbed his hair, flung his head back and, with a quick flick across his throat, cut Nikita's jugular, and he bled to death on the ground floor of that apartment block in Prague.

A deep red stain darkened on the floor.

Chapter Fourteen: Tommy VII

When I was born, so the story goes, my father didn't see me for ten days, let alone he wasn't present at the birth. People forget that stuff. I think the way it worked was visiting was only on alternate days and the first day of visiting he took my mother's mother and let her see my mother and me. That's it - only one visitor. So he didn't see me then. No visiting the next day. Strictly forbidden. On the fourth day my mother's older sister arrives, so she was the visitor and my dad didn't see me. Next day - no visiting. The sixth day my dad's mother arrived, so she was the visitor. I am amazed he got to see me in the first year at all, but of course my mum did bring me home eventually. On the bus from Greenwich to Deptford. The tourist route. Very scenic.

How that's all changed! Now people film the whole shebang and you're likely to find the DVD of your grandson's birth in your Christmas stocking and the afterbirth mixed in with your ratatouille. Or posted on Youtube. Will it go viral?

I've been lucky or unlucky enough to be present at the births of all mine, my huge, rambling, raucous brood. Lucky - because it's so beautiful, so precious, such a miracle that such a complex thing as a human being can be produced from such an act of love – well, I hope so. Biology, life – what a wonder!

Unlucky because of the sheer terror and panic at what the woman goes through. Oh yeah, I can joke about it. The first, Seth, yeah - that was bad for me. In fact, my wife held my hand so much that my wedding ring really cut into my finger and they didn't let you smoke! Yeah, it hurt, but it was worse for her. Also from her point of view - when there are three people urging you to push, push, push, and you're in the worst pain you are ever going to experience in your whole life, you're not in the mood to be told what to do. It's no wonder that she screamed all the swear words there were at me, the person that had got her in that maternity suite to give birth to my son and no wonder that she threatened to cut off my genitalia if I should ever come within, what, two or three hundred miles of her at any time in the next fifty years. I am not surprised. Even in the so-called developed world, women can still die in childbirth. Healthy women can die in childbirth.

So each birth, each new life, each spark of diamond humanity should be loved and cherished and cuddled and celebrated and worshipped for the miracle it is. And told how much it's loved every minute of its life. And it's sad that some must be the products of rapes, gang rapes, drunken fumbling, mistakes, a lack of love, a desire to please, a revenge bonk, the casualest of shags - who knows? It's probably best not to think of those things. I try not to remember those things now. I remember each birth: each one is different, but Seth's was special because it was the first.

It was a hot, violent, grating night in London. The night was hot and the heat was the night. Everywhere you felt the heat of the night. The city was hot. (Thanks, Ernest!) I had nearly not made it in time. I'd dropped Sue off at the hospital and had been told that nothing would be happening until the next day at the earliest. As it happened, I'd got a sort of gig that night in the upstairs room of a pub in Notting Hill which I needed to do for the money. So I gigged the gig, had a few pints and arrived home to find the telephone screaming in the flat. It was happening now and where was I? Very quickly I was on my way – sharpish – driving to the hospital and praying I wouldn't get stopped by the police.

To be fair, the police had other things on their minds. This was July, 1981. Look it up, sunshine. Most of London looked like a war zone. No – it <u>was</u> a war zone. It was high summer, but at four in the afternoon the shops began to pull down the metal shutters, the police began to outnumber shoppers and pedestrians, and an air of violent menace started to descend pall-like over the whole city.

I was stopped on my drive to the hospital. A rozzer flagged me down. I had a mouth full of Polos to disguise the booze, but he wasn't bothered about that. He was dressed in full riot gear: the helmet with visor, a thickly padded jacket and a thick wooden pick handle. Dressed for war. No number.

"What the fuck d'ya think you're doing?" he demanded through the window. "Don't you know there's a fucking war going on? Where the fuck are you going at this time of the fucking night."

I explained that my wife was about to give birth for the first time. That I was on my way to the hospital. That I was neither a rioter nor a looter – just a soon-to-be Dad.

"All right, laddie, you can go, but stick to the main roads, keep your fucking windows shut and don't stop for anyone except the police. There's people fucking dying tonight."

Behind him more policemen in riot gear formed a human barrier to King's Street in Hammersmith. From behind them came strange uncouth sounds: chants, random shouted curses, bricks hitting metal, shattering glass, and in return the police pick-handles began to beat out a rhythmic thudding tattoo that rose to a crescendo as they moved forward into the mayhem that I could not see. The air smelt of smoke and the cordite left from rubber bullets. Sirens swirled their sinuous sonic spell through the bitter heat of the night.

I drove on – past burnt out cars, smouldering shops, ambulances treating the wounded, police vans half-full of handcuffed young men and women, black and white – and everywhere the depressing detritus of that searing night of a scorching summer of hate: a trainer in the gutter, a battered police helmet on a pavement, a broken pick axe handle, smears of blood here and there on the pavements.

The maternity room was even hotter and was filled with equally distressing smells and sounds.

And what I'd seen on the streets was soon forgotten.

Sue upbraided me: "Where the fuck have you been?"

"I've been out. You heard them tell me that nothing would be happening until tomorrow midday at the earliest."

"If you'd missed this, Tommy Wilkinson, I – ."

"If I'd missed this, I'd have done so because the medical staff told me, told us, that nothing would happen until tomorrow lunchtime."

Seth, you must have heard that conversation, although your head had not emerged at that point. It wasn't a good atmosphere, but, sadly for Sue, her pain distracted her from any anger aimed at me.

And I too felt an enormous calm as soon as you were born and out and kicking and screaming, because isn't every father the same - the pride, the love, the unreserved, uncomplicated love, the desire to protect this frail, new version of you who suddenly comes screaming, crying, pink and red and bloody and smeared with stuff and shit into this world? And in those days the pre-natal scans were more rudimentary, so the birth itself was more of a surprise: I didn't know Seth was a boy for a good three minutes because I was too busy counting: head, limbs, fingers, toes, nose, ears, eyes.

After it was over I stood at the window and looked out over the London sky-line. Sue was being cleaned up and being treated to that great British all-purpose placebo – a nice cup of tea. Cynical though I am, there's something sweetly admirable about the calm stoicism of that catch-all response to disaster: I'll put the kettle on.

The Second World War has started and we're going to do really rather badly for quite a while.

Never mind. I'll put the kettle on.

The Second World War has ended and, although we've won, the economy is fucked and I think we'll have to give the Empire back.

Never mind. I'll put the kettle on.

The entire planet is about to be destroyed and we're all going to die horribly.

Better put the kettle on then.

I spoke to Seth. I think you've got speak to them properly and not do that baby talk shit, not oo ga ga ga ga ga goo because if you only do that that's how they'd end up speaking, so I spoke to Seth. Properly. In sentences. Later when he was about four months I read *Emma* aloud to him. And threw a rugby ball at him. I was naïve: at that stage of my life I just thought all you needed to be successful in life were good ball-handling skills and an elegant prose style. Then I discovered neo-liberalism and the global capitalist conspiracy: you need a Kalashnikov as well. Trust me. I am your father and this is the way things are.

"My dearest son, you are not even an hour old yet. You are asleep cradled in my left arm, and your mother more tired, and yet more happy than I've ever known her, is having a cup of tea. When you are older we will tell you that you were born on a summer night when London was aflame with riots and arson and fighting. That I worried about the world you were being born into and that at that moment as I stood at the window I wanted to say, and I did say, my dearest son - welcome to our world. This is your world. And my world. Make it better. Make it as good a world as you can. I hope you have a good story to tell.

"To the south of us there are fires in an area called Brixton and all over south London. To the west of us in Acton and in Southall there is a general glow of burning. And if the windows weren't shut, my dearest son, we would be able to hear the cackling, cacophony of sirens, the sounds of urban unrest and insurrection, the cries and screams and curses of angry people. In the distance, in the outer suburbs, plumes of smoke rise. My dearest son, there are flickers of fires everywhere I look. The fires blaze in the garish streets, lighting this wonderful, beautiful, diseased, corrupt human city.

"A famous woman once wrote, 'Protest is when I say that this does not please me. Resistance is when I ensure that what does not please me never happens again.' I can't tell, Seth, from this distance whether what is happening to my city is protest or resistance. I hope it's resistance.

"And tomorrow, I hope, they will tell us that we will take you home. And we will drive through these wasted, destroyed streets back to the flat where we live, where a room is waiting for you, specially painted and decorated. Your coming, Seth, has turned me upside down and inside out. In a world of materialism and lies and ambition and selfishness and ego it's easy to be drawn in and play games with our lives and lose our way, to believe that what we do and what people say about us is reason enough to act in crazy ways.

"My dearest, darling son, until now I think I have just been practising to be a man, but now, looking at your sleeping face, so close to my own, I'm amazed that I could ever have imagined that success and riches and glory were sweeter than life. And dearest son, while I continue to practise to be a man, I will help you practise to be your

154

own man. I am so happy and so frightened of what the future might hold for you. There's sadness in any birth too. Your mother has just gone through such pain to bring you into this world. And your great grandmother, my grandmother, is not here to know you and she would have been so proud of you, she who had suffered so much and seen so many men fail or die around her, and yet carried on. My dearest son, you look sleepy and tired. There are so many things to tell you and I will, but on this night, this night of riots and love and birth, somewhere in this big, alert, electric hospital there are deaths as well. On this night just one lesson: never, never, never give up, because pain is only temporary, but giving up lasts for ever.

"And one last thing though, Seth (I always say that and I usually lie), I will be talking to you for the rest of your life… which is a mixed blessing. And one last thing - when you let out your first cry in this room, this delivery room, and I became a father, my thoughts were of your great-grandmother, and, although I know it's impossible, I hoped that in some way she could hear across the infinite space between the living and the cold, dark land of the dead, your jubilant wail of arrival.

"For if she could hear you, she would recognize and love the distinct and continuing voice of family, the sound of hope and new beginnings and new life that you and all your newness and you-ness and freshness have brought to this world."

But outside, all over the city, hung the sick smell of rubble and blood and death and decay. London smouldered and smoked by day, and by night it glowed and blazed. And, in a way, I had already lied to my first-born child.

Chapter Fifteen: Yuri

You know, it's ironic, given all I've been through and how I think and feel about it all now, but I can still remember the words of the oath you take when you join the Red Army. And I promise you that when I said those words out loud, I really meant them: I meant them from the depths of my heart. My dad had been a soldier and my grandmother had died during the Great Patriotic War, so I had the army in my blood. To volunteer seemed to me like destiny, a family tradition. What you had to do to prove you'd been here.

"I stand ready to defend my Motherland, the Union of Soviet Socialist Republics, when ordered to do so by the Soviet Government and, as a soldier of the armed forces of the USSR, I swear to defend it with courage, skill, dignity and honour, not sparing my blood, and even my life for the achievement of total victory over our enemies."

But – guess what - it wasn't quite like that in reality. But I suppose nothing ever is. Except for sex – that is much better than anyone lets on. Your teachers, your parents, everyone – they just keep how good it is such a secret.

We were so short of things in Afghanistan. We didn't even have a bowl or a spoon each. My platoon had one big bowl and one spoon. And, at the end of the day, all ten of us would attack it. Apart from the horrors of the fighting, just getting enough to eat was a daily struggle. Wasn't there an English general who said that a good army marches on its stomach? Well, in Afghanistan we marched on vodka and the local dope.

During action you pray to - God probably – I'm not really sure, *Please let the earth or this rock open up and swallow me.*

But no amount of praying ever changed a thing as far as I could see.

At night the mine-detecting dogs whined and moaned and whimpered as they slept. They were killed and maimed and wounded too. You would see them lying right next to the men, those that were dead or with their legs blown off: the cruel and casual insouciance of death. Their blood just merged to form one red stain in the snow, but by morning men and dogs and blood were covered in the purest, whitest snow- almost as if nature felt that their deaths were an abomination that should be covered in the purity of whiteness. That was how I consoled myself.

We used to throw all the captured weapons into one big pile. American, Pakistani, even Soviet sometimes, English, Chinese - all intended to kill us. I soon discovered that fear is more human than bravery. On my first patrol I felt so scared and I was full of a rather futile self-pity, but I had to force my fear back inside so no one could see it. I spent the whole patrol trying not to think that I might end up lying there, small and dead and insignificant, thousands of kilometres from the people who loved me. I buried my fear, forced it down, because of the others: you can't lose face in front of your comrades and besides - there is no point in showing it – it wouldn't serve any purpose. We are here, I used to say to myself. We are here. If not us, then it will only be someone else. Might as well get on with it.

Funny old world. There are men flying around in space; we can make the desert bloom; but down here on this troubled but beautiful planet we go on killing each other just as we've done for the last thousand years, and before that for tens of thousands of years - with bullets and knives and stones. In the villages, they killed our captured soldiers with pitchforks... if they were lucky. That was our worst fear – being captured alive. Worse than losing a limb or four; worse than losing your bollocks. At the height of battle that is what I truly thought and prayed for: *Let it be quick! If I'm going to die, please God, let it be quick!* I felt like standing up and shouting at the top of my voice: *Hey, Bullet! I'm here. Come and get me if you want me!*

I was sent over there in 1981. The war had been going on for two years, but the general public were poorly informed about it, because it was all kept very dark, not much on the television (and what was on television was heavily censored and selective and sanitized), and people kept quiet about what they did know – perhaps from relatives who'd come back and told them the truth. In our family, for example, we had faith in the system: we just assumed the government wouldn't be sending our troops to another country unless it was absolutely necessary and vital to the spread of socialism and liberty. My mum thought that; so did the neighbours. I can't remember anyone thinking differently. The women didn't even cry when I left, because in those days the war seemed a long way away and not very frightening.

It was war - and yet not-war - and something remote with no dead bodies, no prisoners. In those days no one had seen the zinc coffins. Later we found out that the coffins were already arriving in the town with the burials being carried out in secret at night. The gravestones had 'Died' rather than 'Killed in Action' engraved on them. But no one asked why all these eighteen year olds were dying all of a sudden. From too much vodka was it? Flu? Too many oranges perhaps? Their loved ones wept; the rest just carried on until they were affected by it themselves. It was kept very dark.

The newspapers talked about how our soldiers were building bridges and planting trees to make friendship with our allies (as they called them) and about how our doctors and nurses were looking after Afghan women and children in new Soviet-built hospitals. When we read articles in the Soviet press about our achievements we laughed, then we got angry and then we used them as toilet paper. But the strange thing is this - now I am home after my two years out there, I search through the papers to find articles about achievements and actually believe them. At least I want to believe them. I want a good story to tell.

I'll be honest: I fainted the first time I saw casualties. Some of them with their legs sawn off at the groin with huge holes in their heads. Everything inside me was shouting, "I want to be alive!" One night someone stole a dead soldier's sub-machine gun. The thief was one of our own soldiers too. He sold it for 80,000 Afghani and showed off what he'd bought with the money. Three cassette recorders, some American T shirts and a pair of fancy denim jeans. If he hadn't been arrested, we would have torn him to pieces ourselves. In court he just sat there crying. We knew he'd have a hard time in prison.

The terrain caused us a lot of problems. On mountain operations, well, you carry your gun, obviously, and a double issue of ammo: that's about ten kilos, plus some mines - that's another ten kilos, plus grenades, a flak jacket, and rations. It comes to about forty kilos. I've seen men so wet with sweat they look as though they've been standing in torrential rain. I've seen the cruel crust on the frozen faces of dead men. I've seen friendship and cowardice. What we did – well, it had to be done. In the mountains it was kill or be killed: a world without mercy or pity. We were there - who else would do it? There are a lot of clever bastards around now, telling us what a bad, misguided war it was, but, I ask you - why didn't they tear up their party cards or shoot themselves in protest while we were over there? Ask them why they did nothing.

I remember one twelve-day patrol in particular. We spent almost the whole time running away from a group of mujahedeen and we only managed to survive on dope. On the third day one of my platoon shot himself. He started to lag behind us and then, without warning or a single word, put his gun to his temple and fired. You know the worst thing: we had to carry his corpse along with all his equipment: his back pack, flak jacket and helmet. We were not especially sorry for him. He knew we would have to take him with us. But I did think of him on the day we flew back home for good. In fact, I often think about him and I wonder what his family were told about his death.

The worst thing to witness and the thing we all dreaded was being hit by a dum-dum bullet – the ones that explode inside you. I saw one terribly injured lad. He'd had both his legs blown off at the knee, and the bones were left sticking out, white and jagged. Both ears had been ripped away, his penis and testicles had gone, his eyes were blown out and he'd taken a dum-dum in the stomach. I started trembling and shaking when I saw him. I applied tourniquets where I could, staunched the blood, gave him as many pain killers as I could find just to let him sleep. Next was a soldier who'd lost both his arms and had taken a dum-dum in his stomach - his intestines were dangling out. I bandaged him, tried to staunch the blood, and then gave him a massive pain killer too. I held him for four hours and then he died.

When a bullet hits a person, you hear it. It's an unmistakable sound you never forget, like a kind of wet slap. Your mates next to you fall face down in the sand all of a sudden like they're obeying an order you didn't hear - sand that tastes as bitter as ash. You turn him over on his back. The cigarette you just gave him is stuck between his teeth and it's still alight. The first time it happens, you react like in a dream: you run, you drag him and you shoot, and afterwards you can't remember a thing about it, not that you can tell anyone anyway. It's like a nightmare you watch happening behind a sheet of glass darkly. You wake up scared and don't know why. The fact is, in order to overcome the horror, you have to remember it and get used to it.

Within two or three weeks there is nothing left of the old you except your name. You've become someone else. This someone else isn't frightened of a corpse, but acts very calmly when confronted with one and a bit pissed off too. This new you wonders how he's going to drag the body down the rocks and carry it for several kilometres in the heat. This new person doesn't have to imagine: he knows the smell of a man's guts hanging out; he knows the smell of human excrement mixed with blood. He's seen the scorched skulls grinning out of a puddle of molten metal as though they have been frozen in death laughing, not screaming as they did only a few hours before. He knows that incredible, wonderful excitement of seeing a dead body and thinking, *That's not me!* It's a total transformation. It happens very quickly and it happens to almost everyone. And it's sad.

There is no mystery about death for people caught up in a war. Killing simply means squeezing the trigger. We were taught that he who fires first stays alive. That was the law - the law of war. You need to do two things our CO told us: run fast and shoot straight. He would do the thinking. We just followed orders: pointed our rifles and machine guns where they told us to and then fired them when they told us to, because all our training had instilled that unquestioning obedience. And at the time, I'm embarrassed to say now, I didn't feel a thing, not even if I shot children. Both sides were just as bad over there – if they were Afghan we shot them. That is war.

On one occasion our column was rumbling slowly through a steep-sided valley when the lead personnel carrier broke down. The driver got out to lift the bonnet and fix the problem, when a little boy about six years old ran up and got him in the back with a huge knife. Got him right in the heart. That boy was riddled with bullets so that he ceased to resemble anything human, just as, I now see, we too had ceased to resemble anything human. If we'd had the orders to, we would have obliterated his entire village too. And all the people living there.

All any of us wanted to do was survive. Avoid conflict and get home safe – it was simple. There was no time to think. We were eighteen or twenty years old. I got used to other people's deaths, but I was frightened of dying myself. I saw how a man could become nothing, literally nothing, as though he'd never been. When that happens they put an empty full dress uniform in the coffin, throw in a few spadesful of Afghan earth to make up the weight and send it back home. I wanted to live. Looking back the worst thing of all over there – worse than the fear, worse than the appalling injuries you saw, worse than our treatment of the Afghans – was the inhuman and careless attitude to death – except your own of course.

As I've come to realize, you could never reveal the whole truth of what happened: people wouldn't believe you or it would be too traumatic for the listener as well as the teller. Here if there's a terrorist attack or a nutter with a machine gun attacks a school it's all over the television and the papers. Over there things like that happened every day – all over that poor, savage country. During my training I thought it would be frightening and unpleasant to kill a fellow human being, but I quickly realized that what I was really squeamish about was going up to someone and shooting them from really close range. Mass killing from a distance and if you're in a group is exhilarating and fun. Isn't that awful?

In peace-time our guns were kept under lock and key at all hours. Over there you had your gun with you all the time. It was part of you. After dark you would shoot out the light bulbs with your revolver, if you were feeling lazy. It was easier than going to all the trouble of getting up and switching it off or, half-crazy with the heat, you emptied your sub-machine gun into the air or worse - and this is what we were awarded medals for from the grateful Afghan people.

This wasn't the sort of war we all thought we knew about from reading books and watching films – one with a front line, a no man's land, a vanguard and rear echelons, uniforms, flags and regimental colours. You know the word karez - it's the word the Afghans used for the culverts, originally built for irrigation. This was a karez war. Afghans would suddenly come up out of them like invisible spirits, at any time of day or night, with a sub-machine gun in their arms pointing at us, or a huge knife they'd just slaughtered a lamb with, or sometimes with simply a big rock. He might have been the man you'd been haggling with over the price of dope in the market a few brief hours before. But when you saw the sub-machine gun, he ceased to be a human being for you because he was about to kill you and your mates. He was now just a bloody mess of dead flesh flung by the force of the bullets to the ground. My best friend's final words were, "Don't... don't write to my mother, please. Don't tell her how I died. I don't want her to know." And to the Afghans we were just Russkis - not as real human beings.

Still I wasn't sent there, as far as I was concerned, to kill people. Why wouldn't the people of Afghanistan see us as we tried to see ourselves? I can remember their children barefoot standing in the snow and ice while we handed out rations and shoes. Once I remember seeing a little boy run up to our personnel carrier, not to beg as they normally did, but just to gawp at us. I had fifty Afghanis in my tunic pocket so I gave to him. He said nothing – just stood there in the sand at the roadside and didn't move at all until we'd and driven away.

On the other hand, you heard of some of our troops stealing a few kopeks from the kids who brought us water and so on. No one came out of Afghanistan unscathed. I remember once our platoon was slowly walking through a village. I was on patrol with another lad who pushed opened a door with his leg and was shot point blank with a machine gun. A full clip. In that situation sheer fear and hatred take over. We shot everything – cats and dogs – anything that was alive in that village. In fact, I felt that shooting the animals was the worst. I actually felt very sorry for them. Sometimes I wouldn't let the dogs be shot. They'd done nothing wrong, had they? But we destroyed the village, razed it to the ground, set fire to the wheat fields, slaughtered even the chickens. That upset me. I'm a country boy at heart. I hadn't gone to Afghanistan to kill farmers and their families. But I was there: if not me, then who?

When I was serving in Afghanistan I discovered that I only remembered the really memorable things about life back in the USSR, especially things from my childhood, like the way I used to lie with my brother and my sister on the grass among the buttercups and the daisies: or how we roasted chestnuts over an open fire in the autumn and ate them. In Afghanistan I'd remember those autumn fires when we burnt the farmers' wheat fields: the heat was so intense that it melted the corrugated iron on the roofs of all the nearby buildings.

The wheat was engulfed by the flames in a flash and everywhere smelt of bread. And that reminded me of when I was a boy too.

In Afghanistan night falls sharp and sudden like a curtain or a quick blink of your eye. One moment it's bright, attenuated light - the next impenetrable darkness. A bit like all of us, I was only a boy when I got there, but I very quickly became a man almost after my first taste of action. That's war for you: I'm sure it's the same for everyone and it's been the same for millennia I imagine. We used to watch Soviet television shows by satellite, showing life at home going on as normal, but it slowly became meaningless – distant, irrelevant, an irritant.

Sometimes I want to write down for posterity everything I saw, even the worst things, so that future generations will learn and wars will be entered into less casually and with more awareness of the reality - like the young lad from Novosibirsk who'd lost his testicles, both his arms, both his legs and his best friend. I sat next to his bed trying to write a letter for him to send back home to his mother. I could barely hold the pen still in my hand because I was trembling with a strange pitiful horror. Words. Words. Words. What words could I write to his mother? What words could possibly give her any comfort? That he was here and that there was no one else?

And the little Afghan girl who'd accepted a bag of sweets from a Soviet soldier and had both her hands hacked off by her own people as a punishment. I'd like to write it down exactly as it was without any comments – just so that it isn't kept dark.

When it was finished, when our tour was over and we were about to go home we expected a warm, rapturous welcome, flowers and open arms, but we were an embarrassment: we discovered that people couldn't care less whether we'd survived or not. That hurts. It really hurts. And the lies. And the misinformation. And the horror. And everything being kept dark.

And it still hurts.

It always will.

Chapter Sixteen: Tommy VIII

Looking back, something died that day, but I'm not quite sure what it was. The country was having a heat-wave and it still seems a too gloriously beautiful day in June in England for anything to have died. But something died that day.

Jack had urged me, had been urging me, to go for several weeks. He said it was our duty. He said we had to be where the action was, the frontline, where it mattered. We had to stand together or things would only get worse for us all. And I agreed with him but selfishly thought that it might also be good for my work in some vague and ill-defined way that I could not yet see. It was being kept far too dark for my liking.

So we headed north. My car was crammed with food and drink and toys and sweets – all paid for by Jack before we left. We knew that we would have to take a circuitous route to say the least – all sorts of rumours were flying around about cars heading north being stopped by the police and certain people being arrested on suspicion, so we avoided going through the Blackwall Tunnel – which is my favoured and favourite route across or over or beneath the sweet Thames (run softly till I sing my song), and I followed the South Circular westwards and we crossed the river at Chiswick. We were heading for South Yorkshire, so it would have been logical to take the A1, but Uncle Jack knew that road well enough to realize that the roundabouts would give the police plenty of opportunities for roadblocks, so we took the M1 instead. We left the motorway near Derby and then by a circuitous route of B roads and winding country lanes finally reached our destination: a small village between Doncaster and Sheffield. I won't mention its name: the police have long memories, according to Uncle Jack.

In the village we headed immediately for the social centre. It was a beautiful summer evening with that hazy heat prolonged by so many hours of daylight and seemingly attenuated by the idyllic pastoral setting of an old English village surrounded by the plenitude of the full and richly fertile wheat fields that surrounded us. We were greeted with great warmth and gratitude, and the contents of the car were swiftly ferried into the village hall with obvious glee. The village hall was abuzz with people and activity, voices and laughter, conspiratorial whispered conversations and muttered exchanges, children and grandparents, all generations.

We had been on the road all day and we were thirsty. There was no need for directions to the local pub – we had passed it on our way in – and Uncle Jack and I ambled towards it, the rapturous sound of larks providing a triumphant chorus to our progress towards our pint. Despite the difficulties the village was undergoing, as we sauntered through its heart, we were invited into various houses. A cup of tea here, a can of beer there, everywhere a warm reception – and it took us nearly an hour to walk the short half mile to the pub where we found an even warmer reception. Uncle Jack seemed to know everyone, or perhaps everyone knew Uncle Jack. He was in a jovial mood, asking everyone how they were all doing and gleaning groans of amusement when he insisted on herbal tea, since, he asserted, all proper tea is theft.

Certainly I felt instantly at home in the warm camaraderie of our welcome. We did not pay for a single drink that night in the pub, and Uncle Jack allowed this to happen – although we both knew the dire straits that the villagers were experiencing. It was with great delight that Uncle Jack pinned a new badge to my battered leather jacket.

"Think you better wear this, sunshine, so everyone knows which side you're on. You can't be too careful around here with the accent you've got, Tommy," he cajoled.

I was delighted, needless to say – say it anyway!

Where I grew up it's easy to be London-centric; to believe the stereotypes of the North – Here be monsters!; to feel that the North begins at Watford Gap, Watford, at the end of the Northern line, at Marble Arch – or even, as John Baxter used to assert – half way across Southwark Bridge, but I have never been like that... Though there have been times when I have pretended to be like that for comic purposes perhaps. But what unites us as human beings, whichever petty patch of this glorious globe we originate from, is far more important than what appears to separate us – don't ever forget that, sunshine. So I will not tediously pretend to you that I had packed my cloth cap and my pigeon-racing guide for this trip to the heart of England, to the engine of Empire, to the South Yorkshire coal-field. I had come because I felt impelled to do so, to bear witness, to record.

Uncle Jack and I were escorted back to the village hall where we beerily camped out in sleeping bags on two mattresses laid out in a side room to one side of the low dais that probably served as a stage for various entertainments and functions. We fell asleep quickly, exhausted, but full of a summery joy and hopefulness for the next day and our anticipated success.

A glass of shock shrieked through my sleep and hauled me from dreams too deep to remember. Something, someone, somehow had battered through the doors, crash-smashed the windows and in the deathdark of that night had bellowed into our room.

"What on earth?" started Uncle Jack. "What on earth is going on? Tommy! Tommy? Are you all right?"

"I'm fine, Uncle Jack. I'm fine, but I can't see a thing."

From the body of the village hall came a floundering thunder of noise. Sudden quick lights lit up our faces. I felt a panic of fear: what on earth was happening?

"Up! Up! Up! Get up, you little Northern wankers!"

I was still scrabbling for my glasses, when the lights were switched on and I realized that the village hall had been invaded by members of the police force. Jack and I were hurled to our feet, dragged half-standing out on to the dais and then into the body of the hall which was swarming with dark blue uniforms which held truncheons and staffs and crowbars and torches; which were taking, stealing, everything that was liftable, and breaking everything that could not be lifted.

"Who are you two? Not seen you before. Quick – names?"

When they finally let us go, Uncle Jack and I sought refuge in my car, but sleep now was hard to find – like Australia before we could do longitude quickly. Uncle Jack was livid.

"Tommy, I can't believe it! It is like a police state. We have done nothing wrong. All we were doing was trying to get some kip after a few beers. What law had we broken? I'll tell you, Tommy – we have broken no law. We are just standing up for what we think is right. Since when has that been a crime in this country?"

"I know, Uncle Jack – I know. But let's get home safe, eh? I can't drive yet – I'm over the limit, but in a few hours I'll be all right. Let's just go home."

"No chance, Tommy. I came here to picket and I'm not going home on the say-so of some jumped up little boys in blue who don't know their arses from their elbows cos they don't know what the fuck is going on in this country."

"Uncle Jack, please calm down. What difference would it make whether we stay or go? There's only two of us."

"Tommy, I can't believe you said that to me. There's only two of us? Suppose everyone took that attitude? Then we might as well go home and live on our knees for the rest of our lives. You go home if you want to – I am staying because every individual, every drop of water in the ocean, every grain of sand, Tommy, makes a fucking difference – and if you don't believe that, Tommy, my son, then I don't believe you've ever listened to a single bleeding word I've said to you. Besides – where you think you're going in this car? You think the rozzers will let you leave the village? Remember, Tommy, the only thing necessary for the triumph of evil is for good men to do nothing."

I was still too in awe of Uncle Jack to say that doing nothing seemed a very attractive option at that moment of my life. It was a freeze moment. But I pulled myself together and said, "I will stay, Uncle Jack - to make sure you're okay."

"I'm fine, Tommy. It's you I'm worried about. What's got into you? You have got to show a bit of bottle, sunshine. Sometimes you have to make a stand. This is one of those times."

"Okay, Uncle Jack. I will stay. For you and for the cause."

And so we stole a little sleep before the early dawn and the cheeping, raspy racket of the birds roused us.

Uncle Jack had planned our trip very precisely and we even had two seats on the coach, which arrived in the village shortly after six, to pick up the men who were going to the picket lines. There was little surprise at Uncle Jack's account of our night's disruption and the sacking of the village hall – just resigned recognition that this was becoming the norm.

"This sort of thing has been happening for months, but the rest of the country knows nothing about it. For us it's been like living in a police state: coppers always at your doorstep - stopping you from leaving your own home, stopping you from leaving your village. Get away with all sorts. Nothing mentioned on the television or in the newspapers. Who is telling our story? No one!"

But as the coach wandered its way through the narrow country lanes towards the coking plants, the atmosphere became celebratory, almost jubilant – with every prospect of a successful day ahead. Apparently thousands of men were expected from all over the country – from Scotland and Wales, from County Durham, from Kent, from Nottinghamshire – and these men had all taken part in successful and peaceful pickets before today, so there was no reason to suppose on that blissfully blue-skied summer's morning that something was going to die later that day and that the sweetly-shining sun which smiled down through the dimming dew of dawn would become a beating, sweaty cauldron of blazing tyranny as the morning wore on.

I was torn. Krav Maga meant I should avoid conflict and get home safely, but I could see no way to achieve those laudable goals. As soon as we stepped off the coach, violent confrontation was in the air. Not on our side, I hasten to add. We just wanted the chance to put our case to the lorry drivers – but the police had other ideas.

We were herded as cattle into a field with the railway line behind us. But the atmosphere was tense; we went through a barrage of abuse, chants and general insults hurled like pellets as we trudged to our appointed place. All this conflict was familiar to me from the National Front marches we had tried to disrupt, but there was on this occasion, it seemed to me, an added vicious edge which was so wholly at odds with the weather and the friendliness Uncle Jack and I had been shown the evening before that I had to pinch myself to make sure I was awake and alive.

So this is England, I thought to myself.

Apart from the railway line at the back, we were surrounded, and by eight o'clock the field had all the appearance of what I imagine a medieval battle would have looked like: the two opposing sides lined up against each other hurling insults and engaging in spirited chanting; the main police lines were to the north – it looked like something out of *Zulu*. We - at this Rourke's Drift - were heavily out-numbered. To our west and to the east, police with dogs patrolled the lines – the dogs keeping up an incessant barking-snarling that mirrored the aggression of their handlers.

This day is not going to go well, I thought, but I still had no notion that something would die.

Uncle Jack gave as good as anything the police gave in terms of insults, roaring back at the police lines every so often: so this was what he was born to do, I thought. And I began to feel a strong sense of solidarity with the other men. They were there to fight for their lives, their communities, their families, the right of their descendants to work.

From the police lines came rhythmic chanting which I could not decipher, which drew a similar response from us. It was, at this point, like a very evil football match. Then the police began to beat rhythmically on their riot shields. They had all the appearance of aliens from *Doctor Who*; you couldn't see their faces. To say it was intimidating would be an understatement. Uncle Jack became more and more impassioned by a lively sense of righteousness.

The first flash point was around nine o'clock as the first coke lorries attempted, and eventually succeeded, in entering the coking plant. Their arrival prompted a massive surge from our lines – the first of three throughout the morning. The police lines held. There were angry shouts, a constant barrage of abuse from both sides and hand-to-hand fighting at the very front. At a seemingly pre-arranged point the shield line of the police broke and suddenly sixty mounted police officers were charging towards us, batons swinging. The pickets fled in panic, but some were too slow and emerged with blood streaming down their faces from truncheon blows. This cavalry charge – for that is what it was – inflamed an already tense situation. Especially as the sun rose and the day became hotter.

Give the bastards swords, I thought, and this might as well be Peterloo. Give us lot rifles and it might begin to resemble a fair fight. Or a revolution.

The horses remained thirty yards or so in front of the police shield line which was by now keeping up a rhythmic war-beat of batons on shields. They had obviously seen *Zulu* too.

What happened next is open to debate. No one can agree on what happened and even the BBC – the British Biased Corporation – managed to cut the film to show the police as victims – not the aggressive, let's-have–a-fight–these-benighted-pickets, as they acted on the day.

From my position what happened next was a blood-curdling shout of aggression from the police lines and another mounted charge and what I saw from my limited vantage point was about two dozen stones and clods of earth thrown with violent intent towards the police lines. I did not see the sky turn black through the mass of objects thrown, as the police officer in command stated on the BBC that night. Some of the stones were thrown back by the police and that certainly did not get reported on the news.

This provoked a further cavalry charge. Jack and I had been at the back for the first push, but now found ourselves at the front and closer to the baton-wielding aliens, the Zulus in blue. We ran, although Uncle Jack, being sixty-four, was not as quick as he might have been or as he once was.

I've still got a copy of the photo now on a window-sill near my desk. In the photo Jack is lying supine in the field; a mounted police officer is out of his saddle with a raised baton which is bearing down towards Jack's head and upper body; Jack's arm is raised as a feeble defence; his face wears an expression of utter surprise and bewilderment. Although a press photographer took this photo and gave Jack a copy, it did not appear in any British newspaper. I helped him back towards the railway line where he washed the wounds on his head and staunched the blood.

For this charge the cavalry were on their own, so no arrests were made and the horses retreated a few yards, but by now the pickets were hemmed into an even smaller area of the field.

It became clear this was no ordinary battle, designed to stop the pickets talking to the lorry drivers in an attempt to persuade them not to enter the coking plant. This was an attempt to provoke, on a national stage, to humiliate and to arrest as many pickets as they could – the vast majority of whom would later have the charges against them dropped.

As this dawned on me, another realization flashed into my mind. It was a legal right to picket if you were a member of a striking union. There were two people in that field who were blatantly breaking the law of the land: Uncle Jack and me – we were not members of the union that was on strike and therefore we had no right of lawful assembly. My heart sank as this realization sank in, and Jack and I resolved to give false names if arrested by the police and hope that the police would assume we were miners from Kent – what with the way we spoke, you know. I dreaded to think what Sue would say if I returned from our mercy mission with a criminal record.

More and more of the strikers had retreated towards the railway line to the south. The arrival of more coking trucks initiated a tentative push forward by us, but there was another mounted charge and this was followed by random charges of short-shield squads – about half a dozen rozzers in each squad – who pushed the pickets over the railway bridge and into the neighbouring village.

That was it, it seemed to me. Everywhere the pickets were relaxing, having taken their T-shirts off to sunbathe, while they enjoyed cups of tea from local houses and lounged about in the sun. Everyone I saw was in jeans and trainers – not the best clothes for taking on riot police with short shields and long batons - not one's preferred choice of apparel to repel an aggressive mounted cavalry charge.

Uncle Jack and I were chatting with some men from the village who were sitting on the kerbside drinking tea, when we heard the thunder of horses' hooves: the police were clearing the village.

It is hard to describe what happened next, even all these years later, without getting angry all over again. Uncle Jack and I and all the pickets in the village sought refuge in people's houses, while the police rioted and ransacked the village. They did not touch businesses – the post office, the corner shop or the pub; they ignored private houses except to smash a few front windows, but anything else they destroyed: garden sheds, the village hall, greenhouses – anything left in the front or back gardens. And anyone who had not found a place of safety was fair game, it seemed: I saw women savagely kicked and beaten with batons, men kicked and punched as they lay bleeding in the gutter; cars set ablaze. And none of this was reported in the press. But hey! What did the man say? "A lie told often enough becomes the truth." Welcome to the UK!

Something died that day. My faint faith in the police force; my faith in the press and the BBC; something of England died that day too.

On our drive back to the big smoke, our conversation was muted. Uncle Jack observed, more than once:

"Arthur Scargill may be a good union man, but he's a shit tactician. Forget the ballot – that's an irrelevance. Why strike at all? They should've staged a work-in at the threatened pits – like Clydeside. That would have kept the pits open and united the country. Why do people never learn from history?"

What was it the man said? "First they ignore you. Then they laugh at you. Then they fight you. Then you win"? Not on this occasion, Mahatma.

In the spring of the next year, as the miners went back to work with banners blaring and brass bands cheerily and illogically triumphant, Uncle Jack cried when he saw it on television.

He said it reminded him too much of the day he left Barcelona at the end of the war.

Chapter Seventeen: Olga I

You're a fool, an utter fool to come here, I told myself every day or rather every night. In the daytime I was too busy working. I was so shocked by the injuries, by the bullets, by the realization that such weapons had been invented. The entry wounds might be small, but the intestines, liver and spleen were a terrible, twisted mess. Apparently it wasn't enough to kill or wound - there had to be torture too.

"Mum!" they screamed. "Mum!" when they were frightened and in pain. Always, always screaming for their mothers.

I just wanted to get away from Ulyanovsk for a year or two. My dad had died in Prague in '68 and my grandparents on my dad's side – well, they were both dead long before I came along. My brothers Ilya and Yuri had both volunteered for Afghanistan, so it seemed natural enough for me to go too. There was nothing to keep me in Ulyanovsk. On the contrary, everything just reminded me horribly of the past.

"Do you want to go to Afghanistan?" the consultant asked me.

"Ok," I said.

To be honest I wanted to see people worse off than I was. And I wanted to make a difference, but I don't think I did that at all. We were told that this was a just war, that we were helping the Afghan people to put an end to feudalism and build a wonderful, egalitarian, socialist society, but there was a conspiracy of silence about our casualties. It was all kept dark.

It was somehow implied that there were an awful lot of infectious diseases over there - malaria, typhus, hepatitis, and the rest. We flew to Kabul in early 1980. The hospital was in the former British stables from the 19th Century not far from a British cemetery where there were lots of British soldiers' graves from another failed attempt to subdue Afghanistan. It seems that we never learn, really learn, from history. There was no equipment: one syringe for all the patients and the officers drank the surgical spirit, so we had to use petrol to clean the wounds. They healed badly for lack of oxygen, but the hot sun helped to kill the microbes. I saw my first wounded patients in their underwear and boots. For a long time there were no pyjamas, no slippers, no blankets.

Then the very first spring, I'll never forget, a pile grew up behind the hospital. A pile of amputated arms, legs, and other bits of our soldiers; dead bodies with gouged-out eyes, stars carved into the skin of their backs and stomachs by the mujahedeen.

Gradually I think we all began to ask ourselves what we were there for. Such questions were unpopular with the authorities, of course. There were no slippers or pyjamas, but there were plenty of banners and posters with political slogans, all brought from back home. Behind the slogans were our boys' skinny, miserable, faces. Each week we attended a political seminar where we were continually told that we were doing our sacred duty to help make the border totally secure.

The nastiest thing about army life was the informing. Our boss actually ordered us to inform. Every detail about every sick and wounded patient had to be reported. It was called 'knowing the mood'. The army must be kept healthy and we must banish pity from our minds.

But we didn't. It was only pity which kept the whole show on the road. We went to save lives, to help, to show our love, but after a while I realized that it was hatred I was feeling: hatred for that soft, light sand which burned like fire; hatred for the village huts from which we might be fired on at any moment. I felt a desperate hatred for the locals walking with their baskets of melons, or just standing by their doors. What had they been doing the night before? Had they been mutilating our boys and cutting their throats in back alleys?

They killed one young officer I knew from hospital and shot up to two tents full of soldiers and poisoned the water supply. One sergeant picked up a small cigarette lighter and it exploded in his hand. These were our boys they were killing - our own boys.

Have you ever seen someone badly burned, face gone, eyes gone, body gone, just a kind of wrinkled thing, covered with a yellow crust of the lymphatic liquid and a growling coming from under the crust? That's what war reduces men to. We probably survived by hating, but I felt full of guilt when I got back home and looked back on it all. I don't like to hate; I want to love, but war seems to depend on hatred.

Of course, many of the Afghans hated us too. Sometimes we must kill and destroy a whole village in revenge for one of our lads. Over there it seemed right - here it sickens me. I remember one little girl lying in the dust like a broken doll and it was only when I looked closer at her that I realized she had no arms or legs. And yet we went on being surprised that they didn't love us. They would come to our hospitals and we would give women some medicine, but they wouldn't look at us and they never smiled.

Over there that hurt, but now I'm home I understand exactly what she was feeling. My profession is a good one, being a nurse. It means saving others, but it saved me too. It made sense of my life. We were needed over there, but we didn't save everyone we could have saved. That was the worst thing of all. We lost so many, because we didn't have the right drugs.

Or the wounded were often brought in too late, or because the field medics were badly-trained soldiers who could just about put bandages on. Or the surgeon was often drunk.

We weren't allowed to tell the truth in the next-of-kin letters. The truth had to be kept dark – perhaps to spare the families' feelings, but more likely to cover up the errors of those in authority. Who cares about the truth? We're just fed the lies they want us to believe.

A boy might be blown up by a mine and there would be nothing left except half a bucket of flesh, but we wrote that he'd died of food poisoning or in a car accident or he'd fallen into a ravine. It wasn't until the casualties were in their thousands that they began to tell families the truth.

I got used to the bodies, to the suffering, to the screams for mother, but I could never, never reconcile myself to the fact that they were ours, our lads, and that the people back home were being kept in the dark.

Once they brought in a boy while I was on duty. He opened his eyes and said, "Oh thank God," and died. They'd searched the mountains for him for three days and three nights.

He was delirious, raving, "I want a doctor, I want a doctor." He saw my white gown and thought he was safe, but he'd been fatally wounded. He didn't stand a chance. There was nothing we could do for him, but pump him full of morphine and hold his hand until he slipped away, while I sang him songs from home.

I saw skulls shot to pieces. All of us who were there have a graveyard full of memories. Even in death there was a hierarchy. For some reason dying in battle was more tragic than dying in hospital. That was how the lads felt. Even though they cried and cried. I remember how one major died in the re-animation unit; he was a military adviser. His wife came to his bedside. He died looking at her and afterwards she started screaming like an animal. We wanted to shut the doors so no one would hear, because there were soldiers dying alone next door - boys with no one to weep for them.

"Mum! Mum!" they'd shout and I'd lie to them:

"I'm here, I'm here, darling."

We became their mothers and sisters. And we wanted to be worthy of their trust.

Once two soldiers brought in a wounded man, handed him over but wouldn't leave.

"We don't need anything, girls. Can we just sit with you for a bit?"

It was clear they just wanted a break and a bit of human company, conversation, a few moments of companionship amidst the hell that they were enduring

Here back home they've got their mums and their sisters and their wives. They don't need us now, but over there they told us things you wouldn't normally tell anyone. In that kind of situation you find out what kind of person you really are. If you are a coward or a grass or woman-crazy or a drunk, it soon comes out. They might not admit it back home, but over there I often heard men say that killing could be a pleasure.

One junior lieutenant I knew who went back home admitted it.

"Life's not the same now. I actually want to go on killing," he said.

They spoke about it quite coldly some of those boys, proud of how they'd burnt down a village and slaughtered the inhabitants. It sickened me when I heard that sort of boasting.

But they weren't all mad. Once an officer came to visit us from Kandahar where he was stationed. That evening when it was time to say goodbye and leave, he locked himself in an empty room and shot himself. They said he was drunk, but I'm not so sure. I just think he had had enough of all the hatred and the killing.

It was very hard living like that, day in day out. One young soldier shot himself at his guard post after standing in the sun for three hours. He had never been away from home before and he just couldn't take it. Lots of them went crazy. To begin with they were on the general wards, but then later they were put on secure wards. Many ran away. They just couldn't bear to be behind bars. They preferred to be with all the rest. I remember one young chap.

"Sit down," he said to me. "Can you sing *Katyusha* to me, please?"

So I just sang and sang until he fell asleep and then woke up.

"I want to go home. I want to go home to mum. I'm so hot here."

He never stopped asking to go home. But it was a futile request – he was going nowhere.

There was a lot of opium and marijuana smoked and whatever else they could get hold of. They said it made you feel strong and free of everything, especially of your own body, as if you were walking on tiptoe. Every cell in your body felt light and you could sense each individual muscle. You wanted to fly and you were irrepressibly happy. You liked everything and would giggle at any old nonsense. You discovered new sights and sounds and smells. For a moment you could believe that the nation loved its heroes. That's what they told me.

And in that kind of mood it was easy to kill – so our boys admitted. You were anaesthetized and had no pity. And it was easy to die too, they said. Well, easier. Fear disappeared and you felt you had a magical flak jacket that would protect you. That's what they told me.

So they would smoke themselves into a stupor and go into action. I tried it a couple of times myself when I was at the end of my tether, but I just had to carry on. I was working in the infectious department which was intended for thirty beds but instead held three hundred, mainly typhoid and malaria. Each patient was given a bed and blankets, but we often found them lying on their army coats or even just in their underpants on the bare ground with a head shaven but still crawling all over with lice.

In the village nearby the Afghans were walking around in our hospital pyjamas with our blankets over their heads instead of turbans. Yes, that's right: our boys had sold them. You couldn't really blame them. They were dying for three roubles a month. That was a private soldier's pay - three roubles a month plus food: meat crawling with worms and some scraps of rotten fish. We all had scurvy. So they sold their blankets and bought opium. Or something sweet to eat or some foreign electronic gimmicky gagdet. The little shops there were very colourful and very seductive. We'd seen nothing like it before. The lads sold their own weapons and ammunition, knowing they'd be used to kill them.

After all that – well, I saw my own country with different eyes. Coming home was terribly difficult and very strange. I felt I'd had my skin ripped off. I couldn't stop crying. I could bear to be only with people who had been there themselves. I spent my days and my nights with them - the zinky boys. Talking to anybody else seemed a futile waste of time. That phase lasted six months. You try and live a normal life, the way you lived before, but you can't. I didn't give a damn about myself or life in general. I just felt my life was over. This whole process was much worse for the men I think. A woman can forget herself in a child; the men had nothing to lose themselves in. They came home, fell in love, had kids, but none of it really helped. Afghanistan was more important than anything else.

I too wish I could understand what it was all about, what it was all for. Over there we had to force such questions back inside us, but at home they just come out and have to be answered. We must show understanding to the men who went through all that. I was just a nurse and it was devastating enough for me, but they saw action, they saw their brothers die and they didn't understand a thing. They were taken from their homes, had a gun stuck in their hands and were taught to kill. They were told they were on a holy mission and that their country would remember them. Now people turn away and try to forget the war. Especially those who sent us there in the first place.

Nowadays even the zinky boys talk about it less and less when they meet up. No one likes this war and yet I still cry when I hear the Afghan national anthem. I got to like all Afghan music over there. I still listen to it. It's like a drug. Recently on a bus I met a soldier who'd been in our hospital. He had lost his right arm. I remembered him because he was from Ulyanovsk originally like me.

"Can I help you in any way?" I asked him.

But he was just so angry.

"Leave me alone," he hissed.

I know he'll come to me and apologise, but who will apologise to him and to everyone else who was broken over there. And I'm not just talking about the cripples. Nowadays I don't just hate the war: I can't even stand seeing a couple of boys having a scrap in the park and, please, don't tell me the war is over now.

In summer when I breathe in the hot dusty air, or see a pool of stagnant water, or smell the dry flowers in the fields, it's like a punch in the head. A jolt to my brain. And in an instant I'm back there.

I'll be haunted by Afghanistan for the rest of my life.

Chapter Eighteen: Tommy IX

By the next morning many of the protestors had been shot. According to the BBC. Not sure they can be trusted really. They already had form for getting it wrong or repeating the lies of whoever is in power – though we didn't know that for certain back then. Remember Bloody Sunday? I do. I remember the BBC reassuring the nation that our paratroopers shot only armed protestors on that sad day in Derry; the official inquiry at the time said exactly the same. Took nearly forty years for someone in the government to put their hand up and say, "Terribly sorry. Turns out all the people we shot that day were unarmed. But times were different then." No, the times were not fucking different! Killing innocent people has always been wrong. Always. When was it ever right? Makes you wonder what else is going to come out from the miasma of official lies our days are dazed and drugged by.

You wait: next they'll be admitting they killed Pat Finucane. Which seemed distinctly dodgy at the time from the perspective of people like me and Jack. Or finally telling the truth about Hillsborough. Or the Shrewsbury 42. Or the banking crisis.

But I digress. I do remember that we kept the television on all that night even though we had a party. It seemed important at the time – those events so far away in a huge land we knew nothing about - though later events the next year were going to put it all in perspective. And it turned out that really nothing changed. Despite the breathless, excited BBC reports urging us to be interested in something exciting, extraordinary and wonderful. Meet the new boss!

You have to imagine parties for English people at that time and with the little money that we had. There was food, of course: cut up French bread in bowls; other French bread with garlic, in bowls; lots of cheese; potato salad; pasta with some sort of herb mixed in - green bits anyway (Sue had seen to that); cold meat, and, if I remember rightly, there was a huge pot of chilli bubbling away on the hob for later when it got dark and the alcohol made people hungry. Lots of booze: cheap boxes of wine, big plastic bottles of cider, a keg of bitter balanced on a table in the back garden – and the other stuff – the weird concoctions that people turned to when everything else had run out. Alcohol – the good old British substitute for insurrection. A legal drug that effectively immobilises revolt. And when that doesn't work distract them with television.

I remember some details of that night so well, but I've only a vague memory of why we were having a party. It was some minor success to do with work I suppose, a very minor success since it did not alter the bickering that had become a daily habit, an addictive need for Sue and me.

"Why can't you get a proper job?"

"But I work every day. I work fifteen, sixteen hours a day."

"But you earn no money. What fucking use is a job without money?"

"I do my best. I earn money."

"Peanuts. Stacking shelves at Sainsbury's - that's not a proper job. I didn't know things would be like this."

"You knew what I did, what I wanted to do."

"Yes, Tommy, but I thought you'd grow up. I thought children would make a man of you."

"So now I'm not a man?"

"What do you do that other men do?"

"I've decorated this house from top to bottom. Every room in the colour you said you wanted."

"But no room is finished. Everywhere something is still to be done: the window-sill in our bedroom; that bit of skirting in Sam's room; none of it finished. Tommy Wilkinson, you don't finish anything. You start things and you never finish."

"I'll get round to it. I have to work, you know. I need to work. If work comes up, I have to do it. It's unpredictable by its very nature. That takes precedence over decorating."

"What else do you do?"

"I love the children. I entertain the children. I do my best by you. Sue, you're never happy. Look at us: we've moved house – what? - six times in nine years. What's all that about? What are you searching for?"

"I'm searching for something you can't give me, Tommy. I'm searching for stability."

"You're searching for a perfect house; you're just materialistic."

"Materialistic - what would you know about that? You, you can't even look after yourself."

"I can cook. I can fix the car. I can put up shelves."

"Which aren't straight."

"Fuck you."

"Chance would be a fine thing."

"Well, you never seem to enjoy it, so what's the point?"

"You're not a man, Tommy Wilkinson, and you never have been. All your life you've just been practising to be a man."

"Yeah, I'll admit that. I don't know what to do. I do my best and my best, I think, is never going to be good enough for you. You want something that I can't give you and what I do give you, you don't respect, you don't want, you don't need. You look down on what I do. Every word from you I hear is criticism. There is no love, not even affection, in your voice. I feel I can't do anything right."

"Well, you're right, for once in your life."

"I'm always right."

"I don't think you can do anything right, Tommy Wilkinson. You did one thing right - well, three things right - you fathered three lovely children, but you, you're a wastrel: you're no good to anyone; you can't work; you won't work; no one buys your work; you work fifteen, sixteen hours a day; you piss it up the wall. And look at how we live, worrying about being able to afford enough money to buy beer for this bloody party which I wish we weren't having."

"You suggested it."

"I was trying to keep you happy."

"There are other ways to keep me happy."

"Huh, fat chance."

Meanwhile on the television ten, twelve thousand miles away a similar game of domination and power was being played out as our party unfolded. It's easy in my version of these events to present Sue as the Government and me as the pro-democracy protesters in the square, but that's not true.

I was the Government. I was the authoritarian, repressive force, stifling dissent, about to send the tanks in, about to shoot the protesters in a metaphorical, very English sort of way. I was in the wrong, but that's not such a good story: I desperately wanted to be the goodie – the hero who unties the helpless heroine from the railway tracks, the cavalry who steam in to save the settlers, the knight on a white Lambretta who arrives just in time to gun down the mobsters. But life is in colour, not black and white, and it's only now that I can see I was the moustache-twirling villain, the deranged slightly loopy serial killer on the loose, the loud stupid kid at school who thinks he's funny, but everyone else knows is just a first-class, well-practised, fully certified twat.

Not that Sue's materialism and greed for bigger, better houses and a stable income were misguided, but that I controlled the situation. Or rather foolishly, I thought I did. Sue had developed what seemed to me like a physical abhorrence to my very touch. And, yes, it pains me to say that there was the first in a series of other women, and, yes, she was there that evening as the tanks rolled in and the protesters were shot and the innocents were murdered, and I know now that I gave the orders.

That night everyone kept checking the television to see what was going on in that far away square and there was much talk, much condemnation of the people who gave the orders. I felt like a hypocrite. Which is a shit sentence, because I WAS a hypocrite. When she walked in that night our eyes held contact for a long moment. Our desire grew, especially as it was against all the rules.

Later I remember vividly there was a moment in one of the back bedrooms where we were alone and looked out at the sun-filled garden where people were quaffing and chatting merrily. In the garden it must have looked quite innocent. Two people, a man and a woman, just friends, waving down, acknowledging gestures of recognition and joy.

But from inside the perspective was different. When we went downstairs we wore masks. To keep it dark.

"Hi, how are you? So pleased you could come."

"Ah, your latest stuff, Tommy. Fantastic! I really enjoyed it."

"Have you got a drink? Make sure you get something to eat. Sue's got some chilli on. Sue makes such good chilli. You must try some before you go."

"Hi, how are you? Good to see you. Thanks for coming."

"Oh, Tommy, thank you for inviting me. So good to see you again. I'm so pleased for you."

"Ah, it's nothing really."

"Yes, but every little helps."

"Yes, every little helps. That's what Sue says."

You'll remember Krav Maga: fight, flight or freeze. When I wasn't fighting with Sue, I froze. I was quite happy with the way things were. Comfortable with Sue, proud to be a father but beaten down by the daily criticism, the constant sense that I wasn't good enough, and I was quite happy to wear a mask. According to Krav Maga, I should have fought but, hell, I got home safe and, by freezing for a few more months or years, I thought I could avoid conflict - which is the second principle of Krav Maga.

The people in the square were not so lucky. They were shot, killed, imprisoned, interrogated - all at the point of a gun or a tank and, though I'd like to see myself as one of the protesters in the square, I can now see that, paradoxically and to my everlasting shame, I was the Government that ordered the tanks into Beijing.

But while we're on the subject when did Peking become Beijing and who teaches this sort of thing to our children? They should know; they need to know. They need to know that once we had two television channels and were very excited at the thought of three. They need to know that once the only spaghetti, the only pasta that you could buy in supermarkets, was Heinz tinned spaghetti hoops. That even people like me once thought that Tiramisu was an island in the Aegean. And Cointreau was a nouvelle vague auteur. They need to know that once we did not have supermarkets.

Who will tell them these things when you and I are gone, maya padrooga?

Chapter Nineteen: Svetlana

I don't really know what to tell you. Should I tell you about love? Or about death? For me they are so intertwined: everything I've ever loved has died. We were newlyweds; we still walked around holding hands, even if we were just going to the shops. I'd say to him, "I love you," but I didn't know then how much. I had no idea. He'd served in Afghanistan. As had his brother, Ilya. And his sister, Olga.

We lived in an apartment in the barracks on the second floor. There were three other young couples: we shared a kitchen. One night I heard a noise. I looked out the window. He saw me.

"Close the window and go back to sleep. There's some sort of emergency at the reactor. I'll be back soon."

I didn't see the explosion itself - just the flames. Everything was radiant, rather beautiful: the whole sky, the tall flame and the strangely turquoise smoke. That was at three in the morning.

Yuri told me just before he died that the smoke was from the burning material the roof was made from — a mixture of graphite and bitumen, Yuri thought. He said it was like walking on very hot sticky toffee or black, smoking lava. They were attempting to put out the flames. They kicked at the blazing bitumen with their feet. Of course, they weren't wearing any protective clothing at all. They went off just as they were in the clothes they were wearing - the truth was kept very dark. It was a fire and and an emergency - that's all they were told.

Four o'clock, five, six. I waited impatiently until it was broad daylight.

At six that day we were supposed to go to my parents' house to plant potatoes. It was forty kilometres from the barracks. Sowing, ploughing, and planting things - he loved doing that. Sometimes it's as though I hear his voice, still alive. Even photographs or his old clothes don't have the same enlivening effect on me as that wonderful voice. But he never says anything and he never calls out to me, not even in my dreams. I am the one who calls to him.

Seven o'clock, eight and nine. I waited longer. Then I couldn't wait any longer. I had to know what was happening.

At the barracks they informed me that he had been taken to the hospital. I went there as quickly as possible, but the militia had already surrounded it and blocked all the entrances, and they weren't letting anyone through, only doctors and ambulances.

A militiaman shouted, "The ambulances are very dangerous. Stay away!"

There were lots of us there - all the wives of the men who had responded to the fire at the reactor were there. I started looking for Lyudmila, a friend of mine who was a consultant at the hospital. I noticed her getting out of an ambulance.

"Luda, please, get me inside."

"I can't, I just can't. He's bad - they all are."

I held on to her. "I just need to see him."

"Alright," she said, "come with me just for ten minutes."

I saw Yuri. He face was all swollen and puffed up like a balloon or as if he'd been stung by a thousand bees. I could not see his eyes.

"He needs milk, lots of milk," Luda said. "They should drink at least five or six litres a day."

"But he doesn't like milk."

"He'll like it now. Or he'll die."

Most of the doctors and nurses in the hospital and especially the orderlies later got sick themselves and died. But we didn't know that then. They kept it dark.

At eleven in the morning the unit's officer died. He was the first - on the very first day. We learnt later that another officer had been left in the debris. They never did reach him. He's buried under the concrete and we didn't know then, but they were just the first of so many.

I said, "Oh Yuri, what on earth can I do?"

"Go, Sveta. Go – get out of this place and don't come back. You have our baby to think of."

But how could I leave him? He's telling me, "Go! Get out! Think of our child."

"First I have to find some milk for you. Then we'll decide what to do."

My friend Tanya came running in; her husband, Ivan was in the same ward. Her dad drove us in his car to the nearest shop to buy some milk. It was out of town in a village about ten kilometres from the hospital. We deliberately avoided town because we knew everyone would be looking for milk. We bought six three litre bottles, so that it was enough for everyone.

But they started throwing up the milk. They just kept passing out until they put them on drips. The doctors kept telling us they had been poisoned by fumes, by inhaling: no-one said anything about radiation. Not a word.

By now it must have been early afternoon. The barracks was inundated with more soldiers brought in from Minsk. They closed off all the roads. In the town the trolley buses stopped running and the trains. They were washing the streets with some white powder. I worried about getting to the shop in the village the next day to buy some more fresh milk. No one talked about the radiation. The people in town were carrying bread from the stores, just open sacks with loaves in them.

It was impossible for me to get into the hospital to see Yuri that evening. There was a huge crowd of people. I stood under the windows of the ward he was on. Yuri put his head out of the window and shouted something to me: I couldn't hear him because the crowd were so noisy – they just wanted the truth. It was all so desperately chaotic. Someone in the crowd heard him. The rumour was that they were being taken to a different hospital in Moscow that night. All the wives grouped together and decided we would go with them.

"Let us go with our husbands. We must go with our husbands."

We punched and clawed. The soldiers, not from the barracks, pushed us back. Then one of the top doctors emerged and announced that they were being transferred to Moscow on a special flight and we had to go home to get their toiletries and their clothes. The uniforms they had worn at the reactor had been burned. I came running back with Yuri's suitcase, but the plane was already gone. They tricked us. So we wouldn't be there yelling and crying.

It was night and along one side of the street there were buses, hundreds of buses: they were already preparing the town for evacuation. On the other side, hundreds of trucks full of soldiers. They'd come from all over and the whole town was covered in white foam. All the women and children were cursing and crying.

On the radio they told us they might evacuate the city for three to five days and so we should take our warm clothes because we would be living in the forest in tents. People were glad - a camping trip! We would celebrate May Day like that - a break from routine. I saw people getting their barbecues ready, taking their guitars with them, their radios, but the women whose husbands had been at the reactor were crying.

I can't remember the trip out to my parents' village. It was as if I didn't wake up until I saw my mother.

"Mother, Yuri is in Moscow; they flew him out in a special plane."

But we finished planting the garden, all the new seeds, new life. A week later that village was evacuated too. Who knew? Who knew back then? Who knew that a village forty kilometres away from the reactor would be evacuated?

Later that day I started throwing up. I was six months pregnant. I felt awful. That night I dreamed he was calling out to me in his sleep.

"Sveta, Sveta," but after he died, he didn't call out in my dreams any more. Not once.

I awoke the following morning with one obsessive thought in my mind: I must get to Moscow, by myself, somehow. I needed to be with him.

My mother was crying, "Where are you going? How can you leave us?"

So I took my father with me. He went to the nearest bank and withdrew almost all the money he had. I can't remember the trip. Except that it was on the train. In Moscow I just asked the first police officer I saw where they had taken the men from Chernobyl. And he told us. Hospital No 6 near the Shukinstaya station.

It was obviously some special hospital and they only allowed certain people in. I gave a bundle of notes to the man who guarded the door and he said, "OK. You can go in." Then I had to pay someone else, and beg and scrape and grovel – just to see my own husband. Finally I made it to the office of the Head Radiologist, but I didn't know then because the truth was being kept dark. I simply knew I had to see Yuri.

Right away she asked, "Do you have other kids?"

What shall I tell her? It was obvious I was pregnant, but they wouldn't let me see him. I decided to lie.

"This one will be my third. I've already got a boy and a girl."

"Ah good, you don't need to have any more. Alright listen - his central nervous system is totally demolished. His brain and his skull are completely compromised."

I didn't really understand what would mean. Would he be a bit fidgety? A bit bad tempered? Will he have a headache?

"Listen," the doctor continued. "If you start crying we will have you kicked out immediately. No cuddling or canoodling. Don't get too close to him. You've got fifteen minutes."

But at that moment I decided that I wasn't leaving. *If I leave then it will be with Yuri*, I swore to myself. I went in and they were sitting on the bed, playing cards and laughing.

"Sveta!" they called out.

Yuri turned around and joked, "Now it's over - even here she found me."

He looked funny. He had pyjamas on for a size 48 but he's 52. The sleeves were too short, the trousers were too short. But his face wasn't swollen any more.

"Where did you run off to Yuri?"

He wanted to hug me, but the nurses wouldn't let him.

"Just sit and talk," one nurse said. "No hanky panky in here."

We tried to turn it into a joke – like being on a first date. And then all the Chernobyl men came over. Everyone from the barracks - many of the soldiers I knew. There were twenty-eight of them on the plane apparently.

"What's going on?"

"How are things in town?"

I told them they had begun evacuating everyone. The whole town was being cleared for three or five days.

"Oh, my God! My wife and kids are there! What's happening with them?" someone asked. But I had no answers.

I wanted so much to be with Yuri alone, if only for a minute. The other guys felt it and gradually they dreamt up some excuse to leave the ward and we were left on our own. Then I kissed him, but he moved away.

"Come and sit near me. Get a chair."

"That's just silly," I said.

"Did you see the explosion? Did you see what happened?"

"You were the first one saved."

"There was probably sabotage. Someone set it up. All the guys think so."

That's what people were saying then. That's what they thought. That's what they believed. The truth was too dark to see.

The next day they were lying by themselves, each in isolation, each in his own room. They were banned from going in the hall-way, banned from communicating with each other. They tapped on the walls with their fingers, in Morse code. The doctors had explained that everyone's body reacts differently to radiation. One person can handle what another can't. They even measured the radiation in the walls where they had them, in the wards to the right and the wards to the left, and the floor beneath. They moved out all the sick people from the floor beneath and the floor above: and all these wards were evacuated, so that the hospital seemed deserted, apart from the soldiers from Chernobyl.

For a week I lived with my friends in Moscow.

They kept saying, "Take the pots. Take the plates. Take whatever you need."

I made turkey soup for six, for six of the soldiers from the same unit. I went to the shop and bought them toothpaste and tooth-brushes and soap. They didn't have any of that at the hospital. I bought them towels, flannels, toilet paper. Looking back I'm surprised by my friends. They were afraid, of course, how could they not be? There were rumours already, but still they kept saying, "Take whatever you need. Take it. How is he? How are they all? Will they live?"

Live? I met a lot of good people then. Good, naïve people who believed what they were told. I can't remember all of them. I remember an old woman janitor at the hospital who said, "There are some sicknesses that cannot be cured. You just have to sit and watch them die."

Every day I saw a change in him: every day I met a new man - the burns started to come to the surface - in his mouth, on his tongue and his cheeks. At first they were little scars and then they grew; his skin started coming off in layers, a thick white scum peeling from his face; his body covered in blotches of blue, black, red, yellow, grey and brown. It's impossible to describe; it's impossible to speak of it.

The one thing that kept me going and kept me sane was that what happened to Yuri happened so quickly. There wasn't any time to think; there wasn't any time to cry. I loved him, but I had no idea how much.

It gradually dawned on me it was a hospital for people with acute radiation poisoning. Fourteen days they say - in fourteen days a person dies. On the very first day in the dormitory they measured me for radiation. My clothes, my bag, my purse, my shoes. They were all contaminated. And they took it all away, even my bra and pants. The only thing they left was my money. In exchange they gave me a hospital robe and some slippers. They said they would return the clothes, maybe, or maybe they wouldn't since they might not be possible to clean at this point.

That's how I looked when I came to visit him. He laughed.

"Woman, what's wrong with you?"

But I was still able to make him some soup. I boiled the water in a glass jar and I threw pieces of chicken in there, tiny, tiny pieces and then someone gave me her pot. I think it was one of the cleaners. Someone else gave me a cutting board for chopping the parsley and, because I couldn't go to the market in my hospital robe, people would bring me vegetables, but it was all futile. He couldn't drink or eat; he could barely swallow water. And I wanted to get him something tasty – Huh! As if it mattered.

Nothing mattered any more.

Imagine a hell that is black.

That's how it felt: black hell.

Chapter Twenty: Tommy X

I hate Christmas. Fucking hate it. And that one was one of the best and the worst. No, not because I'm Scrooge, and, as the song says, I wish it could be Christmas every day, in many ways, but I hate the institution. I hate the fact that no one told me at my little Church of England Primary School that it had always been a pagan mid-winter festival that had occurred for tens of thousands of years all over Europe because it's the middle of the winter and you need to cheer yourself up. I hate the fact that in the supermarkets the Christmas stuff appears on what? - November 1st? - as soon as Halloween is out of the way. I hate Halloween too, but more of that later. Christmas is good for children. Their smiles and shrieks of delight, as they open their presents, especially the presents from that mysterious stranger, Santa Claus. Father Christmas, the man in (it has to be) - red. People don't look around them. The messages are all there: Santa Claus is in red and on the Underground, it says "Keep Left." Do we pay attention? We should obey the hidden messages that we are being given by our culture.

But we don't, so Christmas…. the forced jollity, the jokes from the crackers which I love and loathe in equal measure. Too many Christmases that I can't remember because of alcohol. Too many Christmases that were simply boring and not memorable, just another day. And where do we live and die but days?

But this Christmas, the one I'm talking about, was very memorable, as you will see.

Halloween – well, I'd heard of it, of course. It was an American thing and I'm not sure when it came back to us and I've got nothing, in principle (I wouldn't have, would I?) against the idea of a night devoted to misrule. I'd just prefer that it was on May 1st or International Women's Day - we don't celebrate those much do we? But we should.

So Halloween, an American import. Was it the '90s when they started selling Halloween stuff in our supermarkets? I can't remember - so many changes. When I was growing up, you knew where you were. Christmas, Easter, Mother's Day – oh, and I suppose Valentine's Day, if you're being picky, but now we are surrounded by Hallmark Holidays.

What can we sell the gullible buggers next? I know, let's take Halloween back to the United Kingdom and so now we have a Father's Day when people spend money they can't afford on presents and cards and then Grandfathers' Days, Stepfathers' Days, Step Grandparents' Days, Second Cousin Twice Removed Days.

A Someone I Once Shagged at a Party Day.

I checked some of this on-line. I knew there would be a National Cheese Week; I knew there'd be a National Potato Week, but when you look at it, every day, every sodding day of the year is hiked to some hyped commercialized enterprise. A National Marmite Day. A Bacon Sandwich Week. There is even a National Bad Cold Day. What, I thought, is that a good time to catch one? To pass it on? To have it cured? Be more precise. Be more specific. What do you mean?

So if I were constructing our year I'd be slightly different. I'd go for different dates, different weeks. January 27th, obviously; May 1st, obviously. So we could have an annual rota of celebration which would include – what? – January 30th, February 2nd, February 4th, April 12th, May 9th, June 25th, July 23rd, August 19th, August 28th, October 23rd November 20th, December 22nd, and, by the same token, we'd have national days of mourning and these should be updated, not tied to the religious customs of a late Bronze Age tribe from the Middle East or even their later Islamic brethren and that would include January 27th, February 11th, April 23rd August 16th, – oh, and 23rd March, although that last one, I know, is controversial. And these could be updated - it would encourage people to learn history, to reassess things. Gotta keep moving, man. Out of our grooves, sunshine.

Do you know I'd forgotten November 5th, but then I don't think that matters? Most people I've come across recently think it's some anti-parliamentary occasion, and don't realize that it's actually a celebration of anti-Catholicism and that Guy Fawkes was all for a theocracy run from Rome.

Fantastico! Fucking fantastico! They must have thought in the sleazy men-only bars in the Vatican City when old Guy's text came through and they were sipping their sambucas:

"Am in basement with gunpowder. About to light fuse. LOL ☺ ☺ ☺ ROFL."

Well, that's how I remember it from school. And I bet someone, some flunky, had to break it to the Pope: "No, it means 'laugh out loud', Your Holiness – not 'lots of love'." On some things the people at the top are more in the dark than the rest of us.

And Christmas is so predictable – the same story, no plot development at all. The same unheeded message of love and peace to all people, the same hastily-bought and vaguely inappropriate presents, the same patronizing attitudes to the rural working class, the credulous shepherds. Just once I'd like to see a Nativity play where Mary demands an epidural NOW, where Jesus is given a plastic toy Kalashnikov with moving trigger, and where someone has the bollocks to intervene and say, "Hang on! Just what the fuck is myrrh?" And in which someone remembers Joseph – whose wife has, after all, played away with a bleeding angel of the Lord – and gives him some pathetic, propitiatory socks or a DVD of the 2005 Ashes series. Or a "Best Step-Dad in the World" mug. Or an "I ♥ Nazareth" hoodie.

Anyway that Christmas… a mixed day shall we say? It started badly when I mentioned that we had no cranberry jelly. Funny isn't it - that a marriage can turn on cranberry jelly? What made it worse was that my mother, who lived a short distance away, had some and I didn't realize quite how hurtful it was to get cranberry jelly from my mother to have with my turkey that day. It wasn't meant to be hurtful. In many ways I'm a simple boy: I just wanted some cranberry jelly with my turkey, but that set the mood for the day. Northern chip shops, boulangèries, cranberry jelly – it's been an uphill struggle, I can tell you.

Sue's parents were coming for lunch. Sue was a good cook, well-organized, good mother, great gardener, fantastic in the kitchen, crap everywhere else. But not as crap as me, it turned out. One o'clock came round and Christmas dinner was for one o'clock and it was ready and I had to go, but I didn't want to go.

What I also hate about Christmas Day is that the news is only five minutes long as though nothing happens in the world that is worthy of our attention on Christmas Day. So had I watched the news, I would have been five minutes late for Christmas dinner and I did watch the news. I watched the news. I couldn't tear myself away from it. There was footage of an evil dictator being gunned down by his people, an evil dictator and his wife machine-gunned down, and this act in that year of tumbling walls was the final icing on the cake for freedom. Or so it seemed at the time. Just a transfer of power really. Our own walls haven't even started to crumble. They are as strong and as high as they ever were. Where's Robin Hood when you need him? Probably being renditioned as I write this. Or water-boarded.

"Tommy, are you coming? The dinner's ready."

"I'm sorry. Something really important is happening. I'm watching it now."

"It's the news. You can see the news later."

"No, I can't. There's only five minutes and there's not another one 'til ten o'clock this evening. I want to see what happens."

"But my parents are here."

"Your parents should understand this is more important than Christmas dinner. It's changing the world."

"Tommy, come now or I will never forgive you."

"You'll never forgive me, for being slightly late for Christmas Dinner because your parents are here? I think you've got your priorities wrong."

"Well, they're better than yours. You have no priorities at all. No money, no proper job, sitting around all day pretending it's work. I've just about had it with you."

"The feeling is mutual."

And so thousands of miles away from Eastern Europe I effectively machine gunned what remained of my flimsy marriage to Sue in my obstinacy and pride. There were other things too. Infidelity, extra marital affairs, a bit on the side, playing away - I hate those anodyne or jokey phrases because they are so far from the reality of what happens, so far from the nitty, gritty, physical reality of what happens and also so far from the feelings, the zest, the excitement, the breaking of taboos and then, forever it seems, the guilt, the betrayal, the remorse, the treachery, and the subsequent sinking sense of self-worth.

Some things probably are best kept dark.

But I will say this: such was my confidence, such was my renewed zest for life, that I really thought I could behave so atrociously, so immorally, so selfishly, so hurtfully, so egregiously, and that my children, with whom I had such a close relationship, would continue to love me in exactly the same way.

Don't be fooled. Learn from my story: they will never love you in the same way.

And in their eyes, the eyes of the children you rocked to sleep in your arms, in the eyes of the children whom you spoke to in their first moments of life, in the eyes of the children that you would do anything for, anything except remain faithful to their mother, there lurks an eternal glance of reproach. A flicker of distrust. It will make you cry in your heart forever. It will shake every blood cell with self-loathing and self-disgust.

I always thought I had a good imagination, but I couldn't imagine the effect it would have on my children. I couldn't imagine the many tears that Sue and they would cry in the days and nights and weeks and months and years after I'd abandoned them. Now I feel like Marvell's Mower.

I have so displaced my heart and mind that I will never find my home, even with a map.

Chapter Twenty-One: Ilya

I felt as if I were a free person when I got home from Afghanistan, and, in a strange way, even freer after Chernobyl. When I got posted there, along with my brother, I thought, *Great! An easy billet! That'll do me!* Maybe it was different for Yuri – he was married and was soon to become a father when the reactor blew. I still find it hard to look Sveta, his widow and my sister-in-law, in the eye.

Feeling completely free - that's not something you can understand I expect, something only someone who's been in a war can understand. I've seen them, those men - they get drunk and they start talking about how they still miss it - the freedom, the fights. *Not one step backward,* Stalin's order. The Glorious Red Army - yes, but you shoot, you kill, you survive. You receive the one hundred grams you're entitled to, a pouch of cheap tobacco. But now I think there are better ways to live. No – I know there are better ways to live.

There are a thousand ways for you to die, to get blown to bits, but if you try hard enough you can trick them: the devil, the senior officers, the combatants, the one who's in that coffin with that wound, even God! You can trick them all and survive. I survived Afghanistan and Chernobyl, but my brother Yuri didn't. There's a loneliness to freedom. I know it.

All the ones who were at the reactor know it. Like in a trench at the very front, fear and freedom, so you live for everything, everything that can give you the slightest pleasure. That's not something those who live an ordinary life can understand.

Remember how they were always preparing us for war against the Americans, but it turned out our minds weren't ready: that there were more immediate dangers closer to home. I wasn't ready. Two officers came up to me and picked me out. This was a couple of days after the reactor first went up: I knew my brother was one of the first in, but I had no idea where he was exactly or what he had been doing or what might have happened to him. I only found out much later. It was all kept very dark.

"Can you tell the difference between gasoline and diesel?"

I said, "Where are you sending me?"

"What do you mean where? You are a volunteer for Chernobyl."

They took me straight from the barracks; they didn't even let me go home.

I said, "I have to let my mother know."

"We'll tell her ourselves."

There were about fifteen of us on the bus. I liked them. If we had to go, if we were ordered to go - we went. If it was needed, we worked. If they told us to go to the reactor, we got on the roof of the reactor. *We are here,* I thought. If not us, then who?

Near the evacuated villages they'd set up elevated guard posts. The soldiers sat there with their rifles. There were barriers with signs that said:

"The roadside is contaminated. Stopping or leaving your vehicle is strictly forbidden."

Grey trees were covered with decontamination liquid. I thought I was going insane. In first few weeks we were all afraid to sit down on the grass or pick the flowers. We didn't walk anywhere - we ran. If a car passed, we would put on the gas masks right away for the dust. After our shifts, we would sit in the tents.

After a few months it all seemed normal. It was just where we lived. We took plums off the trees, caught fish, put out simple snares for rabbits. The pike there were incredible. People have probably told you about this already. We played football. We went swimming. We believed in fate. At bottom all soldiers are fatalists, not pharmacists. We are not rational: it's the Slavic mind-set. I believed in my fate. I was there; if not me, then who?

Ha! Now I'm an invalid of the second category. I got sick soon afterwards. Radiation poisoning. I'd never even been to the doctor before. Hah, I'm not the only one. I was a soldier. I killed other people; I was the bringer of death.

It's a strange feeling - land that you can't plant on. The cow butts its head against the gate, but it's closed and the house is locked. Its milk drips to the ground. In the villages that hadn't been evacuated yet, the farmers made vodka. They'd sell it to us and I tell you we had lots of money, three times our salary as a danger bonus plus three times the normal daily military allowance for being away from barracks. Later on we got an order – whoever drinks can stay a second term. So we are thinking, "Does the vodka help or what?" Well, at least psychologically it helps, I can tell you. We believed that as much as we believed anything, and I tell you we believed nothing.

And the farmers' life goes on very smoothly: they plant something; it grows; they harvest it. And they eat it or they sell it and the rest of nature - it just goes on without them. They don't have anything to do with a Tsar or a Commissar, with spaceships and nuclear power plants, with meetings of the politburo and the poor farmers couldn't believe they were now living in a different world, the world of Chernobyl. They hadn't gone anywhere; they hadn't done anything. People died of shock; they took seeds with them; they took green potatoes, wrapped them up.

And we'd arrive and they'd say, "What do you mean destroy, bury, turn everything into rubbish? Burn everything?"

But that's exactly what we did. We destroyed their labour, the ancient meaning of their lives. We were their enemies.

I wanted to go to the reactor.

"Don't worry!" the others told me. "In your last months before demobilization they put you all on the roof."

We were there six months and right on schedule after five months of evacuating people and destroying farm buildings and shooting animals, we were sent to the reactor. There were jokes and serious conversations, but we knew we were being sent to the roof. Well, after that maybe we'd live another five years or seven or maybe ten, but five years was what most people said most often for some reason. Where did they get that from? They said it quietly without panicking.

In the morning there was a shout: "Volunteers! Forward - march!"

In our whole squadron, every individual stepped forward. Our commander had a monitor. He turned it on and showed the roof of the reactor: pieces of graphite, melted bitumen, a chaos of twisted metal.

"See those, boys. See those bits up there - you need to clean those up and here in this quadrant is where you make the hole."

We were supposed to be up there forty, fifty seconds maximum, but that was impossible. You needed a few minutes at least. You had to get up there and back. You had to run up and throw the stuff down. One guy would load the wheelbarrow; the others would throw the stuff into the hole there. You threw and went back: you didn't look down - that wasn't allowed. The newspapers wrote, "The air in the area of the reactor is not hazardous to human health." We'd read it and laugh and then curse a little. The air looked clean, but I tell you we got some serious dosage up there. They gave us dosimeters: one was for five roentgens and it went to the maximum right away. The other one was bigger: it was for two hundred roentgens and that too went off. Five years, they said, and you can't have kids. If you don't die after five years - well, you can do anything. That's what they said.

There were all kinds of jokes, but said quietly and without panic.

I even saw with my very own eyes, one very old lady, sitting by the roadside selling mushrooms.

"Chernobyl mushrooms! Chernobyl mushrooms!"

I stopped and said to her, "Granny, who in their right mind is going to buy your mushrooms?"

"Lots of people," she smiled back at me. "Lots of people got mothers-in-law. Lots of people got bosses."

I had to laugh.

Five years, they were saying. Huh! I've already lived ten. They gave us medals, and all the pictures - Marx, Engels, Lenin.

One guy disappeared. We figured he'd run off, but then two days later we found him in the bushes. He'd hanged himself. Everyone had this feeling you understand, but then a political officer spoke. He said the guy had received a letter. His wife was cheating on him, but who knows - maybe that was just a story to keep us quiet. A week later we were demobilized.

The papers are full of lies. I didn't read anywhere about how we sewed ourselves up in protective gear, lead shirts, and underwear. We had rubber robes with lead in them, but we made lead underwear for ourselves. We made sure of that.

In one village they showed us two whore houses. We were men who had been torn away from our homes for six months. Six months without women. It was an emergency situation. We all went there. The local girls would walk around all tarted up even though they were crying, because they knew they'd all die soon.

We had some really excellent jokes too.

Here's one:

An American robot is on the roof of the reactor for five minutes; then it breaks down, so they put the Japanese robot up. The Japanese robot is on the roof for five minutes and then it breaks down. Then they put the Russian robot up there. It's up there for two hours and it's still working and then it hears a voice coming over the loud speaker. "Comrade Private Ivanov, another two hours and you're welcome to come down and have a cigarette break."

Or this one:

"Heard the weather forecast for Chernobyl?"

"No."

"Eight thousand degrees and very, very cloudy."

Where would we be without laughter?

Chapter Twenty-Two: Tommy XI

"Dad, dad, tell us a story!" Samantha urged.

"What's the magic word?"

"Please."

"OK."

One day Peter was sent to the shops by his mum. She asked him to get six porcupines, five elephants, four Jack Russell terriers, three talking parrots, two space rockets and a banana.

"Ah, how can you remember that, dad?" Seth asked, entirely reasonably to my mind.

"You have to pay attention, so if I don't remember you can tell me, OK?"

It was my weekend with the children. I was living in a rather squalid, single bedroom, struggling with money as usual and finding it hard to keep up the pretence of normality, but it was my own fault. Mea culpa. Mea maxima culpa.

So Peter walked purposefully down the road, and as he passed the park he saw in the distance six porcupines. He ran up to them excitedly.

'Excuse me, my mum has sent me to the shops to get six porcupines. Would you mind getting in my shopping bag?'

And the porcupines did.

"Dad, Mum says that you don't love her anymore."

"Well, Sam, she's right in a sense, when grownups don't love each other anymore sometimes.... sometimes they can't stand to live with each other."

"Dad, will you always love us?"

"Yes, I'll always love you, you know that, and I'll always tell you stories. When you're adults, when you're grown up, then you may understand."

That was a lie - there was no understanding it. I've grown up a lot since then and, you know, I still don't understand it, so – I was lying as usual, the usual me.

Peter walked happily on down the road towards the shops. As he passed the garage he saw, in amongst the cars for sale, five very big grey shapes. Can you guess what they were?

"Elephants."

Yes, they were elephants. He rushed up to them and said, 'Excuse me, my mum has sent me to the shop to buy five elephants. Would you mind getting in my shopping bag?'

And the elephants did.

I broke off.

"Hold on kids! Hold on! What's on the television? I'll carry on with the story in a sec, but what's he saying?"

'Friends, comrades and fellow South Africans I greet you all in the name of peace, democracy and freedom for all.'

"Oh come on, Dad, get on with the story."

"Hang on! Hang on! This is important."

'I stand here before you not as a prophet but as a humble servant of you, the people. Your tireless and heroic sacrifices have made it possible for me to be here today. I therefore place the remaining years of life, my life in your hands.'

"Oh come on, Dad."

"OK."

As Peter walked along the pavement he passed an old lady with a dog when, suddenly, from a nearby tree four small, hairy and mainly white creatures were leaping around playfully. Can you guess what they were?

"Jack Russell terriers!"

"That's right."

They were four Jack Russell terriers. Asking politely, Peter asked if they would mind getting in to his shopping bag and, because they were polite and well-brought-up pooches, they happily did so. By now the shopping bag was getting quite heavy, but Peter pressed on....

"Hold on, hold on what's he saying?"

'I salute the rank and file members of the ANC. You have sacrificed life and limb in the pursuit of the noble cause of our struggle.'

"Oh, come on, Dad, the story! The story!"

With his heavy shopping bag Peter pressed onwards. As he was passing Tesco he heard a strange sound. Three strange voices were apparently calling out his name.

'Peter, Peter, is that you?'

He looked up and saw a strange sight: three talking parrots were perched on a shopping trolley.

'Hello,' said Peter.

'Hello,' said the three parrots.

"Hang on! Hang on!"

'I salute the South African Communist Party for its sterling contribution to the struggle for democracy. You have survived forty years of unrelenting persecution. The memory of great communists like Moses Kotarna, Yusef Dadu, Bram Fisher and Moses Mabiba will be cherished for generations to come'

"Oh come on, dad, come on - what did the parrots say?"

The parrots said, 'Peter, we know all about your mission to the shops and, yes, we will happily get in your shopping bag. In fact, because it is so heavy we will perch on your shoulder and - don't worry, Peter, we will do the talking at the next place we come to.'

As you can see I was really making it up at this stage. I was torn between the desire to entertain and amuse, however poorly, my children, and the desire to hear what was being said all those thousands of miles away in Cape Town.

Peter pressed on with his heavy shopping bag and with the three parrots, one on each shoulder and the third perched on his head. A little further down the road they passed the duck pond and a man in a shiny suit waved from behind a tree.

Mmm! thought Peter. I wonder what he wants.

With his shopping bag still very heavy, and the three parrots perched on his shoulders and his head, he wandered over to the tree.

"Hang on, kids."

'I extend my greetings to the working class of our country. Your organized strength is the pride of our movement. You remain the most dependable force in the struggle to end exploitation and oppression.'

"Who was it? What did he say?"

"Well, remember he was a man in a shiny suit and he had a helmet on?"

"Ah, an astronaut."

"Well, actually he was a cosmonaut. It's the same sort of thing."

Yes, dear reader, you can count on my pedantry even with the under-sixes.

Peter said, "Hello! Welcome to this planet! I'm on the way to the shops for my mum and I have to get two space rockets. Is there any chance you could help me?"

'Perhaps,' said the man in the shiny suit and the helmet. Then he nodded and he beckoned Peter behind the tree. Now what do you expect Peter found behind the tree?

"Two space rockets!"

"Yes, two space rockets."

This was quite a relief to Peter because he'd got nearly all the things on his mum's list and the space rockets would make getting home so much quicker.

"Dad, Mum says the lawn needs mowing."

"Well, tell her I'll be round next weekend to cut it, if it's not raining."

"She also says the car needs fixing."

"OK, I'll arrange for it to go into a garage. Shall I finish the story?"

"No, let's listen to the man."

"Yes, we should. When you're older you might remember that we sat here this afternoon and listened to this man. He's very important - a very great man."

'I pay tribute to the mothers and wives and sisters of our nation. You are the rock-hard foundation of our struggle. Apartheid has inflicted more pain on you than on anyone else. On this occasion we thank the world community for their great contribution to the anti-apartheid struggle. Without your support our struggle would not have reached this advanced stage. The sacrifice of the front line states will be remembered by South Africans for ever.'

"More of the story, more of the story, Dad."

"OK - where was I?"

"Peter just got the two space rockets from the astronaut."

"Cosmonaut."

"Yes, from the cosmonaut."

"Right."

Peter put his shopping bag in one space rocket and he put himself and the three parrots in the other. He pressed the button and both space rockets took off. A Jack Russell terrier was driving the second one. As they flew above the town they could see for miles. They saw the whole earth stretched out before them. It was so beautiful. Everywhere people teemed around. From this distance they seemed at peace, in harmony and happy.

Suddenly Peter saw a blur of yellow out of the corner of his eye. It was a huge banana grove, on Banana Island. Very quickly he and Tilly, the most intelligent of the Jack Russell terriers, landed the two space rockets and everyone got out.

'Gosh!' said one of the parrots 'There are so many bananas here.'

'Yes,' said another parrot, 'that's probably why it's called Banana Island.'

'How do you know it's called Banana Island?' said Peter.

'Because that's what the sign says.'

'Even we can tell that!" chorused the terriers.

And it was true, there was a huge sign. Black writing on a yellow background. 'This is Banana Island! Please help yourself.'

'Aren't we lucky?' said Peter. 'There's only one banana on mum's shopping list. But I think she would like us to take a few more.'

So he filled up the second space rocket with as many bananas as they could find. There must have been at least a hundred. When they were ready the two space rockets took off and headed home.

'Oh dear,' said Peter, 'I don't know the way home.'

'Don't worry!' said the parrot on his head. 'We know the way home. We know everything; we will guide you.'

And they did and Peter arrived home with all the things on his mother's shopping list and some extra bananas.

"Oh Dad, that was such a good story,"

But it was only a story. You don't always find your way home, that much I've learnt. I watched the television and listened carefully.

'I have fought against white domination and I have fought against black domination. I have cherished the ideal of a democratic and free society in which all persons live together in harmony and with equal opportunities. It is an ideal which I hope to live for and to achieve. But if needs be it is an ideal for which I am prepared to die.'

Now that was a man not practising to be a man, like I was still, but a real man.

When you abandon your home and your family, you can't expect to be a man any more.

"Dad," said Seth. "What's a cosmonaut exactly?"

Chapter Twenty-Three: Olga II

What do I pray for? Not much. I hardly pray these days anyway. I certainly never pray in Church. I pray to something I can't describe – a spirit of the past perhaps or a spirit of humanity. I only want to love. Is that too much to pray for? Yes, I pray for love. Am I allowed to remember or is it prohibited? Perhaps I should just keep it dark instead, just in case. I've never read any books about what happened. I've never seen any films about it. At the cinema I saw films about the war – a war you can understand. The Great Patriotic War. My mum's mother and father remembered that they never had a proper childhood. But they had the war. My dad's mum and dad both died in the war. I have this living death.

Their lives were defined by the war and mine by Chernobyl. That's where I'm from. Or at least that is where I was living in 1986 – only because my brothers Ilya and Yuri had both been transferred after they returned from Afghanistan and were in a barracks near town. They were all the family I had left. So mum and I moved to be near to Ilya and Yuri – who was one of the first to the reactor. Yuri died in fourteen days; Ilya lived until 1998. Where's the logic in that? And Yuri was married.

No book has helped me to understand it. The theatre has not helped and the movies have not helped, but I understand it without them though - by myself. We all find ways to live through it by ourselves. What else is there to do? I can't understand it with my mind, but my mother especially was confused. She used to teach Russian literature and she always taught me to live with books because books and culture are important, but there are no books and no films about this. She became confused. She didn't know how to do anything without books. She didn't know how to feel.

"How can you live without Chekov and Tolstoy?" she says. "Am I supposed to remember? I want to remember. But if the experts don't understand and even the writers don't understand, then they can't help us with our own lives, with our own deaths."

That's what my mum said. I think they understand all right – they're just keeping it dark.

But I don't want to think about this. I want to be happy. I lived in Pripyat, near the nuclear station. It was a big prefab apartment building on the fifth floor. The windows looked out on to the station. On April 26th there were two days left. Those were the last two days in our town. The last two days of its existence.

It's not there anymore. What's left there isn't our town. That day a neighbour was sitting on the balcony watching the fire through binoculars when Mum and I ran down to the barracks as quickly as we could to find out what was going on. No one yelled at us not to go, no one, not the militia, not the soldiers. By lunchtime there weren't any fishermen at the river. They'd come back black. You can't get that black in a month in the Crimea. It was a nuclear town.

The smoke over the station wasn't black or yellow; it was bright blue. But no one yelled at us. People were used to military dangers. An explosion over here, an explosion over there. Whereas here you had what seemed to be an ordinary fire being put out by ordinary soldiers.

The lads were joking around:

"Get in a row at the cemetery. Whoever is tallest, dies first."

I was only twenty-six. I don't remember the feeling but I remember lots of weird things. My friend told me that she and her mother spent the night burying their money and gold things and were worried they would forget the spot.

We were evacuated. My sister-in-law, Svetlana, brought that news home from the hospital where they'd taken Yuri. It was just like in the war books. We were already on the bus, when my sister-in-law remembered she had left something. She ran home and came back with two of her new blouses still on their hangers. That was strange. Sveta eventually ended up in Moscow where Yuri was being treated: he was one of the first to the reactor. Ilya went later and lived much longer, as I've said.

The soldiers looked like sort of aliens. They walked through the streets in their protective gear and masks.

"What's going to happen to us?" people were asking.

Why are you asking us? I thought. *We know nothing.*

They'd just step back.

"The big white Volgas are over there. That's where the bosses are. Ask them."

We were riding on the bus. The sky was blue as a duck egg. *Where are we going?* We had Easter cakes and coloured eggs in our bags and baskets. *If this is war,* I thought, *it's not how I imagined it from the books and the movies.* There should have been explosions over here, over there, bombing. It's not even how it was in Afghanistan, I remember thinking.

We were moving slowly - the livestock was in the way. People were chasing cows and horses down the roads. It smelt of dust and horse muck and milk. The drivers were cursing and yelling at the shepherds.

"Why are you on the road with those? You're kicking up the radioactive dust. Why don't you take them through the fields?"

And the shepherds cursed back that it would be a shame to trample all the rye and grass. No one thought we'd never come back; nothing like this had ever happened. My head was spinning a little and my throat tickled. The old women weren't crying, but the younger ones were. My mother was crying.

We got to Minsk. We had to buy our seats on the train at triple the usual price. The conductor brought everyone tea, but to us she said, "Let me have your cups." We didn't understand it right away. Had they run out of cups? No. They were afraid of us.

Where are you from?

Chernobyl.

And they rushed away.

After a month my mother was allowed back to the apartment. She got a warm blanket, my winter coat, the collected works of Chekov, and all her copies of Tolstoy. She couldn't understand why they didn't let her take the cans of strawberry jam that she'd made. And you know, I think she never got used to that. She certainly couldn't get used to the new place. She missed our old home. Within a year, we had buried her in her old village. It was in the danger zone, so there was barbed wire and soldiers with machine guns guarding it.

I realized then with a terrible feeling of bereftness that I will never ever be able to put flowers on my own mother's grave. I understood why I can't, but where can you read about that? Where has that ever happened? At the cemetery on the grass, after the funeral, they put down a tablecloth and placed some food and vodka on it for the wake. The soldiers scampered over with the dosimeter – which reads the radiation levels. They threw everything out - the grass, the flowers, the food - because everything was clicking away like a bomb. They took their chance with the vodka, and I don't blame them. And that's where mum's buried.

I'm too afraid. I'm afraid to love. And that is the worst feeling.

Have you heard of the poor hibokusha of Hiroshima? The ones who survived the bomb. They could or would only marry each other. No one writes about it or about us or about what happened here. No one even talks about it. But we are here. We exist. The Chernobyl hibokusha.

For some people it's a sin to give birth. It's a sin to love. Do you know how it can possibly be a sin to give birth? I've never heard it put exactly like that before. How can we live without love and without birth? How can we live without Chekov and Tolstoy? And why would we want to?

Didn't someone once say, "Love is not what we find; love is what we do"? But I feel I can do nothing.

I think I will try to adopt. Try to live again. Have a daughter to love.

We are here, but we cannot love and so we cannot live. And without love – I don't feel as if I exist anymore.

Chapter Twenty-Four: Tommy XII

Dobroye utro! Once again it had come out of the blue.

That Easter Jack had just said, "Tommy what are you doing in July? Can you take some time off to go on a trip with me?" And what could I say but yes?

Sue had the children, which was good of her, and we went to Grimsby, of all places. And embarked on this merchant ship, piled high with sealed crates containing goodness knows what, bound for Jack knew where. He told me to dress warm, so I did.

But it was a voyage into the unknown, which has always suited me. I think it's in the blood. You see, I think of it like this:

The first people who spoke English came from where - Holland, Belgium, Denmark? - when the Romans left. And they'd left their homes, gone on this voyage, across the North Sea, not really certain of what they would find, and the English or English-speaking people have been doing that ever since. It's like a race memory. We've got to move, we've got to go, we've got to leave. Gotta get out of our grooves! We seem to have forgotten that recently.

There was a while, of course, when we didn't have the technology or the boats, but as soon as the 16th century comes around, Francis Drake, Walter Raleigh, everybody leaves, hence the British Empire, or the English Empire really, and that's why the divorce rate in this country is so high.

We gotta leave, you gotta leave home, you're torn with regrets, you speak with teary nostalgia about the past - Holland, Denmark (for the first English-speaking people), but now it's for the past, an undefined country that we've left. Or an ex-wife and your estranged children.

Anyway, getting on a merchant ship at Grimsby and heading off, goodness knows where, was fun in a way. But it wasn't a tourist jamboree: the seas were rough, the winds were cold and we went north. It wasn't hard to work out - the sun was always at our backs.

We docked in Reykjavik and then headed east. Jack was still very quiet about where we were going. We saw the northern edge of Norway. And Jack, well, Jack talked about books, talked about Robbie more and more (someone I'd never met) and reminisced about Spain.

And, of course, I had guessed by then that Jack as a merchant seaman must have been on the Arctic Convoys (he'd let that out on our trip to Barcelona), but I didn't know our final destination - like all of us, we never know our final destination, but we do, of course. There is only one terminus that awaits us.

He got a bit more expansive when the Kola Peninsula came into view. I'm not bad at geography or at least I like maps - I knew that was Russia. I figured we were heading for Archangel or Murmansk. The sea was grey, the clouds were grey, and I felt a greyness in my soul, just looking at the waves, their occasional flashes of brilliant white reminding me of some better life elsewhere. I'm lucky too, never been sea-sick, love the feeling of the ship rolling underneath my feet. The trick - don't think about your stomach. Keep your legs wide. Move with the rhythm of the boat. It's easy.

I didn't want to land in Murmansk or Archangel or wherever it was we were going without knowing a little bit more. We took a turn round the deck after breakfast, and by this time we could see on the north Russian coastline settlements, concrete blocks, tiny houses, isolated farmhouses set back in a rolling, quite low landscape, completely unlike Norway.

"Uncle Jack," I said, "I'm not stupid. I know you were on the Arctic convoys. Are you going to tell me anymore?"

He looked up at me, tears in his eyes.

"Oh, Tommy. It's all gone and my memories - I'm not sure they're worth that much. The cold... I've never felt anything like it – minus 30 some nights - ships in the convoy got stuck in the ice.

"They used their own depth charges - which were meant for the German submarines - to break the ice around them just to keep moving. I tell you - it was dangerous. If you didn't keep moving, the Germans got you - their planes, submarines. I remember one attack. It was just after dawn, the time the Germans liked to attack. I was on an ack-ack gun, looking out for planes. I swear, Tommy, in one minute I counted sixty torpedoes headed for different ships. You could see the little phosphorescence in the water. We lost a lot of ships. You know we were taking supplies to the Soviet Union."

"Yes, I know that. I mean is it true, Jack, they couldn't have survived without those supplies?"

"I don't know, Tommy. That's what we say, but then we would - that's our story. I like to think we helped. I like to think we helped." He gazed down into the waves.

"So tell me more about the cold."

"Well, we just didn't have the clothes for it. You could try wrapping your scarf round your face but then your breath got stuck to the scarf. The scarf would freeze and, if you weren't careful, it got sort of welded to your face. Even the snot in your nostrils froze, so I'd go out, two nostrils, full of Vick, hard to breath but didn't freeze. But then they tried convoys in the summer and the losses were appalling – too much daylight for the Germans to see in. That's why we went in the winter."

"Hmmmm…and the fighting?"

"Well, not too bad. I'd seen action in Spain. I knew what it was like to be under fire and being on the ack-ack guns… I dunno, when you shot down a German plane, it was a real thrill. I know that's awful, but it was - it was exciting. Even when you saw the pilot: especially when you could see them! You could see them, Tommy, in the cockpit going down in the sea. On the other hand, you can feel a bit trapped on a ship – like there's nowhere else to go to – and if a torpedo's coming for ya, you're fucked. Of course, no one lasted long in that sea."

"What, so if you fell in you were dead?"

"Within a couple of minutes. In winter. Bit longer in the spring and autumn – if our ships had time to stop for you in the middle of a sea battle."

There was silence for a few minutes as Jack rounded up his stray thoughts. He was still staring down at the waves.

"I remember the convoy Robbie died on. The ship ahead of us got struck by two torpedoes and that wasn't the end. They were still getting men into the life rafts. But then a third hit and all the men, all the crew - must have been two hundred of them - ended up in the water. And it was like two hundred yards ahead of us. There was no way we could change course. All these men in the water musta been thinking, *Oh great there's a ship - we can be saved.* Then realizing that we couldn't stop, that we couldn't change course, that they wouldn't be saved, and that they would freeze to death and drown in those waters. And our captain couldn't take avoiding action. Two hundred yards. They're big ships, Tommy. You can't miss 'em. So what he did - I didn't speak to him, but I could see what was in his head - what he did - he just aimed right slap-bang for the middle of this floating patch of humanity. And you could see their faces, some with a brief flicker of optimism at first when they thought we could pick them up, and then terror when they realized we were going to kill them and then - it all happened so fast - and then relief and resignation because by then the cold had started to affect them. I saw one bloke just as we bore down on the main mass of floating men: he lifted his head up from his lifejacket. He could see me. He looked into my eyes, gave me a broad grin, thumbs up and then saluted, and our ship just ploughed through them - killed the lot."

"So how did Robbie die? Well - if you can tell me about it."

"Well, you can look that up, Tommy. It's a point of record – it's in the books. Robbie was on an ack-ack gun like me, and he got hit by shrapnel. It was a German bomb from a plane which hit the main gun turret ahead of him. His whole back was covered in shrapnel. He was bleeding, bleeding to death, and he died in Murmansk hospital. I'm a silly old sod, Tommy, but I never thought I'd see his grave again. When we get there, we've only got a few hours, because once the boat is unloaded, it's back off to England, so just come with me to the cemetery, the British Military Cemetery in Murmansk. I just want to stand there, you know, say a proper goodbye. Tell him a few stories. Make sure he's up to date with stuff."

"So - shrapnel in his lungs. He just bled to death?"

"Well, it was a bit worse than that. He was my best mate. I'd known him all my life. We grew up in the same road. We'd been to Spain together, and we talked about everything, so to see your best mate die in agony.... And it was worse. What was worse...I've never told anyone this. And, oh God, Tommy it breaks my heart to tell you now."

Uncle Jack broke off and with tear-filled eyes gazed at the distant hills. There was a long pause.

"His hands, Tommy, his hands, those hands that had played marbles with me. They had stuck up two fingers to the teachers at school; they had pulled a trigger in Spain. Those hands, that he moved so expressively when he was talking - his hands were frozen to his ack-ack gun, so before he could be treated we had to get his hands off. Silly sod hadn't put his gloves on."

"Ah!" I said. "What did you do? Break his fingers? Thaw him out?"

Jack looked into the distance again. His whole body shook. There were no tears now, no physical drops of water from his face. Just a hard grey look as hard and grey as the Arctic Ocean, but his body shook and his head nodded up and down seeming to confirm my guess, but I was wrong.

"No, Tommy, it was worse than that. We didn't have time to break his fingers, to thaw him out. I doubt if we could have thawed him out. We had no time. There were submarines and German fighters coming at us from all angles. I kept saying to him - it was right about here, off the Kola Peninsula - I said to him, "Robbie, Robbie," I said. "It's alright. We're going to make it, kid. We are going to make it, make it to Murmansk. It'll be all right."

Jack broke off again, turned and looked into the blankness of the north, away from the land.

"And we did, but Robbie never came back. He died in Murmansk."

"So.... so how did you get his hands off the gun?"

"Tommy, you're an intelligent boy - you can work it out. I didn't want to do it. How could anyone do that? How could you do that to your best mate, but he begged me. He said, "Jack, just do it, I want to live. Just do it! Get my hands off this sodding gun and get me down to the sick bay." Tommy, in war you do terrible things."

"Oh, Christ!" I said.

"Yeah," Jack said. "I got no words. What do you do when you're faced with saving the life of your best mate? I got down to the galley. Got this big meat cleaver. Tommy, I can't talk about this anymore...."

And Uncle Jack stared stonily once again into the wild and whirling waters of the white-topped waves.

"Oh Jack!" And I thought: all these years - you should have told me earlier.

And once again I had no words to solace, to console or to comfort. No words.

The next morning we docked in Murmansk and Jack, in a strange way, was kind of cheerful, as though he was looking forward to going to the cemetery, paying his last respects. It was only July, but he'd put on a smart raincoat, shirt and a tie and, on his lapel, I noticed something unusual.

It was a medal. The predominant colour of the ribbon was crimson, but then there were black and mustard stripes. I know what they mean now. But what was most striking was a turquoise stripe, very thin on the edges of the ribbon. The medal itself had a rather touching picture of a soldier, with a gun flanked by obviously a civilian and a women with a gun which reminded me of the photograph in Jack's flat. The writing was all in Russian.

"Uncle Jack, I'm not being funny, but are you allowed to wear that?"

He said, "Yeah, I certainly am. This is a Russian medal. In 1985 they offered this medal to anyone who served on the Arctic Convoys. Our government wouldn't let us accept it, but, well... I got hold of one. This is the first day I've worn it and Tommy this matters here. The

Russians will see this and they will know; they will know what I did. Not acknowledged in my own country, but they will know, you wait and see."

And that was it really. We were only four hours in Murmansk. I didn't even speak to a single Russian. I don't know what the deal was, but we didn't have visas - perhaps it was because we were on a merchant ship, but we just slipped out of the docks, walked a couple of miles, went to the British Military Cemetery, found Robbie's grave.

Robert Thompson. HMMN. Able seaman. July 23rd, 1920 – February 4th, 1942.

Jack stood there doing nothing for thirty minutes. Then we left, so my impressions of Russia were limited. Imagine Grimsby, designed by Stalin. You get the picture. And then we were back on the boat.

I liked being at sea. I got a lot of work done. There's something about the rhythms of the sea that helped me in my work. But we were a bit isolated. This was what '95 and no internet - no way of communicating. I worried about the kids; I worried about the dogs. But I worried less about Uncle Jack. I felt at last I knew why he'd been crying, why every day as a butcher hacking dead meat he'd been reminded of that moment when he hacked off his best friend's hands in a futile attempt to save his life.

I could imagine the deep red stain of Robbie's blood spreading on the ice-covered deck.

But of course I was wrong: I still didn't understand, not really. Not everything.

Chapter Twenty-Five: JACK AND TOMMY

Arbeit Macht Frei

No words, and yet so many. Arbeit Macht Frei. The gates. The trains. The tracks leading to the heart of the camp. The ramp down to the gas chambers. Steam from the train. Clouds from the crematoria. Two lines. One for men. One for women and children. A room full of empty, discarded Zyklon B canisters. The room where it started with the Red Army soldiers to test out the new system. Auschwitz II – Burkina – bigger capacity. Five crematoria. 4,576 corpses a day. The Death Wall – how many were shot here in a futile gesture of escape? Cell 18 to deal with subversives and would-be mutineers – starved to death. The orchestras playing as the trains arrived and unloaded their human cargo. Snatches of Mozart that they could hear as they were hurried down the ramp. Not enough words. Words no good. The ash lake, revealing nothing of the past in the placidity of its mirrored sheen. Canada – the apotheosis of Nazism, the Shoah and capitalism. Not just genocide. The industrial capitalism of the human body. The assembly line of hate and racism and intolerance.

Words. Zyklon B. Canada. The sauna building. The lake of ashes. The cremation pits. The brick built crematoria. The punishment block. The barracks. The wall of death. The gallows. The electrified fence. The basement of Block 11. The death block. The penal block. The trolleys to transport the ashes.

By the lake of ashes Jack and I sat down and wept.

The Jews.

The Freemasons.

The Roma.

The Socialists.

The Communists.

The Trades Unionists.

The Danish Police Force.

The Polish Roman Catholic clergy.

The Red Army soldiers.

The Soviet citizens.

The Jehovah's Witnesses.

The homosexuals.

The disabled.

The blacks.

The partisans.

The resistance members.

The Jews.

The Jews.

The Jews.

By the lake of ashes Jack and I sat down and wept.

And wept. Wept, wept, wept.

No words left.

No words.

No.

No.

No.

No.

Chapter Twenty-Six: Halya II

After three nights of travelling, the train reached its destination. They had no sense of time, but they knew it had been dark on three occasions since it had pulled out of the railway siding.

Hauled out of the cattle truck. Harsh, glaring lights. Barking, snarling dogs. German guards with guns, truncheons, revolvers, machine guns. Mozart playing somewhere. Men in white coats. Divided into men and women with children. Divided again. Some to the left. Some to the right – down a ramp. Down the ramp. Clothes off. Heads shaved. Down another ramp. Showers.

Hurry, Jews, hurry. Nothing to be afraid of.

It was all so quick, running, running, running.

Dead bodies were flung all across the road; corpses were hanging, decaying and forlorn, from the barbed wire fence; the rattle of shots rang in the air continuously. Roaring flames sprang into the sky; a giant, murky cloud hung above the whole place. Starving, almost human skeletons stumbled around everywhere, uttering incoherent sounds of misery. Some fell down in front of Halya and the new arrivals, and retched out their last breath.

"Please, put your clothes on the hanger and remember the number on the hanger. Tie your shoes together so they do not become separated. Pile your other clothes in one place beneath the hanger. You will be able to collect them all later. We know you are tired and thirsty, but coffee is waiting in the camp when you have had your shower. Hurry up or the coffee will get cold."

Finally they were all in one room together. Halya realized that it had got as bad as it was going to get. The rest she could control. Her strong indomitable spirit roused itself for what she knew would be the last time.

Halya raised her head and cleared her throat, and shouted, "Quiet!" to get everyone's attention.

"Comrade sisters, this is the living hell of fascism. This is the true face of our enemy. We do not have long to live, sisters, but we shall not die now. The fascists cannot really kill us because we shall live forever in the minds and the spirits of our people and in the glorious history of the Soviet Union and in the history of all good, freedom-loving people everywhere. The history of our nation will immortalise us, and our initiative and spirit will live and flourish in those that succeed us to wreak the people's revenge on the Nazis and their inhuman brutalities. Long live the Soviet Union! Power to the people!"

And then she turned to the Jewish members of the Sonderkommando who were still busy herding the last stragglers into the room and said, clearly and firmly:

"Remember that it is your duty and your obligation to revenge us – the innocent. Tell our people, our brothers, tell our sisters, tell our nation, tell the world - that we went to meet our deaths in full complete awareness and pride, and in the sure and certain knowledge that our tormentors will be defeated by the will of the people."

After that, in a voice that quavered with emotion and seemed to catch and claw its way through the words, Halya began to sing:

Stand up, ye children of oppression.

The door of the room slammed shut. There was a collective moan, a huge tear-filled sigh. A child whimpered to Halya's left; to her right several children moaned and screamed in the plunging, evil semi-darkness.

Halya sang.

For the tyrants fear your might!

In the ceiling above them tiny metal grates were snapped back. Almost everyone was howling and screaming with fear and panic.

Halya sang. Louder still to overpower the wailing that threatened to overcome her voice.

Don't cling so hard to your possessions,

The tiny metal flaps in the ceiling were snapped back down.

You have nothing if you have no rights!

The faintest whisper of what might have been mist started seeping out from the tiny mesh containers in the ceiling.

Let racist ignorance be ended.

Halya grabbed the arms of two small children near her and hugged them to herself.

"Be brave, children. Hold my hands as tightly as you can."

Halya sang.

We'll live together or we'll die alone!

The mist became a menacing fog. Wailing. Crying. Screaming. An immense collective whine of mothers and grandmothers, and aunts and sisters, and wives and daughters facing the ineluctable remorselessness of an insane and inhuman malignity.

So come brothers and sisters,

"Sing, my sisters, and breathe deep. Let us die with dignity!" Halya roared. "And sing! Let us die singing!"

For the struggle lingers on.

Halya wept for it all, for them all, and for herself. But still she sang. They all sang.

The Internationale unites the world in song.

Halya lost consciousness as she uttered that last syllable and, united in death with her sisters, fell to the rough concrete floor. The hissing gas, snake-like, slithered and snarled and slurked its way around the room.

A dark pool of bodily fluids darkened the floor.

Chapter Twenty-Seven: Tommy XIII

I felt like a child again faced with all this Cyrillic, a weird code that I could not break and I actually acted like a child, deliriously happy when I could read words in public like 'bank' or 'mini market' and saw that *CAPMEH* was playing at the Opera House. I knew *Carmen*. I'd seen it the summer before in London, but it seemed as if I knew nothing else. Everything in this city, to begin with, seemed to be kept dark.

The first night Jack and I walked back from Katya's apartment to our hotel. We were struck at how dark it was - a city of over a million people shrouded in black. Figures would emerge from the half-darkness and, worrier that I am, I felt the tremble of fear before I realized that we were safe. I stumbled on the unmade pavements, not because of the pavements, but because I do stumble and it was dark. Even on the better pavements I misjudged steps and slight rises because it was so dark. That first night, racing through my brain, as I kept up the conversation with Jack, was the thought that I didn't know where we were precisely; I didn't have enough Russian to even say, "We are lost." I didn't have enough Russian to ask the way to our hotel. I could say "Please" and "Thank you" and "I am not American." That was all. Of course, being fully conversant now with Krav Maga, I carried a glass bottle with me – seemingly casually, but ready to be turned into a weapon if needs be. I didn't need to.

And for so much of our stay other things were kept dark. I would stop and look at smoked glass double doors with a tiny laminated notice in them. They could have been someone's house and someone would say, as I peered with curiosity at a smoked-glass door, "Ah Tommy, you want to get drunk?" or "Ah Tommy, you want to go disco dancing?" or "Ah, Tommy, I didn't know you were interested in stamps." Well, I had been interested in stamps, but really now I was just trying to work out was going on behind the doors.

And each shop was like that. You couldn't tell what it was, or at least I couldn't.

But when you opened that smoked-glass door you stepped into a Tardis, a cornucopia of goods and people and services waiting to be bought.

The people were the same, stone-faced, no eye contact on the street. I had learnt how to ask politely for a coffee.

"Good morning, how are you? May I have a coffee please? May I have a milky coffee please with sugar?"

But I watched and I learnt and I saw coffee bought at the street kiosks with the exchange of one word. "Coffee." That was all. It's sometimes all you need.

Why? I thought. Was it all those years of repression, not just under Communism, but the Czar before that? And yet in their homes the Russians proved to be the warmest, most hospitable, most wonderful people I'd ever come across. So willing to give you so much when they had, by our grossly overblown Western standards, so little.

I exploded a few myths. I could remember as a teenager reading several scathing reviews of Intourist hotels that had no bath plugs. The implication was clear: the Soviet system is corrupt; Communism does not work; they can't produce enough bath plugs. Why did no one tell me that actually it's a cultural practice? They believe that washing under running water is cleaner and more hygienic and so they do know how to produce bath plugs. There's probably a factory in Siberia churning them out. But they choose not to use them. Why did no one tell me that? Why was I misled by those articles in *The Sunday Times Travel Section*? My motel room had no bathplugs, but at least now I knew why. Stories – you just can't trust them. Just keep the facts dark to feed the prejudice, sunshine.

And in a sense those bloody matryoshka dolls, or whatever they're called, the ones you see in all the tourist shops, are quite a good symbol for Russia: endless dolls, and I spent my time trying to penetrate beneath the surface of what was really going on. That's true for the people and the country. While I was there I remarked that one day I'd quite like to go to Yekaterinburg. Everybody erupted with laughing.

Huh, Yekaterinburg, that's a long way from here, they chuckled.

And of course, it was. It was endless - Russia; no wonder Russia had never been conquered. No wonder it was so hard to rule; no wonder parts of it were so backward. So Russia had two weapons of mass destruction: its size and its winter.

Backward, yes, but good in other ways. For the whole week of our visit Jack and I saw no CCTV cameras. We heard no sirens; we saw no policemen. On the roads we saw wrecks that would never have passed an MOT. But we also saw pedestrians stepping onto crossings and the traffic, always calm, always slow, stopping urgently rather than hit a pedestrian. We saw young soldiers helping aged women off trolley buses with their shopping. We saw one MacDonald's: the city authorities have allowed them to build only one. We saw a human city, a city defined by walking and – boy! - did we walk. But it was a pleasure to walk in this city, although the juxtapositions of wealth and poverty, public grandeur and private squalor, as well as the bewildering Cyrillic code, were constantly bewildering and astounding to our western eyes.

A good indication of what it was like was the hotel that we stayed at. Their attitude to paper work and bureaucracy was very casual and it was only on the fifth day of our stay that they bothered to look at our passports and that was when they realized we were British. They had had no idea before then apart from the fact that we were from Western Europe. I smiled and said, " Ya nye Amerikanski" (rather proudly as it happens) and, despite what we had been led to believe, there were statues of Lenin everywhere - at the airport, at the post office, on the streets, in the parks - everywhere Lenin.

Jack, of course, was in his element. I knew we were there to meet with someone Russian whom Jack had met when he fought in Spain. That much I knew. It was only at the airport when we arrived that I realized the Russian was the woman called Katya, almost as old as Jack, who was accompanied by a younger woman, her granddaughter I assumed, who was called Olga and who had large dark almond eyes, a shock of short black hair and walked in a flowing smoothness of motion that I found beguiling.

And the airport itself - well, that was a culture shock. We'd passed through Sheremetyevo at Moscow - which if anything looked more modern, more slick, more efficient than Heathrow and where the Cyrillic was tempered by English underneath. You couldn't get lost at Sheremetyevo, but in this city, Volgograd, there was no English.

Cyrillic everywhere and the Arrivals Hall was in a field and to get to the Arrivals Hall we walked from the tarmac. All do-able, all easy really, but unexpected and dark in contrast to the bright modern glare of Heathrow and Moscow.

Jack was re-born, it seemed, through his enthusiasm, the spring in his step and his zest for each new monument we visited. It seemed as if he had found his home, and I wondered whether this was partly what he had been thinking of as he sobbed in the back room of his butcher's shop on the Old Kent Road. He could never imagine then that one day he would visit it with a grown-up me. A me half-full of a partial understanding of why he was there. Spain – yes. Robbie's death – yes. And the horrific manner of it. The American lies of the Cold War. The sinister creep of neo-liberalism and the erosion of social justice. But there was something else, I was sure. I just couldn't see it all clearly. Too much was kept dark. Perhaps it was his lengthy separation from Katya. That occurred to me. That must be it, I thought.

But, on the other hand, there was no keeping some things dark in this city. The main monument was so big that it dominated the landscape from miles away. It loomed over the city and left you in no doubt about the outcome of the battle.

On our first morning Jack and I had walked the dusty couple of kilometres to Katya's apartment. Then, by a seemingly tortuous system of walking and trolley buses and taxis, we got there. But it only seemed tortuous at the time. The next day I bought a map. Now I know the way by heart and I think I could probably find my way there in the dark.

But on that day I'd not quite got my bearings in this strangely calming yet mysterious city. So it was lucky for Jack and me and it made it quicker for us to have Katya with us, our guide, our translator. But the messages this place sent out were unfathomable and mysterious: the message of the monument needed no translation in a way, but the other ones needed every syllable to be understood and felt in the heart and in the blood and in the spirit.

In fact, that first morning Katya had walked to our hotel and walked us to her flat on Krasnoznamenskaya Street. It was an easy route I now know, but on that first morning I was dazed by the foreignness of it all: mouth and eyes and heart and mind and soul wide open, every building, every street, coffee kiosk, every strange letter of this new-to-me code. I was like a daffodil bursting from the ground, open-mouthed, surprised, to be shone on by sunlight and bewildered by this new universe. I saw the rubbish, the dusty pavements (had Lenin banned tarmac?). The lack of eye contact, the lack of speech, the ubiquitous graffiti and the brand spanking new apartment blocks with BMWs and Audis parked outside, the spick and spanness of the new banks mushrooming next to the morose post-war blocks of flats.

кредит, credit - a universal word now. What had happened? What had happened to the people of this city? Had they all been struck dumb? Were they so astonished to be living here that their only response was sheer wonder and awe? Or were they just miserable, wary, frightened or (and this is a distinct possibility) was I the Englishman abroad seeing what he expected to see, blind to the bleeding obviousness of it all. What was going on?

I kept my hands on my *Russian for Travellers* but there were no words for what I wanted to say:

Sorry, Katya. I'm sorry, Katya. I'm sorry that you suffered in the war. I'm sorry for your people, for your city, for your country. Katya, I don't really know why I am here. I don't know why my Uncle Jack has brought me here to this city. Katya, I'm sorry I do not know. I'm sorry I do not understand. Forgive me that I do not know. Ya nye amerikansk! It's all dark for me. So much is hidden, Katya. Tell me. Help me. Show me.

But the phrase book - which was so useful for ordering red cauliflower soup with paprika and asking for the bill and which would allow me to explain that my rental car had a flat tyre, and might enable me to ask where the nearest theatre was - had no answers, no words for me.

Me! Me! Me! I wanted to shout. I have lived my life with words and for words and through words and by words and here I cannot read my own name again. Like a child, a stupid child, who is teased in the playground because he cannot read his own name - at my age! And you will see later why here in this beautiful, awful, wonderful, human, flawed city learning to read again prompted, though I didn't know it at the time, a kind of re-birth.

At one point on that very first morning I noticed a tiny tabby kitten cowering next to a sapling in the dirty excuse for a pavement which was actually a scrap of dust and dirt. It meowed. I stooped to pick it up and it meowed again, a tiny, dinky, pitiful sound. Katya watched me.

"I cannot look after it, Tommy. I have no room and I live on the second floor. What is wrong, Tommy?"

Katya's eyes were full of pity for me and my innocence, for the kitten, for the past. I didn't know. I looked at Olga. Her eyes were full of a stern, stony sadness too.

Katya continued: "Would you take all the cats in Russia back to England, Tommy? To Sophia, and Hannah and Sarah, maybe little Phoebe would like a sweet kitty to warm her feet on at night?"

I looked around helplessly. Where are the RSPCA when you need them?

Katya continued, "Tommy, would you have a world for cats and not for people. Look around you Tommy, would you help them all, the dogs, the cats, all the strays in Russia and leave no room for people?"

"But, Katya," I said, "we can't just leave it here."

"We can. We will." She smiled slightly but with resolution and strode off. Olga shyly slipped her arm into the crook of my arm and I felt a sympathetic squeeze, and Jack and I followed Katya, but I was troubled for days and nights by the kitten who haunted my dreams and disturbed my sleep.

Aren't I stupid? Still learning after all these years.

Katya's flat, and every flat we visited in that week, was warm and inviting and cheerful and felt like home. So different from the alien difference of the street. So easy, so natural, so normal.

To tell the truth when we stood at the foot of that monument on a bright, warm day towards the end of October I was worried that Uncle Jack wouldn't make it to the top. While I pondered the sheer difficulties of getting his corpse back to England, Jack and Katya stopped. From the ground it looks as if the top of the slope is empty and all that faces you are steps, steps, steps but what memorable steps!

Uncle Jack paused at each City Hero plaque and gazed longest and hardest at the Murmansk plaque on the right. Then, as if nothing else could surprise me in this most surprising of all cities, Jack stopped and bought some blood-red carnations from a street vendor at the foot of the hill. Ah, bless him, I thought. He's gone all soft at last and I genuinely expected some awkward, kack-handed, very English proffering of carnations to Katya. I swear to God, that's what I thought. It might have made a good ending, but I was still a fool, still learning, still stupid, still slow. The carnations it turned out, as we ascended the monument, were for the dead, not for the living, and Jack duly placed them at different places on our ascent. The first one at the plaque commemorating Murmansk – Hero City.

We started to slowly make our way up the steps, Jack urging me to photograph everything, quite insistent in his demands. Me being me, of course, wondered if there was some significance to the number of steps. And in the half-arsed, desultory way began to keep count, but I gave up, partly because it dawned on me that I was completely wrong, yet again, but also because I started to lose count after a thousand and also because some parts aren't steps as such. Just a slowly rising slope which Jack found easy.

"I don't feel old," Uncle Jack would say. "I don't feel anything until noon. And then it's time for my nap."

Nye vashna - his phrase of the day. *Nye vashna* - nothing seemed to be a problem to Jack, but I wasn't so sure - I saw problems everywhere. And it has to be admitted that in this very special place, forty acres of memorial park devoted to the defenders of the city, everything was immaculate, well kept, well-tended. I was still struggling with the Cyrillic code but even I could see CCCP in huge letters everywhere I looked - the monument left you in no doubt about who had won the battle. Not Russia, not the Allies, but the Soviet Union. After the not-quite-endless steps there was a level area, beautifully paved, surrounded by birch trees, about the size of a football field and in the centre a lake - the lake of remembrance.

Olga broke the silence. "We say that the silver birch tree is an emblem or a symbol of Russian womanhood. Slim, white, beautiful, resilient and everywhere."

Some women have more front than the British Museum; Olga had more depths than the deepest ocean. She seemed far out like something lost in space. I smiled regretfully. I had no words.

Beyond the birch trees were rough footpaths which you could use instead of the official route. By now we could see the monument itself. Huge, the spirit of Russia, Mother Russia, brandishing a sword which in itself was ten times the size of Nelson's Column.

Why had I not heard of this place? Why had we never been told about this place? To come here made sense of so many more things. Beyond the large still lake, another water monument, in which coins were thrown for the memory of the dead and for life, and then a huge interior hall, the walls gilded in bright, shiny, gold leafed plaques with the names of the defenders etched forever. A huge hand rose out of the floor and held in it a torch, like the Olympic torch but bigger. The opening was the size of a large dining room table and from it rose an eternal flame, guarded by Russian soldiers every hour of every day and every day of every year.

Jack laid some more carnations and we went round the circular building along the slowly rising ramp to yet another level where, in the first concession to tourism, you passed through a rocky ravine sculpted, covered in faux graffiti (copied from the era of the battle), slogans of victory, of triumph, of dedication to the cause against fascism and from somewhere came the sounds of battle, screams and wails and crashes and shells exploding. The ping of snipers' rifles, the rattle of machine guns, the boom of crumps, the shatterbang of shells, the shouts of suffering humanity, the whizz of mortars assaulted our ears in a ravine shaped by man but natural, and now that we were closer to the monument itself I could see its sheer size. There were individuals near the pedestal and they seemed a quarter of the size of the pedestal. Again me, being me, I wondered how it stayed up, but Mother Russia had wide billowing skirts and, though I understand nothing about design and monumental sculpture, I imagined its extreme height was possible because of its wide base at the bottom.

I mentioned the Hero City plaques at the foot of the hill on the pavement. In the memorial hall were the names of individuals. After the rocky ravine with its sound effects, you trace a meandering tarmacked path up a grassy mound to the monument itself. On either side of that path, lying flat on the grass, are marbled memorials to individuals, the most important individuals, and the most valiant units. Uncle Jack laid a carnation at Vassily Zaitsev's grave and then another one to the 41st Soviet Sniper Unit and slowly we got to the top.

As we looked back we could see the Volga and to the east a flat plain that for all I knew stretched all the way to the Urals. From the top you could also see, hidden by larger birch trees, invisible from the main part of the park, a tiny Russian Orthodox church where we went and lit candles.

Katya asked me, "Are you lighting them for the living or for the dead?"

"For both," I said and indeed there were different places in the chapel for the living and for the dead. Jack did the same.

Jack and Katya sat on a bench outside the church and spoke while I, Englishman abroad, took photos of the church, the view, the memorial park beyond the monument - everything. And what struck me as odd, but refreshing too, was that there was no gift shop. I wanted a physical memory of this place, an object, but there was no commercialization, no gift shop. I know - I looked for it. How different from our life! If it had been our monument there would have been a gift shop, I'm sure, where you could buy a Mamayev Kurgan hoody or a Mamayev Kurgan t-shirt or a key ring, a pencil, a pencil sharpener, or chocolates with Mother Russia emblazoned on the front but there was nothing, nothing at all. In fact, more generally in the city there was nothing at all. Except people. I liked it. My kinda place.

Samantha had asked me to send her a postcard. She wanted no present brought back, but could I find a postcard? No, they did not appear to exist.

That day at Mamayev Kurgan will always stay in my mind. I was close to tears throughout our ascent to the top, and Jack and Katya, while restrained in their body movements and hand gestures, spent the whole two hours there fighting back the tears. Only Olga was completely overcome with emotion: I put my arm round her shoulders, foolishly, because her sorrows and her grief seemed so far beyond any redemption or comfort I could offer.

And this was just the start of our week, our first day. Everywhere we went there were reminders of the war: a memorial to the tank dogs; a memorial to General Zhukov; a memorial to the Soviet Maritime Corps who guarded the boats on the river; a memorial to the Red Air Force; a memorial that showed the limit of the German advance - just two hundred metres from the Volga - so close and yet so far. There is no memorial to the bunker where Paulus was finally captured. They built a department store over it instead. ☺

The city square, the one that you get to from following the broad avenue up from the Volga has another eternal flame, not as large as the main monument's, but always there were wreaths, carnations, hand-written notes. People say the English are obsessed with the war. I tell them, "Go to Russia! See how obsessed with the war they are." And, of course, they have every right to be. All these eternal flames, I couldn't help joking that I would never need another lighter for all the time I was in the city - I could just stoop down and light my fag whenever I liked.

One evening Olga took me to the theatre: I think Jack must have mentioned I was very interested in the theatre. Fantastic show! It helped that it was a musical and very visual, so I could follow the plot easily: set in the Second World War, officer in the Red Air Force is given a new unit to command – a unit of women! You can guess the rest: they all fall in love with him and he's caught in a series of embarrassing situations. A musical comedy. And as I watched and laughed, the real truth of what I had always sensed struck me like a lightning bolt: take away the differences, the flags, the languages, the ideologies, the religions – take away that ephemera which people have such petty allegiance to, and we have so much more in common than what we are told separates us.

Another day Katya took us to the Stalingrad Museum near the river. Surrounded by original Soviet planes and tanks and very busy, it seemed, on the day we went there. I can't help myself. I'm always joking. I knew that Britain had given the city of Stalingrad a memorial sword in honour of the city's efforts in the war and I joked with Katya as we went up the steps.

"If I present my British passport, can you tell them I've come to get our sword back?"

Katya smiled. I chuntered on.

"I think you must have been really disappointed. You get a big parcel from England when you need bread and concrete or maybe more weapons to fight the fascists. It's wrapped up, it's from the King of England and you were really excited. 'What is it? What is it? Is it a new weapon to fight fascism? Is it some more bricks? We need bricks. We need to rebuild the city.' And I can imagine your disappointment. 'It's a sword. What are we going to do with a sword?'"

More seriously, there's a gallery, an entire gallery, in the museum devoted to gifts from other countries and gifts from other cities, so famous was Stalingrad then, but then everything changes, doesn't it?

I'm not normally jingoistic at all, but I have to say our sword was probably the best present and the Americans' present was the worst. The Americans sent a letter. It's there. I read it and I laughed. This is what it said:

"In the name of the people of the United States of America I present this scroll to the City of Stalingrad to commemorate our admiration for its gallant defenders whose courage, fortitude and devotion during the siege of September 13th 1942 to January 31st 1943 will inspire for ever the hearts of all free people. Their glorious victory stemmed the tide of invasion and marked the turning point in the war of the allied nations against the forces of aggression.

Franklin D Roosevelt, Washington DC."

And I laughed because, you know, I think we did forget, somewhere along the road, we did forget Stalingrad. Was that the Cold War? Was it our version of history that made us forget this amazing city and its astonishing, brave people?

And certainly the Americans forgot. And to think the richest country in the world sent a letter – sorry, a 'scroll'. I'd have been really pissed off to get only a letter from the Americans. You can imagine the suspense:

Is it a Cadillac? A gold-plated Cadillac? Is it a food parcel? Hmm. Doesn't feel like a food parcel. Go on – open it then and see what the richest country in the world has sent us. Oh… a letter. Well, more of a scroll, I suppose. But they didn't use a stamp so we have to pay the excess postage.

Some things should never be forgotten. Everyone should come to this city to understand the past seventy years and to understand the future. Some things, perhaps all things, should not be kept dark.

Americans! My maternal grandmother always used to say, her eyes dewy with sentiment, "If you can't say anything nice about anyone, then just tell them to fuck off."

The space programme says it all really for me. Now I'm a dog person, me. Some of my closest relationships have been with dogs: dogs are sociable, biddable and want to please. There are bad dogs, but they've been badly trained or treated. All my dogs have been sociable, friendly hounds. So it is no wonder that the Soviets chose to put pairs of dogs into space: two dogs work well together, and the flickering images of Belka and Strelka in the capsule show two happy pooches on an outing, occasionally looking at each other, and no doubt looking forward to the sausages they would receive when the capsule landed: watch the clip on Youtube. It's all in the eye contact really: dogs do eye contact, and, while they can misbehave, they can be trained to behave. To toe the Party line, as it were. Now turn to the chimpanzee, my learned colleagues. Have you seen chimps behave? No eye contact - and they are manic, solipsistic, ill-disciplined brats – especially when there's anything around to eat or anything they want. An apt choice, one could say, for the first American in space. A fitting symbol of the nation that sent him. And their foreign policy – the most oxymoronic idea that I can think of in the world. My Russian hosts were fond of boasting about the size of the Soviet Union's nuclear arsenal, but would always add, with raised eyebrows, the question:

"But, Tommy, which is the only nation on earth to unleash this enormous power on actual human beings, real people?" I did not need to answer. There would be a pause and they would smile sadly and add, "And they did it twice!"

Jack and I spent the rest of our week doing much as we did on those first two days, visiting memorials, monuments, museums. Jack would walk around to Katya's flat every morning while I stayed at the hotel and worked and sent things to England, e-mailed the children.

Occasionally I'd meet up with Olga for coffee and cake. She intrigued me. But whatever had happened, she was keeping it dark. All I managed to discover was that she was a widow and that she had only one daughter. She referred to Katya as 'Auntie Katya', but there was no mention of any other relatives. Her English was good if a trifle reserved, and I found myself gazing at her face, at her big brown eyes, and thinking: *What is it? What is there that I have seen before? Who does she remind me of? Where have I seen that face before?* Another unresolved mystery.

One of the highlights of the week was the Veteran's Association Dinner. I got so drunk. I'd not been drinking all that week because I wanted to feel alive, I wanted to crack the code, to make the most of my time in this city, but at the dinner it seemed to be rude not to. I say 'dinner' - it was a meal that lasted seven hours and a lot was eaten and neat vodka was drunk almost non-stop. My glass was never empty. When I first picked it up, I took a tentative sip and, so concerned were my hosts that I didn't like it, that I downed it in one as I did all the others. The spirit of the meal was light-hearted and funny and serious too. The Russians love their toasts. Given those present there were many toasts to each other's countries, to the dead of the war, to particular regiments, to the Red Army, the British Navy, the British Merchant Navy. But the Russians have a wickedly humorous side too. After five hours people were getting slowly to their feet and proposing toasts to "My daughters." "His sons," and, after six and a half hours, the toasts were "To your son's ear," "To your daughter's left kneecap," and "Tommy, to the dogs who await your return to Velika Brittania." It was fun.

What I couldn't get over was the number of medals they wore. I asked Katya about this. One man seemed to have over twenty medals and he had obviously just been an ordinary infantryman like the others there. Katya explained.

"Well, that one is for the defence of Stalingrad; that is for the liberation of Warsaw; that is for the liberation of Berlin. Then that one is to commemorate victory in the war and then all those others, because he's so old, are the tenth, twentieth, thirtieth, fortieth, fiftieth, sixtieth, sixty fifth and seventieth anniversary of the victory over fascism. Oh, and that silvery one is for extreme courage."

"But what about the ones he's got on the right side of his chest, what are they for?"

"Ah well, after the War he worked in the tractor factory, and so that one is for ten years' service in the tractor factory, that's for twenty years' service, that's for -"

"I get the picture. Tell me, Katya, the workers in the factories where they make the medals - do they get medals too? 'Valiant Medal Maker for the Glory of the USSR'?"

Katya smiled.

"For making that sort of remark, Tommy, you would have been sent to the Gulags."

Chapter Twenty-Eight: Julie

My brother Tommy? What can I say? Witty, funny, charismatic. Can light up the whole room when he's in the mood, but in other respects - a total fucking wanker. And I say that with sisterly affection – honest.

When we were kids at school, he always looked after me and Caroline. He was always there for us, although if he were here he'd say, "We didn't say that then." Used to protect us, so to speak, in the playground and then, as we got older, because we were all at the same secondary school and most of the girls went out with the boys in the years above us, he'd give us the lowdown on certain boys he knew and would warn us about certain characters. In a way he's always been like that: in my twenties I was seeing this real lowlife bloke, into petty crime and drugs, and anyway one drunk Saturday night he hit me. Well, when Tommy found out, he came round, marched in our flat with a cricket bat, hauled this guy to his feet, dragged him outside and, well, I don't know what was said or what Tommy did, but this guy cleared out all his things, left me two grand in cash and never gave me any more trouble. And yet Tommy is such a peaceful man normally, it has to be said: so placid, but he'd do anything for his family and his sisters and his children.

I know he had a rough time at school when he first started. He is no oil painting, but kids can be cruel and I know that he was called all sorts of horrible names about his appearance and then having all that time off in hospital couldn't've helped. But he just got on with things. Learnt to make people laugh. Learnt how to put the bullies down with a few words. Worked hard at school. Read a lot. Full of useless information. If I had a fiver for every time he started a conversation with me with the words "Did you happen to know...." or "Sis, I found out something amazing the other day about Fanta..." followed by something that he just discovered and was fascinated by and kinda wanted you to be fascinated by too - well, I'd be very rich. And he's still at it. And he knows it's annoying, but he can't stop himself. He's still at it now. And he has to know why. Not just the facts, but why some things happened the way they did.

"Jools," he'll say to me, "I just can't help myself, I'm just in-fucking-satiable." And he swears for England – despite his education or maybe because of it. "Look, Sis," he'd say to me when my kids were little and he'd just mouthed off a stream of filth, "they're just fucking words. Only the bourgeoisie find them offensive – the real intelligence is knowing when to use them for maximum effect." And you know I've never heard him swear at anyone directly – except for politicians. And even then not in the flesh, so to speak.

Give him his due, if he's been a little inconsistent in his personal life, he's never wavered in his politics. And there's the one thing he'll argue about if anyone riles him. That's racism or any sort of intolerance. When I was with my second husband, Mick, Tommy couldn't stand him because of his racist attitudes. Nearly came to blows. He'd launch into one of his tirades, index finger jabbing, passionate and intense:

"It's just not logical, Mike. How can you say you don't like black people? Have you met them all? Are you personally acquainted with every single one and if you haven't and you're not - just take a wild guess here - then I think you should shut the fuck up. What's more, you conceited little prick, you don't know your own history, do you? We're all immigrants in this country, so if we follow your logic and everyone should go back to where they came from, then most of the English will have to move back to Holland and there will be Welsh people living in your house. What do you say to that? Does that thought appeal to you?"

He might take a little breather, but when he was in that sort of mood, tirade full on, there was no chance of debate, because as far as Tommy was concerned there was nothing to debate.

"What you're also ignoring you evil pig-ignorant little racist, in your single brain-cell fucking excuse for a brain is the Anglo-Saxons were not the last people to migrate to these islands. You say you're proud to be English, but England has always been a sanctuary and a refuge for the outcasts, the unwanted, the refugees from Europe. And that makes me proud to be English because it sums up for me what being English is all about – tolerance, generosity and compassion. You ought to research your family history – I'll laugh if it turns out that your ancestors were French Huguenots who intermarried in the 19th century with Jewish refugees from the pogroms! That might change your primitive attitudes!"

The problem was that Mike was a few graves short of a proper cemetery, more than one litre short of a wine-box, and he had no defence, no response to my brother's articulate and angry passion.

He did try to defend his position.

"But they're taking our jobs is why."

"Taking our jobs? What the fuck are you talking about? That's a political issue. The company you work for – all the companies in this country use you as a wage slave. They've got no patriotism. They just want profit and when they can make more profit by having factories overseas, then they do just that and to hell with British workers. Profits to their shareholders come first and you are telling me that immigrants are taking your job, when what you're really telling me is that the whole economy should be restructured, so that the wage slaves have some control over their destiny and the workings of their company. Ideally they should only - ."

"Fuck off, you fucking Commie!"

And that would really rile Tommy.

"What did you call me, you shag-wanking, cunt-bollocking disaster of a human being? You're so stupid you can't even get your insults right, can you, Mikey boy?"

There was silence. I wondered what Tommy was going to say, what he was going to define himself as – but he was always one to resist labels. Never one for joining any organization – just like his favourite uncle – Uncle Jack.

"You make me feel sorry for you, Mikey boy. You just read all the shit in that crappy little paper you buy and you swallow it whole – hook, line and sinker - but it's all designed to distract you, to keep your eye off the main thing, so you end up hating black British people instead of the bosses, the fat cats, who own and control everything. You're just a fucking wanker cunt-moron."

Funnily enough it was often Mick who would go to hit Tommy at this stage of events, because he had no weapon except his fists to fight

Tommy's words. In a way I was relieved when Mick and I divorced – he was just an embarrassment. Now I'm with Linton whose parents are from Guyana, and Tommy, being Tommy, is just so cool with that.

"Go for it, Jools," he joked with me. "Stir up the gene pool. You and Linton will produce beautiful children and in the future maybe five hundred years from now I reckon we'll be all be mixed race anyway, and racists like Mick will be a distant memory like the dinosaurs."

And he was always good with my kids. Always made them laugh. Was childish enough to amuse them and play games, but never spoke down to them. He wrote a whole sequence of nonsense verse for them and sometimes would arrive and grab their attention immediately:

"Sorry I'm a bit late, but on the way I met this wizard – just now on the South Circular – and he insisted on a Battle of Wits and Magic. But luckily I won and managed to shrink him: I've got him here in my pocket. Would you like to see him?"

"Yes! Yes!"

"Ah! You've forgotten that magic word that you know."

"Yes, please, Uncle Tommy! Please!"

"What? I've forgotten what you wanted now."

"To see the wizard! The wizard that you shrinked."

"Ah! The wizard that I shrank. Well, here he is."

And with that he'd produce some wizard finger puppet from his coat pocket and he'd make up some silly conversation between the wizard and him, or let the kids ask the wizard questions. And he always got them good presents when he had a bit of money and not always books either: ordinary toys, things that he guessed they would like and enjoy. One thing I never really understood was that he carried one particular toy with him everywhere and made a point of giving one to all the kids. It was daft really: just a wooden monkey suspended between two bits of wood on a piece of tautened string – the monkey did somersaults if you flexed the wood properly: I have no idea why my big brother was so obsessed with that toy! So, a little weird at times, but from my point of view and from the kids', he was a good uncle, a generous man – with his time and with what money he had.

And because our parents died relatively young, Tommy's friendship with our Uncle Jack was good for my kids. Kept them in touch with that generation. And Uncle Jack was so generous to my children as well – all of them - especially during those periods when Tommy himself was borrassic. He and Tommy used to take them up West to all the museums and stuff. And I know my sister Caroline would say the same: both of them were generous to a fault. Especially when I was a single mum and working all the hours I could find.

But something went terribly wrong between him and Sue. When I first heard about it, from Sue, I just couldn't believe it. If you'd asked me beforehand I'd've put money on Tommy being the last bloke on this earth who would cheat on his wife. Mind you, it was clear that they didn't get on any more: lots of little rows and arguments, petty bickering, snide remarks – even in front of family. But still, Tommy struck me as so devoted to the idea of family and to his children, that I couldn't believe he'd do anything to jeopardise that: how wrong I was.

Of course, since then he's not really been able to settle down. He's forever turning up at family barbecues or meals or just popping round to see the kids, and always with someone new. I don't think I've seen him with the same woman more than once since him and Sue broke up. Of course, Tommy being Tommy, he'll just breeze in with wine and flowers, a big smile, and something for the children and say:

"Hey, Jules, this is Conchita. I remember telling you all about her. She's from Venezuela. Conchita – meet my favourite woman in the world after you – my sister, Julie."

Or Hennie from Holland or Mashka from Moscow or Luisa from Lisbon. Or Dolly from Grey Star. Molly from Dublin. Honest to God - I lose track of them. It's a mystery to me, because as I said he's no oil painting. But I do worry about him as he gets older; I wonder how he sleeps at night, despite his breezy chutzpah.

He said to me once, "Sis, don't tell anyone this, cos if you do, according to the oath I swore, I'll have to kill you, but the fact is I have secret funding from the United Nations. It's a sorta global love project kinda thing. It's all hush-hush, you know."

See what I mean – total bollocks most of the time.

I've kept in touch with Sue, naturally, because my children are close to their cousins, I'm close to Tommy's, so we often run into each other. Of course, Sue can never forgive or forget all the suffering and the betrayal that Tommy put her through. But even she'll admit the happiness they had before it all went wrong. They had some very happy times and Tommy was a good dad and still is in some ways – despite the fact that he abandoned her and the children. And she'll admit that he always made her laugh and can still do that, even today.

Tommy can be outrageous. Sometimes – just to shock. We'd all gone as a group to see my youngest, Zach, and Tommy's granddaughter, Phoebe, in the school nativity play. Zach was a camel and Phoebe was an angel. Anyway, as we were walking away from the school, Tommy got into conversation with a pretty young mother taking her own children back home on her own. They had quite a long chat; we waited on the opposite pavement. Eventually, Tommy crosses the road and Sue, as always she's simply got to say something, she goes barging in, saying in a disapproving tone: "Still talking to strange women. That's the story of your life and the source of all your problems."

Now it's not like my brother to take that sort of remark lying down. Tommy just grinned and goes:

"Who are you calling 'strange'? That's not very nice. It's not a nice thing to say about someone you barely know. And, you can take it from me that she is definitely not strange at all, although she makes some very weird yet strangely attractive sounds when she reaches full orgasm."

Just like Tommy – has to have the last word.

Incorrigible!

Chapter Twenty-Nine: Tommy XIV

"If crematoria can be lovely, this is truly lovely. Firstly, it is situated in a great parkland, with trees, benches and a sense of peace. We were there on a beautiful autumn day, which no doubt added to the beauty and soothed our sadness."

When I first read what it said on the *Internet Guide to British Crematoria*, I was very tempted to mock. Don't get me wrong. I'm with Milton on censorship. For me anything goes, but the plethora of trivia that clogs our lives is too much for one brain to hold, for my brain to hold. And the sentiments expressed in the review seemed so at odds with my own feelings when Uncle Jack died.

But I have to admit they are right: it is a beautiful crematorium, but the manufactured perfection of its pastoral setting — an oasis in South London — only intensifies the sadness one feels at the loss of a loved one. The day that Katya and I were there was astonishingly, heart-rendingly beautiful. Early March, a chill in the air, but bright sunshine; the daffodils were out and there was a small lake on which ducks peacefully, placidly, floated, magically - it seemed. So, if there was an appropriate place to put my Uncle Jack to rest, then this was it.

Me, being me, I thought of the ash lake at Auschwitz and how this little lake in South London was much more peaceful and inviting than anything the Nazis had devised.

Only Katya and I stayed after the service for a quick chat before joining the others for the wake at the Frog and Whippet. Jack had no friends, only acquaintances, and they were all dead. In the family he had out-lived all the others of his generation and had lost touch with the younger branches — apart from mine. So Julie and Caroline were there with their husbands and all my nieces and nephews — and my own children of course. But none of them knew Jack as well as I had done. None of the political organizations that he had so keenly supported sent anyone because Uncle Jack had never joined a political organization - not as a card-carrying, full-blown, yes-I'm-definitely-in-it member.

I'm writing this in the peace and solitude of memory in a room far from South London and so I am calm like the little lake. But I cried and howled all through the service, a secular one, of course, where there was a tape of *Jerusalem* by William Blake, because Jack, above all, knew what it meant and he knew that I knew what it meant. A simple service sheet, his dates and one quotation on the front. "The great appear great because we are on our knees: let us arise!" And then inside the Order of Service. *Jerusalem, The Internationale* and *Katyusha*, a Russian song from the war. My Uncle Jack - iconoclastic to the last.

Wasn't it Mark Twain who said that we laugh at christenings and we weep at funerals because we are not the ones involved? What an old, mizzog tosser! How wrong to suggest that life is such a struggle that we should be envious of those we bury! Every day above the ground is a good day, as far as I'm concerned. I felt empty, forlorn, lonely.

What Mark Twain should have said was that every day above the ground is a wonderful, exhilarating, bountiful day because life on this beautiful earth is so full of promise, so full of hope, so full of expectancy, and, if anyone tells you different, sunshine, then they just haven't found the right way to live.

As Katya and I sat on the bench overlooking the lake. crying and speaking of Jack, nature seemed to reflect our feelings. Huh, the pathetic fallacy, how pathetic to think that nature cares! Yet we always project our feelings on to externals. Do we somehow validate our feelings as a result? So egocentric. We must get out of our grooves, maya padrooga.

In some ways the spring weather was not appropriate to bury my closest remaining relative and my closest friend, so deep, so miserable, so empty were my feelings. But, hey, you can't have rain every day and the spring weather could be said to have reflected Jack's hope, his belief that some things could be better, that everything could be better, if we only managed our affairs the right way. As you get older you seem to attend more funerals than marriages. And the weather, well, sometimes I wish I'll be buried in a cold, gloomy, January so people can think *Yes, pathetic fallacy! It really works!* But on other days I'd rather be buried in the heat of summer, where everyone is relaxed and their spirits are unloosened, and ice cream and balloons and the smells of hot dogs and candy floss fill the air. But then I don't suppose I get a choice. No one seems to get a choice, despite what they tell you.

Don't get me wrong. I'd been inconsolable with grief when my own father died, but this is Jack's story and with my father it was different: there were more of us to share the grief. Jack was childless, friendless, no acquaintances, even from his work. And you know, mate (if you've got this far) how deep his influence was on me. After we buried my father, my brothers and my sisters and I sat at my parents' kitchen table and drank whisky until all four bottles were empty. A grief shared is somehow made easier, more articulate.

What I couldn't understand was what had happened between Jack and Katya? Why, with so much in common, with so much affinity, they had never fallen in love? Not even got together in the latter stages of their life as companions. Was it me? Was it the iron discipline and reticence over personal affairs that people in the past seemed to have? I mentioned this to Katya. Through her tears Katya smiled and then laughed.

"Katya, what's so funny?"

"Oh, Tommy, you know so much and yet you know nothing. You know so little. Why did Jack and I never fall in love? That is such a funny question, Tommy - to ask it now on the day of his funeral is so ironic."

"But in what sense do I know nothing? I know that Robbie was in love with Halya and even had a child by her, but you and Jack were there and it seemed natural, two Englishmen, two Russian women, united fighting the same war, the same beliefs - were you not his type?"

"You could say that. That would be a dignified way of putting it. I was not his type... and he was not my type."

"Huh, as simple as that then?"

"No, Tommy, not as simple as that at all. Robbie was Jack's type. Jack was... what word do you use now? Jack was... gay. He was not interested in me because I was a woman. But he was a good friend – the only true friend I ever had – apart from Halya, of course."

"Uncle Jack - gay? I've never seen him show any interest in men or in sex for that matter."

"Oh, Tommy, you're so naïve. You still know nothing. Think of what it was like for Jack when he grew up in – what? - the 1930s? Homosexuality was against the law in your country. You could be sent to jail. Am I not right?"

"Yeah, you're right and in the Soviet Union too, I imagine."

"Yes, in the Soviet Union too and there is much prejudice still in the new Russia."

"Well, I think that there is still great prejudice here though we have made great progress, but I still don't understand about Jack. Why did he never tell me? Why was it all kept dark?"

"Tommy, look at your history. Who do you know from the past that was gay? From that period."

"Um, well, not exactly from that period, but... um... Oscar Wilde, Wilfred Owen, Siegfried Sassoon, W H Auden, Noel Coward."

"Yes, Tommy, and they were all from the upper classes or from the cultured élite. They had the freedom to do as they chose. Tommy, you know the streets Jack was brought up on, the culture he was brought up in. To be gay in that culture would have been suicide and, Tommy, I don't think he knew himself until he met me in Spain."

"Ah, so you are some amateur psychiatrist are you, you immediately see someone and assess their sexuality. I'm not really that prejudiced myself. I don't care what people do or where they put their genitals as long as they don't hurt someone else or do something against the will of another person."

"Tommy, the sight of you on a high horse is silly, particularly when it comes to personal and private matters. After a few days of knowing Jack and spending time with him, I guessed. I just felt that he wasn't interested in me, as a man is interested in a woman, as Robbie was interested in Halya. But I don't think he knew himself until he met me in Spain. He could not admit his own feelings to himself, so strong had been his upbringing and culture."

"And yet you are his closest friend?"

"Well, you could say that I am sympathetic. Like you I think what people do in private with the other person's consent is a matter entirely for themselves but...."

"But what, Katya?"

"But similar people recognize similar things in others. I have never married for the same reason that Jack never married."

"Oh Katya. Oh Katya, I'm sorry."

Still learning. So stupid.

"Don't be sorry for me. Why would I want to marry? I like women. But like Jack I grew up in a society where homosexuality and lesbianism were frowned upon and still are, and I never openly loved anyone because I knew that I would be in trouble with the authorities if I did. I would have been sent straight to the Gulags for committing crimes of sexual deviance. So, like Jack, I've lived a life full of secrecy and lies and deception."

"Oh Katya, I don't know what to say," and I blinked back the tears of my remorse and my stupidity.

"Tommy, you are not shocked that your Uncle Jack was homosexual?"

"Not shocked in the slightest. I couldn't care less; I'm shocked at my stupidity. Now a lot more makes sense. So he was so close to Robbie... he went wherever Robbie went - which is why they were in the Navy together."

"Yes," said Katya. "You're right."

"And he never said anything to Robbie?"

"Tommy, of his class, of his time, and Robbie so obviously heterosexual in his every action and thought. Believe me – I met Robbie and liked him enormously. He oozed charisma. But I am sure Jack would never have told Robbie. Besides, by the time Jack realized what he himself was and what he felt, Robbie had met Halya. Jack was not a man to cause unnecessary suffering to those he loved."

Unlike me, I thought.

"Tommy, what would have been the point of saying anything to Robbie? It would only have ruined a friendship."

"But, Katya, homosexuality was legalized here in 1968. Why didn't Jack do something then?"

"Tommy, I think it was too late for him - he was nearly fifty - how could he change? People knew him as the local butcher- how could he alter his life then? It would have taken great courage, great fortitude. Also I think, Tommy, his heart had grown cold and incapable of love. What did you want him to do? Go on a Gay Pride march and wear pink t-shirts. I don't think that would have suited Jack."

"Mmm, but something did change in Jack around that time."

"Yes, so he's told me, Tommy. But, of course, he was pleased that it was no longer illegal, just as he was pleased that the death penalty was abolished. He thought things were finally coming round to the way he thought they should be, but his heart was too hard to love. He'd fortified it by then against all the knocks and, to be honest, I think he was probably still in love with Robbie."

"Katya, I think at last I understand. As the light dims, as the stars come out and night approaches it does get harder to say I love you with any real conviction."

"Ha ha, Tommy – you always spout such sentimental nonsense! But you're right, you still don't understand everything. There is always something more to learn. And you still don't see the whole picture."

"So help me, Katya. Help me see. Don't keep it all dark, please."

"No, while we live, some things are best kept dark – trust me."

"Katya, let's go to the pub now and get blindingly drunk."

Katya grinned and stood up. "Trust me, Tommy. Keep some things dark. It's for the best."

Chapter Thirty: Olga III

Dear Tommy,

It is with the deepest sadness that I write to tell you that Katya died two weeks ago. I know you would have wanted to be at her funeral, but I also know that you would not have been able to get a visa so quickly to come.

Katya said just before she died that I should write to you only after she was buried. So I have. She died without pain, Tommy, and wanted to be reminded to you.

She has left many letters and documents that she wanted you to read: some are in English, but many are in Russian. I will not read them until you are here. If you can come to Volgograd, I will help you read the Russian ones and I can suggest some good cheap hotels for you to stay in. Katya also wanted you to have her medals. I can speak some English as you know, but I cannot read the English documents.

Tommy, I know you are always busy with your work, but I remember that when you last was in Volgograd you said your work was very flexible. So perhaps you can come quite easily. You already know me and other people in the Veterans' Association. They will be pleased to see you again, I am sure.

I hope to hear from you soon.

Olga

Chapter Thirty-One: Tommy XV

Dear Olga,

I find it hard to believe that Katya can be dead: she seemed so strong, so resilient, so indispensable. When I received your e-mail, Olya, I cried and I went to the crematorium where Jack's ashes are scattered, and I told him the heavy news from Russia. I hope he heard me, but he was a confirmed atheist, so perhaps he wasn't even listening.

I cannot say I will be delighted to return to Volgograd – the circumstances are too sad – but I know from before that I will be made welcome. And part of me loves the city and longs to be back there. As you know, Uncle Jack and I came the last time in autumn and I would like to see the city in the summer and swim in the Volga.

I am also very interested in reading any papers that may shed light on the past. At Jack's funeral Katya told me something very important about Jack, but there are still mysteries about Robbie that I feel compelled to try to uncover. Olya – too much has been kept dark and perhaps together we can bring to light whatever secrets lie in the past.

As for my work, all I need is a hotel, no matter how basic, with an internet connection. Apart from that, I can come as soon as I can get a visa. I do not have much money, so please recommend the cheapest hotel you can find.

Best wishes -

Tommy

Chapter Thirty-Two: Olga IV

Dear Tommy,

Thank you for your so quick reply. I think the Flamingo Motel on Marshal Rokossovsky Street will be perfect. It has an internet connection. It is very cheap. It is possible walk to my apartment. You will know the importance of the street's name too: Katya told me you always understood the little things in life. So you will enjoy living on Marshal Rokossovsky Street for a few weeks: there are many papers and letters to read.

Katya also told me that you are someone who is passionate about life, kind, loyal, sincere, trusting, caring, and someone who has a beautiful soul. In you I believe I see kindness and much beauty. I strongly value wisdom, strength, love and a degree of openness.

I will meet you at the airport and make sure you arrive at the motel.

Warm wishes -

Olga

Chapter Thirty-Three: Tommy XVI

Dear Olga,

I have booked the motel and will arrive at Volgograd Airport around midnight on June 6th. You will understand the significance of this date for an Englishman, just as I appreciate your choice of hotel – an excellent location.

See you in a month.

Tommy

Chapter Thirty-Four: Tommy XVII

All that summer Tommy stayed in the motel on Marshal Rokossovsky Street, poring through the piles and piles of documents that Katya had left. It was like an archaeological dig, Tommy thought, as he delved further and further into the past. There were a few official documents, certificates awarded along with medals to Halya and to Katya, but most of the hoard of treasure was handwritten. Notes from Jack and from Robbie, a letter from Halya on yellowing, pencil-filled paper that smelled of time and age and death. And right at the bottom a typed document from Katya, signed and dated only ten years before.

Tommy's days quickly established a rhythm, a pattern, which, being addicted to patterns, he enjoyed and relished, and fell into almost without knowing it. He would rise early, do some work for England and use the internet connection to send it off, descend to the bar where breakfast was served and, after a couple of coffees, and the most wonderful bread rolls stuffed with jam or honey, he would go back to the room again and work on the documents.

"Work while the day lasts, for the night of death cometh in which no man can work," had always been his credo.

For lunch he would meet Olga at a coffee shop in the centre of the city and then it was back to the hotel room, usually for more desultory work, a mixture of his own work for England and the documents themselves. Every time he met Olga and looked at her face or gazed into her eyes, something jolted in his brain and he was reminded of something or somebody. *What was it? Where had he seen that face before? Whose eyes did Olga's remind him of? What was it?*

In the evenings he would eat at Olga's. Olga and her daughter had a tiny flat, by English standards. When Tommy first went, he mistook the built-in cupboard doors for doors to other rooms, so surprised was he that two people could live in such a small space. And as time went on he realized that they had all they needed and that anything more would have been extravagant and a waste. Tommy responded to the regular meals and the regular human contact with a joy and a sense of contentment that he had not felt since after Jack's funeral, and that, in truth, he had not felt for more than two decades. Regular meals, human contact, faces - his Russian improved enormously, although, of course, he needed Olga's help to transliterate the Russian documents.

Having only been to the city before in autumn, Tommy was amazed to see it transformed in summer: the heat, a dry almost desert heat, dominated every day. In the last four or five weeks he abandoned work in the afternoon and he and Olga would prolong lunch or walk along the Volga, or visit one of the many memorials and sites to the fallen, or simply shop for food. They went boating on the Volga. Tommy, his slightly pallid, embarrassingly bloated form a source of shame to him, went swimming in the Volga. Swimming in fresh water or sea water was something that Tommy had always loved.

And it seemed, newly baptized every afternoon towards the end of the day as the evening's shadows darkened before fading forever and the night made all things dark again, he arose from the Volga, re-born. And he listened in amazement to Olga's stories of the free three week holidays to all parts of the Soviet Union that workers and their families were given every summer during the period of Communism and the apartments that were given to you after ten years' service at your workplace. These things had been kept very dark in the West during the Cold War. No wonder, Tommy thought to himself.

But he was here to discover the secrets, the mysteries of the documents that Katya had left, and there were many surprises in store. He tried different ways of arranging them: chronologically, English and Russian piles, and then piles for Robbie, for Jack, for Halya, for Katya, but that didn't work because Halya's pile was so tiny, as was Robbie's. He decided to start with the English documents first. All were handwritten; most were in pencil; he was astonished to find what appeared to be a poem by Jack dated September, 1937. It read:

In days unborn when tales are told,

Of freedom's vanguard, strong and bold

When over all the world a hush is spread

And we pay homage to our dead

A cry will ring in every heart

Salud, brigade, salud

They in our hearts will never die

Who carried freedom's banner high

And fighting died and gave their all

To break the strangling fascists all

That cry must live forever

'Salud brigade, Salud'

We who are young must all unite

A deeper fire yet we'll light

To show the path that we must tread

If we with honour, face our dead

They will answer in response

'Salud comrades, Salud'

Tommy was amazed. He never realized that Jack had once written poetry, but by now nothing could amaze him about the past, though he felt sad at the irony that the International Brigaders were essentially forgotten, that fascism had been destroyed, but that a newer form of fascism had somehow insinuated itself across the globe economically.

Dated September 1938 there was another poem, less celebratory, more morose and, Tommy noted with interest, terser, more succinct.

Faces of men running, yelling, screaming

Voices of men shouting, swearing, howling

The fearful eyes of the dying, those of the dead

The faces of cowardice and of the scream-driven mad

Men had been hoping, wanting, waiting

Minds of men loving, fighting, hating

The faces of the wounded drowned in red

Faces of the dying, faces of the dead.

Tommy was surprised to find several letters from Robbie to Halya, though they ceased abruptly in the late summer of 1939, for obvious reasons, Tommy could imagine.

It was clear from them too that another piece of the jigsaw had fallen into place. Robbie knew that he was a father, that he and Halya's son was in the Soviet Union being brought up, he imagined – no, he knew - by Halya's parents if Halya was on military duty. In Tommy's eyes this added not just another piece of the jigsaw, but a rather serendipitous symmetry to everything. It was only right that Robbie should know that a little bit of himself would be united with Halya for ever and was safe from the fascist onslaught on the Soviet Union.

But Tommy knew the dates: he knew that Halya would have died, not knowing of Robbie's death, and Robbie would have died not knowing of Halya's capture and eventual death. And Tommy wept that evening for the terrible murk and fog of war that split lives and shattered families, and made a human bonding such a fraught and dangerous and bloody affair. And yet Robbie's letters exuded the optimism of youth. They were full of love and socialism and hope for a brighter future, a determined sense of inevitability that Hitler would be beaten and that one day he would join Halya and Nikita in Russia.

Halya's documents were sparse and there were only four: a letter that she had written to Nikita and which had arrived many months after her writing it. It arrived at Ulyanovsk by hand and was given to her parents. That night after they had eaten, as Olga falteringly translated the smudged and faded Cyrillic into English, they sat at the kitchen table and wept. The other three were posthumous medals and small cards giving them official verification and then the medals themselves, pristine because they had never been worn: one for the defence of Stalingrad. The ribbon was shaped in that typical inverted polygon shape that Soviet medals have and the ribbon was a pale, the palest cream, with just a hint of green and, right in the centre a thin, single line of red. The Volga, Tommy thought, the Volga running red with blood. The face of the medal itself showed soldiers, women, tanks, and aeroplanes all facing leftwards, westwards, to repel the fascists, Tommy imagined. The other – a beautiful silver one - was for bravery and the third was very impressive: the Order of the Red Banner. And Tommy cried at the futility of the medals, at the human need to commemorate and to memorialise and yet at the shared triviality of these dignified but nonetheless gaudy gewgaws. Even a million of these could not sum up the suffering of the city of Stalingrad, but Tommy understood the human urge to remember, a paltry attempt to simplify the past through objects and to recognize the heroism of simply being there. What else do we have to keep our memories alive? To pay tribute to the past? To prove that we were there? That we existed, although we were never meant to.

Katya's medals lay in a big pile by the time Tommy had sorted them out because of her length of service and because she'd fought all the way from Stalingrad to Berlin. So she had one exactly like Halya's, but then she also had a gaudy ribboned one, red, petrol blue and yellow that marked the liberation of Prague; a black and aquamarine ribboned medal for the liberation of Konigsberg; a black and muted orange for the liberation of Berlin; and then for every ten years after the war the commemorative medal marking the victory over fascism. She even had a Fortieth Anniversary medal, which Tommy realized was not (as Jack had told him) the Arctic Convoy medal, but was in fact the medal for the fortieth anniversary given to everyone and which was also offered to British sailors and merchant seamen, who had been forbidden to accept it by the British government.

Halya's son, Nikita, of course, left few records and no medals. Even the Soviet Union, Tommy realized, would hardly strike a medal for the repression of Prague. But Ilya and Yuri had two matching medals for the misadventure in Afghanistan and another two: the Chernobyl Liquidator's Medal, a beautiful medal, an attempt in simple, almost abstract form, to convey the horrors of a nuclear meltdown, simple and beautiful, elegant and useless, and Tommy knew that it didn't work. Like the others it was futile.

Things were going well at work that summer for Tommy. He reflected that without the internet a summer like this would have been impossible. Very often in the hazy heat, even at midnight, he would be working away and sending things back to England, but he loved Volgograd that summer. The city was transformed. Its heartbeat seemed to match the rhythm of people walking and the flow of the Volga, teeming with river-craft and boats of every kind, boats carrying goods up and down, north and south, pleasure craft, pleasure steamers.

He and Olga spent several afternoons on long leisurely cruises around the islands that dotted the river to the north and to the south of the city. Everywhere people bathed in the Volga. Small children gasped at the feel of the water and then with delight and with love immersed themselves in it. Families, young people, larked around splashing each other, while lovers walked along the Volga Boulevard and gazed benevolently at all this human activity. And it struck Tommy that it was, above all, a very human city. Everything, it seemed to Tommy, responded to the rhythm of human life, work, play, transport - even the river was there for the delight of the citizens.

One of the last documents Tommy read was Katya's type-written one towards the end. It was long and because it was typewritten Tommy could read some of it and make out some words more clearly and, as he deciphered it and then later, over four or five nights, Olga translated it, Tommy felt something in himself die.

This was one secret he had not known. Had never even guessed. The document, Katya's account, addressed 'To whom it may concern', was Katya's account of her time in the Gulag prison system. And Tommy read or heard from Olga's translation, with a sinking heart, of the paranoid brutality of the old Communist regime, and Katya's condemnation of the system that he thought she had loved, the system she'd fought so hard for, the system that Jack had revered and adulated for so long, and Tommy almost chuckled to himself. This was a woman who'd won so many medals, who'd fought from Stalingrad to Berlin and who then, it appeared, had been incarcerated by a brutal totalitarian dictatorship for eight years because she had done a very human thing - she had told a joke about Joseph Stalin.

And even more moving and revealing was a brief hand-written note in Uncle Jack's sloping, spidery hand-writing, paper-clipped to the final page of Katya's testament which simply read:

Auschwitz: Arbeit Macht Frei

Soviet Gulags: Through Labour Freedom

British Detention Centres in Africa: Labour and Freedom

The same lies. They're all at it. Accept no authority but yourself. "If there is a state, then there is domination, and in turn, there is slavery."

Somewhere and sometime that summer, without noticing how it began, without being conscious that it had begun, and, without knowing exactly what they were doing, Tommy and Olga, very tentatively but rather frightened of what might be happening to them and wary, not of each other but of the feelings that slowly wound round in their souls and their bodies, fell in love.

Love? Yes, let us call it that. Words. Words. Words. So much time did they spend together; they saw things in such similar ways; their outlook on things that mattered was in complete accord, and Tommy's gradual discovery through the documents that he dissected that summer that their lives were so intertwined and that there was a beautiful, calm and symmetrical serendipity, some would say inevitability, about their coming together.

Although wiser heads than Tommy's would asseverate, in those mysterious yet uncharted regions of the oceans of human action, nothing is inevitable. They had decided by then with conviction that they did not know much about anything really except each other and what began as a series of meals and coffees and snacks and visits to the supermarkets took on the lineaments and rhythms of the nearby river and the rituals of love.

And inevitably, Olga became Olya, Olenka, Olyushka. Tommy, of course, being Tommy, invented new words: 'Dinkeedoolichka' as a term of endearment and 'Chaynaplitsya' – the afternoon sleep taken after a post-lunch cup of hot black sweet tea – like the tea Jack had relished so much in Spain. Every afternoon they napped together chastely; they walked in time, in step, along the streets and always wanted to do the same things. Tommy's wary, frightened guardedness fell away – a skin sloughed off and left lying on the dusty street sides.

They thought the same things and used a vocabulary that was eternal and universal and known only to them.

One mid-morning, having been sitting thinking, a snaggy thought tearing at his mind, his eyes fixed on the documents, his eyes bedazzled and whirling at all the Cyrillic, Tommy leapt to his feet, a great thought in his mind – the final part of the jigsaw! He had realized whose face Olya's reminded him of.

He shaved and showered hurriedly and, disrupting his normal routine, raced around excitedly to Olya's apartment. He strode breathlessly up the stairs and rang the bell excitedly, bursting with his new found knowledge, his jigsaw piece.

"Olyushka, Olyushka – this may sound crazy, but – but – prepare yourself for a shock. You are Robbie's granddaughter!"

Olya stared for a frozen minute at Tommy's wild-eyed craziness, before she said,

"Yes, I've known that for years. My dad had worked it out and my mother had told me. Robert Thompson was my grandfather. He's buried in the military cemetery in Murmansk. I'm surprised Jack or Katya hadn't told you."

Chapter Thirty-Five: Olga V

Dear Tommy,

Maybe today it was not the best day for a walk, but I decided to walk around the streets of my city and I decided to speak with my city about everything that was inside me. My city - how beautiful you are! There are so many beautiful parks and gardens with my favourite light; it flies into the sky and it seems that it will not be hurt by snow or rain. The stream of cars goes by the wave and carries along, but the sound of unique music makes the body return to the world.

You do not even imagine how much I dream to walk hand in hand with you, my dear man: it should be our parks and alleys, and it should be our light. We can talk, we can argue, we can be also silent, especially it can be so romantic just to be silent next to you.... And in these intervals will lie this special holy feeling, which words cannot express: it is something that people cannot understand because they cannot listen through our silence.

Can you imagine such moments? We can see our small bridges, crowded streets and again silence and music. The astringent taste of tea or heady tang of blood red wine. Can you imagine all these sweet things? We can have these terse sentences; awkward touches and talks about nothing, it can be talks only about the little things that we are afraid to confess like they are the most important in our life.

I am so tired to be single and I want to feel silence between us; it should be music for both of us; it should be a walk without words, and your eyes will look into my soul. I hope that you will come back soon and I will be waiting for you here!

Warmly Yours,
Olya

Chapter Thirty-Six: Tommy XVIII

They still talk about it as the coldest winter and I missed the lot. Part of me thinks that I should have mentioned this earlier, but even I hadn't really seen the truth until now. It wasn't that what happened to me was kept dark – but it certainly wasn't talked about much. And when it was over I just got on with life – until recently really.

Yeah, cold enough to freeze the bollocks off a brass monkey (which is why they make such inappropriate pets in the northern Europe – I've never been tempted). Always dogs – they're easy to frighten and lie to. Like your kids. But I'm not into frightening. Ever. Or a bit parky – great word from Gujerati. I never knew that until I bothered to look it up in the big Oxford. A bit parky – don't you just love the English predilection for litotes?

What a deal! We go round the world, stealing countries, beating people with sticks and making them build very, very complicated railway systems; and in return – words - and in the case of India, the best cuisine ever to grace this sorry little island.

And the doosra. Bargain! Shookria, Talha!

Not to mention the rest of the stuff we stole. Nice marbles, Mr Elgin!

You meet all sorts of people who claim very early memories. I remember nothing before that morning when I was five. There's stuff I think I remember, but it's all from photos and anecdotes. That morning I will remember forever. January 30th in the worst winter ever. Normally a date for joy and celebration. Sylvia Plath was to live a little longer; somewhere in west London Mick and Keith were honing their blues-playing skills; and in Britain it was the big freeze. And I woke up and couldn't walk. My dad got really angry with me – but it's because he was scared. He couldn't believe it.

So they strapped me to a stretcher and ferried me out to the ambulance. By this time I could only move my head and my hands. I can't remember what I was thinking or feeling. Perhaps I didn't understand how serious it was. Perhaps I had faith in the doctors, in Britain. Don't laugh! Three months in isolation at the South London Unit for Infectious Diseases – in those days the choice was easy death or a vegetable. I've always loved brussels. And leeks. Ah! Trumpton! Antwerp! What? Word association football.

Which reminds me:

What's the hardest part of eating a vegetable?

The wheelchair!

Anyway I spent three days lying face down while they did stuff to my spine. Never said a word. The doctor and nurses praised my fortitude. My stoicism. My fortitude and my resolution. My grit and pluck. But shit and fuck! I was there: who else was there? I may have been having the third lumbar puncture when poor Sylvia was finally going a few miles away. Life and death. Always a fucker – suffering no matter which way you turn.

For those three months I did not see a human face. Everyone wore masks.

Even my parents - the only family who could visit me – wore masks. The specialists wore masks; the women who brought my food wore masks. Only the nurses looked at me face-to-face, and the nurses were all black. You should always forgive a wrong, but never forget a kindness. I have never forgotten their kindness.

Looking back, my parents must have been worried out of their lives. They knew that there was every chance that I would die. I was completely, blissfully unaware (Oh! Collocation - don't you just love it! Allusion! As you like it, sunshine!) totally unaware of the danger I was in. Or perhaps that is a tribute to the very rare compassionate necessity of keeping some things dark. If my parents lived in fear of the outcome, and if the doctors and nurses knew the likely outcomes, then they still managed to display a cheery optimism whenever they saw me.

I was bored. I remember having two toys - a flexible plastic puppet about six inches long - a policeman - whose legs you could insert your index and middle fingers into and he would walk across the board on wheels (a table, so to speak) that was always near my chin and lay across the bed. The other puppet, the other toy, is harder to describe: it was an ingenious device, but one that may have been around for centuries. It consisted of two thin parallel sticks, about two inches apart and in the middle suspended on a tiny piece of tautened string was a small monkey. If you held the two sticks at the bottom and squeezed sharply, the monkey performed somersaults, just by the pressure of your hand. I have no idea how it worked. I didn't then and I don't know now.

I was paralysed for three months. After a week of invented conversations and games between the plastic policeman and the somersaulting monkey, I was even more bored. I was bored, bored, bored (zeuxis, since you ask, my friend). I was Mr Bored. The Right Honourable Mr Bored. Lord Bored of Ennui. Duke Dull of the Doldrums. Marquis of Monotony. High Grand Master of Lassitude. My large close knit family could not come to see me. I was very infectious, but each day a small hillock of postcards arrived from all my cousins, all my aunts and uncles, my grandparents, my great aunts and uncles, all my extended family. But, Brownsville Girl, I could not read and so I was doubly bored. They say people who suffer together have stronger commitments than those who are more content. But what happens to you when you suffer alone? How do you re-connect?

Because I was paralysed, I lost control of my bodily functions. Which is a euphemistic way of saying that each greyish white, snow-draped dawn, discovered me lying in a little lake of reeking piss and clogging, claggy, warm shit. A foretaste of dying. Which I was, in a way. Dignity? Not a chance, mate. Right out the fucking window.

One day a huge envelope arrived with over thirty near-identical letters to me from my classmates at school. The ones I had known for - what? – just a term.

Dear Tommy,

I hope you are well.

My brother has lost a tooth.

Yvonne.

They were all a bit like that. My mother has kept them.

So what changed? In a world where all you have is words and an unreadable code you can't crack, it's like being born into a raging, screaming ocean where you swim relentlessly, flailing your legs and arms in hope of rescue, in the hope of reaching a shore line that you can never see, no solid ground beneath you, never a resting place. I had no way of keeping afloat until I taught myself to read. Perhaps I asked a nurse the meaning of one or two words. I can't remember, but I know that one cold snow-filled day in February I cracked the code. I felt a solid, wind-wept, tear-swept but beautiful island rising beneath my feet like the gargantuan back of some great leviathan and, as more and more words emerged and were born into my brain, I felt I could finally, and with a sense of peace, rest. I had a place to stand for the first time in this bright, tiny room in this big hospital.

The island grew into a country with each word I deciphered until an entire continent became visible and navigable – one inhabited by people who had addresses and whom I knew and who were mapped into my sub-consciousness. I read all the clichéd words of hope and good cheer from my extended family and suddenly through language, through words, my paralysis was gone; my joy and my tears and my pain could be shared with anyone who could read, and I could do all this alone. Alone – even in my little lagoons of piss and shit. I could do it here! Now! Anywhere!

I was no longer a prisoner of demons eating away at me and slowly chewing my flesh before my very eyes; no longer a victim of pain and fear that had made me clench my fist white with frustration, grit my teeth into silence and smile helplessly at the nurses who took such good care of me. Words now pleaded back with a happy lucidity of absolute and ice-clear cogency. Through words, through reading, I was free. I could respond, escape, celebrate, indulge, criticize, embrace or reject this country, the earth, the entire cosmos if it was my whim, and, without knowing it, I was launched on an endless journey without any boundaries or rules in which I could and would salvage, clean and re-forge the floating, febrile fragments of my past, and my future, and be born afresh in the spontaneous firework ignition of understanding some concealed aspect of myself, of other people and of my world.

Each word I read steamed and burbled and bubbled and shouted and hissed and fizzed with the hot lava streamings of my lexical re-birth, and crawled their way out onto postcards, letters, stanzas, dripping with birth blood, re-born and freed from the pain-plagued stasis of my hospital bed.

That small, paralyzed child in that bright, light room of isolation who could not reach the light switch, who could not go to the lavatory without the help of a stranger, who could not feed himself, found himself, and found words, and words have changed my life. And then, back then, words struck me with lightning cackle-crackles of elation and joy and leaping-up-and-down ecstasy, and I didn't know, I could not see, that later they would also violate me and betray me with rolling thunder and storms of grief, cyclones of laughter, the drizzle of remorse, the seeping, weeping fog of confusion and lies.

And the next step, of course, was to ask for a pencil and paper, and then I started and - I haven't really stopped.

Some bursts of hope exploded from the lead tip of my pencil: words that propelled me into an awareness of who I was and where I might be going and where I had been and where I really was and where I wanted to go. Words that peeled back, torn back to a burning, searing, searching core of bleak terror, an embryo floating in a cosmos of water that cracked out of his shell wide-eyed and insane and dancing with the joy of life and laughter. Dancing brand-new and sparkling like a newly-formed star in the infinite cosmos of my personal hell. Trees, misty, enchanted mountains, wonderful fertile plains and glorious savage waterfalls grew out of the ends of my fingers, the threatening, leering, loutish otherness of life dissolved, and I became one with the air and the sky, the dust, the glass and the concrete, the tarmacked roads and the invisible airways of the sky - and now there were no longer any differences between me and others, but this knowledge made me different in itself.

Words made bright, incandescent, shimmering rope-bridges of bright red purging fire in the crucible of my brain between everything I saw and everyone I knew and everyone I met and everything I thought of. I entered the blade of grass, the snowflake, the football, the child's soul, my father's boots and every night, with a pencil in my hand, I flew. I conversed with fiery spirits in my isolation room. I visited strange houses where lonely women brewed sweet black tea and rocked in rickety rocking-chairs, listening to Shostakovich. I travelled, swift as time, across unknown, uncharted oceans, over undiscovered bourns; I flew and spiralled through the air. I was everywhere. The pencil was Mephistopheles to my Faustus. The apple to my Eve. And I was there; I was there with my grandfathers, my father and Uncle Bill at Monte Cassino. I was there with Gagarin on his first flight. I was of my time and of all time.

Poekhali! I was there with my pencil, ready to record it all. And though I didn't realize that at the time, my pencil would become my weapon – impotent and perpetually disappointing, but mine. And it would enable me to perform magical transformations. I could become an Asian in Europe, a landless peasant in Mexico, a black under Apartheid, a history teacher under Pol Pot, a housewife alone at night with screaming children to pacify, a Jamaican in a Brixton Police Cell, a worker who's being made redundant, a Quaker under Cromwell, a dissident under neo-liberalism, a Zapatista in the hills, a worker fighting for his rights, a Jew during the Shoah, a Palestinian in Gaza, an emaciated child begging for mercy, a frightened woman everywhere, in every city and every town all over the world it seems, crying, "Please, please, no, no, no," and, above all, it could allow me to be me.

But at the time, truth to tell, the documentary evidence suggests that it only produced this:

Dear Yvonne,

I am all right.

Tommy.

Chapter Thirty-Seven: Katya's Statement

This is a half poem

For the half of my heart

Which beats fast when I'm frightened

And for the other half which is braver,

Beating loudly, brimming over in anger

And rage for my life which is for ever falling apart in half

Pieces before it comes together again as a whole,

For the way there is usually more than one truth,

Often more than one half of the

Halves that don't come in half sizes.

This is a half poem for the half

Of me that is most unacceptable,

Least public at any given time

And for that half of the population

Who've always had the

Biggest, kindest widest ha-

lf of my heart.

Looking back now fifty years later, I still find it almost impossible to believe it happened. It was towards the end of May in 1945. We were billeted in barracks in the suburbs of Berlin. Life was good; we'd just had a massive victory against fascism. There were rumours that we would soon be sent to the Far East of the Soviet Union to help Great Britain and the USA in their continuing fight against the fascist

Japanese. But one night, an hour or so after midnight, the door to the barracks opened and my name was called out.

"Put your clothes on now. Quickly – don't bring anything else and leave your weapons. You're coming in for interrogation."

I thought, "Why is it always at night? Don't they do any work during the day?" I was so naïve: I didn't realize then that this was done deliberately because night interrogations terrorized us. It's odd to remember now, but for some bizarre reason I was not terrified in the slightest. At that time my trust and unquestioning faith in Soviet authority was intact. Usually people will tell you about being beaten or tortured, but it isn't always the case. I wasn't beaten up or physically assaulted at all. No one laid a finger on me. I think I wasn't beaten because of my war record, but who knows? I certainly don't. The interrogator was very pleasant, very urbane and very polite, but inexorable and unrelenting. He called me by my first name and patronymic throughout and was very polite to me. To begin with, of course, I had no idea why I had been arrested and dragged in for questioning.

"Ekaterina Alexandrovna, please tell me how a brave and valiant war hero like yourself, who are now under arrest, tell me how you, a good Russian woman and party member, can grow such hatred towards Comrade Stalin, one of this country's great leaders? We want to understand. We want to understand how you can think of such things."

It was over four days of this before I realized what it must have been.

While we were getting in position for the Victory Parade on May 9th in Berlin I cracked a joke with my unit about Stalin: someone must have informed on me. But it took me several days to realize that. They did use sleep deprivation to break me down: they deprived me of all sleep for nearly a month. Their methods were probably developed in consultation with doctors perhaps on medical advice – or it may just have been a question of common sense. They allowed you to sleep for one hour every day and one night each week, and it's said that some poor prisoners went slightly mad, but not wholly. I think it must have been possible to lose one's sanity completely, but they needed to keep us in a semi-lucid condition.

I was taken out for interrogation every four or five hours. When I returned to my cell I never slept properly – it was just the delusion of sleep. I was falling somewhere and afterwards went the entire day without sleep. Every so often they looked through the spy hole, and I couldn't even lean against the wall and then another night of interrogation followed. When I slept for more than an hour, a guard would come into the room and shake me awake. I was in solitary confinement, of course, and even now, if I close my eyes I can still see every contour, every scratch and every bump on the walls of my cell, painted in the favourite prison colours, brownish red half-way up and a dirty grey above. Sometimes when I'm walking on a pavement somewhere I still feel the cracks on the stone floor of my cell. Number Three, the second floor, north side.

I still remember the physical exhaustion and inertia, the apathy of my muscles, as I moved or tried to move in the cell in which I lived for those three long and tortuous weeks. I think I found it so frustrating because throughout the war every day I had been physically very active, so this forced idleness broke my normal routine and came as a shock. It was five paces long and three across – you see, I can remember precisely. I was taken out of my cell only to be interrogated. The interrogator's ridiculous, senseless slander was actually more insulting than being incarcerated. But since I understood that I was dealing with such an idiot, with a mentally limited clod, I became indifferent to stupid, loud-mouthed accusations. His urbanity slipped after a fortnight and he had obviously decided I would 'benefit' from a change of interrogational style.

"Such insolence," he'd bellow, "you dare state that Stalin is worthy of jokes and can be laughed at. There is no place for you on Soviet soil. You are an enemy of the people. Shoot her! Shoot her!"

But no-one did. They were just empty words. Furthermore, I did not consider myself an enemy of the people in the slightest: I had fought with bravery and distinction all the way from Stalingrad to the centre of Berlin; I had won a medal for courage – and they don't hand those out like confetti in the Red Army I can tell you. Perhaps that was the problem: perhaps it was hubris that made me tell the joke. But then again you have to imagine the atmosphere amongst the fighting battalions who had seen so much death, so many brutalities, so many atrocities: what harm could a few words possibly do?

I felt the complete futility of my situation – they had obviously already decided I was guilty since the act of arresting me was proof in itself – they never made mistakes…. Or at least they never admitted to them. I've heard that some people after interrogation are willing to confess to anything – just to please the interrogators and so get back to a normal routine. But this interrogator made me bolder and more stubborn: I'd helped defeat the fascists at Stalingrad and driven them back to their own corrupted centre – I wasn't going to co-operate with a jumped–up NKVD officer who had never been under fire from the real enemy.

I shouted back at him derisively at the top of my voice.

"It's you who have no place on our blessed Soviet soil, not me. It's you who should sit behind bars, not me. Shoot me right now if you dare! I don't want to live. I'm a war hero."

He went very quiet then and, I'm probably wrong, but I told myself that I detected a glimmer of respect for me. Certainly on that occasion he picked up the telephone receiver and said with indifference, "Come and take the prisoner away."

They took my cherished uniform away and gave me new clothes; not a word was uttered about where I was going or what would be going to happen to me.

After that, on a train packed solid with all sorts of other prisoners, they took me back to the Soviet Union, and I was interred in a transit camp, where the men and women were separated by a barbed wire fence and which was located somewhere near Minsk, I think. We weren't really harassed or bothered by the guards. We used to loiter by the barbed wire fence which separated our compound from the men's. We gazed spellbound at the long, never-ending line of male prisoners who passed us silently with their heads bowed, stumbling clumsily and wearily in prison boots, similar to our own. The men's uniforms were also similar, but their trousers with a brown stripe were even more like convicts' than our drab, shapeless skirts. You might have thought the men were stronger than we were, but they seemed somehow more defenceless and we all, even I, felt a maternal pity for them. They seemed to stand up to pain so badly. It wasn't just me: this was everyone's opinion. They wouldn't be able to wash their clothes on the quiet as we could with our under-things. Above all, they might have been our fathers, our brothers, our uncles, deprived of our care in this half-way house to hell. I couldn't help wondering what they'd done: surely they hadn't ALL told jokes about Stalin?

I spent my eight years' detention in two different camps. The first was the worst: awful, back-breaking, soul-sapping labour. I wasn't totally sure where it was, but it was in the closest part of Siberia – we passed the Urals to reach it. We had to leave the camp every morning at six and work for twelve hours chopping down trees. Each night we would return to the barracks completely soaked to the skin, plastered with mud up to our waists, and, in winter, frozen to the bone. Our skirts were sodden and clung to our legs. Those with reasonable boots tried, to begin with, to protect their legs from the icy water, but feet with boots on sank still deeper into the glacial quagmire that the ground consisted of. We no longer had the strength to fulfil our output targets and so our rations were steadily reduced, and so our targets were 're-adjusted'. Food, or the absence of it, was the major problem in both camps. Those who fulfilled their work target received 600 grams of bread. Those who didn't received 400 grams. The difference of 200 grams was a daily matter of life and death, because it was impossible to survive on 400 grams of bread a day when you worked in the cold of minus 50.

The winter of 1948 was very bad – the worst and heaviest snow for years, I later learnt. The rations were reduced from 600 to 500 grams. Besides bread, we got soup with bits of black cabbage and herring heads, and three tablespoons of watery porridge with half a teaspoon of vegetable oil, and for dinner we got a finger sized piece of herring tail. All this time we worked twelve hour shifts in the cold of minus 50. People simply started wasting away. You'd speak to someone at morning roll call and never see them again: they simply did not return from work, keeling over in the snow and being ignored by the guards.

But there were kindnesses and humanity even in the camp. The zeks helped each other, and at that first camp the doctor was an angel. There were rumours that she saved the lives of dozens of women by keeping them longer in the infirmary, making sure they were excused from work or prescribing extra rations for them just so they would be stronger and more capable of surviving when they went back - as they inevitably did.

And the guards could also be friendly. Many were there for self-interest and other perverse, selfish reasons. If you were attractive enough, you could barter sex for extra food or even a luxury like chocolate. That didn't appeal to me for obvious reasons: also I had my pride: most of the guards were too old for active service or had some slight physical impairment that had made them unsuitable for active service: I, on the other hand, had been a crack sniper with an impressive kill rate. Anyway, some of the guards formed relationships with the younger, more attractive prisoners, some of whom even had children by them. But it was a marriage of harsh convenience, shall we say. The women who slept with the guards got extra food and extra food ensured life. It wasn't love – whatever that is – it was survival.

The second camp I was sent to was centred around a sewing factory not far from Samara. When we arrived about thirty long tables were arranged in several rows: sewing machines stood on the tables in dense, tightly-packed rows, very close together allowing one to turn the handle and throw the women next door a sewn piece of sleeve, a pocket or a collar, or whatever it was we were supposed to be making. Bright lights under the low ceiling blinded our eyes; the sewing machines hummed and rattled and whirred; the air was full of dust and small fibres from the fabric which made up the sewn uniforms. That's what we made mainly - army uniforms - and it was better than the first camp because we switched to eight hour shifts and we worked indoors, but the food was still a problem. At least we no longer had to contend with the weather.

The barracks, of course, gave you no privacy, but we were just zeks after all. It was all bunk beds, made simply of rough planks. Each bunk bed was designed for eight people, four at the bottom, and four at the top. At nights the barracks were locked and we had to use zinc buckets. When we first got there we were given mattress covers and coarse straw to fill them, pillow covers and more straw for the pillows, blankets and even rough sheets: you see, compared to the first camp it approached a sort of zek-like luxury. Things got easier after 1950: we had the right to correspondence and then, a few short months after Stalin died, everything changed and I was released.

People often ask me now who was in the camp. Well, there were some ordinary criminals - embezzlers, forgers, bank robbers – the real zeks who tried, sometimes with success, to bully the more naïve prisoners who were there for political reasons and because they had been denounced. There was even a rumour that the men's camp had someone who had murdered his wife and children in it.

But most of us were 'political' prisoners. I use that term very loosely. We had all been convicted under Article 58, so it was hard to tell the difference between someone like me, who simply told a joke, and people who were genuinely guilty of counter-revolutionary, Trotskyite activity – someone who had done something much more seriously threatening to the Soviet state.

This all sounds very petty now, but totalitarianism can brook no dissent. The deserters, the cowards, the turncoats – they'd been shot without ceremony on the long, gruelling surge to Berlin.

But I can tell you there were lots of fervent Christians in the camps: Orthodox, Catholic, and Protestant. People who had spoken out, or criticized their superiors in any way. They were all in under Article 58. The beliefs and ideals of the religious zeks were totally alien and foreign to me, but I will admit that I left the system with an admiration for their fortitude and stoicism, their sheer courage for the sake of an ideal – until, many years later, I realized that I too had fought hard and long for an ideal, albeit an attainable earthly one.

And then, certainly in my time, in both camps there was a huge influx of other nationalities from the territories we captured from the fascists: Czechs, Hungarians, Bulgarians, East Germans, Poles, Lithuanians, Latvians, and Estonians, who all seemed to search each other out and provided strong support for each other. They managed to bring us some news of the outside world, but we'd always heard snippets from the guards too. For example, we knew that Smolensky had been executed in 1951, but for me the day I finally lost all faith was the day the news filtered through that General Zhukov had been purged. How could that happen? In my eyes he had single-handedly been responsible for defeating the fascists. It was his strategy which turned things at Stalingrad. It was his strategy which had worked in the drive for Berlin. I'd met him - I'd spoken to him. He pinned my award for bravery on my battle tunic. How could they purge Zhukov? I couldn't imagine a more committed Marxist, and a better General. I cried that day. And I don't cry very often. It's easier that way.

I could write on for hours and many more pages, but I won't. You can read about camp life elsewhere and everyone in the camps has their own story to tell, slightly different from mine. Many have no story to tell because they died in the camps, and they are the ones we must remember.

I have two regrets. Firstly, that the joke I told was such a bad joke, so to spend eight years in the Gulags for a not-very-good joke, really upset me. Secondly, I wish now, as I write this, that I had been more outspoken on my release and told more people about the terrible system that existed in our country. I should have become a real dissident. Perhaps with my impeccable war record I might have got away with it.

My one consolation was that I had no family. My parents were both dead. I had no brothers or sisters, no husband, and no children, so they were not stigmatized, nor did they suffer in any way because of my feeble joke. When I was allowed to write, I wrote to Halya's son Nikita, but he had been a toddler when I had last seen him.

What did I learn in the camps? Well, if you live in a dictatorship - don't tell jokes about the leader. Totalitarianism depends on terror and violence for its rule. And it cannot tolerate mockery or humour or laughter.

And the joke itself? Don't be too disappointed - it's not very good:

A crack unit of expert snipers have performed so well in the fight against the fascists that they are given a personal audience with Stalin. Everything goes well: the atmosphere is jovial, celebratory and benign. Medals are handed out; compliments are traded; reassurances of victory are reiterated. After twenty minutes the unit leaves.

However, shortly after they've gone, Stalin looks around for his pipe, but he can't find it. He immediately picks up the phone and speaks to the NKVD officer in charge of his personal security.

"Vladimir Ossopossovitch, I've lost my pipe. Those snipers are so crafty! One of them must have swiped it! Before they leave the building, try and find out who it was. I want my pipe back!"

An hour or so later Stalin is rummaging through the drawers on his desk and - lo and behold! – he finds his pipe. Immediately he calls the NKVD officer to tell him the good news.

The NKVD officer says, "That's a shame! Five of the snipers have died under torture and the other five have given us a full confession."

Chapter Thirty-Eight: Halya's Letter to Nikita

My Dearest Son,

If you get this letter you must know that I, your mother, will be dead, but I hope it will bring some comfort to you to read these words of mine. If you get this letter it will be thanks to the courage and perseverance of the railway driver that I gave it to you. Nikita – the world is full of wonderful people – never forget that when you hear about the terrible things the human race has done and the awful atrocities that have happened in this war.

My only consolation is that you are safe and that the fascists will eventually lose this war. Listen to what your grandparents say. Be a good boy for them, and grow up into the son that I know I can be proud of. If grandpa and grandma have not told you, then I must tell you this. Your father was an Englishman - a wild, beautiful, handsome Englishman. An officer and commissar in the British Brigade in Spain and we fell madly and passionately in love. But when the war was lost, we were parted. You must forgive me for not giving you a proper father and now, because of the war, I have deprived you of a mother as well. Nikita, I saw terrible things in Spain, and here in the defence of Stalingrad, and I know that war is barbaric, soul-destroying, inhuman, but I also know that this war must be fought, because the fascists that we fight are more barbaric, more inhuman, and more capable of terrible acts than any other soldiers I have ever come across. When we win – and I cannot conceive of a world in which we do not win – the world must know the story of the evils that the fascists have committed. Since my capture, Nikita, I have seen sights that I cannot bring myself to put into words, but I trust that you will grow up knowing of the cancerous evil that the fascists unleashed upon our country.

I am writing this on a scrap of paper and will give it to the railway driver – he is Russian and I think I can trust him. I am about to be put on a train – the destination is unknown. Perhaps the letter will reach you by hand one day, my son.

I was captured on November 19th in Stalingrad. I was stupid. I had become separated from Katya. It was my own fault and that day I broke the golden rule of Russian sniping. I became separated from my partner and I had no escape route. I'd fired three shots from my sniping position. The noise from German explosions was terrific. I wasn't completely sure where Katya was, but I had to move after three shots. I had to move! Normally I would move after one shot, two at the most. As I leapt down from the first floor of an old apartment building, there was no floor. I landed in a ground floor apartment and found four Wehrmacht soldiers grinning at me. They knew immediately I was a sniper, and they could tell from my red collar tabs that I was a Commissar as well.

"Tovarishch Commissar," they saluted me ironically. "Name?"

"Halya Reznik," I answered.

"Reznik!" This made them laugh more. "A sniper, a Commissar and a Jew. What fun!"

Nikita, I won't horrify you with stories of what has happened to me since then, but know this: it is the end of May, and your mother is still alive and well, still fighting the fascists. I have no weapon and I am about to get on a train which some people say will take us to camps where we will be exterminated. My fate is immaterial, but let me tell you this.

For three months I was part of a work detail outside Kiev. We spent three months, Nikita, three whole months, digging out tens of thousands of corpses who'd been shot and thrown into mass graves. It was our job to dig them up and burn them in huge pyres and even now the stench of human flesh clogs my nostrils. These German fascists are not human, and it is my hope that when you get this letter, the war will be over, or close to being over, and freedom and humanity and sanity will rule again.

And I hope even more that when you are old enough to read this letter for yourself, you will understand why I volunteered to fight in Spain. Why I had to be at Stalingrad to stop this tide of evil from conquering the motherland, from polluting the life-springs, the civilized streams of living that run through our lives and water our gardens and that we wash and refresh ourselves in every day. Nikita, have a good life: know that your mother loves you and loved you with a gentle tenderness and a fierceness of heart that will never be quenched.

Nikita, know too that your father was the best man, is the best man, I have ever met in this life. I don't know where he is, Nikita. I don't know where he will be when you receive this letter and when it is read to you, but I know somewhere he will be involved in the fight against these fascist oppressors. O Nikita ! Keep the spirits of your mother and your father intact. Shine on, shine on as you walk this endless highway of hope and tears and dreams, as you climb the winding staircase of life.

And of course, Nikita, I would have loved to see you grow up. I was looking forward to walking with you to school every morning, with your lunch parcel under my arm, your hand in my hand. I was looking forward to teaching you to swim. To playing in the parks with you, to cooking your favourite food for you, to teaching you how to read, to showing you what a wonderful world we live in, to take you into our beautiful Russian countryside to collect mushrooms. To bathe in the streams, to climb trees, to shoot rabbits, but the war has decreed that that will never happen, that I will never watch you grow up.

Nikita, don't be downhearted. Today as we were marched to this railway station the sun was shining, the birds were singing, blue skies without clouds were everywhere. I picked some forget-me-nots from the roadside and, Nikita, whenever you see forget-me-nots think of me, your mother, and think too of the ideals for which I fought and died.

And don't forget, Nikita, don't forget, they are the best ideals that one can ever live by or fight for and remember this famous quotation, "It is better to die on your feet than to live on your knees."

I don't yet know, Nikita, where I will die, but I will not die on my knees. There will be no memorial for me, just as there is no memorial for the thousands of corpses we dug out of the ground near Kiev, so I want you to be my memorial. Live well. Stay true to our socialist ideals. And in May always try to pick some forget-me-nots.

Your Mother –

Halya Reznik

Chapter Thirty-Nine: Tommy IXX

Waagwaam?

Waam!

And that is really all there is to say. I don't feel the need for words anymore. I just want to sit here sipping my coffee. I watched the news on Al-Jazeera in the hotel this morning. Tottenham in flames three nights ago. Last night Lewisham. And people wonder why! As if no-one can learn the obvious lessons of history. I don't think nicking some trainers is as bad as the MPs who fiddled their expenses; I don't think ransacking Halford's in Catford is as bad as the systematic oppression of the population through the right-wing press. Rioting – it's part of the English tradition. Give everyone a free Satnav – why not? Better still: double the minimum wage, scrap VAT and people will *buy* a sodding Satnav. We all need to know where we're going. Taken me long enough and I had a sodding map – though for too long I looked at it upside down. And with my eyes shut. And in the dark.

And the financial crisis. Europe at the crossroads. Austerity Avenue or New Deal Drive. Well, you can forget the latter with the banker-wankers pulling the strings. Me – well, you know what I favour - Krasnaya Street forever... but first, perhaps, a stroll down Buenos Aires Boulevard – just to put the frighteners on everyone else.

Words. Words. Words. After all my nattering, you'll be pleased to get some peace. Though cos I've never written anything this long, I won't try it again: it's been a heck of a lot of trouble.

And today. Today will change my life – I'm convinced of that. I've been to Sugar Town and I've shook the sugar down, but it doesn't compare to this city.

How do I know? Well, I don't, of course. But ever since landing at Sheremetyevo Airport on this trip to this country, I've felt at the end of a quest that began that morning where all this started with me seeing Uncle Jack cry. Yes – a quest. For the missing piece of Uncle Jack. For his untold mystery. And for the yearnings of my own heart. A broken, battered organ. All my own fault.

Although I wish I'd known then where it would lead me. I'd've come back sooner. Some valuable time would have been saved. And it will be only a few minutes before the circle is complete.

I know what you're thinking. At my age. I know. I know. But there comes a time in every man's life when he has to face his destiny and hold it fast and hard and true. And never let it go. Never let her go. Never.

And that is why I'm here. To complete the circle. To start a new life. And to see Olya. Olenka. Olyushka. Maya edinstvenniya. Transformer of landscapes. Heart doctor. Word weaver.

I don't know this city well enough to be able to tell which direction she will come from. I've got my bearings. About time, you might say. I'm gazing out of the window onto the main avenue leading up from the Volga, which is down there on the left – you can see it from the street. The pavements are busy. Small knots of people are heading towards the Volga River, while to my right is the central square and I'm facing the general direction of the War Memorial and the Eternal Flame – but I can't see it from where I'm sitting. Too many trees. You can never have too many trees. I think Bakunin said that. Or was it Groucho Marx? My money is on Bakunin – but then it always is.

As I've come to accept, everyone is stone-faced, keeping dark the warmth and fire inside. Within the knots of people, especially the younger ones, there is some laughter, but it is very restrained.

But I'm looking only for Olya. For her laughing open face and the fire of life in her eyes. And the softness of her skin. And her common sense. Don't let me cry. Please don't let me cry. Even with happiness. No crying. Only laughter.

And there she is! And my story is over. You know the rest. You do. Now get lost, sod off, dufah ho, and get your own fucking map.

Poekhali! Let's rock and roll! ☺ ♥

Chapter Forty: Afterword

And there on that sunshine-bursting late morning in Volgograd, on the Avenue of Peace, Tommy picked out on the other side of the street Olya's tentative smile and the fire in her eyes and her confident gait and her head held high, and her face beatified by an openness of heart, and his own heart surged and he tried to stand up, but failed, as the past fell behind him in waves of non-regret.

And from across the other side of the road, as Tommy sipped his coffee, perched on his window seat at the table of the Kafé Shokolada, кафе шоколада, their eyes locked and they knew in that instant, in that tiny snap-shot of time, that there would never be the shadow of another parting for them in this life. Their eyes grinned and their faces broke into tiny smiles of recognition and homecoming.

Home to the sanctuary of the hearts that cared. The hearts that cried. The hearts that had suffered so much.

And impelled towards Tommy (see words can say what you want!), Olya checked the lights on the zebra, before tentatively hovering one foot over the white and black lines, waiting for the traffic to stop and crossing to the coffee shop.

Tommy wanted to jump to his feet and leap onto the pavement and hug Olya tightly and dance all day to the rhythms of the heart, but he had learnt many, many lessons and he wanted to fit in, so he stayed in his seat and waited while Olya entered the café and silently approached his seat, their eyes locking for a brief, yet lingering, wordless stare. And only two words were exchanged:

"кофе? Kofyeh? Coffee?"

"Пожалуйста. Pahzhahloostah. Please."

A slight, mutual nod.

But behind the railway station to the west, if anyone had noticed, hundreds of thousands of white doves burst flying into the air. Tommy reached into his jacket pocket when they were on the pavement and one hundred thousand red rose petals flew into the air, buoyed up by the eddies of Tommy and Olya's long-wished-for reunion. And, when Olya opened her hand-bag, millions of multi-coloured butterflies at once shimmered into the hot noon air and spiralled upwards, their wings a kaleidoscope of harmony.

And their eyes locked and they could not talk.

Words. Too rare and precious to waste. So they did not need to talk at that magical moment.

But many hours later, they walked along the Volga Boulevard and gazed into the depths of the river, which had run red before Katya's mother's tear-filled eyes. It was dusk. In front of them, unseen, kept dark, the huge mass of the Urals and Siberia turned into night, while to the West, behind them now, European Russia glowed rich with the promises of the future and reminded them of the now quiet, silenced ghosts of the past. So many. So many mourned. So many missed. And all the ghosts from Mamayev Kurgan rose and silently, gravely, saluted them with a flicker of their eyes and a slight nod of approbation and acquiescence. Vide, aude, tace, they whispered. Tace in your stoicism, but make sure our story is told. Tell the world. Always.

And did they think of Halya and Robbie, of Jack and Katya, of Yuri and Ilya, of Svetlana and Nikita? Of course they did, and Tommy squeezed Olya's hand as the river flowed on, and the moon rose, and their tears added silently to the deluge.

And did they think, as they walked along the river, of all the people somewhere on this seething, troubled planet, dying and suffering and in pain, and the others being born, and the ones who were hungry, and the ones who were homeless, and the ones who were landless and oppressed, and all the ones everywhere who were kept in the dark, and the couples kissing somewhere on this teeming, life-bursting planet, and everywhere, in every street, in every city, in every country, the anguished, agonized voice of a damaged, frightened child begging for mercy, or a fearful, sobbing woman, saying, "No, please! Please, please, no! No!"?

Of course they did, because they had learnt the importance of keeping nothing in the dark.

And that evening, without words, Olya and Tommy dreamed and saw a better world, a fair and honest world, in which there was no need for armies or governments; a world in which no child cried for food and nothing was kept dark, because the people, salt of this earth, had decided it should be so; a world in which no one yearned for freedom, justice and peace, because they had all come to pass and were as natural as the trees and the birds and the tender kisses of lovers beneath the moon.

And Tommy took a carnation from his pocket and launched it onto the river, wordlessly, expression-less, stone-man, his eyes leaving Olya's for only a second, and the frail flower was borne away in the river on its own lone, lonely, long and longing quest to the sea, as we all are, borne away on the waters, desperately seeking peace, floundering and flailing through the darkness until the plangent, frail and falling voice of an angel calls us home.

TOMMY'S POEMS

The Trees I

After Philip Larkin

The trees now start to shed their leaves

Because they know that they'll soon die.

Each year, like this, they fall, but I

No longer have the strength to grieve.

Is it that my heart's grown cold?

No. They're only leaves we tread

On, trampled underfoot, too dead

To waste our tears on, so I'm told.

Yet still each autumn, winter looms,

Presaged by these browns, yellows, reds,

In each leaf's fall we see our dread

Of falling in the growing gloom.

Mother's Day, 2010

Mother, this is your sonnet. I give you

Words. You gave me the precious gift of life

Over half a century ago. To

Think that these words suffice, my father's wife,

Shows, perhaps, the power we think they own –

As if mere sounds made with lips, tongue and teeth

Could replicate or reveal or make known

The feelings' rich seams lying underneath.

Some dig for diamonds. There are mines for gold.

Black coal is hacked out of the earth's hot heart.

Hewing at the language, so deep, so old,

Do these sounds from my heart turn into art?

No words can work on this most special day:

No precious metals from this man of clay.

Empire

These hands that hewed the coal for you and built your ships and brushed your clothes and tended

your gardens and picked you up when you fell and swept your floors and ploughed your

fields and fired your guns and shined your shoes and cooked your meals

and clapped your fine words and made your engines and

built your cars and carved your monuments

and whipped your slaves

and wiped your eyes

and saluted your flag

and defended your

colours and

delivered

your

messages

and

ticked

your

boxes and

sailed your ships and

took your meagre wages

and felt your scorn and prayed to your God

and hacked at your enemies and staunched your blood and

fought your wars and flew your planes and guided your voyages and

built your nation and now outstretched and now ask for alms and forgiveness and

charity and are folded not in prayer but now are grown into these wings to fly away to freedom

Revolutionary 2011

Every day I go to Argos

Undercover

Deep cover

A sleeper

I look like an ordinary shopper

But I am a revolutionary

An urban guerrilla

A socialist terrorist

The people's freedom fighter

On the front line

Where the heat is

Where you can smell the cordite

And the fear

And so every day

I go to Argos

And

While fussing over the catalogue

And investigating 'store availability'

I steal pencils

Capitalist pencils

Tools of the oppressor

Which I use to write socialist poems

Communist poems

Trotskyite poems

Stalinist poems

Anarchist poems that break all the roools

Poems that kill Fascists

And make lists of those who

Will need 're-education'

After the revolution.

The ones who voted Tory

The ones who voted Lib Dem

The tax-dodgers

The bankers

The wankers

The arms dealers

The child stealers

And anyone not in my immediate family circle.

I've tried banks

But their pens are chained

Like the proletariat.

Fuckers (the banks).

So you have to go with

Huge metal clippers

And run like fuck

From the fascist defenders of the state,

Rozzers, pigs, the fuzz.

Ikea is another good source

Of revolutionary pencils too.

And it's Swedish.

We left-wingers are so internationalist

In our outlook.

And green too.

I recycle my shavings.

So when the barricades go up

You'll easily find me

Comrade

I'll be wearing my red bandana

Like the others

Comrade

Carrying my Kalashnikov

Like the others

Comrade

But I'll be the only one with

A bandolier of pencils

Comrade

To write the new rules.

The New Cross Road

As I walked down the New Cross Road

Near the street where I was born

I saw tears in the eyes of a child

And in all who passed me by

And the words I wrote were on paper

That was all tattered and torn

Just all tattered and torn.

As I walked down the New Cross Road

Near the street where I used to live

I heard the beggar's cry

And I wondered why

When I felt her sigh

That I had nothing left to give

Nothing left to give.

As I walked down the New Cross Road

Near the street where I was born

I felt the chill of the air

And the strangers' stares

In the coldest light near dawn

And I just felt old and forlorn

And my words were just tattered and torn.

As I walked down the New Cross Road

In the late wet shut of the year

I heard an angel sigh

And a devil cry

And I tasted their fear

Near the dead wet door of the year

And I could not hold back their tears

Couldn't hold back their tears.

As I walked down the New Cross Road

Near the street where I used to dwell

I saw the signs of hate

In every face and in every place

In the woman's gaze

And the child's face

And in every place

And the stranger's gaze

And from every place

And in your face

And in my face

And I knew I had travelled to hell.

Mark Duggan

Born on a Monday

On these streets

Raised on a Tuesday

On these streets

Played on a Wednesday

On these streets

Schooled on a Thursday

On these streets

Worked on a Friday

On these streets

Arrested on a Saturday

On these streets

Killed on a Sunday

On these streets

These streets

Black bin-bag windy city

Cries vomit stains and truncheons

On my heart

'The Bathers at Asnières' – Georges Seurat

You remember that afternoon,

The melting ice cream colours,

The air floating icing sugar,

The cool love of the water,

And the sun casting its snoozey spells.

Nothing lasts.

The air hung like frosted multi-

Coloured treacle and slowly moved the world

And watered our wondered imaginations as we lay.

A static kaleidoscope of joy.

A blob of vanilla ice cream fell

On your knee. I licked it off.

Nothing lasts.

We got lost in other afternoons.

The sodden grey tears of November,

The betrayals of winter,

The air cursed and crying -

The words fled, dead and empty.

Nothing lasts.

The searing screech of city traffic,

Heavy like death and hatred,

Jangling wounds seizing our ears

And the air an explosive, toxic

Taste cackling our brains.

Nothing lasts.

Separated by the screams of rituals -

Ceremonies of the untruth, cowards, victims,

The bitter wailings of the innocent

Caught in the ordinariness of the quotidian,

Daily killed by being the ideas of others.

Nothing lasts.

I want to return to that

Candy floss, icing-sugared world

Where ice cream drops forever on your knee

And the water-haze like amber

Holds our better, glad-face selves.

Forever.

To Tilly

I see your tail wagging from afar –

A blur of white upon a field of green.

Oh Tilly! You're my canine superstar

The most clever Russell the world's ever seen!

Mega-pooch! Agile, graceful, loyal hound!

Oh terrier terrific! Jack Supreme!

You swim in the river and dig in the ground,

Chasing the world in your sweet doggy dreams!

Small-child defender, the world is agog

At tales of your courage, your wonderful deeds,

You roller in duck shit, you sweet-talking dog!

You walk at my left leg without a lead!

Belka and Strelka have nothing on you!

You dancer for cheese, you eater of poo!

Birth

It seemed that I emerged from my begetting,

Twigs and leaves in my hair, naked, scarred,

Beaten and harried, hunted, scoured

With the bites of animals and the forest

Scratches of my birth. The earth stenched me.

Battling through undergrowth I found

A clearing – sunlit and snowdrop-full. The

Sun cracked tears and mud on my cheeks

And in my matted hair. And one was

There like me – torn, scorned and ravaged –

But alive. She bore the scars of life and

Death and broken dreams. Tears and

Laughter carved her face. 'Sister,' I said,

'Where is this place and what is to become

Of us?' She raised a finger to her lips:

'Fear not. Enjoy this forest that

Covers and protects us with our blooding scars.

Lose yourself in its sweet labyrinths of

Snowdrop-promise. Wipe the blood from your body.

Ignore the rain that brings sweet life

And hides your tears. Listen! The birds!

The birds!'

Five Ways to Love a Woman

You can give her diamonds

Plundered from the depths of the earth,

Shimmering in their transparent beauty

For her to dangle from her ears

Or display on her fingers.

You can select roses ransacked

From all corners of the earth -

Red for passion, white for fidelity,

Yellow for friendship - and shower

Her body with their scented petals.

Pearls can be pillaged

From the deepest ocean's floor

Black and white, night and day,

To constantly orbit her neck,

A rosary of love that never lies.

Opera and an expensive meal

Can work – something romantic –

Tosca, say – those formal clothes

And champagne and oysters

And sophisticated chat at the interval.

Gold does it too – especially

When combined with designer

Luxury – Gucci, Versace.

Louis Vuitton, before you carry

Her off in your Mercedes.

simpler

more honest

more memorable

is

to wait for the moment

(you'll know when the time is right)

when the moon shines on the river

and the stars are singing for you both

and the living earth beats your blood

and the swallows have returned again

and reach your living fingers

slowly

gently

tenderly

tentatively

to push the hair back over her ear

and whisper to her heart.

Whitney Houston

No matter what they do to me

They can't take away my dignity.

Dignity?

Our tears dripped into that bath

To be with you and

Fall like dew of angels' blood

To match that voice.

Plastered on the world's front pages:

Celebrity, exploitation, manipulation.

No more auction block, babe?

Just a new one, girl.

The Forms of Poetry

Six-sonnet girl, do you long for a haiku?

Or yearn for a romantic pastoral?

Simple postcards saying that I laiku?

Post-its with amorous doggerel?

Your own love-ode in rhythms trochaic?

Craftless and artless – another sonnet?

Or a txt msge = shrt n prosaic?

Poems to your body... written on it?

A LURVE epic? A short winsome lyric?

Your very own iambic elegy?

A satire or a glowing panegyric,

Penned by your poetic prodigy?

"Stuff your sonnets, wanker, and go to hell:

Write me a pornographic villanelle!"

The Frogs in the Garden

Green jumping star!

Emerald dancer!

Jumping sage!

Khaki cavorter!

Lime leaper!

Jasmine jack-in-the-box!

Froggy Diaghilev!

Jade sky-shooter!

I like you!

Last night after weeks of dryness

the sky poured goblets of heavy rain

massive gobs of wet

drops of living damp

sheets of soak

slops of wetty splodge

and the patio became alive with you!

Each step I took released

a jump of frogness -

cavorting

leaping

somersaulting

pirouetting

prancing green dancers

in the half-light of that wet dusk.

But dawn and morning found you

belly-up on the lawn

pale cream now your jumpness gone

your leapery diminished.

And I will leap

and jump

and dance

and sing

forever

to preserve your memory

to mourn you

my little green dancer....

Without You Here

Without you here, I can't be said to function.

Without you here, I'm Ginger without Fred.

I'm Waterloo without my Clapham Junction.

I am the night without the living dead.

The Great Escape <u>not</u> featuring McQueen,

Jagger sans Richards, Morecambe without Wise,

Saturn with no rings, Torvill without Dean,

Uncastled Elephant, Derek without Clive,

I'm Long John Silver, stable on two legs,

Oliver Twist, so working class and stout,

I'm *omelette nihiliste* with no eggs,

Hamlet with the soliloquies left out.

Without you, I'm Starsky without Hutch.

Without you, love, I don't amount to much.

Liverpool, April 2012

In Bold Street

I feel at home

in the radical bookshop

timidly browsing the poetry magazines.

In Paradise Street

I defy augury and precedent

to buy three temptatious apples

and scoff the lot!

Near the Cavern

I hear fading, dying strains

barely audible beneath the casual glatz:

four forgotten working class heroes.

Leaving the spickspan-ness of the Albert Dock

in the middle of the Mersey

this blownback crashing day I hear

the creak of the rigging

the crack of the whips

the moans of the slaves

the heaving, unstoppable snarl of slavery ships.

Trees II

After Philip Larkin

The trees will leaf again next year

To resonate throughout the earth.

All nature will burst out in birth,

So there's no need to shed your tears.

Will I get too tired of waiting?

Hope I don't! The planet's alive

And everything that lives will thrive,

While human dreams keep failing.

The snowdrops' white, the tulips' red

Proclaim this earth will never rest.

When swallows come to claim their nest

The past will come...is gone...is dead.

Nothing Left

Words, words, words.

Got no words left to say.

Love, love, love.

I've got none left today.

Rain, rain, rain.

It hides the tears I cry.

Heart, heart, heart.

Keep beating while I die.

Smiles, smiles, smiles.

All my smiles have gone.

Life, life, life.

At least will soon be done.

To the People of Egypt – February 2011

Like a volcano firing lava into the sky

Like a phoenix from the flames

Like a gush of oil from the deepest earth

Rise up

Throw off your chains

Like a mighty, monstrous wave

Like an explosion of magical fireworks

Like the surge of fresh spring water

Rise up

Rise up

Throw off your chains

Like a shooting star bursting across the sky

Like a torrent of bird song at dawn

Like the roar of a tiger that's suddenly free

Rise up

Rise up

Rise up

Throw off your chains

And find your voice again

Acknowledgements

Thanks are due to so many people. To Jean Bean who typed a fair proportion of the first draft and did so with interest and enthusiasm, aided by her husband Keith, often pointing out factual inconsistencies; to my mother and my son who read early drafts and gave fulsome encouragement; to Natalie Twigg who read the first draft and whose enthusiasm encouraged me to continue; to Flora, my daughter, who discussed the plot with a wisdom beyond her years; to Dick Joyce for his very helpful and constructive suggestions; and to my mother who proof-read the final draft with ceaseless and indefatigable enthusiasm. Many friends read early drafts of the opening chapters, and their encouragement kept me going. Any errors of fact or faults of taste are mine alone.

I owe an enormous debt to the following books and would recommend them to any readers who want to discover more about particular events or periods covered in the novel. Vasily Grossman's novel, in particular, deserves to be more widely known, although during the writing of *Keep it Dark*, I deliberately read only short excerpts from it – I did not want to be over-influenced by one of the greatest-ever war novels. I did a lot of research for this novel and I am certain that what happens in the plot could have happened; nonetheless, any errors of fact or detail are my fault.

George Orwell: *Homage to Catalonia*. ISBN: 978-0141183053

Laurie Lee: *A Moment of War*. ISBN: 978-0140156225

Antony Beevor: *Battle for Spain: The Spanish Civil War*. ISBN: 978-0753821657

Peter Darman: *Heroic Voices from the Spanish Civil War*. ISBN: 978-1847734693

Jim Jump (ed): *Poems from Spain: British and Irish International Brigaders on the Spanish Civil War*. ISBN: 978-1905007394

Vasily Grossman: *Life and Fate*. ISBN: 978-0099506164

Martin Gilbert: *The Holocaust*. ISBN: 978-0006371946

Alastair MacClean: *HMS Ulysses*. ISBN: 978-0006135128

Jan de Hartog: *The Sea Captain*. ISBN: 978-0689100642

Jon E. Lewis: *Voices from the Holocaust*. ISBN: 978-1849017237

Jonathan Bastable: *Voices from Stalingrad: Nemesis on the Volga*. ISBN: 978-0715321768

Antony Beevor: *Stalingrad*. ISBN: 978-0141032405

Svetlana Alexievich: *Zinky Boys: Soviet Voices from Afghanistan*. ISBN: 978-0393336863

Svetlana Alexievich: *Voices from Chernobyl: The Oral History of a Nuclear Disaster*. ISBN: 978-0312425845

If you have enjoyed *Keep it Dark*, please tell your friends. The opening four chapters are available very cheaply as an e-book on Amazon, as are Chapters 5 to 8, so readers can get a taste of the novel before buying the whole thing.

Chapter Three: Jack II contains the text of a speech delivered by La Pasionara, Dolores Ibárruri, on November 1st, 1938 in Barcelona on the occasion of the departure of the International Brigades from Spain.

In Chapter Four: Halya I, I use an English translation of a Soviet partisan song.

Chapter Twelve: Tommy VI uses two songs which come from the BBC television series *Trumpton*.

Chapter Twenty-Two: Tommy XI contains the text of a speech made by Nelson Mandela in Cape Town on the day of his release from prison – February 11th, 1990.

Pages 222 and 223 are deliberately left blank.

In Chapter Twenty-Six: Halya II, I use an English translation of *The Internationale*.

Chapter Twenty-Seven: Tommy XIII uses the text of the letter that Franklin D Roosevelt sent to the city of Stalingrad and which is displayed in the Stalingrad Panorama Museum.

The opening paragraph of Chapter Twenty-Nine: Tommy XIV is taken from the Internet Guide to British Crematoria.

Ironically, given the remark on page 263, in 2013 the Russian government did strike a medal for the 45th anniversary of the repression of Prague – or 'Operation Danube' as it was officially called.

Lyudmila Pavlichenko

Printed in Great Britain
by Amazon.co.uk, Ltd.,
Marston Gate.